Robin D. Owens

Keepers
of the
Flame

LUNA™
www.LUNA-Books.com

LUNA™

KEEPERS OF THE FLAME

ISBN-13: 978-0-373-80262-3
ISBN-10:   0-373-80262-5

Copyright © 2008 by Robin D. Owens

First printing: January 2008

Author Photo by: Rose Beetem

This edition published by arrangement with Harlequin Books S.A.

® and TM are trademarks of Harlequin Books S.A., used under license.
Trademarks indicated with ® are registered in the United States Patent
and Trademark Office, the Canadian Trade Marks Office and in other
countries.

www.LUNA-Books.com

Printed in U.S.A.

Praise for the novels of

ROBIN D. OWENS

"Owens has an easy and engaging writing style, which, when combined with her intriguing characters and interesting setting, makes for a fast and compelling read."
—*Romantic Times BOOKreviews* on *Protector of the Flight*
(Book Three of The Summoning)

"Fans of Anne McCaffrey and Mercedes Lackey will appreciate the novel's honorable protagonists and their lively animal companions."
—*Publishers Weekly* on *Protector of the Flight*

"[A] multifaceted, fast-paced gem of a book."
—*The Best Reviews* on *Guardian of Honor*
(Book One of The Summoning)

"The story line is action-packed but also contains terrific characters.... Robin D. Owens enchants her readers."
—*Affaire de Coeur* on *Guardian of Honor*

"Owens takes...elements that make Marion Zimmer Bradley's Darkover stories popular...and turns out a romance that draws you in."
—*Locus* magazine

Other books in
The Summoning series,
available from

ROBIN D. OWENS

and LUNA Books

Guardian of Honor
Sorceress of Faith
Protector of the Flight

To readers,
May hope always be your friend.

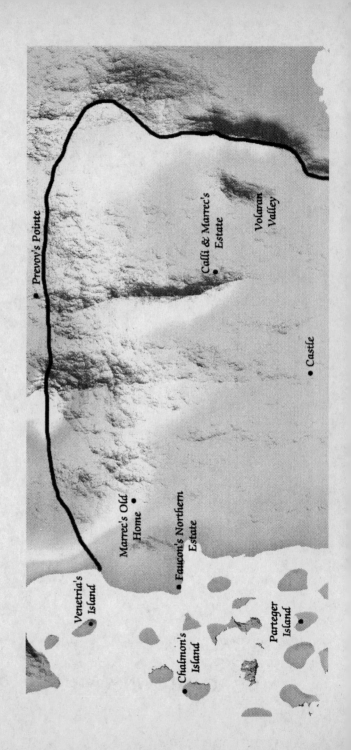

Prevoy's Pointe

Calli & Marrec's Estate

Volaran Valley

Castle

Marrec's Old Home

Faucon's Northern Estate

Venetria's Island

Chalmon's Island

Parteger Island

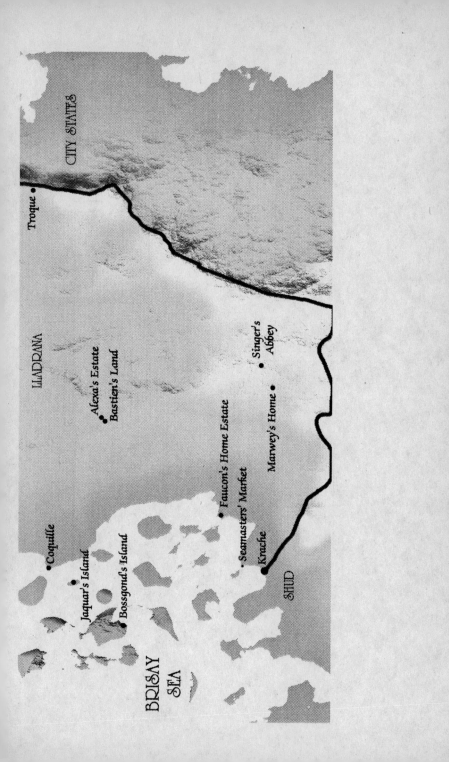

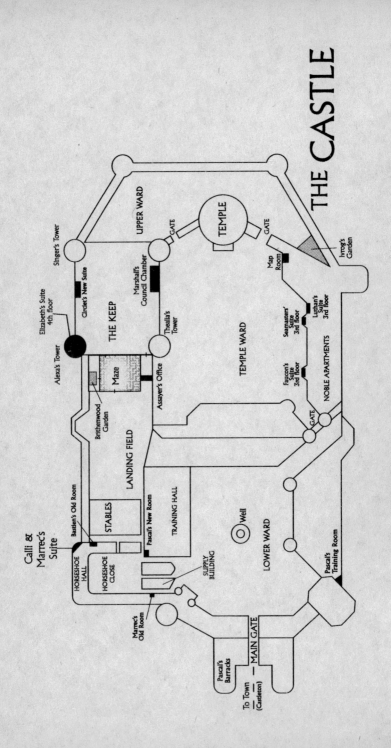

THE CASTLE

Acknowledgments:

All my fellow LUNA authors, my critique group, and the health care professionals in my life who know what I'm talking about, Morgan de Thouars, and Rita Mills, and Mountain Mehndi for Bri's design.

I

Denver, Last of May, early afternoon

He wasn't worth it. Elizabeth Drystan stomped down the grocery store aisle, pushing her metal basket hard. The damn thing had a wonky wheel, of course, and Elizabeth reveled in the necessity of using force.

The man wasn't worth her heartbreak. Heartbreak? More like her heart had been ripped out, leaving a horrible, bloody, aching core. As a newly board-certified doctor starting a job in Denver Major Hospital next month, she knew her physical heart still beat. But, oh, her emotional one was shredded into pieces.

The jerk, Cassidy, had said she was "crowding" him. He "needed space." Just when she thought she could plan the rest of her life—starting with a wedding. After a year,

Cassidy had broken their engagement. Because he needed *space*.

Elizabeth had told him to go to Wyoming.

And the inexplicable auditory illusions—chanting, gongs and chimes—were taking her to the edge of temper and sanity. Even now she had to block the sounds from her mind.

She took a corner fast and crashed into another cart. The jolt sang up her arms. She opened her mouth to spew and saw her twin sister, Bri, who was supposed to be in Sweden—purple-streaked hair and all. Elizabeth burst into tears.

Bri reached for her, hugging and soothing. "I knew something was wrong. I had to came back."

Elizabeth didn't care where her free-spirited sister had been, only that she was holding her. Her tears were dripping down Bri's fallen earbuds and she wondered if salt water damaged them. The silliness of that thought made her gasp, choke, and stifle the water flow. Digging into her cart for one of the already opened boxes of tissues, Elizabeth wiped her eyes and blew her nose. "God, am I glad you came."

Bri patted her on the shoulder. "I knew you were sad." Her jaw tightened. "Man problems, right? That Doctor Medical-Prodigy-Slick-Hunk-Son-Of-A-Bitch. I told you he was an arrogant snob of a bastard. Finally showed his true colors."

Elizabeth hugged her again. "I'm glad you're here."

"Actually, I'm back for good."

That was startling and Elizabeth welcomed the distraction, even if she didn't believe it. "Really?" She stepped back to scan Bri's face under her spiky hair of brown and purple. There was an unaccustomed seriousness in her hazel gaze along with…uncertainty?

Shrugging, Bri flushed. "No place like home, right?"

"So they say." But lately Elizabeth had begun to feel a change of venue might be good. She could reconsider her decision about starting at Denver Major Hospital. Take a long break, call around to some of her other offers. Her feet were actually tingling. She wondered if that was what Bri called "itchy feet."

"Elizabeth?" Bri was smiling. "You went away on me."

That was usually Elizabeth's phrase to her twin.

After one last blow into her tissue, Elizabeth tucked it away into a plastic baggie in her purse, took out an antiseptic towlette packet, opened it and wiped her hands.

Looking amused, Bri rolled up her earbuds and slipped her player in her purse. "Feel better?"

"Always, when you're here."

Bri looked away, then back, hunched a shoulder. "You know why I've been gone. I had to see if other places were more accepting of…our talent."

Elizabeth never wanted to talk about that subject. "The folks will be glad to see you. They were hoping you'd come home for Dad's birthday."

"This time the favors I called in were solid. Got here this morning. Everywhere's been interesting. Denver and home is better."

Touching the puffiness under her eyes, Elizabeth winced. "My God, look at me, breaking down in a grocery store!"

Bri glanced around, "You wouldn't be the first, and you picked an appropriate place. Supplies all around. Tiger Balm's right behind your shoulder and aspirin on my side of the aisle." Bri grinned. Elizabeth always thought Bri had gotten the prettier smile. Bri said since they were identical, Elizabeth had it, too. That wasn't true. Bri's smile was special. Maybe because she was such a free spirit.

"'Scuse me," said a tall, wiry black woman with salt-and-pepper hair, walking down the aisle. Her face showed irritation—that part which wasn't covered with a package of frozen baby peas. "I need one of those instant ice packs." Her visible eye rolled to other items on the shelves. "And one of those herbal sinus pillows, too."

Bri moved her cart. "Let's see," she said. "I'm a massage therapist." She tilted her head toward Elizabeth. "And she's a medical doctor. What happened?"

A corner of the woman's mouth quirked as she walked past Bri to Elizabeth. "Volleyball." She took the peas from her face.

Elizabeth winced in sympathy, checked the woman's eye, then carefully felt around the bone. "No other head injury?"

"No."

"Blurry vision?"

"No."

"Looks like a big black eye."

The woman snorted. "Got that."

"Here," Bri said, ripping open the box and twisting the instant ice compress to initiate the cold. She placed the pack on the woman's face.

Then Bri did the unthinkable. Elizabeth *saw* an aura of green pulse from Bri's hand through the pack and bathe the woman's face for long, long seconds.

"I think you'll find it looks worse than it is," Bri said, releasing the compress after the woman dropped the peas in her basket and held the pack herself.

"Thanks. It feels better already."

"Here's your sinus pillow." Elizabeth hoped her voice was less stiff than she felt.

"Thanks again." The woman nodded and left.

"Are you crazy!" Elizabeth whispered. "I want to talk to you!" She jerked her cart around and headed toward an empty corner of the store.

Smiling, Bri sauntered after her, tugging her smoothly rolling cart. Elizabeth got her temper under control by the time her twin reached her.

"What were you doing!" Elizabeth demanded.

"You know what I was doing. Just because you deny our gift of healing hands doesn't mean I do."

"You used it in *a grocery store*."

"What, you think healing should only be confined to clinics?" Bri glanced around. "Let me tell you, this store is pristine compared to some of the places I've been." She lowered her voice. "The refugee camps I've…*worked*…in."

Elizabeth clutched the handle of her grocery cart until her knuckles whitened. "Someone could have seen!"

"Seen what? It was only a little burst of energy." Bri's smile widened. "And well done, if I say so, myself. That bruise will fade in record time."

Again Bri glanced around. "So how many of our fellow shoppers can see healing auras, do you think? It's not even an organic store."

"*Someone could have seen*," Elizabeth repeated, unable to put enough distress in words.

Bri was frowning now—maybe she'd come to her senses. "You saw how the lady came straight to you, the doctor. People trust doctors with medical degrees, not those of us with healing hands. That's why I've decided that you got it right, working within the Western medical establishment."

Elizabeth still didn't know what to say, and must have appeared as confused as she felt.

Bri patted her shoulder, but her face went impassive. "I promise I won't let anyone know you have the gift, too."

Elizabeth winced and rubbed her temples. She could barely hear her sister for the cacophony once again inundated her mind. "Sorry to snap at you. These damned chimes are driving me mad!"

Eyes widening, Bri said, "Chimes? You too?" Her voice dropped. "What about a gong…and chants?"

Elizabeth knew her mouth opened and closed like a guppy's.

"You hear them, too," Bri said.

"What?" Elizabeth whispered, clutching the handle of her cart again.

"Chanting voices more persistent than the chimes and gong. I thought something was wrong so got checked out in Sweden by both medical and alternative health practitioners. No observable or understandable physical or mental problems."

Swallowing, Elizabeth said, "I attributed it to emotional trauma."

"Well, you've had plenty of that. How long?"

"Three and a half weeks."

"Me, too. Did you have your hearing checked?"

Elizabeth sighed. "Yes."

"Let's give it another week, then decide what to do." Elizabeth turned to finish shopping, but Bri put a hand on her arm, snagged her gaze with the same changeable hazel eyes but showing a different pattern of specks. "It might be a sign that our healing powers are changing. I've noticed mine are a little more reliable and slightly stronger."

Elizabeth flinched.

Bri said, "Is that one of the reasons Cassidy broke up with you? Because he discovered you using your gift?"

"I don't *use* a gift. Sometimes something just seems to flow from me. Nothing important. But our last argument was because he'd noticed…" It hurt to remember. She waved a hand. "Past and done." She looked at their carts, then back at her sister, then they both stared at the sack of potatoes in each other's cart and shook their heads in unison. "I see you had a craving for potatoes, too," Elizabeth said.

"Yes," Bri said, "those really unhealthy shredded potatoes loaded with cheese and sour cream. Mickey potatoes." Mickey was the friend of their mom's who'd given them the recipe.

Trying to lighten the moment Elizabeth closed her eyes and groaned theatrically in pleasure. "As medical professionals, we shouldn't consider more than a bite of those cholesterol bombs. A nice baked potato with a smidgeon of butter—"

Bri reached under a stack of greens and held up a couple of small plastic sacks. "Chocolate for my sweet craving." Bri shook the nuggets so little metallic wrappers rustled as the candies tumbled against each other, glittering. "Our favorites."

"You got dark chocolate for me." Elizabeth was touched. "You're so sweet. So bad, but so sweet." She glanced at her watch. "We have just enough time to settle you in, cook, dress, and go to the folks."

Bri nodded at Elizabeth's cell thrusting from her purse's outer pocket. "You should find about three messages from me on that."

"Oops." When she looked at the readout, it was blank. "Forgot to charge it." Another result of stress. She was tired of hurting because of Cassidy and forced the thought of him away again. Enough wallowing. Get on with life! Straightening her shoulders, she said. "I want you to stay with me."

Under lowered brows, Bri watched her, that uncertain look back in her eyes. "For real?"

"For real. You can have the guest room." She bit her lips to stop them from trembling, cleared her throat. "It'll be good to have you living with me, like when we were kids. Especially since I'm on vacation." She wanted her sister more now than ever since they'd become adults. Bri's first walkabout had been during freshman summer vacation in college. Elizabeth had never admitted how much she wished Bri hadn't gone her own way. Perhaps she'd stay now.

"Okay," Bri said.

Elizabeth relaxed, smiled. Everything would be better now that Bri was home.

A few hours later Bri and Elizabeth left their parents' home. "Mom and Dad *loved* our gift of an all-expenses-paid two-week vacation in Hawaii." Bri was very pleased at how the dinner had gone—except for a tense few minutes when they skirted around Cassidy Jones, who'd usually celebrated with them.

Her parents had been delighted by Bri's announcement to settle in Denver and become a nurse.

She shifted the foam freezer chest full of ham, Mickey

potatoes, crudités, baked beans and fruit salad that she carried.

Elizabeth hauled two sacks of potatoes. Apparently their mother had had the same craving as the twins. "Leaving tomorrow. All this food," their mother had grumbled, pressing it on her daughters.

Night had fallen and wispy clouds draped the black sky. Only a few stars could be seen from the city. Bri inhaled deeply. Their parents' house backed onto Cheesman Park and the scent of thick grass and roses came on a cool breeze. Sweden's air had still carried the last of spring. For a moment she just stood and let the city sounds and scents and very atmosphere caress her.

There was no place like home. Finally her itchy feet had stopped tingling, bringing her back to her family.

"You're tired, let me drive," Bri said to her sister.

"You must be jet-lagged."

"I was, but I got my second wind." As soon as she put her head on a pillow tonight she'd crash for sure, but right now she was in a state of hyperawareness. She unlocked the doors, opened hers and they stowed the chest and potatoes in the back seat, and got in.

Elizabeth stared at her.

"What?" Bri asked as she turned the key in the ignition.

"You really are going to nursing school," Elizabeth said.

"That's right. I finally decided your way was the best." Bri pulled away from the curb. "I've learned a lot, but I'm tired of the traveling. I can use my gift in the established medical community."

"I see," Elizabeth said, but the car was dark and Bri thought that Elizabeth had shut her eyes.

"You'll be a dynamite doctor with the benefit of our gifts. It's too late for me there, I don't want to take the time to go through med school, but nursing…yeah, I can do that."

More, heavier silence.

"All this time I've been sneered at because of my 'flaky' ideas and you've been the good twin because you followed Mom's path through medical school and didn't make waves."

"A little resentment there?" Elizabeth asked in a steady voice.

"Okay. Maybe. But I honestly think you need to admit to yourself that you have a special gift and you chose a career to use it…and you hide that you use it. I don't mind you hiding it—"

"Liar."

"Okay, some resentment there, too, but I've come to accept that you must hide it."

"My way is not your way."

"Oh, honey, I know that! But I want to hear the words from you. Just once. Come on, it isn't difficult. Just say, 'I have a special gift for healing.'"

"You don't want much," Elizabeth muttered. Her voice broke.

Bri pulled to the side of the road. Tapped her head on the steering wheel. "Stupid, stupid, stupid. I'm sorry, you have too much else to handle, and here I'm demanding more. Twin, you need this vacation."

"Tell me about it." Elizabeth was blowing her nose again. "I'm too damn sensitive to every word. Every glance. And being at Denver Major where Cassidy is…."

"And now your gift reminds you of him, too. Damn it!" Frustration welled through Bri. Her twin needed her comfort, but Bri, too, needed something from her sister—support, understanding. But here and now wasn't the time to demand it. She'd been impatient. Releasing her tight grip on the wheel, she opened herself to what she thought of as the healingstream, let the power soothe her, tingle into her hands and warm them. She set her palm on Elizabeth's shoulder, feeling her sister's energy field, more, her struggle against anger and depression. Bri sent the warm flow into Elizabeth.

After a moment, Elizabeth said, "Thank you."

"I have a special gift for healing."

Elizabeth sighed. "Yes, you do." She leaned her head back on the seat rest, but said nothing about her own gift and that hurt Bri.

She rolled her shoulders. She wouldn't give up, she'd just let the tender subject go—for now. She rubbed her hands to absorb lingering energy, then touched the steering wheel to ground herself. She checked the street and pulled out into light traffic.

Elizabeth said, "Cassidy is incredible. He's a better physician than I am."

"No!" The word exploded from Bri. "Never. He's not. He may be more brilliant. He may have gone through the damn programs like a rocket, but he is not a better doctor than you. You're twice the physician he is. And you know why? Because you have heart."

Elizabeth blinked. "I hadn't thought of that. Heart. Huh."

"Huh yourself."

Bri drove down streets overhung with leafy branches.

Elizabeth's breathing evened. Bri felt her sister's glance, but said nothing. Elizabeth inhaled, let her breath out slowly. "Don't ask me to go in a direction I'm not ready for. I don't want the topic raised again."

Bri found her teeth set, and deliberately relaxed her jaw. Again. There was no place like home and family, and no one who could push her buttons so easily as Elizabeth.

Bri turned the car east and a wave of sound washed over her, through her. "The sounds of chimes and stuff is getting louder."

Elizabeth said nothing, but she'd stiffened.

"Chanting mostly. Sheesh, don't even need to turn on the radio." She cocked her head. "Maybe I should have said *merde*. Sounds like French."

There were a couple of minutes of uneasy silence, then Elizabeth finally said, "Never did like those French classes in school."

Then she *did* hear it, too! Bri kept her tone light. "When you visited me in Cannes, you spoke French with a better accent than mine." A tinkle of chimes rippled, then settled inside her, coiling. She flexed her fingers. "Do you recognize that?"

"What?" The word sounded dragged out of Elizabeth.

"The chimes are the tones associated with the seven chakras: C, D, E, F, G, A, B."

"Leave it to you."

A gong sounded in her mind. Elizabeth flinched beside her. "Put on some speed. Let's get home."

"Right."

The rest of the drive passed in a rush, both physically and emotionally. Chanting blocked out all other sounds—

except for the chakra chimes and the occasional gong. The rhythm was odd, Bri couldn't catch hold of any pattern, but it wound her so tight she was near panting.

Elizabeth gave a little moan, rubbed her temples. "I can't anticipate the beat." She squirmed. "It seems to be having a physical effect. My skin prickles."

"So does mine. Nerve endings do you think?"

With a choppy exhalation of breath, Elizabeth said, "Probably. I have my medical bag up in the loft. We can check this out." She sounded as if she was reassuring herself as well as Bri.

"Of course," Bri said, pulling into the underground garage and parking in Elizabeth's space.

They got out. Bri grabbed the freezer chest and Elizabeth both bags of potatoes. As they hurried to the elevator, Bri realized her whole body trembled—the chanting was spiraling, rising with excitement, with demand. She glanced at Elizabeth and saw a huge flickering multicolored banded aura. Bri's breath whooshed out. She noted her sister wouldn't look at her. "This is scary."

2

"Scary," Elizabeth said, jabbing at the elevator button. "Everything will be fine in a few minutes. We'll figure this out." She tilted her head in Bri's direction. "I'm glad you're here with me."

"Likewise." The sounds had affected her heartbeat; the chanting sped it up, the chakra chimes tugging at different internal energies. She didn't like the sensations.

The elevator dinging melded with everything else and she didn't notice it until the steel gray doors opened and Elizabeth hustled in. The black rubber-edged doors nearly closed before Bri hopped inside, stumbled to the far wall and braced herself.

Elizabeth pressed thirty-four and the elevator rose.

Too slowly. Bri's vision was morphing. Sound seemed to take shape, with pastel clouds of pink and green and coral whirling around them. Bri gulped.

"Just a couple of minutes," Elizabeth chanting herself.

"This ain't good," Bri whispered. She wondered if she should dial 911.

The elevator went up and up and up. The chanting and chimes and gong filled it.

There was a slight hesitation, then the upward motion continued.

"We've passed the thirty-fourth floor!" Elizabeth cried.

Bri shuddered. "Isn't that the last one?"

The walls and ceiling vanished.

A wind whipped them into its grasp. They shrieked in unison. Bri wanted to drop her load and reach for her sister, but her fingers were frozen around the chest. She saw Elizabeth's pale face, arms clutching the potato sacks.

They flashed through a rippling field of blinding rainbow light, an enveloping wave of sound. Nothing under Bri's feet. She fell, jarred, as if she'd missed a couple of steps descending a staircase.

Her screams mingled with Elizabeth's. They were together, at least. Chanting came around them, along with the chimes that pushed all Bri's chakra buttons, the gong that had her dropping the chest and shuddering. She flung out her hand, found Elizabeth's. They grabbed each other, clinging.

The chanting stopped. "Well, how about that," said an accented voice. "Two for the price of one. And they brought *spuds*! Did we get this right, or what?"

Elizabeth hung on to Bri, who was trembling as much as she was. The chimes continued to rise and fall, touching her inside—her chakras if she was to believe Bri—stirring her. Everything echoed in her head: her thumping heartbeat—and her twin's?—her ragged breath, whimpering.

Blinking again and again, Elizabeth saw a large circle of people surrounding them, holding hands. There seemed to be four different groups. Some obvious couples were dressed in matching colored tunics over chain mail and had a weapon at each hip. Others had silver or gold bands around their foreheads and wore long robes. A third group wore leather clothes and sheathed swords, a fourth bunch wore colorful pants and shirts or dresses. Most of the people appeared Asian. Golden skin, black hair with slightly different colored highlights, brown eyes. Silver or gold streaks in their hair at one or both temples. Beautiful features. Beautiful people.

I've got a bad feeling about this. Bri's voice came in Elizabeth's mind! She stared in shock at her sister.

Bri!

What!

I can hear you in my mind.

Me, too. A whisper.

"Welcome to Lladrana," a woman said.

The gong sounded again and it was as if a surgeon clasped her beating heart. She and Bri screamed and swayed.

"It sounds as if they're hurting. It's not supposed to hurt that much, is it? I don't recall. Marian!"

Elizabeth focused on the different voice. She saw a blue-eyed blond woman in leathers staring worriedly at her and Bri.

"Ohmygod," Bri said thickly, turning her head. "Lladrana. I didn't do it, twin!" Childhood words of utter truth tore from her. *My itchy feet didn't bring us here!*

The chimes ran up and down the scale, once, twice… seven times. Noises wrung from Elizabeth merging with

Bri's. After the last tone reverberated, they huddled together on cold stones.

Bong! The final thump on the huge silver gong had them twitching.

Silence.

Shoving her sweaty hair away from her eyes, Elizabeth stared at the people again. They'd unlinked their hands.

Three women came to stand near them, outside a glowing green circle around a star on the floor. These three were Caucasian, though the tall, voluptuous woman with red hair and blue eyes appeared to have an Eastern European heritage.

She gestured and the green circle surrounding them subsided. "I'm Marian Harasta Dumont." She touched a golden band around her forehead that showed lightning bolts and clouds, whorls that looked like wind, curvy waves. She, too, had a large streak of white in her hair. "I'm a Sorceress, called a Circlet of the Fifth Degree.

"Welcome to Lladrana, another dimension. We have Summoned you here on behalf of the Cities and Towns. A strange fatal illness has come and they requested medicas—doctors."

Bri sat up straight, glowered at them, crossed her arms. Elizabeth kept her mouth shut.

The smallest person there, a woman with silver hair and wearing chainmail and hip sheaths spoke. "I'm Alexa Fitzwalter, come from Denver last year. I was an attorney. Here in Lladrana I am a Swordmarshall and use the Jade Baton of Honor." She pulled out the baton. It flared green and silver and bronze. The flames atop it turned from metal to real.

Impressive.

Does her name sound familiar to you? Elizabeth asked Bri.

No, but attorney...would Uncle Trent have said something about her?

Maybe I want them to do all the talking, though, Elizabeth said.

Good plan.

The willowy blond cleared her throat. She wore a leather outfit. "I'm Calli Torcher Guardpont. I am the Volaran Exotique." Her brief smile lit her face. "Flying horses." She inclined her head to others dressed as she was, "and the knights who ride them, Chevaliers."

I think I hit my head on the stones, Bri said.

Elizabeth turned to her and sent her fingers roaming over her sister's skull. Without thought she *drew* power into herself, sent it flaring around Bri's head, checking for any damage.

Breaths caught in gasps around them.

"You're a doctor?" Alexa asked.

Neither of them answered. *You're fine. You have a hard head*, Elizabeth said.

I'm having massive hallucinations.

You aren't the only one.

"We know this sounds crazy, but it's true," Marian said. "We can prove you're in another land. A place that needs you very much." She pulled a stick about as long as her hand from her pocket. It grew and shaped into a wand. Then as Elizabeth watched, the piece of wood lengthened and thickened until it was a staff.

"They're not believing us." Marian sighed.

"It takes a while," Alexa muttered.

"Yes, but it should be *easier* with a welcoming party like us," Marian said.

Bri snorted.

"Neither one of them looks like the woman we've been having those intense dreams about." Alexa shrugged, peered at them. Then said, "How long are you going to sit there and let us stare at you and talk about you?"

I vote forever, Bri said to Elizabeth. *Hallucinations have to end sometime. Someone will find us in the elevator.*

Elizabeth chuckled.

The blond woman's, Calli's, eyes narrowed. "Do you get the idea that they're mentally talking to each other?"

"Twins," said the short one, Alexa, philosophically. "And they're very Powerful, you can *hear* the strength of their Songs. Telepathy might be the first thing they notice."

Good guess, Elizabeth said to Bri.

They're all sharp. And now that she mentioned it, I, uh, hear tunes coming from everybody.

Elizabeth tilted her head. She was concentrating on her own vital signs, her pulse, her breathing, and Bri's, but beyond that she *could* hear small tunes emanating from each person. Sometimes it was comprised of more than one melody. She focused on Marian's and discovered the tune became less of a string and more of a woven rope—and led to a black-haired, blue-eyed man standing behind her.

Bri had followed her thoughts. *Interesting.*

"Time for plan B," Alexa said. She gestured to a tall man with powerful shoulders dressed in gray raw silk shirt and trousers. He gave them a half-bow. His expression was serious, his eyes haunted. He left.

Bri's fingers twined in Elizabeth's. *That bad feeling is back. Yes.*

"The baby thing worked for me," Alexa said conversationally. "Twice."

I definitely don't like where this might be leading, Elizabeth said.

"Children worked for me, too, in a different way," Calli said softly. She held out her hand and a man came up and stood with her. A definite couple. Their Song spiraled out and snagged Elizabeth, so strong and loving and tender that she had to block it out because it reminded her of what she'd lost with Cassidy. She turned away from the sight of them.

Bri squeezed her hand. *They look very married, and he's definitely a native. Marian's guy, too.*

Elizabeth shivered. At that moment the large door opened and the man wearing gray strode back in. He held a small, limp body in his arms.

"Oh, no!" Elizabeth and Bri said.

He walked straight up to where they sat and carefully laid the boy of about three before them. The man's expression was stark. "Mortee." *He dies.*

3

Elizabeth and Bri went to opposite sides of the boy, reached for him. His breath wheezed, his face was pale and grayish compared to the golden-peach complexions of the healthy adults. He opened his eyelids. A horrified noise escaped Bri at the milky film covering his eyes.

"Do you recognize these symptoms?" Bri asked, staring at her sister. She pushed the boy's limp hair back from his forehead, gently turned his head to look in his ears, opened his mouth. His tongue showed a white coating too.

"Um," Elizabeth unbuttoned the boy's shirt, put her hand on his chest. "Erratic and thready."

"Don't give me doctor-speak comparisons. Do you recognize this?"

"You never left people without hope," Elizabeth muttered.

"Twin," Bri said, "there's magical energy all around us."

"Illusion." Elizabeth glared. "He needs a hospital."

"We've already tried everything. People are dying every day." Tears dribbled down Calli's cheeks. She and the other two women who spoke English kept close.

"We can help him with our healing gift!" Bri said.

Elizabeth lifted her palms from the small boy. "I can't do anything without my instruments. Antibiotics, drugs!"

Alexa shifted her weight, looked at Elizabeth, met Bri's gaze. "We've done all we could."

Elizabeth folded her arms, held her opposite elbows tight. "Everything's too strange," she whispered. "Magic doesn't work."

With a set mouth and steady stare at Elizabeth, Bri stretched her arms, flexed her fingers, placed her hand on the boy's forehead and groin. She blinked as the air around her glowed, hummed.

Bri looked at Elizabeth, neat and tidy. It would be so much easier with her sister helping. Too bad. She'd have to fling herself into the healingstream alone, as usual. Elizabeth hunched her shoulders, glanced away. She wasn't used to working outside a clean hospital, depending on the healingstream and herself. Focusing on the boy, Bri opened herself to the healingstream. Only complete dedication would save the boy's life. She *grabbed* for the current.

Energy slammed into her, through her. She thought she heard Elizabeth gasp. Bri's hands turned fiery with green flames. The boy's body arched and jumped. Oh, God, oh, God, she'd killed him.

She flung herself back. Her legs tangled. Her head hit hard stone. Commotion erupted around her. Her mind spun, she was afraid to look at her hands. Her fingertips must have blackened from the force of what she'd taken hold of.

She was used to a stream of healing energy, not a raging river. Awesome.

Fearsome.

Her heart stopped thundering the same time her vision cleared—or she had enough sense to blink. She stared up at a circular room, with windows high in the wall. Stained glass alternated with clear. Rough beams were studded with opaque white crystals. Stones that held energy like batteries. Too many crystals to count. She'd plugged into a huge power source.

Would any place on Earth have such a potent psi-magical energy current? Doubt gnawed. The more she ignored it, the stronger it became.

The flow had held a tang of *otherness*. Usually she'd tap into the healingstream, taste what she only knew as Mother Earth. A current of energy straight from the core, smelling like molten lava, tasting like the richest soil. Those sensations had been absent, other sensual cues had come instead.

"Twin," she croaked, and turned her head.

Elizabeth didn't look at her. She was on her feet, next to the man who'd scooped up the boy. Bri felt her mouth drop open. The kid was squirming like any healthy and active youngster. Ohmygod.

The boy's eyes were wide open, bright and brown. His skin looked rosier than most everyone else's. Pale and trembling, Elizabeth had turned doctor and was lifting her hand from his forehead. Then she stuck out her tongue at him and he returned the gesture. Appeared red enough to Bri.

Ohmygod.

Not God, you, Elizabeth said stiltedly in Bri's mind.

Bri swallowed and watched her twin trail her fingers over the boy's cheek. Now well hydrated, almost chubby.

Elizabeth shuddered. *You saved a life.* Slowly, she met Bri's gaze, her own full of shocked disbelief. *You saved a life with…with….*

Healing hands. She glanced down, they weren't black.

The man holding the boy said something and the redhead—Marian—translated the twisted French-like words. "There are other sick outside in the cloister walk. We brought everyone from Castleton, fifteen sick. One died before you came."

Elizabeth stared at Bri, hands fisting. Bri sensed her yearning to help. But Elizabeth would have to admit to having a gift. Which she'd denied since they were teens. Would she help?

Elizabeth stretched out her hand. "Twin?"

Bri rocked to her hands and knees, levered herself to her feet. Swaying, she reluctantly lifted one foot, then the other, stamping them down to ground herself, connecting again with—*not* Mother Earth. She ignored a heart twinge, took a step, saw Alexa sidling toward the bags of potatoes and had a flash of insight.

"Those potatoes are ours! So's the food chest." She glanced around. Who could they trust to guard their "treasure"? As she focused on people, she heard tunes coming from them. Most were fascinated, many were grateful, only one had an essential defining characteristic of pure honesty. She nodded to the guy dressed all in white leathers. "Will you keep our belongings for us?" she asked in careful French, gesturing to their pile of stuff, including Elizabeth's healthy back bag and Bri's solar-paneled backpack containing her cell, her PDA, her music player. All those would help in discovering whether the others spoke the truth and she and Elizabeth were in a different place.

The man nodded and came to stand near their things, careful not to touch them. His nostrils flared, he closed his eyes and shuddered, but his face remained impassive.

Narrowing her eyes, Alexa shot Bri a speculative look. "You heard enough of his Song to choose him to watch your stuff."

That deduction jolted Bri, emphasized the strange things that were happening.

"Bri," Elizabeth called from near the big door.

Bri turned and scanned the round room. She and Elizabeth might have to return here, recreate the setting. So she stopped to soak in details before her mind focused on other, more critical matters.

The gong was gigantic and polished silver about nine feet in diameter. The altar had lamps made of precious gemstones containing flickering candles. A small mallet lay by the lamps. Since they were in the colors associated with the seven chakras, Bri figured they served as light and the chimes. Her stomach quivered as she recalled their effect on her.

The room was a huge cylinder of white stone, with sections partitioned off by tall, fancily carved wooden screens like she'd seen in India. The large rectangular pool she'd skirted smelled of herbal water—acacia, lavender, something resinous—Balm of Gilead?

Built-in stone benches circled the room, their hard lines broken with colorful pillows in all sizes.

People had gathered in clumps, usually those dressed alike, and were studying them. The way Alexa, a small woman, strode through the chamber let Bri know that she expected most people to get out of her way, and they did. An attorney from Denver, huh? Well, she'd certainly made a name for herself here. The thin scar on her cheek, the toughness of her body and the weapons that she wore made Bri's bad feeling return.

One more step and she reached Elizabeth and the man, who was a lot taller than Bri expected, with big shoulders and a body that looked as if he did hard labor every day— but not with the air of a soldier that Alexa had.

"So," Alexa said with a measuring look. "Your name is Bry? Brianna?"

It was Brigid. Bri shared a glance with Elizabeth. How much to say? Were names power here? Should they hide their names? When neither of them answered Marian sighed.

The man handed the child to another guy dressed in pants and shirt. He put his fingers near his heart and bowed deeply. "Sevair Masif," he said. Looking straight in Elizabeth's, then Bri's eyes, he spoke and Bri got the gist of heartfelt thanks since his words were halting and full of rich tones.

Marian translated, "Thank you. We have lost several from this dread disease, but not one so young. He is an only child of a widow and his mother treasures him. Thank you."

Bri inclined her head. Elizabeth pressed her lips together. In regret that she hadn't helped cure the boy? In denial that she *could* have helped with…magic?

Marian's mouth curved in a smile that Bri distrusted. The

Sorceress held out a little bottle. "One drop of this would banish that language barrier for an hour, though you both seem to know French."

"A little," Elizabeth said.

"Some," Bri said.

"No," they said together as they stared at the bottle.

Marian's smile faded. She tilted her head in the direction of the door. "Additional patients await you outside. It will be more efficient if you can speak well to direct us."

Alexa said, "We all work in healing circles, but we haven't been able to effect any cures. More cases surface every day, more deaths every week."

Do we dare leave here? Elizabeth asked.

Bri licked her lips. *They sound as if they need us.*

"Why does everyone have to be bribed to take the potions?" Marian said.

The blond woman who was dressed all in leathers, Calli, smiled at this. "Oh, just because we're not stupid." She glanced at the twins. "It *does* work."

Cocking her head, Bri said, "What's the bribe?"

"I answer *every* question you have for two hours," Marian said promptly.

"If this is really a different place, you promise to send us home," Bri countered.

"Can't be done," Marian said, with a finality that left no argument. She gestured to the groups of people drifting toward them. "It took all of us to Summon you here. Returning you is an even greater feat."

The big door was flung open and a hysterical woman shot in. She saw the boy and shrieked, grabbed him. Bri and Elizabeth moved instinctively, then checked as the woman began kissing his face all over, hugging him tight, tears pouring from her eyes.

Moaning came from outside. *Twin?* asked Elizabeth.

Bri squared her shoulders, tried a hard expression as she looked at Marian. "You three know English and this mangled French. You can translate."

"Three days," Marian said. She drew herself up. "I'll be at your disposal for three days."

"Take her up on it," Alexa advised.

Bri's hand met Elizabeth's and they linked fingers as if they were little girls again. Bri felt wonder, the willingness to heal…. "We don't anticipate being here three days," Bri said. "Someone will find us in the elevator."

"Elevator?" Alexa sounded fascinated. "You came here by *elevator?*"

They left the room for a covered outdoor portico. Before them was a huge courtyard surrounded by dark shapes of buildings like a medieval Castle in excellent condition.

The air! Elizabeth said.

Much more humid than Denver.

No traffic sounds.

The smells are different, too. Rain, wet stone, even the people smelled subtly different than any other culture Bri'd visited.

Sevair Masif turned right, toward the sound of moaning. A tide of pain swept to Bri from Elizabeth, who'd gotten hit first. Her twin doubled over. Bri bent down and hugged her, *reached* again for the energy flow, felt it rush as if a faucet had been turned on above her. The current washed away the echoes of pain, let her put a thin bubble of protection between her and their patients' hurting. She helped Elizabeth erect mental shields.

Sevair had stopped and turned to observe them.

Bri became aware of reverberating sound—this time thready melodies that pulled at her heart with a yearning to mend. She was still considering the strange notion that she could *hear* tunes coming from people when Elizabeth straightened, squeezed her hand, then crossed the stone courtyard with a steady step. Her sister headed to a covered walk along what looked like a Castle keep—cloisters, with lacy stone half-walls and open "windows."

Elizabeth looked down the walk, her emotions amplified and easily felt by Bri. Pity. Hope. Most of all, the desire to help, to heal. She looked at Bri.

"Are you with me?"

They exchanged a glance. Bri could almost see the reflection of herself in Elizabeth's eyes, knew Elizabeth thought of her as a new-age rebel exploring fringe healing. Did Elizabeth sense how Bri saw her—a buttoned-down doctor?

Someone cried out. Elizabeth flinched. "You saved a life." *And I stood aside*, she added mentally, blinking hard.

Don't beat yourself up. I took a familiar risk.

Elizabeth sighed. *I'm willing to risk it with you.* "Can we heal fifteen?"

"We won't know until we try. We'll give it our best shot."

Elizabeth nodded. Bri hurried over, all too aware of *otherness* surrounding her. She joined Elizabeth and saw cots set up all along the walkway.

Elizabeth sent red-headed Marian a cool glance. "Take us to the worst cases, first." Marian spoke to a man and a woman who wore red tunics with white crosses on them, and they went to the far end of the corridor. Elizabeth and Bri followed.

Glancing down as she followed her very impressive twin, Bri saw that the people were definitely different from those who'd been in the round building. Their clothes were shabbier, seemed more lower and middle class. She clenched her jaw; she wanted to help. Elizabeth had positioned herself on one side of a pallet. Bri took the opposite side. Elizabeth had also set her teeth.

Relax, she sent to Elizabeth, opening her own mouth to ease her jaw muscles.

I am relaxed.

Check your jaw and shoulders.

Elizabeth stiffened, then moved a little, loosening her shoulders and her stance. She took a slow breath in and relaxed her muscles as she exhaled. When she looked at Bri, her eyes gleamed from a pale face. All this strangeness was getting to them both, but the restless shifting and the sheer *hurt* of the sick people around them demanded their attention.

Other people had followed, most standing in the courtyard outside the cloister windows. The three Caucasian women—Alexa, Marian, and Calli—remained near.

Bri stepped up to their first patient, an elderly woman. The woman had a slow, thin tune with little embellishments. Bri put her left hand on her head.

Yes, said Elizabeth, *you take her head. I don't trust myself to send the proper amount of energy to her head.* A shiver rippled through her.

It was cooler here, especially in the stone cloister walk, than in Denver. Or maybe it was just later in the night.

Elizabeth spread the fingers of her right hand over the woman's heart, Bri extended her own right-hand fingers, with one finger touching Elizabeth's over the woman's abdomen, felt loose flesh, the laboring of lungs. Milky eyes stared up at her. Bri swallowed hard. The woman was as tall as the rest of these people. Elizabeth set her other hand, spread to touch Bri's, over the woman's crotch.

Bri and Elizabeth matched gazes, breaths.

"Ready?" asked Bri.

Elizabeth nodded. *You handle it.*

Fear puddled in Bri's stomach, but she shut it away, hoping her sister couldn't sense it. She opened herself to the energy. She *pulled*, gently, gently. It rushed through her like a river. She felt the briskness of the night, an effervescence that twinkled like stars in the sky outside the walk. She swayed.

A woman clasped her shoulders, helped ground and steady her, though she didn't seem able to grip or work the healingstream. Marian.

Incredible, echoed in Bri's mind from the sorceress, went to Elizabeth. *I've never sensed Power like this.*

Elizabeth, mind sharper than Bri's, monitored their patient, cut the healingstream when they were done. Bri wriggled her shoulders and Marian stepped back.

"She's still very dehydrated and undernourished," Elizabeth said, looking to Sevair Masif who stood near, and Marian translated. "You'll ensure that she gets additional treatment?"

"Of course," said a female dressed in a red robe with a white cross. A medical person.

"Good," Bri said. The one word was harder to form than she expected.

"Next?" Elizabeth said in a too-brusque voice as if

squelching fear. The healingstream was new to her. Elizabeth might have used a surge of healing energy from herself, or touched on the stream, but had never opened herself to it.

Bri had been the one kicking around the world, finding herself in villages or refugee camps with people who needed help while she only had her hands and the healingstream to depend upon. Many times that had not been enough. Then she grasped a wispy thought of Elizabeth's. She was thinking how she'd shut herself and her talent off and had depended only on her medical training, not her gift, except in rare instances. Many times all her knowledge and training had not been enough.

Once again Bri followed Elizabeth, and they began to establish a balance to handle the cycling energy. Elizabeth learned to open herself, Bri learned to limit and direct the healingstream. Marian stood behind Bri with her hands on her shoulders, steadying, supporting, but unable to join them.

By the time they'd helped six, Bri began to feel the whole jet-lagged incredible event-packed day wearing upon her and moved by rote, summoning the healingstream, sending it into sick bodies. She felt the shadow of Elizabeth's thoughts as she studied and dismissed different diagnoses. Nothing was familiar about this sickness.

Somewhere between two hours and infinity they were finished and Bri was swaying on her feet. Elizabeth stood with the straightness of a woman refusing to give in to exhaustion then swung an arm around Bri's shoulders and they were drawn to a moonlit opening to the courtyard. The cloister had been dark, too dark to work in, why had they?

"Light hurts the sick's eyes," Marian said, and Bri realized she and the other woman had shared enough of a bond for the Sorceress to pick up on her thoughts, even if they weren't linked anymore. Dangerous.

"No," said Marian. She bowed deeply, keeping her gaze on them. "I promise I will never hurt you. Either of you."

"Huh," said Bri. She started to lean on the edge of the stone door opening and missed. Was falling. Something oddly shaped set against her and pushed her upward. In the brief contact, she felt a different sort of energy wash through her, tingling from top to toe, clearing her mind, giving her own energy—and Elizabeth's—a boost.

"Thank you—" She turned to her savior and gawked. A horse stood there, eyes huge and liquid and gleaming with… with…with *magic*? It whinnied and stepped back. Others like it stood in the courtyard. The smell of resinous amber crumbling into perfume wafted to Bri.

"They're curious." Calli walked past them into the stone courtyard and rubbed the horse's nose. "They say you're using Power they only dimly sensed and didn't know how to access. One has gone to report to the alpha pair in Volaran Valley." She pointed. Bri followed her finger to see a white horse. With wings. Soaring over the buildings on the opposite side of the courtyard and off into a night sky that held too many stars.

Impossible.

Elizabeth stiffened into rigidity. *Impossible*.

Another whicker came and Bri looked to the horse that had propped her up. Slowly it opened wings at its sides, spread them—huge feathery things.

Ohmygod, Bri said.

Ohmygod, Elizabeth said.

"Ohmygod," she and Elizabeth said together.

"You're not in Colorado anymore," Alexa said.

4

Elizabeth was holding onto sanity as if it was the unraveling edge of a ratty blanket. Too much strangeness. Everything—the people, the humid air, the sky showing too many stars, and most especially the winged horses.

One was still rubbing against Bri in mutual admiration.

Sevair Masif, the man who'd come from Castleton, was ensuring the care and comfort of his people with efficient orders to soldiers and servants. The knot of the more ostentatiously dressed people—including two of the three Coloradan women—attracted his attention. He gave one last order and joined them, crossing his arms and raising his chin.

"We agreed that should the Summoning of the medica be successful and if she fulfilled our great and desperate need, she would stay here at the Castle tonight. The ladies are tired. Why are they not being led to their quarters?" The soft translation came to Elizabeth's ear and she turned her head to see Calli smiling at her.

Calli lifted a shoulder, sighed. "They argue. Sevair's a good man, just obsessed with frinks."

"Frinks?" Elizabeth asked.

"Metallic worms that come with the rain. The dark sends them, too."

Elizabeth wished she hadn't asked.

"One of your tasks will be to smooth the way between the City and Town segment of society and the rest."

Elizabeth shook her head, looked at Calli, then at Bri who was examining one of the horse's wings. She seemed familiar with the animals, at least was probably familiar with wingless ones. Another change. Somewhere, sometime Bri had learned about horses. No doubt she'd traveled where a horse was still considered a necessity. Elizabeth gestured to the horse and Bri. "Why aren't you supervising?"

"You're sharp," said Calli. "Remembered that I'm the one who was Summoned for the volarans and Chevaliers." She followed Elizabeth's gaze. "I can see auras, you know."

"No." If she denied all this it might go away

"Yes. Most folks here depend upon their ears and their Power to hear Songs. I hear the Songs, but auras are easier for me. Thunder is a curious volaran, and it's difficult to ignore the fact that the horses have wings. Not something you'd see on Earth. Thunder is giving your twin sister some energy." Calli narrowed her eyes. "Some of that is passing into you." Nibbling on her lip, Calli continued. "It takes a while to become used to Lladrana. We, the other Exotiques and I, hoped to make your transition easier. It didn't seem to work."

Elizabeth raised her eyebrows. "With sixteen people in the throes of sickness needing medical help?"

Calli winced. "I suppose that would have been the equivalent of me riding most of the Castle volarans." She met Elizabeth's gaze steadily. "I'd apologize, but I'm not sorry. The townspeople are desperate. None of the medicas in Lladrana have found a cure for this new disease and people are dying." Calli squinted at Bri, then back at Elizabeth. "You and your twin had a basic similar layer of green in your auras when you came but different upper layers. That's interesting. But the bond between you two when you arrived wasn't nearly as strong as it is now."

Elizabeth didn't want to hear any of this.

A man dressed in such an understated and tailored style of leathers that proclaimed him wealthy joined them. He bowed, then looked expectantly at Calli.

"This is Faucon Creusse, a nobleman and Chevalier."

"Chevalier?"

"Knight, like I said."

Faucon said something, and Calli translated. "An impressive display of Power by the new Exotiques, as usual."

Before Elizabeth could answer, the discussion between the leaders got heated.

An older woman snapped something, and Calli delivered the words but didn't match the tone. "Of course we have plenty of space, but we only prepared for one and it's evident that they will not want to be separated."

Masif stood solid. "We townspeople have many places where the Exotiques can stay. We paid to have them Summoned. They are our—" he glanced from Elizabeth to Bri, who were both watching him, nodded in acknowledgment and finished "—guests. They should stay in the city."

"Not tonight," said the woman.

Calli added, "That's Lady Knight Swordmarshall Thealia Germain, she's the head of the Marshalls and runs everything."

Faucon gave another half bow to Elizabeth then turned and stepped up to the group. "Of course the sisters would prefer to room together. Which is why I requested a suite be prepared in Alyeka's tower for them."

"I'd like to keep them in *my* tower," Thealia said. The streaks of gold at her temples were so wide they nearly reached the middle of her head. A sign of nobility? Both Faucon's temples showed swaths of silver.

At that moment a horrendous siren went off.

Elizabeth jumped.

Bri stumbled as the volaran she was leaning against hopped away.

The courtyard was full of people and now every one of them was moving. Some were racing away to a point Elizabeth couldn't see; the healthy townsfolk had stepped back to crowd the cloisters. Volarans alit in the courtyard and the Chevaliers—those in leathers—jumped on their backs, along with some of the younger people who had a sheath on each hip.

Thealia, the older woman, turned and scrutinized the action like the head of the hospital checking the emergency room in a crisis, and Elizabeth's stomach tightened as she sensed there was a disaster in progress. "What?"

"I wondered." Marian, the sorceress, circlet, whatever, reached Calli at the same time as Bri. She looked at Calli, jerked her head to the small white-haired woman who joined them. "Four Summonings. Four times the Dark has attacked very soon after."

"Connected," the small woman, Alexa said. Her serious gaze watched the refined chaos and her left hand went to the cylindrical leather sheath at her side.

Bri had linked arms with Elizabeth and she could feel nerves thrumming through her twin.

A slightly shorter, muscular man who moved with grace whirled Alexa up in his arms. "Let's go!"

"We fight? It's not our rotation," Alexa said.

"I have a bad feeling. I don't want Pascal and Marwey to lead the youngsters. We'll do that."

Alexa met Elizabeth's gaze, then Bri's. "Later. This is my husband, Bastien, by the way."

Elizabeth wanted to call them back.

"Must you?" cried Bri.

But Alexa and Bastien merely waved.

"They'll triumph, as usual," said Marian.

"Yes," added Calli.

But both women's faces showed anxiety.

"How many will we lose?" murmured Calli. "Who will we lose?"

Elizabeth stepped closer to Bri. Again she thought she should offer to do something—what?

Bri said, *What in God's name could we do? We know NOTHING about this place.* But they shared flickering along their nerves as if they should spring into action, too.

The activity in the courtyard separated into patterns— those who flew away and those who stayed.

Thealia, the leader, snapped out a few orders and said something to Calli and Marian.

"Another interminable war council in a few minutes," Calli said.

Bri flinched beside Elizabeth, and Elizabeth finally let herself realize what she'd sensed all along—these people had many reasons for Summoning them, and the primary one was because of a war.

A disease was one thing, a war quite another. She didn't want to be here.

As if she'd read Elizabeth's mind—could they do that?— Marian said, "They don't fly to fight other humans. They fly to fight monsters and save a world. A world we need your help to save, too."

Worse and worse.

Bri leaned against one of the fancily carved columns of cloister "windows" opening onto the courtyard. The stone was cold and hard and had the unmistakable feel of reality. She much preferred being propped up by a winged horse and tingling with energy, stuff of dreams.

Calli kept up a running commentary and translation.

At that moment the man in the white leathers appeared carrying the cooler they'd left in the huge, circular room. Atop the chest the sacks of potatoes were neatly stacked. Elizabeth's bag's strap crossed his chest, and the loop of Bri's big backpack was over his shoulder. He carried them all easily.

Calli frowned at him. "Luthan, you're not fighting?"

His jaw clenched and he nodded, showing no emotion. "I have instructions from the Singer to remain at the Castle or in the town for the first two weeks after the Exotiques arrive." His voice gave nothing away, but a ripple of shock passed through the others.

"She said two would be coming?" asked Marian, seeming to throb with irritation and curiosity.

Luthan said, "She said at least two."

Silence draped the cloister. He let the statement hang, then bowed—with cooler—to Elizabeth and Bri. "I am Luthan Vauxveau, brother to Bastien, the pairling of Exotique Alyeka. I am also the representative of the Singer, the oracle of Lladrana, to the Marshalls. I sit on their councils to inform her what transpires here."

"It would be good if she kept us equally informed," Thealia said.

"The Singer is the Singer," Luthan said.

"Not the same as the rest of us, that's for sure," Calli muttered. She caught Bri's eye. "A prophetess."

The leaden weight of exhaustion was ready to flatten Bri. Despite the spurts of adrenaline since she'd arrived, and the various sources of energy that poured into and through her, there was only so much a body could take. Except for a quick nap at Elizabeth's that afternoon, she'd been going nonstop for too many hours.

"Where do I put this chest?" Luthan asked expression-lessly. From the faint sheen of sweat on his forehead, Bri thought he was under a mental or emotional strain. His hands were sheathed in gauntlets.

"I can take that—" she offered, pushing away from the wall, but the handsome Faucon stepped forward.

"I will carry the ladies' treasures." He took the cooler and potatoes from Luthan. "Marian and Calli, if you would show the new Exotique Medicas the way to the suite under Alyeka's."

Calli sniffed. "We argued, all wanting you near. Thealia

won, but that was when there was one of you." She shrugged. "Circumstances change rapidly in Lladrana." She shot a glance at Bri. "A lot of stairs. You hanging in there?"

"Yes." She had to shift back and forth to feel her feet, but she figured she could manage stairs. The weariness would hold off for a few minutes more.

Faucon waited for Marian and Calli and their men to precede him then took his place between Bri and Elizabeth as they followed. Luthan, still bearing the twins' bags, fell into step.

They entered the keep and trudged up an endless number of stairs around a tower, went through a door and marched singly through a narrow security corridor to enter a wedge-shaped bedroom in purple. There was one huge bed and a smaller one.

"My valet has arranged for the extra bed and wardrobe," Faucon said, sweeping the room with a glance. "I will put the food in the dining room." He disappeared and Bri heard the opening and closing of more doors. When he returned he glanced at Bri and Elizabeth and winked. "Most defensible." So he'd seen how Alexa had salivated over the potatoes, too.

"Where do you want these, ladies?" asked Luthan, removing the bags and holding them at arms' length.

Elizabeth gestured to a low wooden chest at the bottom of the big, curtained bed. The room was crowded with the smaller bed, two large wardrobes, a set of chairs, and love seat, all shoved against the large circular wall under a row of windows.

Bri tottered a little and Elizabeth was there, wrapping her arm around her waist, and it felt good to be with her sister again, not alone in this strange dream.

"Thank you all," Elizabeth said with the authority of a hospital physician.

"You're welcome," Marian and Calli said at the same time.

"We'll leave you alone now, but if you have any concerns, just holler," Calli said.

"We'll be back tomorrow morning," Marian said.

Elizabeth nodded at the same time Bri did.

Faucon stopped before them and raised Elizabeth's hand to his lips, kissed her fingertips. "Vel-coom to Lladrana," he said in heavily accented English. Bri got the impression it was his *only* English and he'd been saving it.

Then he kissed Bri's hand and she sensed great satisfaction from him. He was pleased he could provide the new Exotiques with amenities. She caught the thought—more emotion really—*Which one is mine?*

Uh-oh.

But he was gone the next moment, closing the door behind him and Bri was left staring at it and doubting what she'd thought she'd heard. Sensed. Felt. Oh, hell.

They were alone. At least inside the suite, Bri hadn't heard as many footsteps leave as those who had accompanied them. Guards?

She supposed she could send a mental probe and figure out who was there. Just the idea that she was contemplating such a weird action made her stomach twist.

"Bri?" Elizabeth's voice was laden with concern.

"I'm hanging in there. Been a long day." She wondered if anything would happen if she braced a hand against the wall that the bed was against. It was either that or collapse in a heap, so she did so. The pretty pattern wasn't paper. It was silk. She shook her head to banish gray exhaustion from her vision and saw that Elizabeth had checked out two doors and left them open.

"Study." Elizabeth pointed left. "Bathroom." To the right. "Then dining room."

Bri stared at the bed. Bigger than a California king. Of course the Lladranans were a big people, larger than American average, or American big. They pampered themselves, with beds that big and a damask comforter filled with down atop it.

Elizabeth sniffed. She had a tissue in her hand.

"Oh, Elizabeth!" Bri stumbled to her, found her and they held each other and rocked, as they'd done often when life had overwhelmed them in childhood. Privately, because this was their own twin thing.

Bri, I'm frightened.

Me, too.

You're the adventuress. Do you think we're really somewhere else?

Either that or the elevator crashed and we have massive trauma and are either in comas or dead and not moved on yet.

Choking, Elizabeth said, "That's what I thought. Am thinking. I think."

"Therefore you is. You always think. But both logic and emotion lead me to believe we're alive and functioning and in a different, uh, realm. We're together, you're not in my dream. Or maybe you are. Should I say something I know that proves to you that I'm me and here?" She thought a little. "I found this really excellent rock group in Sweden and had an affair with the drummer and even followed him around on a European tour."

"You!" Elizabeth's head jerked as though from a blow and her arms loosened. Her eyes were wide with shock.

Heat flooded Bri from her feet to tickle her scalp. She winced and gave an embarrassed chuckle. "Yeah. I'm susceptible to lust and infatuation just like anyone else. He found someone who'd flatter him more and dumped me." Not the whole truth.

Elizabeth's eyes narrowed and she swept a glance up and down Bri. She raised her hands. "Hey, I'm all right. I can be sensible. No sexually transmitted diseases. No pregnancy."

With a final scan and a blink, Elizabeth crossed her arms. Bri held out hers again, and they hugged, stepped back, but kept their hands linked.

"All right," Elizabeth said. "That sounds so you, but I never would have imagined it. Never."

"Your turn," Bri said. "You pretty much acted like I'd expect if this was all my dream. Prove you're you."

Elizabeth's jaw clenched. She dropped Bri's hand, looked away, blushed a fiery red, and Bri heard her answer telepathically. *Cassidy was—is—into light bondage. And I liked it, too.*

Bri's mouth fell open. She stared. Elizabeth's arms were crossed again and she still wasn't looking at Bri.

"You're right. That's something I'd never think of." Her turn to study her twin. "But you were both wound too damn tight. I can see…no, I don't think I want to see. Just let me ask. One or both of you, um…"

"We took turns." Elizabeth's voice was stifled. She finally met Bri's eyes and said, "And you reacted just like I'd expect you to."

They stared at each other, then cracked up, falling together again. When they'd finished with the bout of hysterical laughter, Bri took a tissue, wiped her eyes, then blew her nose.

"For the record," Elizabeth said in a serious tone. "Sexual preferences aren't necessarily determined by stress or how 'tightly' a person is wound."

"Huh. I heard that sometimes high-powered professional women such as yourself—"

"So, tell me, Ms. Free Spirit. Haven't you ever done it?"

Again heat rose in Bri. "I'll take the fifth, but I will say it never became a standard sexual practice."

Elizabeth smiled wickedly. "We aren't identical."

"One last thing, what's your favorite number?"

Bri waited a beat, then said, "Forty-two," at the same time Elizabeth did. "I think I have to sit down."

"The beds—"

"Definitely not the bed," Bri said. "If I hit a bed, I'm gone, and we need to talk. You got any chocolate in your purse?"

Going to the chest, Elizabeth took her black healthy back bag and clutched it. "Maybe."

"Me, too. I've got a feeling that we'll have to be careful of it or those others will pinch it or expect us to share. Let's see how much." With slow steps, Bri reached the chest, then hefted her backpack with the solar panels on it. "Boy, am I glad I invested in this." She carefully spilled the contents. Her music pod, PDA, digital camera, cell, and everything else she needed for a three-day hike.

Elizabeth pulled items from every pouch of her bag and lined the objects in little rows, glanced at Bri's heap. "That's it?" she gasped. "Two small candy bars. That is the extent of your chocolate cache!"

Bri winced. "I was hungry on the plane. I ate some."

Elizabeth took Bri's pack, shook it. Rustling came. She rolled her eyes. "You just dumped the bag, didn't check the compartments." Nimble fingers delved and found the unopened bag of the miniature bars Bri had purchased as well as two credit card holders and a lucky koala bear key chain.

"Oh, thank God!" Bri snatched the chocolate bag. Tears welled in her eyes. "You are a wonderful woman, twin." The words were out of her mouth before she realized that Elizabeth's chocolate stash was about twice the size of her own. Elizabeth still had the unopened bag of her dark chocolate treats, too.

"I wonder whether the others prefer milk or dark," Elizabeth said.

Putting down her bag, Bri sorted her stuff. Electronics, pens and paper, food, water bottle, wallet and coin purse and loose change, keys, instant coffee, herbal tea bags…. "I bet it won't matter. Chocolate is chocolate after all. We don't let them know we have it."

"You don't think they have chocolate here?"

"I don't want to take the chance."

Elizabeth was packing her purse up again, sliding things in their proper pockets. "You're right, and my chocolate is mine and yours is yours."

Bri sent her a wounded look. "Would I take your chocolate?"

"Yes."

Sniffing, Bri said, "You're right. Better hide it."

"When I get home—" Elizabeth stopped, choked, dropped her bag, put her hands over her face and folded onto the love seat.

"Oh, honey." Bri grabbed her own packet of tissues and sat next to her sister. "I know you're scared. I am, too. But we're in this together."

"I don't want to be in anything. Even if you are here."

Bri rested her head on Elizabeth's. She didn't dare let go of her control or she'd be asleep in two seconds. "I'm sorry." She blinked and blinked again to keep her eyes open.

Elizabeth's muscles tensed as she gathered her own control. It wasn't often Elizabeth broke down, and Bri could only imagine the emotional roller coaster her twin had been on lately. Not surprising this hit her hard. It might be hitting Bri equally hard if her mind wasn't so fuzzy.

"I love you, sis, but I don't know what to say," she said. "I don't know how to help you."

After wiping her eyes and blowing her nose, Elizabeth threw away their tissues in a wastebasket, then said brusquely, "Just weariness. Now let's get serious. What sort of meds do we have?" Once again she opened her bag and brought out a small gold-toned pill box that Bri had given her on their last birthday. She flipped it open and showed a few over-the-counter analgesics.

Bri winced. "That's it?"

"You know I don't carry any sort of drugs on my person, and make sure everyone in the hospital knows that."

"Yeah, yeah, good idea." Bri fumbled through her stuff, withdrew a generic mega-bottle of American aspirin. "I used local remedies in Sweden."

"That's good."

Bri separated a few baggies with a mixture of pills. "Herbs and vitamins."

"What kind of herbs?"

"Um, Rhodiola Rosea."

"Excellent," Elizabeth said.

The only thing that looked remotely mainstream medical was a series of tin-foil–wrapped packets with little bumps of pills in them.

"What are those?" Elizabeth asked.

"Swedish cat antibiotics. I was taking care of a friend's cat. It got better after one week instead of two."

"What are the ingredients?"

"I don't know."

They stared at each other.

"We'll have to keep them for emergencies."

"How can you think of using—"

"If it came down to cat antibiotics or death, what would you chose?" Bri said brutally.

"You have a point." Too anxious to sit still, Elizabeth stood and paced along the lined-up furniture, looking at the night-dark windows facing…what? She'd lost her sense of direction.

But the rooms of the Castle didn't bother her as much as the people, the suffering people, she'd found here. "Do you really think we can turn this epidemic around?" Elizabeth asked, not at all sure, frightened of failure.

But Bri was asleep. She slumped against the back of the love seat, listing toward where Elizabeth had been sitting.

Elizabeth swallowed hard. Even exhausted, Bri had handled this whole thing so much better than she. Of course Bri was used to new people and places, learning to fit into a new culture.

Elizabeth went back to the couch and sat, studying her

twin. Bri had really meant to settle down in Denver. How ironic that now her itchy feet had finally stopped, they were *somewhere else*. Elizabeth glanced at their pitiful cache of drugs. Aspirin, vitamins.

And *healing hands*. That thought tightened her throat. She'd denied her gift for so long. Suppressed it.

All she'd ever wanted was to be a good doctor.

Cassidy had discovered her secret. It had been the inciting incident of their last fight which had led to the end of their engagement.

If she let herself, she could hear murmuring around her—like a film soundtrack. And she was sure her retinas still held images of the auras she had actually *seen*. Automatically, she repacked her bag and Bri's backpack. Then she changed herself and Bri into nightclothes and persuaded her sleepy sister to bed. Maybe this would all be a dream.

5

Bri woke and savored the coziness of sheets and warmth, definitely not the tiny, chilly apartment in Stockholm. Elizabeth certainly did herself proud. Did the family proud, including Bri herself. During college she'd had no doubt that Elizabeth would sail through medical school and become a brilliant physician like their mother. Now if Bri could only buckle down and master nursing school.

She yawned, stretched. The day before had been hard, the worry that she'd get home to Denver all right on standby. Those incredible dreams. She snorted. Imagine that, flying horses. She hadn't dreamt of them before.

Opening her eyes to a canopy overhead showing an embroidered huge winged horse, she got the nasty feeling that she still hadn't dreamt of them. She jackknifed up and the covers slid down, and the room was warm. She was covered in a large shirt, obviously not her own. There were buttons on the *shoulders*. A soft whuffling moan caught her attention and she looked over to see Elizabeth in the huge bed with her. Beyond the posts of the bed were windows set in a circular wall showing gray sky.

Tears had her eyes stinging. She wanted to be *home*, and not just Denver, but her old room with her old waterbed. A room that had been redecorated years ago. But at least she was *supposed* to be home in Denver. The yearning for it had gotten bigger and bigger in the past year and developed into a horrible homesickness. She wriggled her feet, not just to get her circulation, but to test. No signs of itchy feet.

She glanced at Elizabeth, who was wearing a pristine nightgown. Slipping from the bed, she went over to the large freestanding wardrobe that featured two doors with a couple of drawers beneath them. Opening the left door she saw only a smaller shirt and a larger shirt. Brought by Faucon? Or in case a man was Summoned? Opening a drawer, she found handkerchiefs, took one and blew her nose.

"Bri?" Elizabeth mumbled.

Bri froze. If she was feeling this bad, how would Elizabeth the homebody feel? How was she going to comfort her sister when she had little emotional strength herself?

But Elizabeth was sitting up in bed, looking around, eyes bright. She smiled at Bri, rolled her shoulders, linked her fingers and stretched. "Not in Colorado anymore."

It occurred to Bri that to Elizabeth, leaving Colorado and her grief and problems might be a relief. Bri blew her nose louder, saw a large wicker basket with a linen sack that she figured was a laundry hamper, and tossed the used hankie inside. "Lladrana." She remembered that much.

Recalled also that she had some power bars in her backpack. Padding on thick carpets to the love seat, she grabbed her pack.

She hopped onto the high bed and under the covers and opened her satchel. Elizabeth probably would have put the food—yup, she unzipped the pocket, dipped her hand in and tossed a bar to her sister, while ripping the wrapping off one herself. "Thanks for sleeping with me. If I'd been alone, I mighta freaked."

"I didn't want to be by myself last night, either." Elizabeth studied the wrapper. "What's in this?"

Bri spoke around a mouthful of granola, raisins and yogurt bits. "Only healthy stuff, I swear, sweetened with rice syrup."

Hastily Elizabeth peeled off the wrapper, dropped it over the side of the bed, took the shreds of Bri's wrapper and did the same. Must be a wastebasket there. Elizabeth chomped down, made a humming noise. Chewed. Swallowed. Turned to Bri with crumbs on her lips. "This is really good."

"Yeah." Bri had already gobbled hers and wasn't going to eat another one of what now must be rationed. She slipped from the bed and went to the windows.

"What do you see?" asked Elizabeth.

"Green fields and hills." A movement caught her eye and she craned her head to the left. "Castle wall, garden, big dirt field. Pretty bustling down there. Soldiers. Those knights, Chevaliers, a couple of…of volarans. That city guy, Sevair Masif, all neat and tidy and pressed, watching this tower."

"Any sign of The Three?"

Snorting with laughter, Bri withdrew from the window. As kids they'd always had nicknames for those in their lives, twin shorthand. "Nope."

"How late is it?" Elizabeth was frowning, staring at the window.

"Hard to say. No sun, though I think the windows face west. A gray day."

"How long do you think they'll give us alone this morning?" Elizabeth asked.

"If they can sense resting versus waking energy patterns—"

A strumming came at the sitting-room door, then the rapping of a knuckle. Bri finished, "—I'd say not long at all."

Hopping from bed, Elizabeth said, "Gotta pee," and headed to the bathroom.

Bri never drank much on a travel day, but now that Elizabeth mentioned it…

More harplike notes.

She recalled the polished rosewood door to the suite had something like a Swedish door harp affixed to the door, without the little wooden balls, and with vertical strings.

She went to the outer door. "Give us a break, folks, we're sharing a bathroom. And we don't want you in our bedroom."

There was some mumbling. There seemed to be a lot of life signatures beyond the door, and Bri was able to sense them easily. Scary.

"May we come in?" a voice asked in English.

Definitely at least The Three.

"Who all's there?" Bri asked.

"Bri?" came Alexa's voice.

Good ear. This being an aural society, they probably all had good ears, or like Bri had guessed before, they sensed energy patterns, too. Though Bri's and Elizabeth's energy patterns might be very similar, they wouldn't be identical.

"Who all's there?" she repeated, heard a flush and thanked God that there appeared to be modern plumbing. Water ran as Elizabeth washed her hands.

"Marian, Alexa, Calli, and our husbands," Marian said. Bri had a good ear, too, and the voluptuous redhead's voice was deeper, throatier than the others.

Bri backed up a couple of paces as Elizabeth walked into the room, dressed in her clothes from yesterday and not seeming too pleased about it. She'd have washed out their underwear, of course, before they fell into bed. "'The Three' have turned into 'The Six.'"

"They brought their men? Why?"

Shrugging, Bri went to the bathroom. "Don't know. At a guess, to show us a benefit of the place? Hunky husbands?"

Elizabeth snorted. "The last thing I need is a man in my life. Let me go through the bathroom to the dining room where there's another door to the hallway." She hustled past Bri, closing the door behind her, then faced the outer door. Her panties were still damp and she resented wearing them. If the women had been perspicacious enough to have night-gowns made, why couldn't they have provided some decent underwear? All Elizabeth had seen were long-underwear type leggings and tops and she'd had enough of those all the last miserable winter long.

The Six. Huh.

"Elizabeth? This is your morning briefing. By now you would have realized that you're here for a while. And we thought we'd help you get on," Alexa said.

Elizabeth crossed her arms. "Bri is in the bathroom." She heard sputtering water. "Showering. Come back later. With breakfast. I'll take an egg white omelette and a piece of dry toast. Bri will have eggs scrambled with cheese. If this be-nighted land has coffee, bring two cups, hot and black."

A male chuckle came as if in approval. "I don't think they're as disturbed as you expected them to be. You go get the food. We will stay here," the man said. In *English*. One of the men knew English. Elizabeth couldn't figure out whether that was a good sign or a bad one.

Marian said, "They have each other for support, so of course they are less affected than we were—being stranded in a strange dimension all alone."

That's what *she* thought. Elizabeth allowed herself an irritated sniff.

"But a discussion over food will be fine. I will, indeed, go, Jaquar."

Who was Jaquar? Calli's husband or Marian's?

Alexa said, "I'll hang here with the guys. A coupla croissants and butter and an omelette sounds good to me, too, with that cheese. And mushrooms!" Alexa called. "Too bad we don't have hash browns."

"I'll go with Marian," said Calli.

"Much running around," said another male voice in English, very heavily accented.

Shifting from foot to foot, Elizabeth stared at the door, wondering if it would be beneficial to let the others in, four instead of six. Would it throw off their rhythm?

"It might," Bri said next to her ear and Elizabeth jumped.

"Sorry," Bri said. "You were thinking really loud."

"Alexa and the men are out there."

"Ah. Well I have the feeling that Alexa would be a hand-ful by her very self."

"True." Elizabeth looked at Bri. She was wearing the

leggings and the smaller shirt, with her bra underneath. Both Lladranan garments were made of cream-colored silk. "You look good."

Bri shrugged. "The outfit works for the moment." She smiled. "I didn't want to put on damp panties."

Elizabeth grumbled, "More humid here than in Colorado. Our underwear would have been dry if we were home."

"Yeah." Bri's smile became a wicked grin. "Bet at least one of them is leaning against the door?"

"I don't know." Elizabeth frowned. "These are warriors. Would they do that?"

"One way to see." Bri strode forward.

Bri yanked open the door.

6

No one fell into the room. Instead, with twinkling eyes and a smile as wide as Bri's, Alexa strolled in. "Good morning. The greeting here in Lladrana is most often 'Salutations.'" She waved to the men following her. "I don't know if you remember the guys. Bastien, the one with the black-and-white streaked hair and the baton at his hip is a Shieldmarshall and mine. The taller one with blue eyes—ancient Exotique blood mixed with Lladranan—is Marian's soulmate, Jaquar, a Sorcerer-Circlet, as you can see from his gold headband."

Jaquar walked in, and like Bastien, gave the room and the open doors a quick scan. Neither of them would miss anything. Then Jaquar bowed, first to Bri who still held the door, then to Elizabeth. "Salutations," he said. He spoke English well.

The last man was equally tall and had an easy amble that

Elizabeth recognized was similar to a cowboy's walk. He carried six books.

Deceiving, that last one, Calli's man. He's even more aware than the others, Bri said to Elizabeth.

Hands on her hips, Alexa studied them. "You're talking to each other telepathically, again. Rude."

"We think we should have all the advantages we can get," Elizabeth replied. "And you will no doubt be speaking Lladranan before us." She gestured. "Make yourselves at home."

"Don't mind if I do," Alexa said, heading for the angle between walls where the chest sat with the leftovers from their father's birthday dinner.

Bri jumped in front of it at the last minute. "Ours!"

The third man holding the books gently closed the door. He made a short bow. "I am Marrec. I am with Calli." His expression turned considering. "You will read in Calli's book that I was in Co-lo-ra-do with her."

With an effort, Elizabeth kept her mouth from falling open. Possibilities spun in her mind. "If you were in Colorado, then there's some way to get back and forth. We can go home." To her surprise, her heart didn't leap in her chest in delight. She blinked and took a few instants to probe her own feelings. She wasn't sure she wanted to go home right now.

Jaquar, wearing an ankle-length midnight blue velvet robe and looking every inch a very masculine man, took a seat on a long leather couch. Bastien hitched a hip onto the arm nearest the confrontation of Bri and Alexa opposite him. Marrec sat on the other end of the couch, as if leaving space for Calli and Marian. Still, Elizabeth could almost *feel* that these men trusted each other, more, were bound together through their wives. And their love for their wives?

Bri and she had grown up with parents who deeply loved each other and their children.

"We can go home!" Bri's choked exclamation echoed in mind and words.

"It's not that easy," Marian said from the hall. Calli held a plate with one hand and the door knob with the other. Marian carried a large tray.

"You'd think with all the magic you have here, you could just beam that over," Bri said.

"It's not that easy," Marian repeated.

The smell of eggs and coffee and ham made Elizabeth's mouth water.

"Alexa, your omelette. With cheese and mushrooms," Marian said.

"But you haven't been gone very long, and the food looks fresh, so magic *was* used," Elizabeth said.

"That's right. Magic, which is called *Power* here, and more like the extension of psi powers—"

"Power can heat the food, but it's harder to translocate things," Calli said. "Especially more than one item at a time. And there's an energy cost. You always have to figure what energy you might need for something else later." She handed Elizabeth the plate. "Sit. We can talk over breakfast."

"We often have breakfast discussions with our parents," Elizabeth said.

Everyone looked at her then Bri.

"You have parents."

"Of course," Bri said impatiently. "Will one of you pass me my plate, please?"

Calli had gone directly to a gate-legged table against a wall. Marrec joined her in setting up the table and soon there was a crowded table for eight. Opening lower drawers of a cabinet, Calli set a cork hot plate down for the tray, then brought out dishes, mugs and silverware. Marrec took chairs set around the room and placed them. Everything looked familiar.

"There've been Exotiques from Earth here in Lladrana before," Marian said. She'd found thick glasses that looked handmade and poured water into them.

"And Marrec went to Colorado," Elizabeth said.

"It's part of the Snap," Alexa grinned. She still stood near Bri and the cooler. "That's Marian's topic."

"Let's eat," Bastien said in the French-sounding Lladranan that Elizabeth barely understood.

Jaquar frowned at Bastien. "I told you we refined your language potion." Since Jaquar still spoke English, Elizabeth deduced that Bastien had been following the conversation.

Bastien grunted, moved to a chair that had its back to the foam chest and held out his hand to Alexa.

She looked at the cooler. At Elizabeth. At Bastien. At Bri. After tapping her foot, she sighed and walked to Bastien, took his hand and stood tip-toe to brush a kiss over his mouth. But she moved to a chair where she could still see the chest.

Bastien rolled his eyes, shook his head and sat next to her. "I have eaten, but my belly can always accommodate one of these." He unfolded the napkin on a large basket. Letting out steam from flaky croissants, he took one, set it on his plate, then ripped it into large pieces.

Alexa cut a third of her omelette and put it on Bastien's plate, then she dug in.

Doesn't look like they're going to poison us, Bri sent mentally to Elizabeth.

Not since we survived the first night, but I'm sure they have plans for us. Images of the people they'd healed came to her mind, were matched by Bri's memories. The flow of emotion between them was stronger than Elizabeth had ever experienced. Of course they'd had "hunches," intuitive feelings about each other, but nothing like this connection that seemed to have thought sharing and definitely included telepathy.

Elizabeth shifted in her seat, picked up a fork, cut into the omelette and ate. Fabulous—and delicately flavored with spices she didn't quite recognize.

"So," Alexa said between bites, "welcome to Lladrana. You are now known far and wide as the Medica Exotiques Summoned for the Cities and Towns."

"Already?" asked Bri, brows lowering.

"Already. The Sorcerers and Sorceresses, Circlets they're called, had a contingent here for the Summoning. Some have flown back to their islands. All of them have crystal balls for communication."

"Interesting," said Bri.

Marian finished pouring coffee all around except for Alexa and stared pointedly at the Swordmarshall. Alexa chewed and swallowed, drank some water, met Elizabeth's eyes, then Bri's.

"I'm the background person, since I fight the horrors every week." An unamused smile flashed, then was gone. "I was originally Summoned a year ago to help defend Lladrana, that's this country, from invading evil. Centuries ago some warrior-mages made a boundary of magical fenceposts with an energy field strung between them to keep the horrors—inhuman monsters—out. The fenceposts started falling and the desperate Marshalls consulted the main oracle-prophetess here, the Singer. The oracle said that if the Marshalls Summoned someone from the Exotique Land, that's Earth, she'd re-discover the method of making fence-posts and re-powering the boundary." Now her smile crinkled her eyes. "To everyone's surprise, it worked."

Bastien leaned over and kissed her cheek. "Not surprising."

"Yeah, it was." Alexa's face hardened. "I was the first Sum-moned in a century. Alone with the Marshalls. Tested im-mediately to prove I could handle the job." She swept a gaze around the table. "You weren't there. None of you."

Marian sighed sympathetically. She pushed back her chair and went to the sofa where Calli's guy, Marrec, had placed the books he'd carried in. Dividing the stack in two, she put one on the table beyond Bri's plate, then one set near Elizabeth. The top cover was dark black hide Eliza-beth didn't recognize, with a green wand topped with flames embossed on it. The spine said, in English, *Lorebook of Exotique Swordmarshall Alexa Fitzwalter.* Underneath was a dark purple book showing sheet lightning on the spine with the words *Lorebook of Exotique Circlet Marian Harasta.*

"Circlet?" murmured Bri.

Alexa answered as Marian resumed her seat and drank the excellent coffee. "The society here is fragmented. The Circlets are the Sorcerers and Sorceresses of this place. They usually live in Towers they raise by magic as *their* final test on islands off the coast. Lladrana has one coast, the west."

Alexa sipped her water, set the cup down, and smiled

again at Marian. "But like all academics, the Circlet politics were vicious—"

"We simply did not cooperate well before Marian," Jaquar said, haughty brows raised over blue eyes.

"Blue eyes," Elizabeth said.

He inclined his head in a nod. "Yes, there has been some interaction between our cultures. Somewhere in my blood-line there was obviously an Exotique ancestor."

"I understand the Lladranan people are golden-skinned and dark-haired with dark eyes," Elizabeth said, observing the silver waves of hair that Jaquar and Marrec had at their temples, "but aren't there other cultures here with lighter coloring?"

"Excellent observation," Jaquar said. "Yes, occasionally we have traders, and it's true I spent my formative years in the south, but blue eyes are most indicative of Exotique blood."

"Okay," Bri said. "So most people look like Marrec and Bastien."

"Ttho," said Bastien in a mock-offended tone, bridling back and staring down his nose. "*No*. I am a black-and-white." He indicated his striped hair.

Alexa pinched a bit of buttered croissant from his plate, waved it. "Black-and-whites are those whose Power— that's magic—is fractured, and they usually have mental problems." She grinned and popped the croissant into her mouth.

"Bastien has been irritatingly brilliant all his life, but…" Jaquar said.

"A loose cannon," Alexa said with relish. "I still like using English idiom. Most people look like Marrec."

Elizabeth and Bri stared at Marrec, his golden skin, black hair with silver streaks over the temples, dark brown eyes set at a very slight angle. He sat stoically under their gaze.

"Yes, our patients had the same cultural features," Elizabeth said.

"I fixed Bastien," Alexa said, stretching to plant a noisy kiss on his jaw.

"Ayes," Bastien said. A side of his mouth quirked up. "Well and truly," he said in English. His eyebrows lifted at Marian's and Jaquar's stares. "I have been practicing."

"Me, too," said Marrec.

Alexa huffed. "Let's get my part over with. Marian was Summoned by the Marshalls for the Circlets to help battle the Dark—that's the really bad entity running the show—making the monsters and sending them here for some physical object that we still haven't figured out." She smiled winningly at Elizabeth and Bri. "In addition to curing the sickness, that could be your task for the world, Amee. And the Snap doesn't happen until you fulfill your task, usually about two months. The Snap is the way back to Earth." Alexa shook her head. "We knew it would take six to fight the Dark in the ultimate battle at the end of this summer. Didn't think of twins. Thought of three more Summonings, the City, the Seamasters, the Singer. With us—" she gestured to Calli and Marian "—that represents the six core factions of Lladranan society."

Bri said, "I'm not sure I followed all of that. But we certainly can't stay until the end of summer. That would drive our parents mad."

Silence shrouded the table.

"You assume that time passes on Amee at the same rate that it does on Earth," Marian said.

Fear squeezed Elizabeth's heart. "No! Don't tell me we've already been here years!" Bile rushed up her throat, her stomach contracted.

"Marian!" Calli scolded. She was sitting next to Elizabeth and put an arm around her shoulders in a tight squeeze. "Yes, time passes the same."

But Elizabeth was trembling. Bri shoved back her chair with enough force to knock it over, marched with unsteady steps to Elizabeth, stood beside her chair and flung her arms around her. She turned into Bri and grabbed her hard in return.

"That was nasty," Bri said thickly. "Get out."

"I didn't mean—" Marian said.

"Marian, sometimes you're just too clueless in that smart brain of yours," Alexa said. Another chair thumped and Elizabeth felt stroking on her head from small hands, and a strong feeling of calm coming from both Calli and Alexa.

"I'm sorry, I'm sorry," Marian said, a sob in her voice. Elizabeth sensed the woman hovering around Bri and her, as shaken as the rest.

"We women from Earth have one major rule around here," Alexa's voice was soft, but steely. "We don't hurt each other. That means we don't manipulate each other and we support each other. *We stick together.* There are enough problems here for us all without infighting."

"I didn't mean to," Marian whispered.

"I know," Calli said. "You were just saying that when a person finds themselves in a new dimension, old rules might not apply. The academic approach. That wasn't what was needed."

"I know," Marian said.

"You owe them for scaring them," Alexa said like a judge laying down the law. "Big time."

Elizabeth was breathing easier, the aftereffects of a strong adrenaline rush fading so she could act normally.

I notice that we are all girls in this group hug. Elizabeth heard Bri's light tone and knew her twin was settling down.

Jaquar and Bastien have gone to the windows. Marrec has his hand on the door knob, Marian's telepathic tone sounded shaky. Her hand had closed over Elizabeth's shoulder as if to steady them both.

Men, Alexa's voice, the first time Elizabeth had heard it in her head. Had the other women been courteously holding back, or was it because they were all touching?

Because we are all physically connected, Bri said.

"This isn't unexpected," Alexa said. She stopped smoothing Elizabeth's hair and Elizabeth missed it. She heard the sound of furniture moving. Lifting the chairs back, probably.

Alexa continued, "Live here long enough and you begin to believe in fate—in the Song. The Marshalls and Circlets and Chevaliers and the Cities all had requirements for the people they wanted to bring to Lladrana. Being able to mesh with the individual group and the culture was the primary one. Since we previous Exotiques have assimilated well with the culture, it's only logical that we'd be friends."

Elizabeth wanted to see. She drew away from Bri, straightening in her chair and Bri let her go. Both of them back on an emotional keel.

Alexa cleared her throat loudly, stared at the cooler once more. "Anything perishable in there?"

Bri met Elizabeth's eyes. *The fruit salad. You handle this.*

You've always been better at negotiations, at haggling in the local markets, than me.

"Fruit salad," Elizabeth said. "Leftovers from our father's birthday party. Melon, papaya, grapes, kiwi, pineapple..." She waved.

Bri strolled over to the cooler, opened it and took out a big plastic-wrapped bowl. She blinked rapidly. "Mom's bowl," she said, placing it on the table and removing the clingwrap.

"Wedgwood," Marian murmured.

"A special celebration," Elizabeth said.

"Well, the fruit won't keep," Bri said. She dished servings out to everyone.

Alexa sat, took a bite and hummed in pleasure. She scooped a portion of Bastien's off his plate, swallowed and said, "You really shouldn't eat this. You might develop a taste for it, then where would we be? Not sure any of this grows here."

"Grapes do," he said, and left them on Alexa's plate as he took more back, and they all dug into the food.

As soon as she took her last bite, Alexa stared at the cooler again, licking her lips. "Two sacks of spuds, white and red. Pretty big cooler. What else is in it?"

Bri wiped her hands on a napkin and went back to the chest. She lifted the plastic-wrapped casserole out and set it aside.

"Oh, man. Oh, man," Alexa breathed. "Is that what I think it is? Potato casserole?"

"With sour cream and onions and loads of cheese," Bri returned sweetly.

Alexa's moan was nearly orgasmic. Bastien's eyes gleamed. "I know my woman and her tastes. Whatever that is, it is wonderful."

"That can go pretty bad if not eaten quickly, too. Probably really excellent for breakfast," Alexa pointed out.

"Yes," Elizabeth said. She lifted her brows. "There's no refrigeration available?"

Marrec said, "There is a keep-cold twiddle-spell and we have ice."

Jaquar said, "We can bespell the cooler free of charge."

Bri said lightly, "Then we might invite you to eat the casserole with us at a later time. You have to talk to Elizabeth about that. It's her cooler." Then Bri lifted out the large dome-covered plate. She smiled, cocked an eyebrow at Elizabeth. "Chocolate cake with vanilla frosting."

The words caused a lengthy silence. All the women's gazes locked on the plate. The three once-Earth-now-Lladranan women nearly quivered.

"I know this choc-lat." Marrec rolled the word on his tongue. "It is good."

"Damn right," Bri said. "Homemade birthday cake. *Now* we'll talk about returning to Denver."

7

Elizabeth waited for reactions. Marian sighed, shared a glance with the other women. Alexa dabbed at her lips with a napkin, folded it and stood. "We always go through this." She cleared her throat, looked tentative. "I don't want to step on toes, I only want to understand." Her chin lifted. "I didn't have much to go back to, so I settled here after the initial shock. Lladrana's been good to me."

Elizabeth felt her eyes widen. Bri's mouth fell open. The woman had a long scar on her cheek. She'd said she fought monsters every week.

Bastien snorted, stood and stepped behind Alexa, wrapping his arms around her. His gaze was fierce. "She is beloved. She has a good estate, wealth which she did not have on Exotique Terre. She is," he glanced at Marian and Calli, "you all are, the crème de la crème."

"We've found our places in life." Calli went to stand

beside Alexa, took her hand. "I hadn't planned on going back with the Snap, either, not after I bonded with Marrec, and certainly not after we adopted our child, children." She smiled softly at her man. He lifted a shoulder and moved to hold her like Bastien held Alexa.

Alexa angled her chin at Marian. "That one was the one who kept saying she had to go back."

"For Andrew, my brother with multiple sclerosis. And I did."

"But you're here," Bri said.

"I brought him back with me. And he's still here. After a fashion."

Cold curled inside Elizabeth. She kept her voice mild. "After a fashion?"

Alexa grinned. "Since you're both medicas you'll be interested. His mind and, um, soul—" she glanced at Marian, who nodded "—were transferred to a Lladranan body."

Wow! Bri's thought echoed Elizabeth's. *Incredible.* Bri said, "I'm not a medical doctor. Elizabeth is."

Marian raised her eyebrows, obviously back to normal. "We saw you save last night."

"She has a unique gift of healing hands," Elizabeth murmured.

Blinking at Bri, Marian said, "So I would postulate that you studied alternative medicine. As I studied New Age subjects." She crossed to the other side of Alexa, and still watching the twins, held out her hand. Alexa took it. Jaquar strolled behind her to stand with the other men, rested his hands on Marian's hips.

"Choose an end," Alexa challenged with a smile. "You're supposed to be here." Then her humor faded. "Bottom line, we need you. We're sure the Dark is sending this disease somehow and we need you to find a cure."

Elizabeth shook her head. "It isn't that easy."

"We know it isn't," Marrec said, his accent thick. "None of the Exotiques' tasks were easy. But they prevailed."

"We're sorry for your problems, but we have loving parents who will miss us in two weeks," Bri said, lowering the cake back into the cooler.

At that moment a long lilting strum came from the door. "Sevair Masif here," said the deep voice of the city man.

Alexa hurried to answer, obviously glad of the interruption. "He's been very patient, but he's waiting for you two. The City and Towns were the ones who Summoned you."

Marian and Jaquar did a little chant and the dishes and cutlery cleaned themselves and were stacked on the table. Elizabeth and Bri watched wide-eyed, then Bri hurried to put the casserole back into the chest and set the top back on it. She smiled. "Plenty of ice."

"Bri, you can't go out looking like that!" Jaquar sounded shocked.

All the women looked at him.

Marian said, "I would never have thought you to be a prude."

He glanced at the other men as if for support. Bastien smiled blandly and replied in simple Lladranan that Elizabeth was beginning to understand, "She looks wonderful."

Marrec leaned on the sofa and said in accented English, "I was in Co-lo-ra-do. In the summer. I saw bare legs." He smiled reminiscently.

Calli blinked at him. "Oh, yes, I left you in the park when I went to the bank."

Bri said, "Before I was in Denver, I was in Sweden, before that, Spain. But I've traveled a lot, I should have realized." Now she smiled at the women, not nicely. "Can you do an instant clean on my clothes? The blouse is silk. Or do you have clothes for at least one of us?"

"Yes," said Marian drawing herself up.

"Yes, what?" asked Bri.

Marian withdrew a finger-length stick from her pocket and with a flick of her wrist it turned into a wand. She pointed it at Elizabeth. A hot breeze hit her, rippled over her, shaking her clothes and leaving them with a fresh scent. Her panties had dried. But Elizabeth wasn't too sure about the efficacy of magical clothes washing.

"Both," Marian said. "I can cleanse your clothes, even while they're on you, and we have clothes for you. Both of you." She went into the bedroom and came back with two robes of dark red with white crosses on them. Medica tunics, one knee length, the other mid-calf. The shorter one buttoned tight around the wrist for several inches, so the sleeves didn't get in the way of anything. The longer one had wider sleeves that came to the elbow.

Another heavy ripple of noise came from the door, obviously impatient. The knob turned and Sevair Masif strode in, followed by a hesitant person wearing the shorter medica robe.

"What is taking so long?" The tone more than his words held meaning. He stopped and stared at Bri. Blinked. Swallowed. A hint of red came to his cheeks. Bri sent him a grin, then slipped the tunic over her head and wiggled into it. The robe fell past her knees and she looked—marginally—like the other medica. Since the tight lower sleeves didn't fit well over the thinner silk shirt, Bri rolled up the red sleeves and let the white show. It was a very *Bri* look: casual, rakish, elegant. Proclaiming to all that she leaned toward New Age. Elizabeth couldn't imagine Bri in a proper nurse's uniform. Meanwhile the medica was eyeing Bri's style.

Elizabeth wasn't about to add to the show. She looked at the remaining heavier robe with short sleeves. "Not one for each of us at all," she said. "Two different robes."

"One for each of you," Marian said easily, "but in the two different styles that the medicas wear. This one is for traveling."

Bri took the long tunic, and tossed it over Elizabeth's head before she could protest, pulling it down over her Earth shirt and slacks, twitching it so it fell smoothly. The hem was long but the sides were cut high for easy movement.

Bri hummed in approval. "Looks good."

Elizabeth had worn a cream-colored silk shirt and dark blue slacks to their father's birthday party while Bri had worn stylish jeans and a turquoise shirt.

"It suits both of you," Alexa said.

"*Prie introd moi*," said Sevair.

"This is Sevair Masif, a City and Townmaster, a stone-mason and excellent architect of Castleton," Marian said.

He bowed. "Call me Sevair," he said. Those were the last words Elizabeth understood of the long stream of sentences, except that the gist was splitting her and Bri up. One for the Castle medicas and one for the City? When she glanced at the medica, she had her hands folded at her waist and was nodding.

As soon as he finished, the medica launched into speech before Elizabeth could ask for a translation. The woman tapped her chest, gestured to the whole Castle, was impassioned. Elizabeth thought she spoke of facilities and training, or an exchange of training, while the man had spoken of need and duty.

The medica paused for a breath and Marian interrupted. "You're not understanding much of this, are you?"

Bri said, "I lived in Cannes for two years and Elizabeth studied French and visited me."

"But it's not quite French, is it?" Marian said.

Everyone stared at them.

Bri looked at Sevair and the medica, inclined her head, and said. "*Je ne comprehends pas.*"

The medica sighed, looked at Marian.

"Just a drop of language potion," Jaquar wheedled, drawing a tiny bottle from a pocket of his robe. It sparkled. "A drop would let you test it for a couple of hours." He flashed a "Trust me, baby," smile. "You'd be able to speak and understand Lladranan well."

Elizabeth decided to let Bri handle this and kept her mouth shut.

Bri said, "How many medicas are there?"

"Five here at the Castle," Alexa said, "the best in the country. The Marshalls can form a healing circle, too." She shifted, appearing disgruntled. "Though none of us have been able to cure those with the sickness, like you did."

"They *are* the Exotique Medicas," Calli said. "They will have skills that the rest of us don't. Like I can speak with the volarans, or you can handle that baton."

Jaquar had strolled over to Bri, lifting a small cork from the bottle. Blinking, Bri could see that the pale lavender liquid inside sparkled a little, even in the tendrils that rose from the bottle. Really odd.

Jaquar waved it under her nose. It smelled *wonderful*, floral, like all the spring blossoms of a tree. She wanted another sniff, but since it was more like a craving, decided against it.

"Say something, Sevair," Jaquar ordered—and it wasn't in English, but sounded perfectly clear and not the mangled French Bri had had to concentrate to untangle.

"We," Sevair gestured to the medica behind him, "have come to discuss matters. Since there are two Exotique medicas, it is only reasonable one stay here at the Castle and one come with me to Castleton." Though he sounded as if he was reporting a compromise that didn't please.

"Split us up!" Bri said, and realized she was speaking French—sort of.

The line between Sevair's brows dug deeper as if *he* tried to understand what she said.

But Elizabeth was frowning, too. "What did you say, Bri?" she asked.

"They want to split us up. Send one of us away."

"Yeah," Alexa rolled her eyes. "All the way to Castleton. Two miles downhill."

Bri felt her cheeks pinken. "Oh."

"Two miles downhill from a Castle on a hill means walking two miles *up*hill for someone," Elizabeth said.

"True," said Bri.

Jaquar waved the vial near Bri's nostrils again. Wonderful scent. She clenched her teeth, then said, "How much would give me language skills for the day?"

Marian's gaze met Jaquar's. She cleared her throat.

"Language skills, ah. You might be interested to know that during sex there is a definite transfer of the language with your partner. That is to say, you'll get Lladranan. They get English too, but there's not much chance to practice it."

Bri moved until she was shoulder to shoulder with Elizabeth. "We look like the easy types to you?"

Marrec shook his head. "No Exotique is easy. Not a one."

"Pity," said Bastien.

Jaquar said, "Two drops for today lasting perhaps until tomorrow noon."

The medica stepped farther into the room and said something that escaped Bri. *You understand that?* she asked Elizabeth.

No. "Please translate," Elizabeth said. She'd tensed up again.

The other Coloradan women shared a glance, grouped together and murmured a bit, then Marian looked at the twins and said, "She speaks in words and concepts that we are not sure of, even though we have done Song healing. Something about wanting to consult you about the rhythmic cycles of each energy point-pulse." Marian didn't look pleased that she didn't get it.

Bri turned a little to Elizabeth. *If I try, I can hear each chakra tune. Can you?*

Elizabeth squinted, then a corner of her mouth lifted. *Not really, but I can "see" different colors of swirling energy. I definitely see auras now, more than I ever did on Earth.*

Chakra auras.

I suppose. Elizabeth held out her hand, and Bri clasped it. They looked at Marian. The sounds Bri heard merged with Elizabeth's sight. Each chakra had a series of notes, a color, spun in a different pattern and to a different beat.

Now that you help, I CAN hear the notes. Probably what the medica was talking about, Elizabeth said.

For sure. And with our link I can see the chakras better than I ever could on Earth. The seven main ones and all the way to the thirteen. Bri felt Elizabeth scrutinizing the medica. *We could learn from them, and teach them, too!*

You got the parents' teaching gene, Bri said. *I think I'll take a chance.*

You always do, Elizabeth said.

Dropping Elizabeth's hand, Bri went to Jaquar, who still held the small bottle. Now she wasn't physically connected with Elizabeth, sounds were amplified and her aura sight dimmer. She *reached* and drew Power from the atmosphere, boosting her sight. Yep, easy to see auras. Jaquar had a shadow in several of his energy pulses, as if a lingering sickness was finally passing.

"What made you sick about a year ago?" she asked him.

He stilled, straightened to his full height. "I lost my parents. A Dark monster drained their Power and killed them."

The room suddenly seethed with sorrow, anger, determination.

"He was sick with grief," Marian said. "Almost mad with it."

Jaquar grimaced.

"Those particular monsters, sangviles, especially like to kill people strong in Power," Alexa said. "Like Circlets. Or Exotiques."

Bri looked back to Elizabeth. *They do need our help.*

And they aren't about to let us go before they get it.

"Two drops only," Bri said, and stuck out her tongue.

Plink. Plink. Oddly enough, the taste wasn't nearly as good as the smell. Bri wasn't sure what she expected, a sweet honey like columbine perhaps, but she didn't get it. She turned to the medica.

"Say that again."

The medica nodded. "We believe this sickness was sent by the Dark in some way, but the symptoms are not the same for every patient. It affects the rhythm and Song of the different energy pulses of a person—chimes—but not the *same* chime."

You get that? Bri asked Elizabeth. *And they call a chakra a chime.* Bri shrugged. *Only natural in such a culture, I suppose.*

But Elizabeth was staring at the medica, then Jaquar. Bri could *feel* her waves of curiosity. She stared at the vial. He offered it, and she sniffed, wrinkled her nose. *Overly sweet*, she said to Bri. *But I know you liked the scent.*

Elizabeth held up two fingers. "Two drops only."

Jaquar nodded.

The tip of Elizabeth's tongue peeked from between her lips. Jaquar carefully poured one drop, then a second.

I like the taste, Elizabeth said.

Speaking of taste, what do we do with the spuds? Bri went to the bags of potatoes and pulled out three of each, then said to Sevair, "Do you have botanists who'd study these? They're a very good crop on Earth, called potatoes."

She thought she heard Alexa moan.

"They are a delicacy," Marian said to Sevair.

Sevair had pulled a folded bag from his pocket, snapped it, then opened it. The man was prepared. How depressing. With a smile, Bri carried the potatoes heaped in her hands over to him and dumped them in the bag, then drew one back out. "You germinate them by the eye." She pointed to one on the Idaho potato. "These are better baked, the others are better boiled."

"That one is excellent fried. Deep fat fried," Alexa said. Now Marian whimpered.

Sevair lifted an eyebrow, took the potato from Bri, weighed it in his hand, glanced at Calli. "Your opinion?"

Calli smiled. "What you have there is about a thousand times more tasty than turnip fries."

He looked surprised, then pleased. Nodding to Elizabeth, then Bri, he said, "Then you have something to barter with. However, I assure you that the Cities and Towns who Summoned you abide by tradition. You will receive property—an estate in the city or town of your choice— and enough money to support you for the rest of your days. Both of you." He slipped the potato into the bag. "You will also receive a bounty on every plant that is developed from this po-ta-toe."

He bowed to each of them. "I thank you both for accepting the language potion. It will make our tasks much easier. With your permission, I would like to adjourn to Temple Ward."

Alexa was staring at the cooler and the potatoes.

"Where's that guy who guarded them last night?" asked Bri.

"That would be my brother, Luthan," Bastien said. "I don't think we've spoken of Luthan."

"Or Faucon for that matter," Marian said.

Something else, here, Elizabeth said mentally to Bri as she walked over to stand in front of the chest, blocking it from everyone else.

Alexa's wistful look turned into a pout. She speared Bri with a disgruntled gaze. "Luthan Vauxveau is a Chevalier, a knight who rides the flying horses, so flies into battle with us. He's a wealthy nobleman with his own estate and the representative of the Singer, who is *the* prophetess of Lladrana, lives to the south in an Abbey, but meddles in our affairs."

I don't like that, said Elizabeth. *We have enough to worry about with the people in this room.*

I don't either, Bri replied.

Alexa cleared her throat. "Some people have instinctive reactions to Exotiques. Either an instinctive revulsion or an instinctive attraction."

"I'll go for the attraction," Bri said.

"That can be a problem, too," Marian said.

Bri waved that away. "Better than the alternative. I've suffered from prejudice before. How nasty is this repulsion thing?"

"Bad enough to get you killed," Bastien said. His usual optimistic expression had faded and turned grim, making him look like the warrior he was. "Alexa had to fight for her life."

8

I saw him, Luthan, shudder last night when he looked at us, Elizabeth said.

Now that you mention it…

"Luthan has the instinctive repulsion," Alexa said, her voice cool, her manner lacking any playfulness. "He is deeply ashamed of it. He would die before he hurt any of us."

Must be difficult to have a brother-in-law who thinks you're repulsive, Bri sent to Elizabeth.

"Ayes," said Alexa, reading body language or energy or Bri's mind. "Ayes is 'yes.' 'Ttho' is 'no.' And Luthan has long since gotten over his first problem with me, as well as Marian and Calli. It's only when he has to meet and interact with a new Exotique that the problem surfaces again."

"But you must be aware that others might have this reaction," Marrec said. "If they have never met an Exotique before, they may not know they have this flaw and may act on it instead of thinking how important you are to us."

"We understand," Elizabeth said. Bri could feel her need to leave the suite and get out into fresh air, someplace not as crowded with others. Bri felt it too.

"Okay, so there's a repulsion and Luthan has it and hates it. I still sensed he was the most honest of all of you." She enjoyed saying that. "Will he watch our goodies for us?"

Marian sniffed, took out her finger length wand again. "I can bespell the chest to keep the food cold. And Jaquar is very good with lock spells. He can put one on the door and all the windows."

"What about Faucon?" Elizabeth asked. "Since Luthan has the revulsion, I would imagine that he has the attraction?"

"Ayes," Alexa said cheerfully. "He's sexy, rich, noble, a good Chevalier and a good guy. He'll want to Pair with you." She shook her head. "Twins. He'll go mad at the choice. I'd advise you to take him up on any offers."

"We aren't staying," they said together. Bri continued, "Our parents—" The thought of their parents grief at the disappearance of their daughters clutched at her gut.

"It's difficult," Marian said. "I couldn't leave my brother Andrew." Then her voice softened, held a wrenching undertone. "He came with me, but was badly wounded, and dying. We transferred his mind and soul into a dying Lladranan, Koz. Now Andrew is Koz."

That still sounded weird.

"There's a cure for MS here?" Bri asked.

Marian grimaced. "We didn't know. We hoped. But my place was here, with Jaquar and the Circlets." She took her husband's hand. "With my mentor, Bossgond, and the school we wanted to found, *did* found."

"I don't believe it." Elizabeth shook her head.

A smile lingered on Marian's lips. "Come meet him, then." She nodded to the medica who was waiting patiently by the door. "Jolie was the main medica to make the transfer, if you'd like to talk with her."

Jolie said, "You did it yourself, Circlet Marian. That procedure is a matter of the soul and the Song. We medicas only kept the receiving body alive."

All Bri's nerves shivered at the thought.

"It was a matter of faith in herself," Jaquar said, kissing his wife's cheek. "She knew her Power was strong, and fashioned to be more of use here than on Exotique Terre."

A definite prod at them, Bri thought. She said, "I have always used my healing hands."

Jaquar switched his gaze to Elizabeth. "And you? You both have great Power here, otherwise the Song would not have reverberated in your mind—the gong, the chimes."

Bri jerked in surprise. "How did you know that?"

"It is the way Exotiques are Summoned." He nodded to the books on the table. "You can learn much from the others' experiences."

"Later." Alexa walked to the door, sent the twins a challenging look. "Can't hide in here all day." She snorted with laughter as if at a secret joke. "Come along. Your new life awaits. If you dare."

Bri spared one last glance around the room, then watched carefully in the hallway when Jaquar bespelled the door.

As they walked down the stairs the medica, Jolie, began asking Elizabeth questions. Soon they were deep in a conversation about medical techniques. Bri blinked. She didn't want to face another new day in another new place. She was supposed to be in Denver.

When the outer door opened onto the wide courtyard of the Castle, they all hesitated.

"One of the twins should come with me to Castleton. We have a house prepared," Sevair said. "The Exotique Summoned was for Castleton and the other cities and towns."

"Sounds like traveling," Elizabeth's voice was strained. She met Bri's eyes. A bad feeling slicked Bri's gut.

I don't want to leave the Castle. Elizabeth was even more hesitant.

Bri couldn't resist the plea. She pasted on a smile and jutted a hip. *Looks like it's me, then. Think this telepathy thing works across two miles?*

Elizabeth's eyes sharpened. *An interesting experiment.*

Yeah. Bri straightened her shoulders. "I'll go." She sent a glance around the cluster of people. "For a while. We aren't chessmen to be pushed around."

"Of course not," Bastien said. "No Exotique can be pushed far." His smile was crooked, his gaze admiring.

Alexa said, smiling, "We get to Castleton often, usually to the Nom de Nom."

"A worthy establishment," Sevair said, but something about the way he said it made Bri think he didn't really mean it.

Bastien laughed. "A Chevaliers hang-out."

Of course he hadn't really said hang-out. Had he? Bri could hardly distinguish the English words from the Llad-ranan, especially since she realized that the Exotiques had already had a definite effect on the language. "Okay" was commonplace. Maybe Bastien *had* said hang-out.

"Lodging, food, and clothing is a priority. We *will* shelter and care for our Exotiques." Sevair's broad hand with scarred fingers gestured to Elizabeth and Bri.

"*Merci,*" said Elizabeth. "It's comforting to know we have a place here at the Castle and in Castleton."

"Not only there," Marian said. "If you prefer Circlet Towers you can live with me or Bossgond."

"Marrec and I have a big house at your disposal, too," Calli said.

"Exotiques are valued," Sevair said, "but I think you will find that no one values their Exotiques more than the Cities and Towns."

At that moment a couple of women strode up to the group. The older one was the Marshalls' leader, the other wore expensive leathers. Bri vaguely remembered them from the night before.

The Marshall bowed brusquely to them; she wore Authority like a surgeon's coat.

"I'm Thealia Germain, Lady Knight Swordmarshall."

Okay, make that the Authority of the head of the Joint Chiefs of Staff.

Thealia jerked a nod at the woman beside her. "Lady Hallard, representative of the Chevaliers."

Bri thought it sounded like the two top warriors in the world. She stepped back. She'd avoided war zones on her travels. Poverty and disease of third-world nations was bad enough without being caught in a struggle between vicious groups.

Elizabeth nodded at them. "Ladies."

Well, Elizabeth had served her time in emergency services and ICUs; she'd have seen plenty of wounds inflicted on people by others.

"Exotique Medicas," Hallard said.

Thealia continued, "It's time for the morning briefing about last night's battle. My husband and Shieldmarshall noticed a different pattern in the fighting, as did other Shields. We also received a message from the horrors, or perhaps I should say from the new Master of the Horrors and Servant of the Dark."

Just the titles had Bri backing up a little more, into the solid shape of Sevair. He steaded her with a hand on her shoulder, then said in voice full of suppressed fury, "You mean my ex-assistant."

Thealia spared him an impatient "get over it" look. "All three of our groups were betrayed last year." She indicated Hallard with a stern jerk of her head.

"Yes, of course." Now Sevair's voice was quiet, even soothing. "My anger and grief are not solely my own."

"The briefing," Thealia snapped.

"What was the message?" Marian asked. "This isn't a good sign."

"I prefer to speak of that in private."

"Hey, Jean," Bastien called to a soldier in the Castle colors, lingering on the edge of their group. "What was the Master's message?"

"'Our Dark plague will take you all.'"

On the receiving end of scathing stares from the Lady Knight Swordmarshall and Lady Hallard, the soldier shrank back into the dark shadows shrouding the cloister corridor in the gray morning.

"So now we know for sure," Sevair said quietly, though he'd left his hand on Bri's shoulder and she felt the tension run through all his muscles.

Scowling, Thealia said, "Unfortunately."

"The Circlets must hear this news immediately," Marian said.

"Broadcast a message by crystal sphere," Thealia said impatiently. "I want you Circlets at my briefing."

"Of course," Jaquar said, slipping his arm around Marian. "We'll join you shortly." They moved away.

"Right," Alexa said, holding her hand to Bastien. He made a face but took it and matched her magically rapid pace back to the keep, outdistancing the taller Marian and Jaquar.

"And you, also, Citymaster, and the Exotique Medicas."

"Thank you, but that is not possible," Sevair said.

A few seconds of startled silence passed. The Lady Knight Swordmarshall was obviously not used to people denying her.

"Castleton has prepared a welcome and thanks for their Exotique Medica. The morale of my city is very important. We have been much harder hit by this sickness than you here at the Castle. My people come first." His hand grew warmer with sheer energy on Bri's shoulder, heating it, reminding her that she was standing in damp, chilly air.

"Of course," Thealia said in repressive tones.

The Castle medica, Jolie, stepped forward. "It's my opinion that the Castle Exotique Medica should see our facilities and learn the basics of our methods, while we speak to her of the Power she used last night. The sooner we understand each other, the better." She swallowed.

So Elizabeth was the Castle Exotique Medica, huh? That made Bri the—

Sevair's fingers squeezed Bri's shoulder gently, released, leaving a quickly cooling spot. "Both Medicas were Summoned on behalf of the Cities and Towns. I reluctantly agreed that one of the ladies stay here for training. But they are both for the Cities and Towns."

"The medicas can reimburse you for the Marshalls fee to Summon—"

"This is not about zhiv," Sevair said. "This is about need and priorities."

"I understand." The medica bowed her head.

"I do, too," said Elizabeth. She smiled. "I'm used to training at one place and working in other departments, and Bri has traveled, using her gift, extensively."

Yep, Elizabeth definitely wanted to stay at the Castle. Still, Bri continued to drag her feet. She didn't want to leave. Even the Castle was better than someplace new. After years of traveling, of being flexible, of modifying her behavior to be accepted into a new society—even if it was an alternative medical structure that she fit into better—she wanted just to be herself in one place with her family.

Sevair's large hand squeezed her shoulder again, then he stepped back and made another very courteous bow. "We of the city and towns are honored to have you here, Exotique Drystan."

She looked at his serious brown eyes, let out a sighing breath. At least there was an upside—she wouldn't have to work to connect with the medical community here, wouldn't have to prove herself. That had already happened. Last night.

Clearing her throat, she said, "Thank you." She sucked in a breath and addressed Jolie. "This is where your... warriors...the Marshalls and Chevaliers return, right? Elizabeth is better with wounds."

Elizabeth frowned. "That's right." She inhaled deeply, too. "Any wounded from last night's battle?"

The medica studied her. "Two. We would appreciate your opinion. It's an excellent way to start." She sounded cheerful.

Elizabeth jumped into conversation with the medica, and was walking to the big round temple where several others waited in their red robes with a white cross.

Bri felt abandoned.

"The morning wears on," Thealia said, turning to Calli.

"Marrec and I are out of this." She raised both hands palms outward. "Until the last battle."

Thealia snorted, pivoted on her heel and left. Her boot-steps echoed through the courtyard as she went to the keep.

"They meet in the Marshalls' Council Chamber," Calli said.

"I'd imagine so," Bri said.

But Calli had tilted her blond head and was studying her. "You know, the destruction spell does demand six, and there are two of you. Maybe we will only need one more to win the final battle."

"We aren't staying," Bri said. She was sure the phrase would be repeated like a mantra in the coming days.

Clop, clip, clip, clip, clop. A large brown volaran danced up to them, neighed, dipped its head. A series of pictures came to Bri, of herself and Sevair mounted on the winged horse and flying down toward a spired town. With the images came a feeling of anticipation and pleasure. The pegasus was talking to her!

She smiled uneasily at the volaran, but stroked her neck. Looking at Sevair, she said, "Did you get that?"

The clouds had returned but she saw a faint tinge of redness on his cheeks. Of course it could have been the coolness of the air.

"Did I hear the volaran? Not very well."

She thought he didn't like admitting what he might consider deficiencies.

But Calli was there, smiling, her blue eyes twinkling. "Mud says she'd like to fly you both down to Castleton. I don't fly with her often and she likes Exotiques. They smell so good."

"Mud?" Bri couldn't think of an uglier name for such a beautiful creature.

Calli's smile widened. "Her name is really, 'Rich-Earth-Warm-And-Soft-From-A-Summer-Shower-To-Play-In."

"Mud." Bri smiled.

"It's not far to Castleton," Sevair said. "It would be a very short ride."

Mud batted her eyelashes at him, whickered.

"Don't you fly?" Calli asked.

"Ayes, but I don't keep a volaran."

"Mud can be yours. I'll call others for you," Calli said.

Another bow from Sevair to Calli, this one a stiff inclination of the torso. "I thought you and your bondmate were settled on your estate."

"We are," Calli said, "but since Bri and Elizabeth have arrived, Marrec and I have decided to come with our children to the Castle—and Castleton—at least once a week.

"Children!"

"We adopted. Continue to adopt." Calli's smile remained in place, but hurt shadowed her eyes.

Bri couldn't help it—she heard a tiny tinkle of chimes in the back of her mind and Calli's Song became emphasized, not the Song of the Exotique Calli, the total person, but just the physical. The murmur of her second chakra was low, or rather, one note of that melody was missing. Calli's ovaries were gone. She couldn't have children.

"You know, don't you?" Calli said quietly. "You can see my physical health?"

"No," Bri said absently. "I *hear* it." She met Calli's gaze. "You are in excellent health."

"Exceptional," Calli said.

"Yes."

Sevair shifted beside her, and Calli's attention went back to him, even as Bri absorbed the shock of being able to *hear* what might be wrong with a person. Mud pawed the ground.

Calli said, "Surely as a Citymaster, you travel."

Nodding, Sevair said, "I have a coach."

Calli looked at the streak in his hair. "You have the Power to call wild volarans. I sense you're an excellent partner."

His expression froze into an impassive mask. "My sister loved volarans. She had planned to call one." He lifted a strong shoulder, dropped it. "Or several. Perhaps become a Chevalier. That didn't happen."

Since he used the past tense, Bri knew what *had* happened.

"Ah," Calli said. "But it would be easier for you to perform your duties if you flew with a volaran. Using their distance magic, your trips would be much shorter. I'm surprised no one has considered this before."

With a lift of one brow, Sevair said, "Are you? The Marshalls have avoided telling the Citymasters much, the Circlets—"

Calli waved that away. "I understand. Lladranan society has been segmented." She lifted her chin. "But we Exotiques are mending the situation. Mud will love to partner with you."

"I don't have room near my house to stable volarans." Sevair's voice was even.

"Contrary," Bri said.

He frowned, then said, "We'll fly to Castleton. Mud, would you like to be my regular mount? Stay in Castleton?"

Mud pranced in place.

Calli slid her gaze to Bri, "Along with the estate and the salary, volarans are an Exotique perk."

Bri didn't answer. She looked at Elizabeth, who was watching their little scene, hearing the shadows of their conversation through their twin link. Bri would be the first of them to fly on a winged horse! Elizabeth might stay in the safety of the Castle, but Bri would fly! She couldn't prevent a grin, and heard an audible mind-sniff from Elizabeth.

9

With a last stroke of Mud's softly feathered mane, Bri said, "I'll get my backpack."

Calli nodded and Bri was off before Sevair could say anything. She walked fast. Her feet weren't itching, but her hands were, wanting to pet that volaran more. Riding a flying horse! That would be worth this trip. She shut down the thought of her parents. They were in Hawaii right now and enjoying themselves, basking in the sun.

Then she was at the door and up, into the suite that was the most luxurious quarters she'd stayed in since she'd left home for college. She grabbed her pack, stuffed her clothes into it, eyed her stack of books and dumped them in, too, then hesitated. She fumbled for the digital camera, checked the memory. She had plenty, had just put in new for her Dad's birthday party.

When she reached the courtyard again, she saw that the clouds had parted and the sun shone bright, gleaming on

Mud's rich hide, lighting hints of red in Sevair Masif's hair, turning Calli's coloring of blond hair, blue eyes, pinkened cheeks into a perfect picture. So she snapped it, and tucked the little camera back into the pack, began to hook up the charging cord up to the solar panel, then had second thoughts. Who knew what spectrum of light this sun had? How the solar power collected would affect Earth devices? She replaced the memory bit with a new one, took the shot again, backed up and took a few pics of the Castle—the keep and Temple. Then she connected the camera to the battery pack, not the solar panel, and headed out.

Calli stared at the backpack and touched a silver grid. "What is this?"

"Solar power, for all my electronics except laptop. Which I didn't bring with me anyway." A little pang of regret, though it would have been useless here.

"I can't believe this," Calli said.

Bri thumbed on the music player, put an earbud next to Calli's ear.

"Wow," Calli said.

"What is that?" Sevair's brows were down again.

Somehow Bri didn't think he'd appreciate her music. Music for itchy feet. Loud and raucous. She sent him a cheeky smile. "Just toys." She put the music player away. "Reminds me." She pulled her cell from the pouch, looked at the power indicator which showed it was juiced though the connectivity showed nothing. She hit redial for Elizabeth's apartment. Futile.

She gulped, turned the phone off, stuck it back in its pocket, made sure everything was protected. Shrugging, she said, "That was a communication device. Nothing."

"Hmm," he said.

"You had to try," Calli said softly.

"Yes."

Let's fly! said Mud.

"Yes. Castleton awaits." Sevair looked at the sundial affixed to a wall. "We're not too late."

Which told Bri that he'd arrived at their suite very early, probably calculating that it would take quite a while to get them moving. Clever man.

"And arriving by volaran will be impressive," Calli said.

His smile returned. "Indeed."

The volaran had been equipped with a long modified western saddle that would carry two. Sevair swung onto the flying horse with ease. Bri handed her bag to Calli then mounted, too. The light robe scrunched high above her knees.

"Your sister is wearing the right tabard for flying," Sevair said. He took the pack from Calli and examined it. "Odd cloth."

"Yes."

"Something from the Exotique Terre machines. Good craftsmanship. Excellent design."

"It's, um, magical." She tapped the panels. "These will capture the sun's power and give it to my toys."

"Amazing."

He strapped her bag onto Mud. The volaran craned her neck to sniff at it. Sounds and a couple of images flickered to Bri, but she didn't catch the details.

Calli chuckled. "Mud says your bag smells of many interesting scents."

"I'm glad she likes it."

Calli's hand grabbed Bri's. "We're only two miles away."

Bri stared down at Calli. "I've been in places where two miles away is like another dimension. I reckon this is one of them."

Flushing, Calli nodded. "Ayes." She held out a small sphere. "A crystal ball for you." Her mouth twisted. "Think of it as a cell phone programmed to call any Exotique. We all have one."

"Thanks." Bri took the inch-sized sphere. It was warm in her hands. Naturally, or from Calli's body heat? Bri started to pocket it, realized she wasn't wearing her jeans.

"Here." Sevair's large, calloused hand slid across her thigh and sent tingles through her. Now that she thought of it, he smelled good too. But he was holding fabric of her tunic apart and she saw a large pocket.

"*Merci*," she said.

He clicked his tongue and the volaran trotted to the center of the courtyard. Sevair braced.

Large wings opened, lifted, and they were off the ground and up, up, up!

They were flying! The sheer exhilaration of it, of zooming through the air was like a fabulous, fantastic dream.

As soon as the initial glee wore off, Bri was inundated with Song. Loud, somehow horsey-beats—clip, clip, clop—and brass came from Mud, along with an occasional flat note reminding Bri of a squelching footstep in wet earth.

Then there was the Song of the man behind her. Now that the only natural sound was air rushing by her, she heard it, thought she heard his steady heartbeat—a little rapid as her own must be—but strong and even. To her surprise she didn't just get a few notes from him, but a long, streaming melody, and she liked the tune. Definitely intriguing. Strong, stable but with an unexpected intricate twine of notes repeating at well spaced intervals, changing minutely each time. As life changed the man?

Personal Songs must change as an individual did. If so, her pattern must be shot to hell, and Elizabeth's, too. She chuckled deep in her throat; the arms around her tightened and glancing back she thought she saw another smile.

Mud was flying slowly. Stretching out her moments of glory? The road from the Castle and its walls to the city of Castleton, also encircled by stout walls, was steep downward, and Mud had hardly dropped. Instead she circled over the city.

"A tour by air," Sevair said. His whisper puffed warm air by Bri's right ear. "Fabulous."

Pride rang in his Song, too, a gleaming silver note. Dedication, a repeating theme of a cadence that reminded Bri of deep stone-like tones, like bedrock singing. What a fancy! But where better to explore fancies than atop a flying horse?

"Lower, please," Sevair said loudly.

Bri saw rooftops of red tile and gray and blue slate. Some buildings were three stories, a few four, and only one was five.

Masif pointed to it. "The Guildhall." Again that silver bell chime from his Song.

As they circled down, Bri saw the part nearest the Castle, probably the oldest part, was jumbled on each side of a very thick gatehouse that sent out equally thick walkways and occasional towers along the walls. Toward the center, the city became more orderly, with houses surrounding parklike squares or circles. Commercial districts surrounded stone courtyards and pumps or fountains. A small stream threaded through the city, and the walls appeared newer and even stronger around the lower third of the city. She thought she could see where an old wall might have been.

Mud heaved a sigh Bri both heard telepathically and felt beneath her. She got the picture. Time to descend. Even the duty-bound Sevair behind her seemed reluctant; she wondered if he ever allowed himself to play.

Images came to her mind, another volaran, two, near Sevair—the winged horse's projections.

Sevair replied with an image of roomy stalls with a feed trough full of hay and grain.

Bri realized negotiations were taking place and was amused and interested.

Mud showed Sevair dressed in Chevalier leathers with a raised sword. Flying down to a battlefield. Yellow and black and gray things Bri couldn't quite discern but which made shivers crawl up her spine were fighting with humans and volarans.

"Ttho!" His negative rang in her mind, must have carried to others. He showed himself dressed in rich pants and shirt, with tabard, flying to other towns and cities.

Whickering in satisfaction, Mud dropped down to the courtyard, and she sent one last vision—of her throat opening and Song flowing from it to other volarans. Bri knew the image and the Song—Mud would tell others that Sevair wanted her kind, would care for them well, would not be fighting. He'd be flying for transportation to other fascinating places. The volaran added a picture of Bri at the end.

Bri laughed.

They landed in what appeared to be the town square, though it was a long, cobbled rectangle. People stood on all sides, looking at her.

Sevair dismounted and bowed.

She was reluctant to get off the winged steed, and Sevair reached up, put his big hands around her waist and lifted her down with ease. Her eyes met his and she saw he was very serious again. As always.

His fingers slid down to hers, then he lifted her hand with his in a gesture of triumph. "This is Bri Drystan who saved widow Marchand's boy last night and healed all who were sick of the Dark disease. Our Exotique Medica!"

Cheers rose from the square. Bri was surrounded by happy faces. Tears stung. She'd known gratitude before, but it usually came from an individual, not a crowd. Awesome.

Bri's minutes of basking in glory lasted only until she noticed Sevair conversing with other well-dressed people and watching her from the corner of his eye. She knew that look. She had purple streaks in her hair, an alternative-life-style fashion statement that she now regretted since it meant that she might be watched all the time.

No one came up to talk to her. When she stepped close to someone, they sidled back. So they respected Exotiques, were glad she and Elizabeth, and the others, were here, but the Exotiques were also obvious aliens in a culture with few differences.

"Let's discuss matters inside." Sevair stepped aside, offered his arm to Bri and took Mud's reins, then led them both to the guildhall. The crowd parted. He planted Bri on the porch with a look that meant "stay," and Mud went happily into a walled and grassy garden. The people in the square dispersed, except the kids who were intently eyeing the garden door.

Then Sevair was back with introductions to the other Citymasters, half of whom were women. Bri made note of them, and figured it wouldn't be as hard remembering what guild they were master of as much as their names. The goldsmith wore an intricate gold ring, the weaver a fine rainbow-colored shawl.

But when they got into the guildhall conference room it became jaw-cracking dull. They talked about the statement that the Dark sent the plague. They spoke of funding a Chevalier team to fight against the Dark, or studies by Circlets. Bri spent the first few minutes looking at the people, then the room—rich wood panels that held a symbol of the craft guilds with ornately carved trim in the shape of fruits and flowers. There were windows, some of them stained-glass as if they were a glazier's ongoing project, high in the wall offering light but no view.

The scent spoke of polish and understated wealth. Of tradition.

They'd seated her at the end of the room in a fancy chair that was so new-looking that it was evident it was a symbol. The back panel had a woman with raised arms and tilted-back head and open mouth, singing. Not too difficult to deduce that the chair was reserved for the Singer, and Bri wondered if she'd ever used it.

She had only shifted in the chair twice—okay, three times—before Sevair caught her eye. A ripple of a melody came from him. He was as impatient as she with this talk, but he showed no restlessness, continued to make his points as steadily as he'd probably made them several times before. Some would consider that a virtue.

She was just about ready to stand and make a circuit of the room, scrutinize the woodwork, when the door burst open and a woman staggered in holding a sick child.

Adrenaline poured through Bri. Her hands tingled.

10

By midmorning, Elizabeth's mind was spinning…no, that was a trite and wrong image. Her mind was so saturated with new ideas and experiences it was like a sodden sponge. Her brain might have sunk to the bottom of her skull unable to hold one more new thing.

She'd been shown the healing rooms, and had watched when the medicas followed up on the injuries from the battle the night before. The claw-slices and puncture wounds on heavily scarred bodies had horrified her, empirical evidence that these people fought *somethings* that tried their best to kill them. She was told again that the Marshalls formed a healing circle after the battle and handled most of the injuries. She garnered that though the "incursion" had been large, only two people had died. Alexa and Bastien had saved the day.

Her whole body tensed at the images forming in her mind, but she asked no questions. Then a Chevalier woman limped in with strained muscles and a broken arm from a too tough practice and Elizabeth helped heal her. That was—strange. Nothing like linking with Bri, but Elizabeth couldn't pinpoint why.

The female knight and her partner in the skirmish had been charged a large sum for the healing for being careless in a time of war, when the medicas needed to be fresh for any battle aftermath the Marshalls couldn't handle. Individuals and pairs were patrolling and fighting in the north and might appear at any moment.

Then they'd all trooped to the inside training hall in the lower courtyard of the Castle to reiterate the policy to the rest of the fighters.

Alexa Fitzwalter rescued her, shooing off the medicas surrounding Elizabeth with flapping motions as if they were a flock of birds. "Give the woman a break!"

Elizabeth shook her head. Had Alexa actually said that? She reran the words in her mind. No. Something equally colloquial, but not those exact words.

Jerking her head toward the security gate between the lower courtyard and Temple ward, Alexa said, "Let's get rid of the extra bed and wardrobe in your room. You don't object to living in my tower, do you?" She started off across the grassy middle of the yard.

Elizabeth kept pace. "Would my objection be listened to?"

Alexa smiled. "Sure. You get to choose where to stay."

"I'd rather go."

Face losing expression, Alexa said, "Got that."

"This is not our fight. Our parents—"

"I'm sorry," Alexa said brusquely in English. "We understand, and we cut Marian some slack, but since then the war against the Dark has heated up. It wants something here in Lladrana and won't hesitate to make this country a waste-land to get it."

"Could you give—" Elizabeth started, but Alexa was shaking her head.

"I think anything a big evil entity wanted badly enough to create monsters and kill whatever got in its way is not something we should give that entity. Like Hitler and the atomic bomb. What we have here in Lladrana starts with genocide, since it's only Lladrana being invaded now. But I reckon it will move to the eradication of the human species." Her smile was grim. "I'd rather not be an individual in an endangered species. Not to mention that we can all hear the planet, Amee, weep. This planet is much weaker than Earth, in energy—Song."

Elizabeth remained silent and nodded to the guards who held open the heavy gate door. She stepped over the threshold curb. "I've never been a proponent in the sacri-fice of the individual for the greater good. Especially when the individuals don't want to be sacrificed. I would have thought as an attorney that you would have agreed. You don't seem to be the type to defend major corporations, but individuals."

"I took any case I could get," Alexa said, heading toward the keep. Sadness passed over her face. "I had a partner, as close as a sister, who died just before I came." She sighed. "I was grieving. We'd just set up business and were scrambling for work." They entered the keep and strode down corridors.

"That reminds me," Elizabeth said. "Our godfather is a judge in Denver."

Alexa's expression changed to wariness as she stopped outside the door to the twins' suite. "Let me guess, the honorable Trenton Philbert the Third." She fingered her baton sheath.

"You know him."

"Yeah. Open the door."

Elizabeth set her hand on the knob, heard and felt a little "pop." They went down the narrow security passage to the dining room entrance. She pushed open the door. Things looked slightly disarrayed. Of course, someone had come to get Bri's gear.

Alexa went to the table and put her hand on the stack of three books. "All of us know the judge."

"What!"

Alexa's smile was ironic. "Denver isn't as large as some of the eastern cities, but it ain't a small cow-town anymore."

Elizabeth blinked. "Calli was a rancher."

"Ayes, and 'Bert' had a spread right next to hers." Alexa's forehead creased. "The Philberts had lived next to Calli's family for a couple of generations."

"Coincidence?" Elizabeth said, then shook her head just as the smaller woman was doing.

"I don't think so," Alexa said. Again she shrugged. "We'll see if the last Exotique knows him, too. A singer," she murmured. "Probably gotta be a singer. He big into the arts?"

"Of course."

"Of course," Alexa repeated.

"Though his new wife is…unusual. Very involved in New Age studies."

Alexa stared at her thoughtfully, "The owner of the metaphysical store in Denver, Queen of Cups."

"Yes, how did you know?"

Tapping the books with her finger, Alexa said, "Marian met her." Alexa's mouth opened, then her lips pressed together as if guarding secrets. "Read them. There may be other connections among us. We need to know."

"I will." Elizabeth scooped up her healthy back bag, slung it over her shoulder. She didn't want to think about connections. She went into the bedroom and stopped in her tracks as she saw a long-haired white Persian cat batting one of the foil paper chocolate wrappers around and pouncing on it.

"How did he get in here?" Elizabeth said.

The cat sat down and draped her tail around her paws. *I AM a she.*

Elizabeth plunked onto the bed. A talking cat. She was going mad. Flying horses, talking cats. She rubbed her eyes.

"This is my companion. She is a magical shape-shifting being, come to help us defeat the Dark."

"Of course she is," Elizabeth said tiredly, but jolted at the sight of the miniature greyhound cradled in Alexa's arms. Futilely she scanned the room for the cat.

I am a dog now.

"So I see." Her shoulders slumped.

The greyhound held out a dainty paw.

Sighing, Elizabeth went over to take it, and Power *zinged* through her body, removing weariness. She stepped back and released the small pads and claws. "I shouldn't be surprised."

"Of course you should be," Alexa said. "You're in a different dimension. I can speak from experience that information and surprises come flying at you—sometimes literally— the first few days." Her lopsided smile charmed. She continued, "I'm down to a surprise every couple of weeks. Marian's still getting surprised every other day or so, but she's a scholar and a Circlet and investigates stuff." She bent down and picked up the wrapper and her scowl was back, along with an accusatory stare. "Chocolate. You have more than the chocolate cake. You have *candy*." She held the scrap up to her nose and sniffed, whimpered. "You had chocolate *last night*."

Elizabeth had. After she'd put Bri to bed, she'd eaten one, or rather had let it melt in her mouth and slide down her throat, savoring every instant. She clamped her bag close to her side. "Yes, I had one. After we healed—" she still wasn't comfortable with the word "—fifteen people."

Alexa blew out a breath. "Guess I can't blame you." She widened her eyes and tried to look pitiful. It didn't work. She was one of the strongest, most competent people Elizabeth had ever met, including her mother and the staff at Denver Major.

When Elizabeth didn't respond to the ploy, Alexa once again donned the manner of extreme efficiency. Looking down at the dog in her arms, she said, "Is there anything else in the extra wardrobe Elizabeth needs?"

Faucon's shirts, the dog said slyly. Elizabeth heard her. She ignored the comment and stared at the greyhound. It had an aura. She was getting used to seeing light flare around people, green most especially for the medicas. This aura was different, radiating a glittering rainbow with golden patches that glowed every few seconds.

The greyhound launched herself from Alexa to Elizabeth and Elizabeth caught her. She was light, as if she was more spirit than flesh. Her fur was soft. The dog looked at her with deep brown eyes that drew her in, made her dizzy, had her sinking into her balance.

You and your twin are needed here. It will take both of you to find the answers.

Elizabeth blinked, but still heard the voice in her mind, thought she saw the dog's muzzle opening and closing as if she uttered words. *Stay. I am Sinafinal, a fey-coo-cu. Call on me if you have need, but guard my name from others. Only the Exotiques and their mates know our names.*

"Our?" Elizabeth managed.

There was a short bark and another greyhound sat on the bed, tongue lolling and wagging its tail.

My mate, said Sinafinal.

It was male. Slightly larger, it was a dappled brown instead of grey like Sinafinal. It held out a paw.

Cautious, but fascinated, Elizabeth took the paw. Another surge of energy through her, but something about this one felt almost familiar.

I am Tuckerinal. I was once a hamster. I came with Marian from Earth and am her companion.

"Um, salutations." Again she eased back from the magical being. Fey-coo-cu, magical shape-shifting being. Former hamster. Right.

Hello to you. Too messy here. Bed and wardrobe must go.

"I'll take care of it," Alexa said, waved toward the bathroom and dining room beyond.

The dog sniffed at Elizabeth's bag. *Do you have nuts?*

"No."

Yes, you do! Nuts, nuts, nuts! He pawed at the bag, managed to tip her cell phone out.

"No!" Alexa lunged for the bed, but it was tall and wide. She hopped on, but not before Tuckerinal's quick paws snicked the case of Elizabeth's cell open and his tongue came out to scoop up the battery and memory chips.

"No!" Elizabeth dropped Sinafinal, but it was too late. She was dazed by what she'd just witnessed, a dog eating electronics.

Tuckerinal burped and grinned at her. *More nuts?*

"No, Bri has the most toys." She snapped her mouth shut.

Br-iii. It was an anticipatory lilt in her mind from him. He swiped a long pink tongue over his muzzle. *Toys. Nuts.*

"Uh-oh," Alexa said.

"No!" Elizabeth scrabbled at the remnants of the phone, knowing it was useless, but trying to put it together all the same. Tears spurted from her eyes and anger and humiliation washed through her.

She is doing that turning red thing, Sinafinal said.

"Out! All of you! How could you? That was my *camera* phone. It had *pictures.*" She whirled to Alexa. "Photos of our father's birthday party. Of our parents! Get out. Now. I don't want to see any of you."

Tuckerinal sat up. He wasn't happy and grinning now. *I can show them. All. I can repeat voice mail.* He opened his mouth.

"Hey, sweetheart." Cassidy's deep tones rolled out. "Can't tell you how much I want you, how I'm lookin' forward to after shift. Later."

Elizabeth moaned and curled onto the bed.

Alexa was there. "I'm sorry. So sorry. You didn't say you'd left a…a lover, too."

"The…the…bas…tard…broke…off…our…engagement… two weeks ago," Elizabeth said between shuddering sobs.

"Oh, gawd," Alexa said in English. The bed dipped as she crawled closer. She sat by Elizabeth and stroked her hair. "I'm so sorry."

"I love him. Loved him." She cried more, couldn't seem to stop. Hadn't she cried enough over the man? "He…saw. Me trying to…use my…my…gift." It was all so horrible. She could remember her despair that a young girl was dying, her desperate hope that she could call down a miracle. Her failure.

"He…was…appalled… A…doctor, rational person…" He hadn't loved her enough.

Two small forms settled on either side of her. One purred near her abdomen. She reached out and tangled her fingers in long, soft fur. Sinafinal, as the cat. A long nose nuzzled the back of her knee.

I made Elizabeth cry. I am very sorry. I will make it up somehow. A doggy sigh. *I could not resist the nuts. A little one comes. We both need energy and Power and Song for it.*

That made no sense to Elizabeth.

Alexa said. "You will take care of all the photos for Elizabeth. Not one must be lost. We'll see what we can do about having them, um, hard-copied."

The absurdity of that—hard-copied from a dog's stomach?—just made Elizabeth cry harder.

The sick child was a girl of about seven or eight, sturdy. Probably too heavy for the mother to carry, but she held her child with desperate strength.

With a careful sweep of his arm, Sevair shoved the stacks of papers aside, then took the child, carried her to the conference table.

"Sevair, this is not the place…" said one hefty man shrinking back to the side of the room. Sevair and the woman—now twisting her hands in her apron—were between the citymaster and the door, otherwise Bri thought he might have bolted.

"This is exactly the place. Exactly our priority. Exactly our duty." Sevair bit the words off. He gently laid the girl on the table, grabbed his overtunic, stuffed it under her head.

"Medica?" His look was a demand.

Bri found herself rubbing her hands. She stopped, shifted her shoulders, drew in a deep breath and went to the child. The girl was unconscious, so no talking to her about where it hurt. Opening her mouth, Bri caught sweet, labored breathing. No coating of white on her tongue. She checked under her eyes. Nothing there, either.

No use. She'd just have to trust in the healingstream, in the magic and Power of this dimension. That everyone was right and her hands would be enough. Sure weren't any antibiotics around. She stroked the child from head to toe, heat radiated from her throat and her abdomen.

Keeping in mind what the medica had said, Bri strained to *hear* the chakra centers, the chimes. Cacophony clashed in her mind, in her ears, rocking her back and making her shake her head to get rid of the sound, like cars crashing. Terrible sound.

One more lung-filling breath. Ease it out and *reach*. Again Power slammed into her. Her body jerked. Strong hands grasped her shoulders, excess energy went through that link.

Heal her, said Sevair.

She looked for the chakras, couldn't make out the jumble of colors. So Bri shut her eyes and prayed. Found the Song again. The Song of the child. The Song of herself. The throbbing Song of the Power flowing through her.

But it needed to be controlled, focused, sent to the right organs in the correct order, so the most important systems were strengthened first to support the healing of the rest. Power flowed through her. Had she reached for it? She didn't know, but knew there was plenty here.

The Songs drowned out all thought. She touched young flesh. She healed. Without thought and without plan and without reason.

Later she found herself shivering, lifted and folded into a chair, Sevair's tunic now draping her. Her vision cleared, and she saw a bunch of people near the table, the citymasters, the woman holding and rocking her girl, tears and snot streaming down her face, a big man in rough clothes.

If Bri could have spared the breath for a sigh of relief, she would have. She'd done it. She was so much stronger here to be able to heal a strange, debilitating sickness in one session.

There was no sign of the hefty citymaster.

Songs washed through Bri, pulsed around her. Still fearful strident notes from the father and mother, the girls' sweet tune, the intricate pattern of the citymasters.

Sevair was tapping a map with his index finger, looking at the man. "You live here?"

"Ayes." The man nodded.

With a brusque nod of his own, Sevair placed another red dot on the map.

"Outlying farm area, again," a woman said.

"Yes," Sevair said.

"I don't see any kind of pattern we can work with." An older man crossed his arms. "Hard to stop such a sickness if we don't know where it will strike next."

"Let alone why," said the woman.

"Who all have you been with today?" asked a different woman of the farm wife.

The farm woman dragged a rag from her pocket, wiped her face and nose. "Ella collapsed in Noix Market Square."

"Wonderful." Deep sarcasm came from the older man.

"We must send people to the farm and the square," Sevair said. "I'll have an assistant accompany these folk home."

Bri stirred, tried to stand, couldn't, she felt like an aged grandmother. After licking her lips, she forced words from a dry throat. "Bring the girl to me." With her quavery voice she even sounded like an old grandmother. At least the typical stereotype. Her own were professional women. And her brain was nattering.

The man in farmer's clothes lifted his daughter and carried her to Bri, setting her across Bri's lap, supporting her.

The girl looked fine. Good color. Bri tested her forehead, temperature seemed all right, checked her tongue and eyes again, all good.

She slipped her hand through the gaping shirt. Again warm skin, her patient's heart thumped with a regular beat, her lungs filled and emptied. After a couple of sips of breath, Bri opened herself to the sound of the chakras. They hummed with what she was beginning to understand was healthful normality.

Incredible.

"She's good," she said to the man watching intently.

He smiled and she saw even, white teeth, then he took his daughter. "Yes, medica, she *is* good. A good girl, good daughter. We would have been sad without her." His commonplace words were backed by Song, and Bri first heard the tones of a loving family: father, mother, two sons, two daughters. All experiencing euphoria at the saving of Ella. All sending Bri their utmost gratitude.

Too much to handle seriously. She cleared her throat, "Tell me, sir, do you raise vegetables?"

His brows winged up at being called sir, then he smiled again, his chest puffed out. "The best chouys in Lladranan."

"Chouys, huh?" Bri caught Sevair's eye. "We will keep him in mind, right?"

"As you wish, Exotique." Sevair did the torso incline.

"My thanks and my woman's thanks," the farmer said formally to Bri, then to the guildspeople.

The farm woman came over to Bri, studied her. "*Merci.*" Reached out her hand. Bri took it and their fingers locked. "*Merci.*" The woman squeezed her hand, let go and followed her husband to the door, she drew herself up and said, "It is good that you Summoned an Exotique Medica for us all." They left.

While Bri was still contemplating these words, Sevair scooped her from the chair.

"I can walk!"

"Can you?"

"Yes."

He set her on her feet, but kept an arm loosely around her waist, steadying her. Her legs were a little wobbly, but the feel of the stone under her feet seemed to help. She straightened, took a step, paused, took another step. Everyone watched her. The women smiled. The old man scowled. "If this is the Power cost of Healing one child, we have big problems."

"Yes," Sevair said briefly.

"They healed sixteen last night," someone said.

"We were together," Bri said. "My twin sister and I. And we were in the Castle with a lot of Power."

"And with the Marshalls, who themselves are greatly Powerful," Sevair said.

"This room is good," Bri said.

The woman nodded. "We will scout out other places of Power that will be good for healing if an epidemic comes."

"When the epidemic comes," Sevair said.

Bri shuffled faster and made it to the door before the argument truly began. She stepped away from Sevair's arm, tilted and had to brace a hand against the wall.

Sevair finished snicking the lock to the door behind them, and held out his arm with old-time courtesy. Bri took it, managed a weak smile, and they walked very slowly down the corridor. Every other man she knew would have been impatient with her, would have picked her up and carried her to wherever they were going, not simply walked step-by-step in silence. Sevair Masif was a real stand-up guy.

When they reached the door, he held it open to show a carriage pulled by a team of horses just beyond the pillared portico. "The Citymasters' equipage to take you to your new home," he said.

Before they even crossed the threshold, there was the sound of hoofbeats, rustling and a protesting neigh from Mud. *Me!* It was loud, demanding, and inescapable.

II

The volaran pranced.

"It's only a few blocks to her new home," Sevair said.

Mud rolled big eyes at him.

Sevair sighed. "Very well. The tailor will be coming shortly and we are, as usual, running late." He lifted Bri and mounted behind her. Sevair projected a pretty square full of mature trees and flower beds, surrounded by three-story town houses set closely together. He indicated one with pillars in the front and a long back garden.

Mud lifted off, as light as a feather caught by a spring breeze. She soared over the square and people cheered again, sent blessings Bri could actually feel along with a rise of Song. Fabulous.

She leaned against Sevair, solid behind her, and observed as they skimmed over roofs.

The square with the house wasn't more than two streets

over, and the neighborhood was smaller than she realized, cozier. A lot of people seemed to be in the park, "casually" watching. No doubt everyone knew she'd be living here.

It was finally sinking in that she was a celebrity. How very odd. She'd been in places where her skin or face weren't the same as most of the local population, and she'd earned respect from people, but nothing like this.

Mud landed softly in the beautifully landscaped back-yard. Sevair lifted her down. This was *her* new home? Her nerves jangled. She'd never even thought of buying a house, let alone something as—substantial—as this one. It was a full three stories and of creamy-colored worked stone, like the limestone she'd seen in the English Cotswolds. Looking down the block, she saw a variety of styles, all melding into a harmonious whole. No doubt all belonging to upstand-ing and sober citizens.

She was in over her head. The soles of her feet prickled. "It's…it's lovely," she forced out.

Sevair's expression lightened. "All of the artisans of Cas-tleton worked to provide the best for you."

Uh-oh. Major expectations. She wet her lips. "Great."

"I'll show you the inside in a moment. Now, Mud…" Speaking slowly, with gestures and clear mind images, Sevair told Mud she could return to the Castle, or be stabled with other volarans in a different part of town.

Bri stroked Mud. "Thank you. I'm honored you'll stay in town." As soon as she patted the flying horse's neck and stepped away, Mud took off. Bri watched the volaran, heart squeezing. Not a sight that she'd ever see on Earth.

Sevair cleared his throat. When she turned to him, he offered his arm. Bri hesitated, but curled her hand in the crook of his elbow. His muscle was like the stone he worked. He led her along meandering stepping stones to a back door that was fancy enough to be on the front of any house. Placing his hand on the knob, he hummed a few chords, and made Bri repeat them to unlock and lock the door.

They stepped into an impressive kitchen of pristine white tile, but he moved her through it quickly, hardly giving her time to look around. "We've arranged for all your meals to be delivered. You need only list what you want daily."

"Um, merci." Guess she wasn't expected to learn magical cooking.

"We wish you to concentrate on your medica gifts."

She'd always done that, but to hear it as a duty was a little off-putting.

The hallway was papered in pale lavender, with a faint pattern of darker-colored leaves and flower sprigs. His gaze lingered on the purple streaks in her hair that she'd begun to regret. "Purple is the traditional color for Exotiques."

"Oh."

"But Alyeka and Marian and Calli have not used the color much in their furnishings. So we, too, limited the use." A small cough. "Except for one bedroom." Again he glanced at her hair, "should you prefer it."

He showed her the rest of the house. The luxury and space of it intimidated her with the expectations the city-masters had of her, the belief she'd stay in Lladrana. Each wooden panel and piece of furniture was carefully crafted of the best materials. A showplace. She didn't know if she could live in a showplace, but to refuse and dent everyone's pride was impossible.

The master bedroom was on the third floor, with a

balcony over the square and a wide window to the north, showing the Castle. She had a prized corner lot. The guest bedroom was an explosion of purple. Someone had put it together with care, with various shades and rich textures, but her eyes watered just looking at it.

Sevair watched her closely. Not time to tell him that she and Elizabeth had finished their purple phase at seven years old. "It's…interesting."

He chuckled, relaxed. "Then we were correct in keeping to a more traditional decorating scheme for the master bedroom."

"Ayes," she said.

Harp strings came at her door. Bri blinked.

"The doorharp is bespelled so you can hear it anywhere," Sevair said. He went to the bedside table and picked up something that looked like a real horn and spoke. "Who's there?"

"Geraint." Bri heard the answer.

Sevair said, "My assistant." Then into the horn, "Ayes?"

"The other citymasters request that you accompany the farmer home after market."

Eyebrows winging up, Sevair said, "Come in," and set the horn down. He hummed the unlock spell on the front door. His expression had gone serious again. "We citymasters had intended a dinner in your honor this evening, then decided after you healed the child that you should rest. Will you be all right here on your own?"

Bri blinked at him. She'd traveled the world over and had been all right on her own. She'd been careful—mostly. "Ayes."

A young man wearing gray walked toward them. He bowed.

"My assistant, Geraint, who attends to my office, will be available to you for anything."

"Salutations," Bri said.

Sevair turned to Geraint and spoke of reassuring the countryside that their concerns were not overlooked. Bri drifted toward the creamy-yellow painted bedroom. Cheerful and sunny, especially on this gray day, she liked it, though it was a trifle too fussy with lace.

Earlier she'd set down her pack on the desk. It looked totally out of place here. High-tech materials against silk and brocade and lace, gender-neutral in a very feminine room. The citymasters had obviously expected their Exotique to be female.

Again harp strings sounded. Bri looked around and found a shell-like horn on the bedside. She picked it up. "Who's there?" That was what Sevair said.

"The tailor, my lady," said a female voice.

"Is that the right greeting?" Bri asked. "Who's there?"

A little cough on the other end of the horn. "Ayes."

"Thank you," Bri said. "The door is unlocked, please come in. I'll meet you in the parlor." There *was* a parlor.

She turned and found Sevair at the door, Geraint hovering behind him.

"Unless you want me to stay, I'll leave now." Sevair's voice was matter-of-fact, but his gaze was warm with a touch of curiosity. When she listened, she thought the vibrations of his Song expressed interest—personal—in her.

He smiled. "Citymaster Nu will take care of you. She's an excellent tailor and already has a wardrobe planned."

Bri glanced around. "So all my needs will be provided by citymasters?" That didn't come out the way she'd intended.

His gaze lingered on her face. "Ayes, anything you wish for will be provided."

"Ah, how about lunch?" Her mind went back to the potato casserole and her mouth watered.

"Of course." He looked at a water clock set on an beautifully sculpted table made especially for it, smiled again. "The clock is understandable and acceptable?"

"Ayes, we know that time passes the same here as at home. The clock is charming." The rush of water soothed her.

"I'd heard that time is the same and so are clocks," Sevair said. "And the table?"

The intensity of his glance clued her in. "You made it? It's beautiful." A short pillar with a delicate stone floral vine covering the underlying flutes. Bri thought she even saw a fairy face peeking out between leaves.

He nodded. "Thank you."

She wondered how much more of his work she'd find in the house. Something to look for.

"As for lunch," Sevair said, "it should have arrived and been placed in the kitchen for you. We have cold and hot boxes to keep the food at the proper temperature. The other Exotiques—all three of them—planned the menus." Amusement laced his tones. "There was lively discussion." He sobered again. "However, the tailor is here…"

She suppressed a sigh. The woman was probably a busy person and Bri was taking up time. "Yes. The tailor first. And I'm a little tired. I'll rest."

"Everything okay?" Alexa asked.

Elizabeth looked around. The extra bed and wardrobe

had been removed, the furniture rearranged. Bri's fragrance, more, her Song, still floated in the rooms, reaching Elizabeth's heart. She'd only had the company of her sister for a few brief hours before they'd been separated again. Not their choice this time. Or perhaps it had been too easy to accommodate the wishes of the Lladranans and they should have thought more of themselves. But they hadn't been given the time.

Going back out to the sitting room, Elizabeth checked the potatoes and went to the chest. Her breath caught in her throat when she saw the clean empty serving bowl that had held the fruit salad. Her mother's special-occasion china.

What would her parents think when they discovered their daughters were missing? Elizabeth's car was in her allotted apartment parking spot, but…. She shut off that line of thinking. There was nothing she could do about it right now, and it would only muddle her thoughts when she needed all her wits to deal with the current situation.

Her mind went back to what Alexa had said before. Elizabeth asked, "Any idea what this item…the Dark wants…is? Is it physical?"

"No, we don't know what it is. Yes, we know it's physical. We think the Dark originally came to this planet through the dimensional corridor and landed in Lladrana, then left and settled in the north on its own cozy volcanic island. But it either lost this object or didn't realize it needed it."

"Hmm," Elizabeth managed.

Alexa said, "So, the Dark wants this item, and we think it's somehow sent this sickness as a plague to wipe the Lladranans out. The monsters haven't been able to penetrate the northern border and take the thing. So killing us all with an epidemic might be an alterative plan." Her steps slowed; she studied Elizabeth with cool eyes. "That's your task, your's and your sister's. To find a cure for the plague."

"Nothing like a little pressure," Elizabeth said.

Alexa shrugged. "That's life on Lladrana. You, what, just got certified as a medical doctor? Did internships and residency? That ain't exactly a walk in the park." She'd switched to English again, and Elizabeth's head began to ache.

Elizabeth said in Lladranan, "No, my training to be an E.R. doctor wasn't easy." 'Training" was a word she'd already learned. "But it was a long ordeal, now over."

"Ah, and now I'm asking you to gird your loins for another long ordeal."

"If most Exotiques fulfill their task within two months for the Snap, Bri and I can do it, too." Elizabeth was feeling overwhelmed, but wouldn't admit doubt to anyone other than Bri.

Blinking, Alexa said, "Fulfilled their task in two months?"

"You said that the Snap averages two months, and one of the prerequisites for the Snap is the fulfillment of a task."

"Excellent deduction." Faucon, the elegant Chevalier said from the door. He looked around. "All is as it should be."

"You did your task in two months," Elizabeth said.

Alexa pinkened. "A little over."

"Marian succeeded in a month," Faucon said, and grunted when Alexa elbowed him. "And Calli—"

"Calli decided early on to stay in Lladrana," Alexa said.

"Bri and I will work hard on our task," Elizabeth said. "But we want to return home. We have our parents to consider.

They'll worry." She lifted her chin. "Imagine how you'd feel if your children disappeared."

Scowling, Alexa said, "We understand that."

"Good. Understand that our food and our belongings are ours."

"Fine, fine." Alexa waved a hand.

"Promise."

"I promise," Alexa ground out between her teeth.

"You seem to be giving us a list of rules and requirements. I'm just returning the favor," Elizabeth said, and the phrase sounded fine in Lladranan.

Faucon indicated the potatoes. "I can arrange for a cold storage box to be put in your dining area," he said smoothly.

"Aren't those expensive?" Alexa grumbled.

Faucon just kept smiling.

"Right, with you, zhiv—money—is no problem," Alexa answered herself.

"I'd like the cold box," Elizabeth said. She sent a look to Alexa. "You were all very free with your bribes to keep us here this morning."

Alexa's chin came up. She touched her baton. "Exotiques who stay get an estate and a lifetime salary. That's the deal. The citymasters have a house for you in Castleton, but if you both stay you can have what you want, where you want."

"We won't be staying."

"I'll let you get settled," Alexa said. Her eyes softened. "Despite all its dangers, Lladrana can be a wonderful home."

"I'm sure," Elizabeth murmured.

Alexa dug into a pocket and came out with a small crystal

sphere. "Almost forgot, this is for you. Communication to any of us, though, um, we may develop a telepathic link as we go along."

Elizabeth took it. Even as she watched the crystal clouded. She hurriedly placed it on the sideboard.

"We also have an internal communication system." Alexa picked up a cow's horn. "Magic—or rather Power. It doesn't use much energy. Feel free to call." She walked to the door.

"Thank you." Elizabeth's mouth dried. Soon she'd be alone. She should cherish the time alone, as she'd learned to do during her medical training back home. But this wasn't home.

From the doorway, Alexa said to Faucon, "Aren't you coming?"

"In a moment."

She snorted again and disappeared into the hallway.

Elizabeth met Faucon's warm, dark chocolate-brown eyes.

"You will have the cold-storage box within the hour." He hesitated, came up to her and took her limp hand. Only when she felt the warmth of his fingers did she realize how cold her own were, though the room was nearly hot.

He squeezed her hand. "Please, call on me if you have any other wishes you want fulfilled. I would be your friend."

From the lilt of sensual Song coming from him, Elizabeth was sure he wanted more. As she gazed at his elegant features, her pulse picked up, surprising her.

Keeping his eyes on her, he kissed her hand, let it go. "Until later."

"Later," Elizabeth whispered.

He went out the door and closed it behind him.

Elizabeth stared at the strange room, full of beautiful furniture, the window showing a landscape of gray and green rolling hills. No mountains. No plains.

The white chest from a place a world away.

She found herself on a new segment of her life, and not the new segment she had planned.

And a new man?

12

Elizabeth spent her afternoon studying in-depth with the medicas, especially the non-invasive healing of muscle and bone. As predicted—or perhaps dreaded—a Chevalier fighting pair had arrived in bad shape.

Calli and the Marshalls took care of the volarans' injuries since the medicas wanted to teach Elizabeth.

The Marshalls' healing circle was more like calling down a blessing, or general healing, not detailed work with the chakras—God help her!—or individual systems of anatomy. The medicas could do this, too, and had participated in such circles to use the Marshalls' incredible strength and team-work. But individually and in pairs and triads, the medicas were more specialized, drawing on what Bri called the hea-lingstream and performing with their minds and magic what surgical teams would do with hands and tools.

Incidentally, Elizabeth learned other things. The Chevaliers she worked on were an independent pair, which meant that they were poor and didn't fly under anyone's banner, like Faucon's people. The image of that man distracted her for a moment, and she had to ask for elucidation of the lesson. The medicas were waiving their fee because they were teaching her.

The Chevaliers were pairbonded which meant marriage, and no stigma attached to homosexuality in this culture, a very good thing.

And the wounds were fearsome.

Elizabeth had never seen anything like them and had to keep her breathing, her emotions detached, her mind focused so she wouldn't vomit.

She learned from the medicas which "horrors" perpetrated each wound. Apparently the Chevaliers had been unlucky enough to run into a combination of all three major horrors.

The long, deep and razor-thin slices were from "renders." The easiest to mend with Power. "Slayers" had duller claws but poisonous spines. Elizabeth helped flush the poison from the Chevalier's system, through the skin pores, which was gross enough to remind her of her beginning days of med school. Little round bumps left from "soul-suckers" showed a deadening of the skin around the wounds. Physical life force had been drawn from that injury.

What was even more incredible to Elizabeth was that sometimes the Chevaliers wouldn't get help if they felt the wounds weren't severe enough.

Any wound was dangerous in Elizabeth's mind. The Lladranans had a different point of view. A very, very tough people.

A people who'd been at war for a long time.

* * *

Bri woke from her nap feeling restless. She tried to reach Elizabeth telepathically and was reassured when she touched her twin's sleeping mind. They'd be able to communicate mentally, then. She wandered through the rooms, feeling like the greatest fraud. This wasn't her; usually she shared small rooms with other women of her ilk. What would she do if she were in a new place on Earth? She'd go out. Even if she was unsure of the language, she'd unpack then hit the streets. Something was always going on outside if she didn't want to stay in.

It was a little melancholy to think that if she'd been back home in Denver, she'd be tucked up in Elizabeth's spare bedroom watching a favorite video. She'd yearned for home, had made some life decisions and headed there, ready to put her plans in action. How ironic that the moment she really wanted to be home, she was here, in another new place.

Which she didn't know much about. Surely she'd understand more about the culture if she went out and looked around. It was midafternoon and the sun had finally come out, burning off wisps of mist and brightening pretty streets. Definitely out.

What did she want to carry with her? She had no money—zhiv, she'd learned that word; her cell phone was useless. She wouldn't get the feel of the people, couldn't interact well with her music player going. She had a fanny-pack for essentials like tissue, chocolate, her Swiss Army knife. She'd have to be careful with the chocolate, ration it if she was going to be here two months.

She strode into the bedroom. A huge hamsterlike *thing*

sat in the middle of the bed. Worse, her cell, PDA, music player and digital camera were around him, some in pieces.

She shrieked and lunged for her electronic tools. The backs of her cell and her PDA were off and various plastic and metallic guts spilled across the bed. Her camera and music player looked untouched. She scooped up the PDA, camera and music player and clutched them to her breast. Her PDA had lost its backup battery and excess memory card. She stared at the creature. What was she going to do?

To her horror, the beastie snatched at the power source of her cell, put the object in its mouth and *munched* it. *Hello Brigid-who-likes-to-be-called-Bri. Your smell adds to the room.*

Bri staggered back to the wall, leaned against it, judged the distance to the door, a few steps. She could run if she had to. Surely she could outdistance such an animal. But it talked. Not simply an animal. "How do you know that?"

Because I met your sister Elizabeth-who-dislikes-being-called-Beth and her name and yours were in her mind.

Bri's mouth fell open but no more words came out. The…the…*being*…scrabbled around in the heap of plastic and parts and picked out a memory chip. Bri whimpered, but that didn't stop it from showing four teeth and biting down hard on the data storage, which disappeared into the enlarged hamster.

"What are you?"

What and who. I am a fey-coo-cu, a magical shapeshifter. I was once a hamster, brought here by Marian, my companion.

That boggled the mind, Bri just couldn't grasp it. She must be missing steps. "What?"

Marian brought me here and I ate some stuff. With little digited plump paws it indicated the remains of her electronics, eyed the ones she still held.

"Go on," she said, stuffing her electronics in her pockets. How glad she was now that she hadn't gotten an all-in-one PDA or phone!

No, the being said.

"No?" she repeated faintly.

I am very good at Exotique telepathy. It preened and stroked its whiskers, shifted to rub its fat belly and Bri noticed it was male. Did he have something stashed in one of his cheek pouches?

None of your data is gone. It is in me. His mouth opened and rounded. "Hello, twin, just informing you that all our plans went through. The trip for the folks to Hawaii for Dad's birthday is paid for and set. I bought a leather carrier for the tickets to give him as a present." Elizabeth's voice projected from the fey-coo-cu. A cheerful Elizabeth of several weeks ago, before her breakup with the moron.

Bri burst into tears.

The hamster drooped. *Not again*.

Staggering to the bed, she reached for her bag he'd rifled. At least he hadn't taken any of her food—probably only ate electronics. Pretty limited diet here. She fumbled for a tissue, sobs still tearing from her throat. Sinking down on the bed, she wiped her eyes and blew her nose, avoiding the sight of the dead items in the middle of the bed.

Suddenly her lap was full of purring cat. She blinked, stared down at it, a long-haired white Persian, perfectly groomed. Big blue eyes looked up at her, full of sympathy. She found herself stroking the cat with one hand, even as she slid the pockets of her robe behind her knees so the creature couldn't get at them or their contents.

I am Tuckerinal. That is my mated name. My mate is a female fey-coo-cu native to Amee. Her name is Sinafinal, and she is Alexa's companion.

Something the women *hadn't* told the twins.

There is much to say and talk and discuss when a new one of you comes, Tuckerinal chided in an arrogant cat-tone.

Bri sniffed tears away, grabbed tissue and mopped up.

I came to say hello to the other Exotique Medica, Bri-Brigid. Hello. He smiled a winning smile, revved the purr.

"Hello, Tuckerinal," she said thickly.

We give our names only to the Exotiques and their mates. He stood, circled her lap, kneaded her thighs a little, then curled up again. *You may call on us any time. Sinafinal likes to take more shapes than me.*

Bri found no reasonable, let alone brilliant, answer.

When Marian gathered the magic to raise her Tower, she gave me excess and I grew and became a fey-coo-cu. Before, my name was Tuck. He butted her hand and she rubbed behind his ears.

Marian. Tuck. Hamster cheek pouches. It made sense.

Coughing, she asked, "You really came to greet me?"

Elizabeth was worried about you. She thought you might wander the streets.

Just as she'd been about to do. She lifted her chin. "She didn't say anything about that to me."

Tuckerinal smiled a catlike smile, eyes twinkling. *I know English and Lladranan and Exotiques and Lladranans and I like to explore. I can accompany you.*

That sounded…okay.

Then he burped, sent a glance at her destroyed PDA and cell.

The penny dropped. "You knew from Elizabeth that I had more good stuff than she did." Bri stood up and dumped the cat.

It growled, sat, shot a leg up to groom in disdain.

"Oh, yeah, that's why you came." She paced to the window, back to the bed, to the window. People were out on the street, going about their business. She *had* to get out.

"You owe me—" She turned and looked at the bed to find all the remnants of her electronics gone and a miniature greyhound watching her.

Her legs gave out. She grabbed the desk chair and sank into it. Rubbed her eyes. "Oh, man."

I am not a man. I am a magical fey-coo-cu, and I do owe you. A pink tongue came out and swiped his muzzle. *Your nuts were most tasty. More wonderful Songs.* He rippled out a few ringtones, *The Ride of the Valkyrie,* the themes from James Bond and Harry Potter.

"Oh. My. God."

We say, "By the Song." I do owe you, and Elizabeth, too. She cried when Cassidy said something. Bri figured that Elizabeth had kept a voice message of Cassidy's.

The little greyhound was there at her feet, a paw stretching to touch her knee.

"I want to go home," she demanded.

Tuckerinal's paw withdrew. *You cannot. Not until the Snap.*

"Fulfilling the task that brought us here."

Curing the sickness. Helping the Cities and Towns be a part of all Lladrana. I will think on what I owe you, but tonight we will adventure together, yes?

Bri studied the walls of the room, noticed that the trim was not a deep maroon but more like another shade of purple. Yellow sunlight slanted through the wide windows. There were people to watch, things to learn. Her feet itched.

She stared hard at him. "I want your magical word of honor…" Did that sound crazy or what? But the dog lifted a paw as if ready to vow. "That you will *not* touch my other nuts, um, electronics, my music player and my digital camera, in any way!"

He blinked. *They will die.*

"No they won't." She pointed to the pack. "That is solar powered—catches and stores—"

I know what solar powered is.

"Don't you touch it!"

Giving her a sidelong look, he sniffed at it, looked mournful. *This, too, would be good to eat.*

She picked up her pack, took out the tissue, her coin purse, a pen and paper though she usually used her PDA for notes. "You do not *touch* this, either."

He lifted his nose. *They will all die eventually.*

"That may be, but you will not eat them." She had no idea how long the batteries would last. Months? Years? She was excellent at recharging them and had done so the afternoon at Elizabeth's. They'd been fully charged by the time she and Elizabeth had left for Dad's birthday party. She thought she'd taken only twenty pictures or so.

She didn't know how long the solar panels that would charge the batteries would last.

I can show things. He wriggled a little, motioned with the lifted paw and Bri saw a three-dimensional hologram of Tower Bridge of London. Sort of. No road. No river.

That is Marian's Circlet Tower.

"Stop!" Bri made the time-out sign. "Too Much Information. No more."

The dog panted. *Very well. Shall we go?*

"You didn't promise. My electronics are very, very important to me, particularly my digital camera. I don't want you to touch them."

He sighed. *I will not.* Then his ears perked. *Though if you WANT to give them to me before they die so I can keep the data, I will be happy to eat them.*

That wrung a half-laugh from her. "Not going to happen."

The dog stood, shook himself. *Maybe. Maybe not.* There was a slyness in his mind tone and his gaze slid away from hers. She remembered with a jolt and a catch of her breath that this world was supposed to have prophecy.

Shall we go? I will show you the Nom de Nom. It is a good place to start.

Bri recognized the name, the place where Chevaliers hung out. "All right." She noticed something else—in all his forms, Tuckerinal was about a foot long. Interesting factoid. "We'll go. After you promise, you sneaky thing, you."

He barked a laughing bark, sat again, balancing on his rump and lifted both paws, dog-as-hamster, she guessed.

I promise I will not touch any of your toys, the solar powered or the ones with the interesting nuts. He glanced yearningly at her pockets and Bri was faced with a dilemma. Did she take her music player and digital camera with her or not?

Not the music pod. There were times, like sitting on an

airplane and dawdling through airports, when it was worth
its weight in gold, but not when learning a new culture. Did
this house have a safe?

Yes, Tuckerinal said.

With one paw he indicated a colorful yard-square tapestry
of town life—buildings and bustling people, just what she
wanted to experience. "Go wait for me in the entryway,
please."

With a sound more mutter than growl the dog walked
from the room. The safe was easy to use. When Bri sensed
it needed a password Song to complete it, she used "There's
No Place Like Home," hoping fervently that the fey-coo-cu
wasn't overhearing her thoughts or knew the tune.

A few minutes later Bri followed the trotting greyhound.
As expected, she got a lot of glances, but also smiles and
waves.

People eyed the little dog with respect. The waves of
energy and musical notes she was beginning to understand told her that he *was* a Powerful creature, that being
with him added to her image, and that no one really knew
much about fey-coo-cus or Exotiques so they treated
them well.

Tuckerinal kept a steady pace, but not too quick that Bri
couldn't take time to look at houses and the green squares
around which they were built that showed summer blooms:
lavender, roses, and a sweet-scented gray-green moss with
bell-like white flowers.

The town was walled, with square and round towers at
intervals, in matched pairs on opposite sides. Some had
belvederes or cupolas on the top. In the distance to the
south she could see newer stone encompassing the city as

it grew. An ominous sign. As Earth towns had grown, they'd overflowed the city walls and the need for such defense.

Tuckerinal stopped outside a tall, narrow and shabby building with a creaking sign that changed from black to white and back again. The Nom de Nom.

The dog sat and wagged his tail, lolled his tongue. *My favorite place here in Castleton.*

13

The door opened and rich cooking odors wafted out.

"Salutations, Medica Elizabeth, shouldn't you—" The female middle-aged Chevalier stopped, stared at the purple streaks in Bri's much shorter hair.

Her companion, a woman with a shield embroidered on her tunic, smiled broadly, elbowed her fellow, did a little bow. "Salutations, Medica Bri."

Evidently they'd met her twin. Bri nodded. "Salutations."

"Your sister helped heal us today," the first said, her brows lowered. "The fine was extortionate."

The other grimaced. "The fine was just." She linked hands with the first. "Come along, we have better things to do than complain." With a wink, they sauntered off toward the main road that led to the Castle.

Bri entered. The Nom de Nom looked like many a tavern

on Earth. To the right was a long bar, with a man tending it. To the left was a series of red-seated wooden booths.

Tuckerinal yipped and wagged his tail when a chorus of voices greeted him, calling "fey-coo-cu," though Bri sensed that many weren't sure which one he was. There were plenty of men and women standing or leaning against the bar, but it didn't appear to be a crowded time of day.

Most of the booths were full, including the last one where people were rising with mugs and plates, apparently moving to an empty place.

That is OUR booth. Tuckerinal's muzzle lifted with pride. *Alexa likes it the best so we always get it.*

Another perk, not too shabby.

Trotting toward it, Tuckerinal said, *Don't look up.*

Of course she did. Monster trophies. Breath strangled in her throat, the edges of her vision went gray.

Tuckerinal barked.

"Here, there." A strong arm slid behind her back. "I guess no one told you about the trophies."

Bri couldn't even manage a squeak.

"Clear the way for the Exotique Medica!" the man ordered and Bri realized that he'd previously spoken in English. Blinking hard to settle her vision, she brought him into focus. Another attractive Lladranan man. Wide temples, skin tanned golden, well-formed features. She realized she was clutching his nice, firm, strong biceps with both hands, but didn't care. "Who?"

"I'm Koz. Marian's brother. Formerly Andrew."

Seemed she couldn't escape Marian's folks. Bri sagged against him. She should have been refreshed from her nap, should have been able to handle the monster parts, but no.

This all was hitting her far more than usual for a stay in a new country. Of course, it *was* a different dimension.

He half-lifted her and toted her to the edge of the bench of the last booth, urged her head between her knees.

"It catches most of us at first. Not exactly elk and deer." His English had a definite Lladranan accent, as if his tongue wasn't used to speaking English words his mind knew.

"No," she forced out between breaths.

Here there be monsters. Mounted heads and paws and tentacles and wings. The big black bristly one that snarled had long curving claws that looked capable of killing with one swipe. Torso and paws were attached to plaques. The equally sickening yellow-furred one had mean little glass eyes of red, shorter fur and spines which, given the state of things, were probably poisonous. A few spines were show-cased, too. The third monster—horror, and they *were* horrors—was not as hefty as the other two, looked more supple, and had gray skin and two tentacles with suckers at each shoulder and a hole for the nose. The last was a beaky, sharp-toothed skull of a flying dinosaur.

"What are they?"

Koz lifted her hand and curved it around an icy tumbler. She raised her head, carefully avoiding looking up.

"The black one is called a render, the yellow a slayer and the third a soul-sucker. It doesn't really suck your soul, more like your energy. The final one is a dreeth."

"Ah." She met his mild gaze. He'd know. He was dressed in Chevalier leathers, and if she wasn't mistaken, had a sucker scar on the back of his left hand.

"Guess you didn't read any of the Exotique Lorebooks before you came."

She took a long, deep drink, grateful for the cool water sliding down her throat, swung her legs in and under the table, propped her elbows on it. "It's my first day here. What did you do on your first day?"

"I died."

Christ. She put her head in her hands.

Tuckerinal growled from her left, likely on the table. Castleton probably didn't have a Health Department, no one seemed disturbed, shape-shifting magical creatures probably didn't have fleas. And all this mental babbling was to avoid thinking, more to escape *feeling*.

Koz curved his hands around hers.

"That wasn't well done of me," he said quietly. "But it was irresistible as a comeback."

For a moment she and Koz stared at each other silently, while Tuckerinal curled up and closed his eyes. Bri thought she *could* see a difference in his expression from other Lladranans. He'd know at a glance that she hadn't exactly fit into mainstream States structure.

He smiled. "I lived in California."

Well, that said it all. Maybe she might have fit in there after all. But she wanted Colorado.

The barmaid sidled up to them with drinks, set them on the table, glanced at Bri's face and hair and slipped away. Bri's nose twitched at the scent of tea. She pulled the cup toward her, sniffed again and smiled.

"Thought you might like a cup," Koz said. "Time-honored girl drink, good for shock and what ails you."

Bri sipped. The tea was hot and strong and of excellent flavor. Narrowing her eyes, she said, "You calling me girly?"

"Oh, yeah!" He leered.

A chuckle bubbled from her.

"The local ladies just don't get me." He looked soulful.

"I bet they get you plenty."

He laughed and Bri understood she'd been trying to ease the tension between them, perhaps even the subtle stress in the room. This was, after all, a gathering place of people whose life spans might be cut short the next battle, and everyone knew it.

She tapped the rim of her cup. "Tea?" Everyone else was drinking ale or liquor.

"They keep it for Alexa. She doesn't drink alcohol."

"And Alexa always gets what she wants?"

A lift and drop of a shoulder from Koz. "Pretty much. She was the first," he said simply. "She's still the most unpredictable in the minds of people and she's of the highest rank in the land, a Swordmarshall."

"And she's little and cute."

He raised his mug in a toast. "Little, anyway."

"Ayes." The woman was a warrior, it would be rare to see her cute, though Bri had caught glimpses of it. No doubt that would wear off, a pity.

She leaned forward. "Tell me, Koz, how does it feel to have your mind and soul living in a different body?"

14

The farm family had sold out of their produce by the time Sevair and the Citymasters' carriage reached Noix Market. Naturally word of the daughter's collapse and healing had spread. Everyone wanted to hear the family's experiences with the new Exotique Medica.

Sevair had ordered the carriage to accommodate mother and daughter and rode with the former on their cart back to their fields. He closed his eyes as he recalled the frantic mother rushing in with her daughter. The girl was large and heavy-boned, yet reminded him of his sister who had taken a chill and died when a child. The helplessness of the adults, he supposed. Except Bri.

Thank the Song for the Exotique healers. They gave him hope that this disease would be beaten before it swept Lladrana with such vigor that it became a plague.

He decided that he and the other Citymasters must part

with some good zhiv to purchase crystal balls for each mayor so they could communicate faster. Each city and town had cherished their autonomy, but now was the time to pull together. Over the last few weeks it had become obvious that the medicas could not cure the sickness and that it threatened them all. Especially the few villages in the north, as if the north, with the invading monsters, didn't have enough devastation. Those places should have the crystals first.

A fleeting thought came—he'd heard mirrors might also be bespelled for communication. The Circlets might prefer expensive crystal balls, but the townsfolk would be happy with mirror-talk. He'd ask Marian, the Circlet Exotique, just how much such workings would cost.

Castleton had a healthy emergency fund, and other major cities such as Troque and Krache might also. Enough to cover the expense for the less prosperous villages.

Speaking with the Exotique Circlet was always the right way to proceed, or even Exotique Alexa. They were more cognizant of the over-riding problems of the whole land rather than stuck in one rut of society.

"Heavy thoughts, Citymaster?" rumbled the farmer next to him—Cley, Sevair recalled his name.

"This sickness makes for heavy thoughts," Sevair said.

"Ayes, indeed." The man's voice trembled, his hands tightened around the reins but did not pull to discomfort the horses. A strong, controlled man, qualities Sevair admired most.

"We are doing our best to eradicate the sickness."

Cley nodded. "Ayes. We of the farms know that." He added drily, "The Marshalls, as the major landowners of

Lladrana, hold the independent farmers as their responsibilities. They have been busy fighting and plotting against the Dark, but they must consider our well-being more. Please remind them of that."

Sevair gritted his teeth. Just what he liked doing, reminding others of a higher status than he of their responsibilities. He remembered the last, disastrous time he'd done that—confronted Circlet Jaquar, only to find that one of his own staff had been at fault.

His former assistant had betrayed the Cities and Towns—and farmers—to serve the Dark, as its new Master, the controller of the monsters.

The new Master who had sent that evil message with the chevaliers the night before. That Sevair had been so wrong in his judgement of Jumme had shaken him, and he still grieved for the man he thought Jumme had been, perhaps had been before he'd yielded to corruption.

"I thank you again for Summoning the Exotique Medica," Cley said.

"Keeping the Exotiques has always been a problem," Sevair reflected as he thought of the battle ahead. He and the other City and Townmasters had gone 'round and 'round that issue. What if the one they Summoned was the one to return? So far Lladrana had been lucky, or fought hard, to ensure that the Exotiques stayed. Someday luck would run out.

The farmer looked at him, a slight smile curving his lips and showing in his eyes. "Ayes, I know people and that Exotique Medica I saw is the type who is always on the move, never still." He snorted, shook his head. "Purple hair."

Sevair winced.

* * *

Koz smiled at Bri, quick and charming, and it lit his eyes. He leaned back against the red leather of the booth and swallowed a mouthful of ale. When he was done, he said, "You are the only one who's ever asked me how it felt to have my mind and soul transferred to a different body."

Bri blinked. "Really?"

He nodded. "Really. Marian doesn't like to talk about it. Since it bothers Marian, no one else does. Not one Circlet or medica. Guess they think it would bother me, too." Shifting in his seat, he said, "It was a traumatic day all around." He grimaced. "She calls me Koz, but still thinks of me as Andrew."

"Aren't you Andrew?"

"Mostly." He thumped his chest. "But the body is Lladranan, and Koz." He shrugged. "I have some shadow memories of the Koz-soul." Sadness draped his features. "He loved his Pairling, his Shield, very much."

"How does it feel?" Bri went back to her original question.

He straightened. Fire lit his eyes. "Good. It feels *good.*" Then he raised a hand. "No, it feels *great.* I had multiple sclerosis, my body was deteriorating. It was only a matter of time before I had to make choices."

Bri understood that suicide was often a decision MS sufferers chose. Her throat closed. She took another sip of tea, let it trickle down, warm her, soothe her.

"And now?"

Koz stretched luxuriously, as if savoring the extension of every muscle, the stretch of every tendon. "Koz was in prime shape." His grin flashed again. "A little older than me, but I didn't mind that at all. He had an athletic life as a Chevalier in Alexa's household. Andrew'd contracted MS early, had never been able to be active." He inhaled deeply, expanding his muscular chest, let the breath out through flared nostrils. "Lots of room in here."

Then he tapped his head. "Hadn't developed as much brain power. I could *feel* new synapses linking."

"You had muscle and motor memory, of course."

"Yeah, and learning that was tough, too. How to walk like a healthy Lladranan, while my mind remembered creeping around with canes. I worked out like crazy those first months, pushed the physical limits of the body, just to determine them." Again he slapped his chest, grinned. "Now all circuits are fully integrated."

"I didn't see the Lorebook of Exotique Koz in my to-be-read stack."

He stared at her in surprise. "I didn't write one."

Elizabeth wasn't the only one fascinated with medicine, interested in new techniques, the only one who'd received the "love of learning" gene from their parents. "Write it."

"Yeah?"

"Yeah." Bri swallowed the last of her tea. There was no pot on the table to refresh the drink; she waggled her cup. "So, what's good here?"

"I like the ale. Marian goes for the mead. More tea?"

"No thanks." Not yet. She'd have to look up and study the monsters before she left, planned on being pleasantly tipsy before she did. "Where's our food?"

As if waiting for that signal, the burgers were slid in front of them. Bri's plate had a colorful side of steamed vegetables, some of which she didn't recognize. She speared a long green thing that wasn't quite a green bean or pea pod. Chewed. Yum.

Pointing her fork at Koz, she said, "Tell me stories."

He gestured to a door across the way, at the end of the bar. "There's a room full of banners and plaques of the ones who have died fighting in the last three years."

She swallowed hard, ordered ale. "Let's start with cheerful stories." Then she turned and looked at the bar, catching most of the Chevaliers there off-guard staring at her. Waving her fork, she said, "All of you tell me stories of Lladrana."

Though Sevair was not much of a landsman, he and his coach driver helped the family with their evening chores. Later they sat at the table when the Song of thanks was sung and ate the dinner another daughter who'd stayed home had prepared. Countryfolk supped early and Sevair walked in the evening while his coachman and horses rested before the trip back to Castleton.

When he looked west, the city was a few slight spires and towers in the distance. The spires from the large church he was decorating, the towers of the old city wall that he'd repaired, or new in the south of the city as it had grown, that he had helped build. His heart tightened. He loved the place. His parents had died when he was sixteen and in his last year as a journeyman, and he'd transferred all his caring to the town. The town would never abandon him like his sister and his parents, never fail him. Another shard of pain as he thought of the young man who was now the Master for the Dark. He had not seen the youth's underlying weakness, the crack that made a piece of stone worthless for sculpting.

He'd begun to care about that one, too, and had been betrayed for the worst evil in the universe.

Now, for whatever reason, he felt a fascination for the Exotique Medica, Bri. He, too, knew her sort—free as the wind, ignoring ties—yet he'd heard the twins were adamant that they must return to the Exotique land because of their parents. That spoke of love and loyalty.

But he watched the sun send shafts of light onto his work in the city and reclaimed his serenity. He had done his best with Jumme, as he did his best with every responsibility set on his shoulders.

The town dimmed into the shade of sunset and now the Marshalls' Castle was lit with gold, a tumble of large blocks. When the sun moved lower and the shade on the Castle and the town moved to dark, he didn't like the symbolism and turned away.

As he walked back to the house, he noticed patches of small-leafed groundcover, the green-gray stuff that had begun appearing in the city parks, neighborhood squares and rounds this spring. The flowers were tiny white bells. He stopped. This was new, as were the potatoes that the Exotiques had brought.

Had the previous Exotiques carried with them seeds of something else? Was this Exotique stuff? He'd read their Lorebooks. Alexa had come from a snowy place, still winter in her land. Marian had arrived nude from her city dwelling. But Calli had been Summoned in full summer, from the outdoors.

He'd seen the plant often. Something Exotique, or something worse? Something else sent from the Dark? Like the horrors. Like the sangviles. Like the frinks.

The frinks that fell with the rain. Small metallic worms, most of which died when they hit the ground. Some that didn't. He'd always been the most wary of men with regard to the frinks.

He narrowed his eyes, picked up a long branch and combed through the sprigs of the plant.

A puff of spores released, glinting in the evening. Sickness could be caused by plants, couldn't it? The runny eyes and stuffed nose and headaches some people experienced during the spring and fall. He worked at the plant, uncovering the top tangle of leaves to see underneath where nothing else grew. Bare earth was revealed, along with the shine of something metallic that caught the last ray of the dying sun.

With his stick, he separated it out, a small circular section of a frink.

His heart lurched, settled, but fear poured through his veins.

Animal couldn't turn to vegetable. Not usually.

But the frinks weren't animal, they were horrors. Who knew the limits of the Dark? Certainly not he. Couldn't a frink carry a seed with it? Embedded in its body, perhaps?

He had to tell others about this. Now.

His jaw set. The sooner he reported this to the Castle, the sooner the whole of Lladrana could be on the watch for this demon-weed and eradicate it. They'd have to find a way to destroy it. Now. Fast.

It seemed even as he watched, new sprigs unfurled from the main stem. How much of this stuff was in Lladrana?

He shouted for his coachman, and the man came running. Stopped several feet from him, looking wary.

"I must return to Castleton immediately. I can't wait for you. Come later at your own speed."

"But…but…" the man sputtered.

Sevair cut him off with a gesture. "Warn the farmer and his family to avoid these patches of vegetation." Sevair pointed to the inoffensive-looking plant. "Frink spawn."

His coachman, who had been peering bewilderedly at the spot, snapped upright and took a step back. He saluted, old habits of a Castle soldier. "How will you—"

But Sevair's mind had already solved that problem. He called mentally *Mud!*

There was a slight hesitation, then a cheerfully excited, *Citymaster?* from the volaran.

I need you here, now! Can you come to my Song?

Ayes! Night flying!

He thought he could almost hear her hooves kick against the latch of her stall, open the door.

I come!

The rest of Bri's meal passed in good company, and with her openness, Chevaliers came and went at their table. As light globes came on in the corners of the room, Bri knew that time passed. The door opened and let in darkness and cold air. Koz finally left since he was on rotation to fly to the next battle, making it evident with a kiss on her hand that he wanted to be more than friends.

With a challenging gaze, one of the male Chevaliers said, "This isn't the only tavern in Lladrana."

She stared at him. Obviously a test of her mettle. A pub crawl. She snorted. As if she hadn't done that a few times. She shoved her mug away. "All right." She stood and he did, too. He was much taller. "Show me," she said.

The tavern roared with laughter and bets. Bri had no intention of getting drunk, she'd just buy—have someone else buy—a drink and take a swallow or two.

On her way out she stopped and looked up again. The magic light let her study the monsters, assess their size, all larger than men, and their danger—deadly.

Then she was swept away. The hour—hours?—grew later and the stars shimmered through mist veiling them and the velvet black sky.

Most of the other off-duty Chevaliers, including her challenger, lasted through four taverns, and Tuckerinal had dragged along.

When Bri and the ex-hamster exited the last club alone, she giggled in tipsy triumph. Blinking, she realized she had no idea where she was.

Before she could ask Tuckerinal, a large hawk lit on the top of a nearby fence and chittered at him.

My mate, he said.

I am Sinafinal, the bird said.

Bri blinked at the hawk. Its feathers seemed to have a deep blue sheen like nothing she'd seen before.

The bird clacked her beak, sending Bri a beady-eyed stare. *Tuckerinal should have returned an hour ago!*

"Not my problem," Bri said thickly. "Didn't know that, did I? No." She shook her head.

She and the hawk stared at each other. Then the world tipped a little and Bri steadied herself with a hand against the cold stone wall of the tavern. A flapping noise came and she watched another hawk land beside Sinafinal. This one had a dark red *magical* color to its feathers. Tuckerinal.

The two seemed to glow oddly, a *dark* glow, as if they

gathered starlight and absorbed it and the absence of the light wavered around them.

It was a good night, Tuckerinal said.

We will talk later, Sinafinal said to Bri, then lifted into flight. *It is time*.

Bri watched the two fey-coo-cus spiral up into the night sky and her breath caught. They were very magical with that dark glow surrounding them, very beautiful. As was the sky, with a brilliant arc of stars that could only be a tiny portion of an arm of a galaxy. Twinkling points of light flung across midnight blue like glittering diamond chips on a gauzy scarf. She stood there gazing into the sky long after the birds disappeared.

Loneliness invaded, for home, the dry air and dim stars of city life. Bri bit her lip. Her former homesickness was nothing like this on Earth. She'd never been in a place or situation she couldn't leave to go home. To run away to, a little voice said in the back of her mind that she didn't want to heed. But she was coming to understand that was her greatest fault. When things got sticky, she ran.

Sometimes that was right. What she hadn't told Elizabeth was that the rock star had gotten violent. Only one blow, and dodging, she'd taken it on her side instead of in her stomach, but one blow was enough.

Two strong arms grabbed her. One around the waist, one on a choke hold around her neck. She struggled, but couldn't break the man's grip.

There were times running didn't save you.

15

Mud arrived quickly, but Sevair didn't get away until late since the farmer called a conclave of his fellows.

He and Mud flew through the night and Sevair practiced speaking with her with small words and images in Equine. Just as the first time he rode her—partnered *with* her—that morning, he thought he could feel the pathways of his Power widen at new use, his hair turn silver.

Fear lived in his gut. He didn't often anticipate disaster, but anxiety about the frinks gnawed at him. He'd been the one charged with finding out about the frinks, had contacted the Marshalls, then the Circlet Jaquar. But Jumme had intercepted his letters. Now everyone paid for his poor judgement.

Frinks. He'd *known* they would be deadly.

The Marshalls and Chevaliers would be awake and lively after sunset, as usual. He'd talk to them, but only after he rang the guildhall emergency bell. His people must be warned first. No frinks would fall with the rain where Exotiques lived. So there were no plants like this on the Castle grounds, but they were multiplying in Castleton.

They landed in City Square and Sevair hurried to the bellpull and yanked hard three times, sending long, low tones throughout the town, notes the Citymasters and guild masters were attuned to. Immediately doors opened around the square. Some of the heads of the guilds occupied the homes reserved for those of their station, which were clustered around the city square and the guildhall.

He nodded to them, then Sang the key to the door of the guildhall and the small council chamber just inside, Sang the lights on, and took his seat.

They were all gathered in minutes, not only the Citymasters, but the mistresses and masters of each guild, too. This year slightly more women held such titles than men.

"I think I have discovered the source of the sickness," Sevair said.

The door opened and Circlet Jaquar walked in. Sevair wasn't the only one who stiffened in his chair.

Jaquar closed the door behind him and bowed. He wore a long velvet robe and his circlet around his brow. Sevair thought he wasn't the only one who felt shabby beside the man.

"With your permission, I would like to stay. I heard the town bell and knew it signified something important. In times like these, all knowledge should be shared."

Sevair felt heat rise in his face. He'd accused this man of not answering his concerns. Apparently Jaquar would not be put in such a position again. Sevair glanced around the table, but most were still staring at the Circlet. "You are welcome. Take a seat." He gestured to a couple of empty chairs.

Inclining his head, Jaquar sat and said, "My thanks."

After clearing his throat, Sevair began again. "I think I have found the source of the sickness."

When oaths and exclamations died down, he explained.

They were all discussing the matter when a strum came on the door harp and the assistant to the head of the Inns and Taverns guild entered, frowning. She dipped a curtsey to them all, eyes widening at Jaquar, then addressed herself to her guild mistress. "I did as you requested and went to the Exotique Medica's house to bring her here." She drew in a large breath. "She isn't there. I heard from a neighbor that she went out late this afternoon, but I haven't found her."

Babbling concern erupted. People shot to their feet.

Sevair's head ached. He closed his eyes and rubbed them.

When he opened his eyes he saw Jaquar smiling. Sevair scowled. "Can you find her?" he cut across the clamor.

Jaquar's eyes widened, narrowed. He tilted his head as if searching for Bri's Song, then sighed. "No. I have not been with her so long as to recognize her Song."

How hard could it be to find one Exotique's Song in Castleton? Sevair didn't ask aloud. "Thank you, anyway."

Shrugging, Jaquar said, "Exotiques. Who knows what they will do next? And she has purple hair. How difficult will it be to find a pale woman with purple hair?"

Awful.

"I'm not gonna hurt you. I jus' want you to listen to me. You must listen to me!" Bri's abductor was big, with a straining belly under rough linen shirt and corduroy pants, and he stank of alcohol. They sat in a tiny room behind one of the seediest bars Bri had ever seen. There was a lop-sided table and two three-legged stools. He'd closed the inches-thick door and locked it with magic. "I'm not gonna hurt you."

She'd tried to get out, but couldn't. She'd banged on the door, but the noise beyond drowned out her cries. The grime-encrusted window was too small for her, too small for Alexa.

She'd attempted to call her twin, but the drunk had some sort of smothering mind-shield on her. He'd yelped when she'd tried to contact Elizabeth, but had held her thoughts at bay. He'd also taken her bag and the little crystal ball, which he'd grunted at and pocketed himself. Otherwise he hadn't touched her after they'd arrived.

His erratic Song rang with single-mindedness. Bri sensed no physical threat. She kept her distance, figured she could push him down and break a stool over his head. He wasn't too steady on his feet. They'd fallen against a few walls on the few blocks, walk to this place, but his grip had been desperate—asexual and panicked.

"Listen to me, Exotique Medica," he said and his tone, his very manner changed. He stood straight and glared at her with a laser-like gaze from amber eyes. She noticed that though dirty, much of his scraggly shoulder-length hair was golden. The streaks denoting magic were so wide there was only a little black in the center of his head. She hadn't needed the golden color of the streaks to tell her he was old. The deeply carved lines on his face did that, and his eyes. They held years of suffering.

Still a strong and vital man, he'd once been well-educated, she'd bet on that. Once been in a position of authority if that tone and gaze were any indication. Her mother had that voice and stare mastered, as did other medical doctors she knew, and her honorary uncle who was a federal judge.

So she sat on the wobbly stool near the table and watched him.

"*Merci,*" he said.

A thought brought a spurt of fear. "My understanding of the language and the ability to speak it will fade soon."

He grunted. "Just listen." He tapped his barrel chest. "What I have to say to you won't take long."

She waited, discovered all her muscles were tense, duh! Relaxed them one by one, keeping her own expression impassive. He went to a shelf and grabbed a bottle, pulled out the cork and took a long swig. Another layer of the odor of yeasty ale was added to the atmosphere. Then he clomped back to the small table, sat on the stool across from her, put down the bottle with a clank and pointed a fat, grubby finger at her.

"You are the Exotique Medica, Summoned to help this town with the worst medical crisis this country has ever seen. Since we have monsters invading from the north and ripping people to shreds, that's saying something." He belched, wiped the back of his hand across his mouth, muttered, "Pardon."

He shifted on his seat and Bri got the idea that not only was his stool as wobbly as her own, it was too small for his butt. She kept her sarcastic smile inward. Shoving the bottle aside, he leaned forward and Bri saw golden, gray and black bristles on his grizzled face.

"The medicas here in town and up at the Castle are goin' about healing this sickness all wrong. If the epidemic gets worse we'll all be in deep trouble."

His finger pointed again, wagged. "They're used to listening to the chimes and healing a person chime by chime, energy by energy. That hasn't worked." Another belch, but this time he was so concentrating on making her listen that he didn't excuse himself. "The medicas don' take a whole-body approach, healing all the chimes at once, slowly, steadily. An' they pay little attention to the chime at the crown of the head." He tapped his own skull, the parietal bone. "The spiritual chime. I think the Dark attacks that first, weakens it, then the evil snakes through the body to the weakest point, invades and attacks that. Jus' like the monsters in the north."

Bri stared some more. "If that's true, why haven't you told them that?"

"I have!" he roared, standing and knocking his stool over, waving his arms. "I have!" Then he turned on her and his voice was rough, bitter. "But they won't listen to *me*, will they? Not Zeres the drunk and the fool and the failure."

His words poked at her own lack of confidence. She knew the feelings of frustration and anguish all too well, couldn't stop her words, "Don't call yourself that." She stood and caught a meaty hand in her own. It staggered her, and not just from the force.

Clear, true tones of Power resounded through her. The cleanest, strongest Power she'd heard from anyone.

"Ayes," he sighed, then smiled. He moved faster than she'd thought he could, caught both of her hands in his, forced them up palm-to-palm, then linked their fingers.

She couldn't break his grip—more, she was whisked into a great blackness with flashing bright smears of light. Whirling, swirling, spinning. She didn't know the right word for her sensation, not falling, but *sucked*. The pressure of the passage of air around her.

Her heart thundered in her chest, darkness shrouded her vision. But her hearing expanded until she thought she could hear all the sounds that ever were in jarring notes, somehow interlaced, but the cacophony staggered her.

She was sitting down again, hard flat seat against her butt, blinking at the old man who slurped deep of his bottle of ale, some of it dribbling down his chin to join other stains on his shirt. She shook her head to clear the aftereffects of the Songs, even as she yearned to hear it again. But the experience was so powerful—as if she'd been plugged into the universe—that she didn't know if she could handle it. For a minute she wanted a good slug of alcohol herself.

When he put the empty bottle down, it hit the edge of the table and toppled over. This time he wiped his whole arm across his mouth before he sat. Once again an amber gaze met hers. "We're connected, you and I." He snorted. "Obvious now why the Song hasn't ended my miserable life before now."

"You are a medica."

He snorted. "Was a medica."

"Your life isn't miserable."

Tapping his temples with his forefingers, he said, "You aren't looking out at it from these eyes, from this bloated body." Then he rubbed his temples. "Thank the Song that won't happen again. Not so pure for a long time. Thank the Song."

He twined his fingers before him and leaned forward, serious. All these people were so deadly serious—except for the Chevaliers, who'd laughed in the face of death, and that wasn't true humor. How was she going to stand it?

With a fist he rapped the table. "Pay attention."

She folded her own hands on the table. "Yes, master."

His mouth stretched in a smile that revealed good teeth and the remnants of an attractive face. "Very good, pupil." His expression closed. "But those medicas will want to train you, and they'll train you all wrong for this time. I sense that you know instinctively how to cure this disease. With my help, you'll figure out how the Dark is causing it, and how to stop it from invading humans, stop it from killing those who already have the sickness." He sighed. "Sometimes the Song is good."

"You said the medicas can't solve the problem of the sickness, or cure it with their usual methods."

"True."

"What of the Marshalls?"

"They heal when they have to, when they deem it a priority to them and theirs. So do the Circlets, having learned from the Marshalls and the Exotique Circlet Marian. But that great healing is more a matter of faith in the Song."

"Spiritual, as you said."

"They are usually led by a medica or two. Ask any Marshall or Circlet how they heal and they will either not know how or give you a wrong answer."

"Arrogant," Bri murmured.

"Ayes, both me and them. All of them." He made a wide gesture, his eyelashes lowered halfway.

"I was Summoned with my sister, my twin."

Nodding he said, "Lucky, that. The Castle healers got ahold of her, they should be satisfied with her, leave you alone. We'll have to confront the city and town medicas, equally arrogant. But you can do that. You'll win."

He sat and stared at her, cocked his head, narrowed his eyes, as if he were measuring her Song, then his eyelids closed and his muttering transformed into a snore. His body relaxed and he slid off the stool right under the table.

Bri stood. Her mind spun and her legs buckled. She was more tired than she'd realized. The fumes had gotten to her, as had the long day, the healing—that fabulous connection to the universe through Zeres.

Now she'd let her guard down, sleep crept up on her. Her body demanded rest. Her brain was in no shape to think and her mental shields had vanished.

Song filled her, pretty notes coming from Zeres, raucous undertones left over from the bar. It was silent now and she couldn't pinpoint when that had happened. How long had she been floating like a star?

She shivered. It was very late or very early. In any case it was dark and she was tired. Zeres had curled onto his side on the floor, his mouth open but not snoring, passed out. The door remained shut. Bri put her head on her arms and laughed-cried. Wouldn't you know it. Even here she'd fallen in with the alternative medicine faction-of-one. She fell asleep.

Sevair hated being at the Castle, disapproved of by all. *Hated* waiting in a small anteroom for Elizabeth to wake. Naturally word had leaked during the long night of searching that the city had misplaced its Exotique. A Chevalier or two had snitched. Circlet Jaquar had continued to be sympathetic.

The Marshalls eyed him with amused disdain. The other Exotiques had refused to awaken Elizabeth, saying that she needed sleep and through her link with her twin, would know if Bri was in any danger. That was something, at least.

So now he sat in his formerly-best-robe for Elizabeth.

Bri had still not been found. They'd traced her movements. She and the male fey-coo-cu had left her house and gone to the Nom de Nom, then other taverns.

Both feycoocus had vanished, too.

Sevair ground his teeth. Why couldn't Bri have stayed *in*?

Because she was a woman always on the move. He shouldn't have expected that she'd stay at home. The Citymasters hadn't planned to leave her alone during the first evening. He was to stay with her until she retired, ready to answer any questions, arrange for any additional needs.

But the guilds had been upset by events and no one had taken his place, something everyone was chastising themselves for now. The Citymasters were holding off on a door-to-door search until Sevair spoke with Elizabeth. His mouth turned down. Every single one of his colleagues had shown relief when it was pointed out that Elizabeth knew Sevair best, and he should be the one to break the news to her. He hadn't seen such a unity among them in the three years he'd been a Citymaster.

At least he waited alone. Everyone else was in a council, talking about the discovery of frinkweed. Sevair figured that the Marshalls would soon be visiting their home estates to see how rampant the plant was. Independent Chevaliers would be hired to examine the north for the frinkweed, especially near the remaining gaps in the border fence line.

The door across from him opened and Elizabeth stood on the threshold, smooth shoulder-length honey-colored hair tidy, dressed in a medica's summer robes. The sun was shining today, had already burnt off mist and was warming the ground. Only Sevair's internal weather was gray and dreary.

"Citymaster Masif," she said cooly.

He stood and bowed. "Please call me Sevair. May I have a word with you?"

She blinked. "Of course." Stepping back from the door, she led the way back into her suite.

The sitting room contained a lot of purple, bright in the streaming sunlight. Elizabeth took a chair, twitched her robes around her. Not clothes she was used to wearing, no matter how good she looked in them.

"How can I help you?" she asked.

Taking a deep breath, he eased it out. "We have misplaced Bri."

16

Laughter rolled from Elizabeth. "Oh, this is rich." She shook her head, still grinning. "Our parents were *constantly* misplacing Bri."

That made him feel slightly better.

Elizabeth tilted her head. "She's fine."

He cleared his throat. "Can you tell me where she is?"

Pressing her fingers to her temples and closing her eyes, Elizabeth was silent for a moment. "She's not answering me telepathically. I think she's asleep. And she's definitely in Castleton." Elizabeth opened her lashes and smiled.

She was so like Bri in looks and the occasional expression, but so unlike in manner, that Sevair swung from thinking they appeared identical to believing they didn't look at all the same.

Elizabeth stood. "Bri's okay. I think I'd like breakfast in Castleton. We can wait for her to wake up, or I can trace her. I'm famished."

Elizabeth's casualness reassured Sevair. "I flew up, and would be honored to show you your home in Castleton."

Wariness appeared in her eyes. She opened her mouth. Sevair forestalled her with a raised palm. "I know, neither you nor your sister intend to remain here like the other Exotiques."

With a little release of breath of her own, Elizabeth nodded.

As Sevair led her to the courtyard, he felt a twinge of relief that the Citymasters had planned that breakfast would be the introduction of the city medicas to their Exotique. Plenty of food. The healers had been told Bri was missing, but he was sure they'd all show up anyway.

Mud greeted Elizabeth with a quiet whicker, and no one else questioned their leaving. The flight down to Castleton was quick and silent. Elizabeth didn't feel at all like Bri before him. As soon as they dismounted, Mud was aloft again, and flying to her stable. Sevair sensed that the volaran was embarrassed that she didn't have enough emotional connection with Bri to find the Exotique.

Elizabeth murmured approval when she saw the house, her Song lilting with pleasure. "It's perfectly lovely," she said.

"Thank you," Sevair said. He paused in the kitchen to tell one of the two serving women to cancel the search for Bri. Her sister would find Bri after breakfast.

The scent of food—eggs and fresh bread—permeated the house, as did voices. When they stopped by the dining room, they saw there was the entire half-dozen Castleton medicas, along with four Citymasters.

Everyone rose and bowed to Elizabeth. She flushed.

"Thank you." She smiled. "I see we haven't started eating yet." She went to the empty chair at the head of the table and sat. Both chairs flanking her were empty; Sevair took the right.

A servant bustled around, lifting the tops from chafing dishes and scooping out fluffy eggs, started the bread basket around the table.

The town medicas near Elizabeth peppered her with questions regarding the day before and her training at the Castle.

The door opened and slammed shut. A moment later Bri stood on the threshold, hands on hips. A strong scent of liquor emanated from her. She appeared tired. Her clothes were wrinkled and dirty. "Glad you're all having a good meal. Looks like you all had a good night. I was kidnapped."

Cool relief was followed by hot rage in Sevair. He dropped his cutlery. Outrage and fury spiked Songs all around him.

Elizabeth remained placid. She gestured to the chair at her left. "Kidnapped or not, I see you've landed on your feet."

Bri snorted, frowned at her sister, and stalked to the table. When she lifted the top of a dish, she smelled mouth-watering eggs. "I can see you're distraught."

"I could tell nothing was wrong with you and underneath your irritation, you're excited," Elizabeth said.

"Kidnapped." Sevair rose, walked over as he examined her. The other people in the room stared. Most wore medica garb. Checking her chakras—chimes?

"I'm fine," Bri said, feeling the ache of her body spent sleeping on a cold stone floor. When she'd awakened, Zeres was still sleeping, and the lock spell on the door was gone. Once she'd found a main street, she'd seen the guildhall and the Castle on the bluff and had wended her way to the house. As soon as she'd drawn near, she'd known Elizabeth was there and a weight had lifted.

"Her chimes ring true and strong and Powerful," said a medica.

Sevair's palms warmed her shoulders, ran down her arms and cradled her hands in his own large, calloused ones. The stone carver determining the soundness of his material?

"A friend, concerned," he said. "A sculptor thinking about the loveliness of a woman." He answered her thought. He'd gotten at least the gist of it directly from her mind. She blinked up at him.

"I heard you spent much of the evening with Koz and other Chevaliers at the Nom de Nom." Dropping one of his hands, the other closed over her fingers and tugged her to the table. Pulling away, she waved him to his seat, then filled a plate. She met Elizabeth's gaze with a smile and her twin eased. Everyone in the Drystan family cherished breakfast.

A female Citymaster lifted the top of a covered dish to show thick slices of bacon.

Elizabeth said, "The dishes are…bespelled to heat." Poor twin, her view of the world was taking a hit. Bri sent her a wave of love heart to heart, received one back.

"You spent time at the Nom de Nom?" Sevair prodded.

"Ayes," she smiled at him. "And the Vert Chevalier, and the Stella Luna and the Bier Cruche, and the Risible Chien." She brushed at her clothes. "I don't know the name of the last one, but I was only in a back room." A flash of images had accompanied her retelling—Koz, of course, from the

Nom de Nom, but also the trophies. Bri eyed Elizabeth. Had she seen the monsters yet?

As if sensing her strain, Elizabeth said, "You're safe, eat."

Bri pushed tired, irritable thoughts away. "Yes."

With one last clench of his jaw, Sevair said, "Tell me who laid hands on you and I'll see that he—or she—regrets every minute for the rest of his life."

Bri looked at him, dressed formally again, she realized. The rest of the table was too—citymasters and medicas. "That won't be necessary."

Sevair frowned. "We were worried about you."

"I can see that." Bri gazed pointedly at everyone who was tucking into breakfast.

"Bri's grumpy in the mornings," Elizabeth said. "I told them you were all right." Her face tightened. "Kidnapped?"

"Yes, seems there's someone alienated from the medical establishment—" she waved at the medicas "—who believes they're handling the sickness wrong and has better ideas."

Elizabeth closed her eyes, gave a tiny shake of her head. "Only you, Bri."

"Yeah, that passed through my mind."

"Who is this person who questions our methods?" asked one of the city medicas stiffly.

After swallowing the wonderful eggs—a touch of cheese and other spices—Bri said, "His name is Zeres. He'll probably be along." If he was really determined to help, if he really believed what he said the night before.

Scowls of disgust circled the table.

"How dare he do such a thing as kidnap you and babble his stupidities in your ear!" one of the male medicas said. His fork clinked his plate as his fingers shook.

"Thought that would be your reaction," Bri said. She ate a few bites more, said, "Please excuse us." To Elizabeth, Bri said in English, "I'm inclined to believe the guy."

"What! Of course you are. You're used to thinking all standard medical practices are hidebound."

Bri finished a piece of bread. "You've got that flip-flopped. Standard Western medical practice thinks what I can do with my gift of healing hands is pure BS." She met Elizabeth's eyes steadily. "If *my* practices had been acceptable, I'd have been right there with you through medical school." She shifted her shoulders, letting past disappointments roll away.

"But here they *practice* like you do!" Elizabeth said. "Must you always be contrary?"

Scooping eggs onto another slice of wonderful bread sprinkled with seeds, Bri said, "The bottom line is, he's right, these people haven't been able to cure the sickness. They called us across *dimensions* so we could do it." She switched to mental and emotional communication. *I felt this incredible connection with him, heard this fabulous Song, like no one else we've met.*

Elizabeth stared at her, her own piece of bread halfway to her mouth. *You've met someone?*

Not a sexual link. Bri frowned. *Almost a familial connection, like a mentor.* She tried to *send* Elizabeth the feeling she'd had when she'd been with Zeres, the strong Song of him, that sucking into darkness, but her memories were dim.

"Oh," Elizabeth said.

A cough called them back to avidly watching medicas. The man who'd spoken earlier, a lean man with stern face and respectable wings of gold in his hair, caught Bri's gaze. "Introducing you to the people yesterday was good. Morale has been low, the atmosphere fearful. But today we must begin your training."

His gaze shifted from Elizabeth, neat and tidy and clean and smelling like good herbs to Bri in her mass of wrinkles, doing the red tunic with white cross uniform no honor. Comparisons again, and here! Exactly why she trained in massage therapy and other alternative medicines some-where else than Denver where her sister went to medical school.

He turned a gimlet eye on Bri and smiled in a way she didn't quite like. "We'll adjourn to the parlor."

Bri muttered to Elizabeth, "Looks like they're still going to try to whip *me* into shape today."

Elizabeth patted her shoulder, smiled widely. "That's because I was such a good student yesterday."

"Uh-huh."

"There is *so much* you must learn." A female medica flut-tered her hands. Equally plain they'd have preferred that Elizabeth had come to the city.

Eggs dried in her throat. She straightened until her spine was as rigid as Elizabeth's, and swept a gaze at the medicas sitting at the table. She could envision them flapping around her like a bunch of red birds, full of "Your training. Your sister. You must do this and you must do that."

Setting her silverware down, she dabbed at her lips with a thick damask napkin, took a sip of water and spoke, "I am not like my twin, who is well-trained in the practices of our land, and an exceptional physician." She glanced around again. "You must have deduced that our portion of our world does not view medicine as you do, and Elizabeth is unaccustomed to using only her hands and innate Power to heal." Bri lifted her hands stared at them, backs and palms. "I have used my healing hands all my life, and trained in alternative medicine."

"Yes, but—"

"I'm sure you're full of things I must do and learn. I healed someone of the disease yesterday—did any of you? Elizabeth treated wounds of Chevaliers—did any of you?"

Brows had lowered again, expressions of wary stubbornness molded the medicas' faces.

"I'm willing to work with you, to learn from you, *and* to discover with Elizabeth and you how to cure this sickness. This is an *exchange* of techniques and information."

Before the silence could thicken, and clash continue, Sevair said, "There's news. We believe we have determined where the sickness has come from. Frinks. A plant we call frinkweed."

Everyone except the Castle medica seemed surprised.

"I found it last night in a farmer's field. A small moss-like plant with white bell-like blossoms."

Bri gestured to the front of the house. "There's some plants like that outside in the square."

"I know," Sevair said heavily. He shared glances with the other Citymasters. "We know. We're spreading the word."

"Probably not as fast as the damn plant spreads," said one of the male medicas.

Sevair's jaw flexed. "We can only do our best."

"As you have always done," an older woman soothed.

"I've given the information to Circlet Jaquar Dumont. He took samples last night. He did not recognize the plant, has seen none on Alf Island."

"Exotique Circlet Marian has lived on Alf Island for over a year," someone said.

"And the frinks stopped falling with the rain where Exotiques were," Sevair said, turning to look at Bri and Elizabeth in turn. "Another blessing bestowed simply by your presence."

Bri blinked. No one had ever said anything so sweet to her.

"So Jaquar and Marian are gone?" Elizabeth asked with a tinge of relief.

"No. They called other Circlets to come from the islands to consult and take samples." He cleared his throat. "I was told that no Circlet has had a gift for botany for generations."

"Perhaps the very reason the Dark chose this method for its plague," a medica said.

"Probably," Sevair set his plate aside.

Lifting her mug of tea to her mouth—welcome after the scent of alcohol that coated her nostrils and tongue—Bri finished the last sip as the serving women came in and cleared plates. They'd have been listening. She used her napkin, then rose. "I'll take a quick bath and change my clothes and be right with you. Are there any more people with this frink-sickness?"

"We do not know," a female medica said primly.

Bri puffed out a breath. "Then we might be ahead of this, for once." Her shirt stuck to her back—sweat, or the residue of ale that had transferred from the floor of the tavern to her clothing while she slept. Or droplets from Zeres's flask and tankard as he'd gestured with it.

Elizabeth stiffened beside her. "A tub. You have a tub?"

"You don't?"

"Only showers in the tower. Baths in the bottom of the keep from hot springs. *Public* baths."

Bri snickered. "I have my own luxurious hot tub and tiled area in the garden level. With opaque stained-glass windows."

"Snot," Elizabeth said.

"You want to share?"

"I showered this morning."

"I will have one of the women bring down your clothes," said Sevair formally. Bri understood she'd disappointed him. She hated that. Her parents rarely scolded. All they'd have to do was give her a disappointed look and it sliced her heart. Even though, after a while, she realized her parents had perfected nuances of expression to use on her.

When Elizabeth made a poor decision, they all sat down like reasonable people—Bri included at Elizabeth's request since she was twin and support—and discussed matters and options. Bri's actions became part of a talk, but she always got disappointed looks as consequences for impulsive choices.

Bri didn't get a chance to apologize to Sevair—which always worked with her parents—because they were in a crowd of people. Unlike most everyone else, he appeared weary, strain living behind his eyes, etching the small lines of his face deeper. He'd probably not slept, been up dealing with this frinkweed and looking for her. His *Song* told her so, with hesitations and lengthening dips in rhythm.

She laid her hand on his arm, and his music came strong and steady and...sweet. No, not sweet, gentle or tender. She wasn't prime this morning either. So she opened the valve to the healingstream and let it sweep through her like a tide, lapping exhaustion from her, settling new energy into her. Transferring some to him.

He stiffened, but was quiet under the rush of Power. Bri could almost see it sinking into muscle and tendon and bone, nothing wasted, all cherished. His eyes met hers and the color seemed lighter now that he was less exhausted. He bowed. "My thanks."

The rest of the medicas and Citymasters observed them. Elizabeth beamed. "Nice trick, isn't it?"

One of the medicas said, "She summons the Power so easily." And Bri recalled that only the Citymasters and Castle medicas had seen her work before.

"I don't think Sevair slept at all," Bri said. "And my night wasn't comfortable."

Sevair's expression solidified into stony anger. "I'll find this Zeres. Where—"

But Bri was striding from the room and heading for the warmth and cheeriness of the garden-level bath. She could already imagine it wreathing her in scented steam and sliding along her skin.

When she got there, she indulged in a good soak until she heard the slam of the front door overhead and the sonorous demand of Zeres, "Where's my student!"

Voices clashed.

17

By the time Bri got dried and dressed and up to the parlor, the medicas and Zeres were going at it.

Only the medicas and Sevair had remained, the latter with stern retribution on his face.

Elizabeth was frowning. She'd taken one look at Zeres and judged him.

As the medicas had judged her by the state and smell of her clothes. She'd been a wandering sheep who had returned, a party girl, a free spirit, not a kidnap victim. Though her feelings had been somewhat mollified as she sensed sheer relief from the Citymasters and had heard of their efforts to find her.

The medicas and Zeres stood in the entryway, voices loud as they tried to impress their opinion on each other. Zeres was attempting to talk about healing the disease, and the medicas were running through all of Zeres's failures. Bri winced.

"That's what we call a 'heated discussion' if it happens in the teaching rooms," Elizabeth said.

"Really?" Bri asked. "Zeres is the only one talking medicine. The others have lit into him."

Elizabeth stiffened. "A physician's manner and methods and...past have bearing on every treatment."

"You think it's fair? How did you feel when Cassidy caught you using your gift?" As soon as the words were out, Bri regretted them. Elizabeth paled. Bri put an arm around her shoulders and hugged her. "I shouldn't have said that. But I'm tired of being judged and found wanting, too."

"You've helped many with your gift!" Elizabeth said, and Bri was surprised to hear the utter sincerity in her voice.

"Yes, I have," Bri said. "Both here and home on Earth."

A long, rising chord echoed through the house and everyone turned to the door, Bri and Elizabeth lagging behind as they realized it was the door harp. If it had been Earth there would have been thunderous knocking, the sound of urgency and desperation.

Opening the door, Sevair revealed what all had dreaded. Three more people with the sickness: an old man with a cane; a teenaged boy leaning on his mother, tall and thin and gray-faced; a limp young boy of about ten in his mother's arms.

"Bring them in," Sevair said.

The "heated discussion" came to an abrupt end.

The old man tottered in. Sevair started forward as if to scoop the guy up, then checked and bowed instead. "Master Mathias."

"I came as soon as I felt ill," the old man said in a mellow voice.

"Very good," said the male medica who led the city doctors. They went to the large front room which had been furnished as a home consulting-room-cum-surgery.

All three patients were placed on beds that looked much like the massage tables Bri was used to, covered with clean sheets and soft blankets.

Everyone entered and someone closed the door, and a shiver of sound swept around the room along with the scent of sage and lavender—a cleansing spell.

For an instant the medicas and the twins and Zeres eyed each other, then Zeres took the initiative. With an elegant gesture from a dirty hand, Zeres said to the cluster of medicas, "Go ahead, heal them."

The physicians stirred. Their robes rustled angrily. "We can't," the head medica muttered, chin jutting. "You cure one."

Zeres nodded slowly. "Very well, I will." He went to a basin and washed his face and hands, humming more cleansing spells, and the sound of his voice caught Bri again—there was something *more* about Zeres than anyone else.

Elizabeth said mentally, *I see what you mean. He isn't like the rest.*

No.

If we can figure out what is different about him and train the other medicas....

Bri stifled a small snort. *Good luck.*

Elizabeth gazed at Bri. *You have it, too, that extra quality to your Song, like Zeres.*

Hunching a shoulder, Bri said, *Yeah?*

Yes. I don't have it.

Then it must be an aspect of the healingstream.

Before they could explore that, Zeres turned from the cupboard, moving like a respected doctor under the scrutiny of all. He went to the old man. "Mathias, you permit?"

The old man's eyes narrowed. He sniffed lustily. "You smell and look stale but not drunk."

Bri crossed to Zeres, but he just sent her a cool glance. "I will not need your help."

She stepped back to Elizabeth, knowing Zeres had to prove himself. It was in the strained set of his shoulders. Zeres passed his hands over the patient, who watched with keen eyes.

"Don't worry, old man, when I'm finished with you, you'll be better than you have been in years."

Mathias cackled and his tense body relaxed into the bed. He closed his eyes.

The medicas muttered, a sarcastic buzz of noise.

Zeres ignored it. He went to the top of the massage table, took Mathias's head in his hands, the same way Bri would have if she were about to start a neck massage.

And then he Sang, and it was beautiful, a low bass with throbbing notes. No one in the room moved. Elizabeth took Bri's hand and she saw colors flow over Mathias. His skin looked finer pored, healthier, his lips ruddier.

"Fini!" Zeres near shouted, then crumpled and lay on the floor, twitching.

Mathias sat up, stared down at the fallen medica, then slid off the table, moving easily.

The other medicas stared at spry Mathias, limp Zeres.

Bri frowned. "He knows how to link with the healing-stream, but can only control it with his Song, can't determine the strength and depths of it or break the link without fainting."

Sevair lifted Zeres, carried him to a large, plush chair in the corner of the room.

"Nice muscles, excellent strength," Elizabeth murmured, then switched her gaze to the medicas, who appeared stunned and unhappy.

Mathias walked over to the chair and perched on the arm. "This is interesting, the most fascinating thing that's happened to me lately. I'm staying." He sent a shrewd glance to Sevair, gestured with his chin to another corner chair.

Sevair said, "I'm staying, too, but I prefer to stand." He joined the twins.

The boy's mother said, "He isn't eating." She was anxiously stroking his head. "His tongue is coated white." She opened his mouth to show them.

Bri met Elizabeth's eyes, "Looks like we're up."

"Yes." She studied the child, bit her lip, then squared her shoulders. "I learned a lot yesterday."

"And I know a lot. We'll be fine, twin, we always are when we're together."

Elizabeth smiled and it lit her eyes. "Yes." She donned a physician's manner and crossed to the bed where the boy's haggard mother was now twisting her hands.

Bri took the opposite side. "I can see his aura and chakras clearly," Elizabeth said, putting her hands on the boy.

Bri smiled. "I hear the tones better, and see the chakras dimly." Their spread fingers touched.

"Ah," Elizabeth said with a tiny, satisfied curve of her lips. "I hear the tones, the 'chimes' now."

"Let's see what you learned yesterday," Bri said. That

would have caused *her* to stiffen up, but Elizabeth was a med school graduate, used to being scrutinized. Their energy connected, strong and clear. Elizabeth glanced up. "Both of us are flaming green with healing energy."

"Ayes," Bri said.

"First Chime," Elizabeth murmured.

"C," Bri said.

"Red," Elizabeth said.

"Root chakra," Bri replied. Elizabeth's questing Power moved up the boy's torso.

"Ah, there it is. Muddiness in the yellow third chime."

"Solar Plexus chakra, musical note of E," Bri said.

Elizabeth began clearing out the gray smudges of sickness.

"Wait, what are you doing?" Bri asked.

Not glancing up, Elizabeth said, "My job. Healing him."

"Without looking him over? Since when don't you examine the whole patient first before you start healing?"

Elizabeth's flow of energy jerked unsteadily. She gazed at Bri with shocked eyes. Bri smoothed out their shared Power. *Let's use our gifts*, Bri sent Elizabeth mentally. Slowly she moved through the boy's body, examining him. There were other minute smudges of black and gray tendrils. Elizabeth saw them, too.

On up to the crown of his head, where a very fine cobweb of gray delicately shadowed his brain. *Oh, my God!* Elizabeth said.

Zeres was right. They are treating one part of the body first, without looking at the whole.

Elizabeth helped Bri with the complex destruction of the web, pulling at a thread, shriveling it with the healing-stream. This house, too, had plenty of Power. Crystals rimmed the walls at the ceiling. Bri used a strong, laser-like current.

An intense half-hour later, they were done. Bri gnawed her lip. *Twin? I haven't been methodical, I just let the healing-stream flood me. Do you think we should do a follow-up with everyone we healed that first night and the girl yesterday?*

Frowning, Elizabeth considered, when her voice came in Bri's head it was cool and logical and reminded her of her parents. *The crucial word is "flooded."* She gestured to the patients around them. *I think that's what Zeres did to Mathias, too.* They both turned and stared at the man. Bri listened to his chakra Songs and his overall "health" Song. She heard nothing wrong, just the slowing of old age.

His aura is clear, Elizabeth said. *I think "flooding" is an excellent cure, but not, ah, energy efficient.*

I agree, Bri said.

Mathias stood and turned with a wicked smile, as if to let them see everything.

They laughed together, then moved to the teenager, who had closed his eyes, a sheen of suffering on his face. His mother hadn't said a word, but clutched his hand in a white-knuckled grip as if she could tie him to life.

Again Bri and Elizabeth spread their hands on the youth, found the gray web in the brain, poisoning the rest of the body, and another knot in the gonads. Bri opened herself to the healingstream. Midway through the procedure, she noticed Elizabeth faltering.

You're using too much of your personal energy, draining Power from the crystals. You need to tap into the healing-stream. Elizabeth didn't answer, so Bri shrugged and hooked her into the Power flow.

Then they were done, the teen rising from the table and stretching and grinning. Before Bri knew it, she was being squeezed and kissed soundly by him, then was released so he could do the same to Elizabeth. He shot them a wicked grin and flourished a bow. *"Merci!"* He held out an arm for his mother and she hurried to take it, sending a watery smile to Bri and her twin and curtseying.

Then they were gone.

"A very interesting exhibition," Mathias said. He, too, bowed to Bri and Elizabeth, patted a snoring Zeres on the shoulder, and tilted his head in consideration at the group of medicas. "Not my place to get into the thick of this. Good day to you all. Keep me informed, Sevair."

"Yes, sir."

Zeres snorted and woke up, wiped a little drool from his mouth and rubbed his belly. "I need food!"

Bri patted his shoulder like Mathias had done. "We had a big, tasty breakfast. There's probably leftovers."

He heaved himself from the chair and strode to the door with an even look at the medicas. "You're going to have to listen to me, you know." He pointed to Bri. "That one's my student." He rolled his shoulders. "Do what you will." He left.

The medicas had bunched together in disapproval. "We will have to think about this," said the leader. He nodded and left, the rest either bowed or curtsied, but followed.

Bri and Elizabeth and Sevair stood in silence. His brows were down in deep thought. Bri didn't care about the internal politics of Castleton. She rubbed her hands. "We've done good work this morning. Want to try out that bath?"

"Yes, before I go back up to the Castle," Elizabeth said.

Apparently she didn't want to get involved in politics in this strange land, either. "Perhaps you can bring me some bread and cheese? I'm hungry, too."

Bri chuckled. "I could eat a bit of cheese. Done."

An hour later Elizabeth had had a complete tour of the house and had congratulated Bri on her new home while stroking the smoothly polished newel post of the stairs in the entryway. Mud arrived and flew her to the Castle to inform the medicas there of the morning's events. Bri and Elizabeth had decided to see patients at the house every afternoon, starting tomorrow.

Zeres and Sevair remained, lingering in the dining room, discussing the frinkweed. Bri came in from the back door, and went to the home surgery to cleanse it. The medicas had done some Song ritual that re-energized the Power crystals, and Zeres had also added a cleaning sweep, but Bri wanted to make sure it was purified the way she liked. She cleaned it physically and Sang under her breath, a little spell that she'd cobbled together. It went well and the room smelled right to her when she exited and found the men in the hallway.

With a raising of his chin and squaring of his shoulders, Sevair became all Citymaster. "I would like to speak to you about your actions last night, Zeres," Sevair said in a low voice that raised the hair on the back of Bri's neck.

The older man turned slowly, as if recognizing danger. Zeres made a half bow. "Citymaster Masif." He cleared his drink-roughened voice. "My apologies." With a sweeping gesture at the elegant surroundings, he said, "I didn't think I would have any chance of speaking with the Exotique Medica." Drawing himself up to a semi-impressive figure, he continued. "It was vital that I talk to her. My theories might be unusual, but they are *right*," he added with an ill-disguised gloat. Then he smiled and was as handsome as any other Lladranan man, likely a lady-killer in his youth. Attractive and arrogant like many doctors, he reminded Bri a little bit of Elizabeth's ex-fiancé, Cassidy Jones. Bri slid a glance toward Elizabeth and saw her frown.

"I couldn't anticipate that Bri would be so open to my ideas, could I?" Zeres said.

Sevair crossed his arms.

"Ah." Zeres's smile faded and a line in his forehead deepened. "I did what I believed necessary for the good of our city and our country, to fight the Dark." His hands fisted. "You, as a Citymaster, must know of difficult choices."

"I do," Sevair replied coolly. "So I will convince my colleagues to delay your punishment until after the crisis of this sickness has past." He stared at Zeres and got a sober nod in return, then Sevair switched his attention to Bri and something in his expression warned her a zinger was coming. "You will be allowed to train—excuse me, *exchange ideas*—with Bri, and will have to work with the city medicas."

Zeres coughed, but Sevair just showed his teeth. "For the good of our city and country and to fight the Dark we must all work together. So, we accept that you will be Bri's mentor." Sevair's non-smile widened. "And Bri will be responsible for you and your behavior. I expect you to stay here in Exotique Medicas' home." He nodded. "Good day to you." He walked to the door, then, hand on knob, turned back to look at them and this time he cracked a real smile.

"The responsibilities for each other should be good for you both. I'll see you later."

Check up on them.

Sevair opened the door. "And if you cannot manage to stay in the Exotique Medicas' house, at least stay together, and carry that crystal ball." He left.

Zeres stared at the door, then he sighed and smiled, winked at Bri. "Guess I'll go get my few belongings." He stared up at the second floor.

"There's a bedroom in the back you can have," Bri smiled back. "It's purple."

Bri read some of Alexa's Lorebook at the desk until even that woman's interesting adventures couldn't keep her head from nodding and the words from blurring. So she stumbled a couple of steps to the bed and fell down on it.

Awoke suddenly an hour later, filmed with cold sweat and trembling from dreams of horrible monsters attacking her parents, dreeths that shot fire at their plane. Bri watched helplessly, from the center of a glowing pentacle, surrounded by chanting figures.

The worry she'd been suppressing surged into a tsunami of panic. She didn't know that she could move. The room seemed to whirl around her, then close in on her. She wasn't home, wasn't on Earth, wasn't near her parents.

She sensed her twin, shouted down their link.

Elizabeth, our folks!

18

Elizabeth's face appeared before Bri's inner eye. *Easy, twin.*

Bad dream. Bri sat up and rubbed her face, grimacing at the dampness of it—sweat, tears. She couldn't speak of it yet, put fears into words. *I'd like to take another look at the Temple where we were Summoned,* Bri said.

Elizabeth sniffed. *I went there yesterday evening. When YOU were partying.*

Getting to know people, Bri protested.

Of course. It was said with twin-exasperation. *I went alone and the place was empty.* She hesitated.

Go on. But Bri had sensed her feelings, the awe at the building and the echoes of Songs, particularly ones that had used energy to heal, linked to a montage of images that had flashed through Elizabeth's mind. How a square pool had attracted her, radiating waves of healing in pale auras nearly colorless but which she could *see.* The vestiges of not only the green pentacle that they had arrived in, in the west of the great circular room, but others. Even smudges of colors that Elizabeth thought were used to Summon the other Exotiques.

Wow, Bri said, almost forgetting her fears as the dream panic wore off.

Yes. That's just the impressions I got. You should definitely visit it, too. Another hesitation. *WE should go together, but you should also go alone. Just to feel and see what it might bring you.*

Bri reeled back against her padded headboard. For Elizabeth, that was a comment *way* out there. *Okay.*

Anyway, I observed the Temple thoroughly,

Bri bet she had.

I don't think we could take ourselves back. There's great energy there, but I don't know whether we could access it to use it to get home. Elizabeth gulped. *I have no idea how to craft a...a...*

Magic spell? Bri could almost see Elizabeth wince.

Magic spell, Elizabeth said faintly. *Unless you studied New Age spirituality as well as healing methods.* For once there was no hint of derision. Her voice had lifted as if with hope.

I attended some Wiccan and other pagan ceremonies, Bri confirmed. *But only as an observer.*

A few seconds of humming silence.

Too bad, Elizabeth said.

Do you think the other Exotiques would help us?

Not until we cure this sickness.

Their parents would return in two weeks to find their daughters missing. They'd have already called to tell the twins that their flight had been fine. Panic came back to spear her. What if their flight *hadn't* been fine?

Calm, Bri. And Elizabeth sent her calm, professional calm as if Bri was a hysterical patient. But Bri knew better. There was a tiny voice locked down in the back of Elizabeth's mind that was screaming too.

How many flights have we heard of that have crashed on the way to Hawaii? Elizabeth said.

Not many. Elizabeth had a point. The constriction in Bri's chest loosened slightly. *Is there ANY way we can find out if they're safe?*

I don't know, but I know who we can ask, Elizabeth said grimly.

Marian.

Marian, Elizabeth agreed. *I'll go right now.* The telepathic-talk link between them stopped abruptly though if she tried, Bri could sense what Elizabeth was doing—running out the door, racing down tower stairs. Elizabeth had learned to move fast as a doctor.

All Bri could do now was sit back and wait.

But she wouldn't, of course. She had to fill her mind with other things. She walked down to Zeres's room to see him snoozing, too, and it occurred to her that she should make sure the house had no liquor in it.

As soon as she'd finished speaking with Bri, Elizabeth went to the Circlet's suite in the Castle keep. She had no doubt Marian was there. One of the new developments of her "Power" was that she could feel where the other Exotiques were if they were in the Castle. Fortunately, this was one of those senses she could turn on and off.

She lifted her hand to run her thumbnail over the harpstrings and a pang went through her as she saw the pale pink she'd painted her nail. A celebration that her schooling was over and she had some good weeks of vacation before she started her job at Denver Major Hospital.

Just thinking those words brought more pain and the image of Cassidy. Bright blue eyes, fearsomely intelligent, black hair, sculpted features. Black Irish, though he'd been an orphan and shuffled through a foster care system that he'd believed had treated him "well enough." But he never spoke of the past, only the importance of the present and future. She suspected he wanted to be as "normal" as she. She'd thought he'd loved her, but perhaps it was only her loving family that he'd wanted.

Standing outside Marian's suite wasn't helping anything. Elizabeth set her shoulders.

The door opened to Jaquar, another blue-eyed, black-haired man: thankfully his features were more gorgeous-Asian than Celtic. "Salutations, Elizabeth," he said in the deep voice that was his most effective magical tool.

She smiled, knew it was thin-lipped but it was the best she could do. "Salutations, Jaquar." She curtseyed. May as well go into this confrontation excessively polite.

He stepped back and let her in, shut the door and bowed.

Marian sat by a window that showed volarans rising and circling down from the Landing Field.

"Salutations, Marian." Elizabeth attempted to brighten her smile but failed.

Marian rose. "Hello, Elizabeth. What can we do for you?"

"Bri and I have a problem. Our parents were flying to Hawaii yesterday morning. We don't know if they arrived safely. Could our cells have received a message from them?" The cells that Marian's damned companion had eaten.

"I'm sorry, no," Marian said. "Cell phones definitely don't work across the dimensions. Both Koz and I brought one and the Circlets performed many tests."

Elizabeth glanced around the room, saw a large clear crystal ball. "Is there any way to find out what is happening on Earth?" It came out more like a desperate plea than a simple request.

Marian hesitated. Elizabeth could hear a lie coming.

She straightened to her full height, not quite as tall as Marian, inches shorter than Jaquar. "Neither Bri nor I will be easy in our minds until we know our parents arrived safely. No one wants upset doctors."

Married-couple telepathy between Marian and Jaquar. Elizabeth wondered if telepathy with her twin was as irritating. She had to keep her hands from fisting. She wanted action. Horrible to be helpless.

Jaquar's brows dipped. Elizabeth flicked her smile back on, realized it was useless.

"We are not accustomed to our Exotiques having very strong ties with Earth," Jaquar said.

"I understood that Marian did." Elizabeth kept her manner outwardly serene even if she radiated stress. She stared into Marian's blue eyes. "You must have worried about your brother."

"He was away on a retreat."

"Then you knew he was safe."

Marian flushed, touched fingertips to her breast over her heart. "Thinking back, I believe I knew he was safe because I had a bond with him. I felt he was safe. Perhaps you should search inside yourself."

Elizabeth felt fiery heat wash up her neck and into her face. "I don't have that skill yet." She took out the small crystal sphere that had been in her pocket all day, cupped it in her palm and said, "Bri?"

Bri's face formed in the ball. "Can she find out for us?"

Holding the sphere between thumb and forefinger so everyone could see each other, Elizabeth said, "Marian believes we should be able to sense their health."

Tugging at one of the purple streaks in her hair, Bri said, "What? Meditation or something? How can I relax if I'm imagining a plane crash!"

"Good point," Elizabeth said, wishing Bri hadn't voiced her own fears.

Bri's looked at Marian. "Can't you help us?"

"*The Lorebook of Exotique Marian,*" Jaquar said quietly.

"I didn't hear that," Bri said. "I'm coming up there!" The crystal showed a couple of misty tendrils that quickly faded. Elizabeth placed it back in her pocket, relieved. Bri was on her way and there would be two people to pressure these magicians.

Marian lifted her chin. "If you'd read my Lorebook, you would have known that my mentor has an interdimensional telescope."

"As if I've had time to read your Lorebook," Elizabeth replied. Then Marian's words cycled through her mind. "An interdimensional telescope. That would mean your mentor—"

"Bossgond," Jaquar interjected helpfully.

"Bossgond can see Earth."

"Yes." A pause. "If he knows where to look. The Hawaiian Islands is a big area to search for two people."

"They spend the first three days on Oahu. I have their itinerary. I'll be right back."

When she turned the corner to their hallway, an intense telepathic humming between Marian and Jacquar stopped. They'd sensed her, she supposed, and were now composing themselves. She was determined that her parents' safety would be verified. Nothing was more important. If she had to find her way to this dimensional telescope and chivvy this Bossgond into looking, she would. They would. She grinned fiercely. Bri was on her way. When they fought together they never lost.

She didn't bother with the doorharp but gave a hard rap on the door, turned the knob and walked in.

Marian was flushed. Irritation showed brightly in her eyes. Jaquar had a stiffness to his bearing. From the corner of her eye, Elizabeth caught a large glowing crystal ball with wisps of mist…. It had been recently used.

Elizabeth closed the door behind her and lifted her chin. "I trust you have been making arrangements to check on our parents?" She was polite and authoritative.

"Ayes," said Jaquar. Relief swept through her. He stepped in front of Marian. "Bossgond is a dedicated scholar, which makes him a very curious man. Most of us are quite curious. If you can give us a location where Bossgond might find them, Marian will help him look."

"I think it's more important to stay here for the council of war early tomorrow morning—" Marian started.

So that was the tension between them!

Jaquar rolled over Marian smoothly. "We can leave immediately and reach Alf Island before nightfall. We may even be able to find them this evening." He shifted a little and Elizabeth got the impression that his next words were for Marian as much as herself. "We can spend the night in our own home. Search for your parents tomorrow morning."

Marian stared at them, then said, "I'll pack." She went into another room.

"Bri and I can accompany—" Elizabeth started.

But Jaquar was shaking his head. "Leave the Power workings to the Circlets, Exotique Medica." Obviously he wouldn't irritate his wife in this. Elizabeth wanted to press, but she and Bri hadn't been invited, had no way to get there or any place to stay overnight without help. Her jaw flexed, but she kept quiet.

"That reminds me." Jaquar went to a small laboratory table in the corner of the room and brought back two small bottles, one tinted a faint orange, the other slightly yellow. "Language potion for you and Bri, good for a week. I have noticed your speech deteriorating."

Elizabeth's lips compressed, but she took them. No harm had come to them so far.

Marian returned with what looked like two sets of light saddlebags, wearing a split-legged gown. "Do you have any idea where your parents will be?"

"Of course," Elizabeth said. She went to the long table near the windows, set her appointment book down and flipped open to the section for her parents' trip. Marian joined her.

Unfolding the color computer printouts, Elizabeth just stared for a moment as more pangs of homesickness struck. The top sheet showed the hotel information and included pictures of the hotel, the beach, and a room.

Marian sucked in a breath and Elizabeth glanced at her to see a wretched expression, softening Elizabeth. Despite the choices the Earth women had made, they'd miss Earth. She certainly would in their position.

"This is where they're staying," Elizabeth said.

Jaquar put his hands on his wife's shoulders and stared with lively interest at the page. "Such a tall building. Fascinating." He shook his head. "I've never seen such trees, such a beach."

Slowly, Elizabeth separated the top sheet from the rest and handed it to Marian. Marian's fingers trembled as much as her own as she took it. "Thank you. I'll take good care of it," Marian said in English.

Elizabeth said, "When do you anticipate looking through the…looking for them?"

"If we leave here within the next few minutes, and considering the strength and Power of our volarans and how much Distance Magic we use, I'd say two and a half hours."

Elizabeth let the sentence with more strange concepts sink in, breathed deeply, and replied, "Hawaii is three hours behind Denver." She flipped to the list she'd made. "If they follow the reservations I made, they will be touring the Byodo-in Temple on Oahu then. Dad is the Dean of Anthropology at the University of Denver. I arranged a special individual tour. They'll spend some time there." Elizabeth drew out the information and printouts of the Temple.

One of Jaquar's long, elegant index fingers tapped the blurry picture. "What is this?" he asked sharply.

"Huge bell, like a gong," Marian breathed.

"Gong?" Elizabeth questioned, then got it. A shiver sifted through her. "It's a big bell." She fumbled for recollection. She hadn't printed anything out about the bell. "But not silver, I don't think."

"Sound from a massive bell is much like a gong," Jaquar said. "That would help Bossgond find the location. What are the chances of your father wanting to ring it?"

Elizabeth closed her eyes. "A certainty. People are encouraged to ring it. He won't just do it once, and he'll make sure Mom rings it, too."

"Some sounds can cross worlds," Jaquar said. "They are there today. It is fated, I think."

19

Peacocks! squeaked a little voice. It took Elizabeth a couple of seconds to understand that the word came to her mind from the hawk now perched on the edge of the table.

"Tuckerinal," Elizabeth said coolly. She hadn't forgiven him yet for eating her cell phone. Her fingers curled tight on her organizer. It was a good thing that she hadn't gone electronic with her life, like Bri had.

She stared with narrowed eyes at the ex-hamster. "I had photos from my Dad's birthday party on my phone. Show them to Marian and Jaquar. They'll be looking for our parents in the dimensional telescope."

The bird's eyes rounded. It blinked, seemed to consider, then projected two smiling heads close together.

A moan came from Elizabeth. Her parents had never looked so happy, so solid, so loving—of each other and of the people their eyes were focused upon—the twins.

To her surprise, Jaquar's arm came around her shoulders and he supported her.

Another photo appeared. This one showed her parents standing together in the wooden-paneled den. Her father's arm was around her mother's waist and in his other hand he held the leather wallet with their trip information and tickets, the twins' gift. Her mother's arm was around his waist and she leaned into him. Again they beamed with happiness.

Elizabeth simply stared. Finally she rasped, "Bri will have more," she whispered. "She brought a digital camera." How glad Elizabeth was they had that!

Jaquar said, "These two will do fine. Tuckerinal?"

The hawk hopped to a sheet of paper, shut its eyes, swayed. Elizabeth watched in amazement as color images appeared under him. They were large, larger than eight by ten, and the resolution was as good as professional studio shots, not grainy as they would have been if she'd printed them out. She made a sound in her throat. He opened his eyes and staggered a little to the side. *Power. Part of my payment for eating your nut.*

Marian cleared her throat too, and Elizabeth saw her misty eyes. "I apologize again for the terrible fright yesterday morning. Consider this little trip of ours repayment." She gave a half-smile. "I can see why you want to check on them. I'll reiterate something else. We Exotiques stick together. I wouldn't have knowingly hurt you and this is the last we'll talk of repayment and favors or anything else."

"Fine," Elizabeth said. She nodded to the photos. "May I have those after you use them?"

"Of course. And Tuckerinal will make a set for Bri."

"Bri is fun to be with," chirped the hawk.

They heard a choked sound behind them and found Bri,

hands at her mouth, staring at the photos. Behind her was Sevair. Bri's hair was touselled; she smelled like the scent of volarans, amber resin.

"They'll help?"

"They think they can check on Mom and Dad. Did you bring your digital camera?"

"No, I didn't think of it. Why?"

"Marian can explain. I take it you haven't read the *Lorebook of Exotique Circlet Marian*, either?"

Bri gulped. "I've started Alexa's."

"Perhaps later you can try to sense your parents," Marian said.

Eyes firing, Bri said, "We'll do that."

The Citymaster cleared his throat. Bri flung out a hand. "Sevair very kindly brought me."

"I board her volaran," he said. "I would like to hear how the Circlets can contact Exotique Terre. It has always been our understanding that such a thing is impossible."

Now Jaquar smiled toothily. "Bossgond. We will be leaving very shortly. You can come if you want."

Sevair hesitated, then smiled. "I have heard he is as irascible as a retired Master merchant who hoards his gold and knowledge and whose gout pains him."

"That's right," Jaquar said. "Coming?"

The Citymaster glanced at Bri, who was still a little shaky, and Elizabeth who felt wrung out and probably looked it. "Not this evening. But you can tell the great Circlet Bossgond that I will accept your invitation in the future."

"We must leave," Marian said, whisking toward the door. She didn't open it in time for the hawk and it flew through it. Then she and Jaquar left.

Bri rubbed her eyes. "I thought I saw—"

"You did," Elizabeth said.

"I knew he was magical, but…."

"I suggest we leave here." Sevair scanned the room. "I don't want to be alone in Circlets' chambers."

"Nope. Ttho," Bri said. "No telling what would happen if we touched the wrong thing."

Elizabeth handed her the yellow bottle. "The language potion."

"Suppose we'd better." As soon as they were in the hallway and the door locked behind them, Bri uncorked the bottle and drank. Her lips curved as her tongue swiped them. "Good. Tastes as good as it smells."

She stared at Elizabeth. Elizabeth would have preferred to wait until her speaking and comprehension skills had actually faded until taking the potion, but Bri's gaze was challenging and Sevair was watching. Elizabeth opened her own. "It smells better." Tossing it down, she licked her lips.

"Jaquar must have refined them," Bri said.

"Yes."

As they walked to Elizabeth's tower suite, Bri asked Sevair, "Can they teleport?"

"What is this teleport?" Sevair said.

"Moving instantaneously from one place to another," Bri said.

Sevair's eyes widened. "Why would you even think of such a thing? Who told you—"

Elizabeth slipped an arm around Bri's shoulders, squeezed, and answered. "In the magical Songs of Exotique Terre magicians sometimes have this power."

"Tel-e-por-ta-tion," Sevair said, as if tasting the word. A corner of his mouth quirked up. "Fairy Songs for children."

"Guess so," Bri mumbled.

"Let me tell you about the dimensional telescope," Elizabeth said. "Come to my rooms and we'll see if there's a picture in the famous and fabulous *Lorebook of Exotique Marian*."

There was. It sprang off the page, a three-dimensional hologram. The telescope was set before an infinity of mirrors. Then the image pivoted, the gears moved, and they were looking through the eyepiece at a small, book-laden apartment.

"Fabulous, indeed," murmured Sevair.

Elizabeth couldn't say anything. Everything she'd experienced caught up with her. Her mouth went dry. A dull thunk reverberated throughout her body. Finally she understood to the marrow of her bones that this was not a dream.

Everything she'd experienced was true.

She was trapped in another dimension.

Bri couldn't help it. After the usual exhilaration of the volaran flight from Castleton to her house, she crashed. Sevair held her arm and she leaned on him, feet dragging. Evidently he didn't believe her cheery forced smile.

"You're tired," he said.

"Not really. I've had a nap." Even though her sleep had been a series of nightmares.

"Really," he said firmly and led her straight to her bedroom, pushing her gently onto the bed.

She sank into the feather mattress. Another slight shove on her shoulder and she was flat on her back, tugs as he removed her shoes. "Maybe I can rest my eyes for a moment."

"Rest your eyes." He rolled the words out, sounding amused. Maybe they didn't have that saying here. Her lashes had already closed, but she sensed his smile. That was good. The man didn't smile often enough. Her last thought.

A tinkling bell woke her up. The water clock. She'd adjusted it to ring at twelve-hour intervals, the least amount of settings. Groggily she stared at it. Six p.m. local time. Of course they probably didn't say p.m. Frowning, she recalled them saying "of the evening" or "of the morning." Then fuzziness vanished and she sat up, irritated at herself.

She didn't believe in naps. They were a waste of valuable time when she should be off doing something new and exciting, but two days in a row she'd fallen asleep in the afternoon, and today, twice! Yesterday, she could justify the sleep after the long day she'd put in the day before, but today…. She slipped from her wrinkled clothes and dressed in fresh ones, bundling the others down a laundry chute. Her mind provided rationalizations: she was still recovering from the time changes, Sweden to Colorado, Denver to Lladrana; she'd worked hard and needed rest; she was coping with an entirely new situation and dealing with many emotional shocks; she wasn't connected to Mother Earth, and for some stupid reason tears flooded her eyes.

A crash came from downstairs. Tentatively she probed the house with her senses.

Zeres. Messing around in the kitchen. Probably eating *her* food, and she was starving. She grabbed her shoes and put them on and headed downstairs.

He was munching a sandwich and vegetable salad in the

dining room and she simply stopped to take in the sight. Big, unshaven, barrel chest and beer belly, shaggy hair, though it didn't appear as dirty. In fact he looked well scrubbed.

Light streaming through the windows lingered on the rough old man and the gleaming, perfectly fashioned table, the delicate china. He didn't look right here.

Hands on hips, she said, "Make yourself at home."

He grunted around a mouthful of food, swallowed, then his keen dark-brown gaze met hers. "*Merci,* I will." He raised his brows at her scowl. "I am your mentor. You accepted me and sent the rest of those red tunics away." Pointing a finger at her, he continued. "Despite all your successes, little girl, and your confident words, you need a mentor here."

Unfortunately he was right. She looked at him, then around the room, thought of the pretty, fussy bedroom, the purple guest room she'd already given him, all the elegant and expensive furnishings. "You don't really fit here."

He glared, but, mannerly, he didn't answer since he was chewing. Shifting from foot to foot, she realized that not only did he look out of place here, she felt strange. The house was beautiful, filled with beautiful things that intimidated her. What if she broke that china, scarred that table? She understood that everything was hers, or hers and Elizabeth's, but it felt like a big responsibility. She had enough big responsibilities right now. And the house wasn't her style—it was traditional, fashionable with the most elegant of the past. Elizabeth and their mother would prefer it.

Furthermore, she felt a small *pull*, a hint of knowledge that there was some *other* place that called to her more. She'd had feelings like this before, walked a city until she found the neighborhood, the building she felt most comfortable in. Sometimes lodging wasn't available there, but often it was. She'd been lucky more than once. She wondered what sort of place in Castleton would pull at her. No harm in finding out after dinner.

So she fixed food and ate. Zeres apparently took his mealtimes seriously and didn't speak. When she was done and Zeres swallowed the last of his apple cider, she pushed her plate aside and leaned over the table toward him. "We aren't staying here."

"No!" He drew the smooth, pretty cobalt-glazed pottery mug toward him. "I want to stay."

Now she leaned back in her chair, the carving of the heavy back pressing into her. "This place isn't my style." Even the fancy patient room was too upscale. She wasn't a doctor, she was a healer.

She gestured around them. "Face it, we don't belong here. My sister Elizabeth, maybe, but not us."

Frowning, he said, "Those medicas at the Castle will never let her go. She should be down here, like you." He glanced at the kitchen. "And there's the food."

"Wherever I go, they will feed me."

He perked up. "That's right. They want you to concentrate on the frink plague. Always knew those things would be trouble."

"You and Sevair Masif."

"A good boy. Trifle stiff, but a good Citymaster." Zeres scratched his cheek. "Pity about the betrayal of his man. Nasty situation, him being the new servant of the Dark and the Master of the horrors. Been a year, probably not much human left."

Bri stood. "Do people blame Sevair?" She took her dishes into the kitchen and put them in the sink, saw no soap or dishcloth to clean them, so she rinsed them off and let them stay, unhappy at leaving them dirty.

Zeres followed her. "No, folk don't, none of the gossip I heard. They admire him, know he took the defection hard. The Marshalls spread it around that the whole mess coulda been worse. The traitor's a less effective Master than that one the Volaran Exotique defeated last year. Philosophical about it."

"Huh." She really *did* need to read those Lorebooks. She shrugged, and the gesture made her think of her backpack. She wanted it while she explored the town this evening, followed the call, soothed her itchy feet.

Zeres set his dishes in the sink and walked away. Sighing, Bri rinsed them, too, called, "Just a couple of minutes and we'll go find our place."

Elizabeth kept busy with training sessions and when the Circlets didn't communicate by crystal ball about her parents, her chest constricted.

Finally she went to her suite, and skipping Alexa's Lorebook, she started reading Marian's. Elizabeth wanted information and fast. She found out Marian had created the best globe of Earth the Lladranans had, and wondered how well the woman had delineated the Hawaiian Islands. Though Marian hadn't seemed to think finding the twins' parents would be a problem, the Lorebook didn't sound as if it was easy.

On this discomfiting thought, Elizabeth fell asleep and woke as evening fell, stiff from sleeping at her desk. But she was used to grabbing sleep where and when she could and had slept sitting up more than once. The first thing she did was check the crystal ball on the table. It was clear. No calls.

For a while she just wanted to hide, but she was hungry, so she tidied herself and left the suite, descending the stairs.

Remembering the scene with the Circlets revived a bruising ache inside her. Despite all the interesting things she'd been learning, the igniting of her gift from a match to a torch, this wasn't her place, wasn't a vacation between her residency and practicing medicine as an emergency room physician. For an instant she wondered what Cassidy would think of the whole situation. If she'd still been engaged to him would she have been Summoned?

So far in the past, two days ago and another life. Life would never be the same for either her or Bri.

A man pushed away from where he'd stood in the shadows at the bottom of the stairs. Her hand went to her throat.

"My apologies." Faucon Creusse, the startlingly attractive man who was instinctively drawn to Earth women, swept her a bow.

She found herself curtseying, though she'd only done that in occasional school plays.

He stepped up to her. "I would never have startled you."

"Why are you here?"

20

Faucon's brow furrowed, then he smiled wryly. "I think I sensed your distress. No one would stop any Chevalier from guarding any Exotique." He held out a hand.

After a moment, she put her fingers in his, and his bright aura flared to her other sight, even as his Song met hers, clashed, wove with hers.

"Ayes," he said and lifted her fingers to his lips. "This is good, the Song blesses us."

Elizabeth took a step back, drawing her hand from his. She'd liked the little sensual shiver as his mouth had pressed against the back of her hand, but was wary of it, too.

"Please dine with me in my suite," he said.

"I don't think—"

"I assure you the food will be much better than what you will receive even in the Marshalls' Dining room."

She believed that. "Thank you for your offer." She hesitated. "Perhaps another time."

"Then may I escort you to the Marshalls' Dining Room?"

Cocking her head, she said, "Are you allowed in?"

He smiled and her pulse quickened. "Of course. I'm richer and of a higher social status and have larger estates than many of the Marshalls. They don't want to irritate me."

"Ah, I'd anticipated a discussion with the Exotiques—"

"Calli is dining with her family. Alexa and Bastien have already supped. But I have spent much time with each Exotique and would be happy to answer any questions, tell stories." He took her hand and tucked it in his arm and led the way down the hall.

Elizabeth said nothing more as they made the long walk to the Marshalls' Dining Room, but she watched his aura from the corner of her eye and listened to the faint melody of his Song. She was very aware of him, his hand covering hers on his arm, the easy muscularity of his body. She was very aware of his effect on her, the heating of her blood.

She stepped away outside the door. "You're here because of your attraction."

"Certainly." He spread his hands. "Behold a poor moth dazzled by flame."

That made her smile. He was handsome, charming, sexy, and in excellent physical condition. Despite his instinctive desire for Exotiques, she didn't think he was a man who lacked control.

"All right," she said. "So you're here at the Castle with me because I'm accessible, as opposed to courting Bri in Castleton." She bit her lip as she speculated on the depth of his liking. She didn't bother to hide her doubt. The man was easy enough in her company that she felt she could be herself. No masks. She wasn't sure how long it had been since she'd lived without a mask. Only those close to her saw her without one, her parents, Bri, Cassidy—

This man was nothing like Cassidy—charming instead of intense.

Faucon chuckled, took one of her hands and squeezed it. "Your sister is very attractive to me, too, but I think I prefer the less—unpredictable."

"Hmm."

He opened the door. "Superficial attraction can diminish or change."

She noticed his qualification.

Bending, he whispered in her ear, "I've made a study of the Exotiques. But nothing in-depth. Yet."

She shivered at the note in his voice, looked at him through her lashes.

The Castle battle alarm sounded. His jaw set. He whipped her behind him, held the door wider for the Marshalls bolting from the dining room. Elizabeth ran downstairs with him. She could have escaped his tight grip, but her heart was in her throat and she wanted to see the mobilization.

He went to the courtyard instead of the Landing Field, dropped her hand, whistled high and long. Elizabeth flinched. His bow was brief, his mind already winging to other things—to battle, no doubt. Her nerves jittered.

"I'm on rotation," he said.

His volaran, large and gleaming, landed in Temple Ward, and suddenly a man and a woman in squire uniforms were before him. One helped him into his armor, buckled on his sword. The other checked the volaran's tack. A group of eight other hastily armored Chevaliers wearing Faucon's colors of red and orange hovered near. He scanned them, nodded.

"All here!" he called. "Go to the Landing Field, mount up, follow me. I will claim no portion of your kills." He swung onto his volaran, dipped his head at Elizabeth and his expression softened, his mouth quirked. "Would you join me for breakfast tomorrow?"

She knew night battles were rare, but didn't know how long any battle lasted, whether this was a small or large invasion. She didn't anticipate sleeping, but waiting, and studying the Lorebooks.

Everything was real.

Keeping her gaze steady on his own, she said, "What about a very late dinner?"

A grin that would melt any woman's heart slashed across his face. "Done!" He waved at the female squire. "Tell my major domo. Neither of you are on rotation tonight."

"Yes, Hauteur." She ran across the courtyard to the Noble Apartments.

Faucon reached down and skimmed a thumb across Elizabeth's cheek. "I'll see you later." He made it intimate, though the ward around them boiled with others readying and flying to fight. She could hear the commotion from the Landing Field beyond. Then he drew on his helmet, secured it, and pulled on thin gloves that Elizabeth hadn't noticed folded over his belt.

"Dreeth skin, very tough," he said. "Good evening, Elizabeth."

She swallowed hard and repeated words she heard echoing around the Castle. "Good hunting."

He nodded and with a muttered word he and his volaran lifted into the sky. Elizabeth watched them fly away north. Then her eye was caught by movement in a lit third-story bow window of the Noble Apartments. Faucon's female squire and another man watched, too. The man's aura flashed with worry and fear; she sensed he wanted to fly with Faucon. The major domo caught sight of her and bowed, then turned away, giving orders. To prepare a wonderful dinner for her and a man who might not return.

Bri had intended to stroll the streets of Castleton to see more of the small city and find the place that called to her. Zeres had a different idea. When he pulled her into the nearest neighborhood tavern, as tidy as the too-groomed square, she knew he'd discovered there was no liquor in the house. She was dealing with a real alcoholic. As she watched him gulp down an ale then fill up his bota bag, after telling the barkeep to charge it to "the Exotique Medica's account," she considered whether she could clear that sickness from him. She'd handled plenty of hangovers, her own included. She'd used the healingstream on people who'd liquored themselves up to take away the pain of injury—and dealt with both the alcohol poisoning and wound.

He shoved away from the bar. "Whatcha lookin' at, little girl?"

"Call me Bri." She opened the door and went out into the last, lingering light of the day before the sun disappeared below the town walls. "Do you know that liquor affects your brain, killing cells?" The word "cell" came out as "note."

Zeres grunted. Bri danced ahead of him, wrinkling her nose. "You smell again."

He shrugged a shoulder.

"I could probably cure you of this sickness."

"It ain't a sickness, it's a choice," he said roughly.

"My world doesn't entirely believe that. It's a sickness and a choice. But I can't help if you don't want to change."

His eyes were stark and burning. "There is an underlying cause. If you can't help with that engulfing night and flashing death I feel every time I heal—" He opened his bota and swigged. She continued to stare at him as he stoppered the bota.

"Yes, I can and will. You were dramatic this morning for the medicas, but Elizabeth and I heal those with this frink sickness as well. Work with us, you won't be alone."

Grunting, he followed her down a narrower, older, more charming side street. "Untrue."

"What?"

Another hunch of the shoulder. "Castleton ain't the only city to have the sickness. All the other towns do too, prob'ly more of the outlying countryside, and the noble estates." He pointed at her. "Mark my words, you and your sister will be out making the rounds. Until we figure out why you can heal and no one else can."

"Except you. Well, I'll help you discover what that darkness and flashes are—that which let *you* heal, too. When you know what it is, it will be easier to accept." She turned another corner where the street became more cobblestone and less large paved stones, and she heard him drink again. He didn't answer so she pressed on, "I connect with what I call a healingstream. It can be wonderful and is very strong here, much stronger than on…Exotique Terre, but it, in itself, doesn't frighten me. I can help you with that." She glanced back over her shoulder and saw his scowl as he returned the bota to his hip. "And the drink."

He opened his mouth, shut it, his face hardened. "I want my old life back, when I was a respected medica."

Bri smiled. "Then we'll get it back for you. You'll be the hero of this age."

"You and your twin will be the heroes."

Her smile disappeared.

"You truly aren't going to stay are you?" Zeres said.

She shook her head. "No. Neither of us will."

He gestured as they turned once more. "Even though we are going to a place that calls to you."

Her turn to shrug. "Places have called to me before. They aren't home."

The Castle claxon rang and everyone on the street stopped and looked up to the hill—volarans were already rising into the sky with armed riders. Bri shuddered. "No, this is *not* home."

Elizabeth returned to the Marshalls' Dining Room to pick up a plate of bread and some cheeses to assuage her hunger while she waited. The keep seemed empty and echoing. A third of the Marshall pairs had left the day before for northern frinkweed duty, now a third had gone fighting. Though the floors and walls of her tower were solid, she'd gotten used to sensing the faint Songs—life forces—of Alexa and Bastien and missed them. They, too, were off to battle.

So she read Alexa's adventures, and had to put the last of

her food aside when she reached three-dimensional images of the horrors. Elizabeth had heard of the trophies in the Nom de Nom, and of the Assayer's Office here in the keep where independent Chevaliers were paid for their kills. But she hadn't actually *seen* them, and she was a visual person.

Alexa's book detailed them in all their dangerous hideousness. For a few minutes Elizabeth thought of going to the Assayer's Office. It would be open since a battle was being fought. Or head down to the Nom de Nom tavern in town to examine the real things. Instead she found herself drifting across the courtyard to the Map Room that would show the progress of the battle. Alexa's book had several pictures of the Map Room, too, as well as a map of the Castle and Lladrana.

She joined others, most of the older, original Marshalls, and saw the blue fire marking the border and gaping holes.

"The incursion isn't bad," said the rich voice of a man, Lady Knight Swordmarshall Thealia's husband.

She frowned. She knew that voice. "You were the primary voice in the chants Bri and I heard on Exotique Terre."

His round face lightened, he bowed. "Guilty."

There was an exclamation and they turned back to the huge map. "Three Chevaliers dead."

She gasped, but forced words out. "Faucon Cruess?"

"No nobles, no pairs, three independents, poor souls," Thealia's husband said.

Elizabeth glanced around. "Calli?" Her voice rose. She strode to the top of the map, saw little shield icons. The largest red-orange one was Faucon, the two blue-green ones Alexa and Bastien. Elizabeth didn't know Calli's colors.

The Marshall's hand came onto her shoulder, squeezed,

massaged. "Calli and Marrec have a family. They won't be fighting until the last battle. She isn't here because their children get restless when an alarm sounds."

Anyone would get restless.

There was a slight cheer. "Four more fenceposts!"

Someone said, "More horrors to the east, we're moving."

"It's going to be a long night," said the Marshall.

Night fell and Bri and Zeres were still walking. Now and then Bri's feet would tingle, but it wasn't *the* place. She was distracted by all the Songs: Zeres's, families' in the well-lit houses, people in taverns, even the river running through the town, the trees and the parks. Maybe even the stone city walls that they drew closer to.

They weren't exactly walking, more like staggering. Zeres had continued to guzzle liquor, and Bri refused to leave him. She didn't think being on her own again at night was wise. Even drunk, Zeres was formidable.

Nor did she think the Citymasters would be pleased if she was alone. They'd met up with Sevair Masif and other guild people soon after the alarm rang. Checking up on her. One of the men had bowed and bowed and offered a dagger, a beautiful leather sheath and belt. Bri hadn't felt comfortable refusing though she'd never used a knife as a weapon in her life. Both the head of the smith guild and the leather workers had beamed at her acceptance of the gift, so someone had been pleased.

She and Sevair had conducted a short, polite conversation, and he'd taken her hand in a formal kiss-the-fingers-goodbye. She'd gotten the idea that he was committing her Song or scent or something to memory so he could track her.

So now she was weaving from Zeres's weight through a mist that had floated in, making the city eerie, coating the streets and buildings with moisture. She shouldn't have been able to support him more than a step or two. She was awed that she was using *magic* in such a concrete way, to hold someone up and walk.

She'd taken care to keep a telepathic line open to Elizabeth, had felt brushes of her twin's mind. Elizabeth was concentrating, nervy, as she awaited battle results. Bri was glad she was in the city; she'd go up when the wounded came in, hoped she'd have enough energy to heal the sick later. She had a deep conviction Alexa would be all right, whatever happened to her, something in Alexa's Song, a determination to triumph.

Elizabeth had also been a bit surprised to feel secondhand Bri's itchy feet.

She'd once sought to understand why places called to her. Reincarnation? Sacred spots? Some hadn't been so very sacred...the hill in Prague, the clearing in Arkansas, that ancient caravansary in Turkey....

As always, she went with instinct. Elizabeth may have been learning a new vocabulary to explain their healing hands logically, but Bri *sensed* the best way to function here was on instinct. Her gut wouldn't steer her wrong.

The streets had quieted as the mist sent people to home or inns. Zeres hiccupped and snored in her ear. She wondered that he could walk, looked down to see that his feet weren't touching the ground.

She lost it. Whatever belief that had kept him upright and moving with her. He slipped into a loose, untidy heap at her feet, and the snoring rose.

But she was here, in a small cul de sac, facing north, in the oldest part of the town. Blinking, she understood that the wall to her left wasn't brick, but huge stones set together, the *west* city wall. Not crumbling, of course, but certainly aged.

In front of her was the projection of a tower built into the wall. The building had an additional small octagonal tower to the right that she recognized housed a staircase. She could barely see the crenellated top rising one more story above the rest of the building. The left side of the place was part of the city wall.

She liked the idea of living in a tower abutting the city wall. How cool was that? Able to look out on…well, whatever the view was. Green fields.

There was also some symmetry. She wriggled her shoulders to ease them from the weight of carrying Zeres. Elizabeth and Alexa lived in a tower that was part of the Castle keep, the western wall of the Castle. Not due north, more east. Bri checked her twin and found Elizabeth's mind slow, still anxious. Squinting, Bri *saw* the twin bond that linked them, unrolling at a good steep angle upward and to the east.

The mist coalesced into the patter of rain. Zeres's snores cut off. He gobbled, blinked bleary eyes. "Gonna just let me lie here in the rain? *Merde,* students these days…." He hefted himself and stumbled toward the tower's door. He set his shoulder against it. It gave in and went down.

Zeres yelled. Darkness billowed from the tower. "Wha's this?" Another grunt, this one of surprise or pain. Bri ran, saw him slide down the angled wall of the staircase tower that he'd staggered against. She jumped toward him, fumbled under his cloak to feel his heart. Strong and steady.

She didn't think she'd be moving him anytime soon. When she stood, her hand went to her new dagger. She pulled it from the sheath. No light gleamed on its blade. The dim light of the street globe half a block down wasn't enough to show the dimensions of the room. Rain splatted hard behind her.

There was…an odor. She sniffed. A powdery dryness coating her nostrils, an underlying hint of…damp feathers? Volaran, or volaran kin? She strained all her senses. No evil like the small motes that still surrounded the trophies hanging on the wall of the Nom de Nom.

Slowly she sheathed the knife. Rolled her shoulders again. Stepped farther into the room, blinked and blinked once more, moved step by step until she thought she was in the center. The feeling of *rightness* was here. She closed her eyes. The atmosphere *flowed* in some way. She'd read of seething and roiling atmosphere, but that wasn't it. Richer? Contained more oxygen? She'd grown up in the Mile High City, but had lived at various altitudes since. More magic? *Yes!*

Like the great round temple in the Castle, there was more magic here. The rafters might be studded with storage crystals. The home surgery at the house they'd given her and Elizabeth had crystals but they weren't as old and saturated as here.

She glanced at Zeres. No wonder he passed out. Whatever sensitized him to the Song might have short-circuited him.

Curiosity nibbled at her. She couldn't tell where the Power source was. She stamped her feet, listening for hollowness, couldn't hear any, but thought there was a basement. If she really believed in the Song she could raise her voice and send it echoing, testing the interior space. She wasn't much of a singer. *A feeler.* Once again she closed her eyes, extended every other sense.

She had to go up.

She tried to recall how many floors. Didn't remember anything except the crenelations at the top. She still couldn't see much, but the stair tower was on her left, angling into the room, with a deep black slab of a door or opening. "Light," she said, and flicked a bit of Power out with the word as she'd been taught. Nothing happened. No prepared torches or crystals or whatever was in here.

Something rustled. She froze.

Zeres snuffled, shifted, groaned. His boots scraped against the grit of the floor as he curled up.

Bri let out a held breath. She peered through the door into the night. Forked lightning silvered sheets of rain, then left the city darker. She couldn't see to the other side of the cul de sac. She shivered. No summer warmth.

She thought of Sevair's grumpiness, the ache she'd sensed in his joints. A low-pressure system had been affecting him. She hoped he was warm and dry.

The outside door lay black-hole-like on the floor. Zeres grumbled in his sleep. The rain hissed. She wouldn't be leaving soon. Another shiver. Surely upstairs would be warmer, or would there be windows open to the rain?

Rubbing her arms, she sidled toward the stair tower until her toe thunked against wood, like the sound of rich paneling. She slid her foot around and found dips and pro-trusions. A door of embellished wood. Since nothing crum-bled or splintered, the tower hadn't been deserted too long.

She opened the door and the dark wasn't so oppressive. Air and dim light came from above.

With careful steps she wound upwards on the solid stone stairs. Then she reached the tiny threshold-landing of the next floor, this one a pointed arch, half open and not quite as dark.

The scent was stronger here, but so was warmth. Bri pushed the door open with a horror-movie *creaaakk* and entered the main chamber. Large windows on three walls showed light from opaque glass, a bare room. Thunder rumbled, and Bri was spurred upward. The next level should open onto the walk atop the city wall. It wouldn't be much sheltered, she wouldn't go out. So she passed that door and went up to the topmost floor. That rectangular door was also half open and beyond was more light, more windows. She shoved it open. Stepped through.

Hot wind whipped it from her hand and slammed it behind her.

What iss thiss? A little human. Female. Tassty?

21

Elizabeth had fallen into the dazed alertness so familiar from her internship, awaiting an emergency to shock adrenaline through her body. Absently she split her attention. She watched her bond with Bri flare and subside with different colors. Noted the coming and goings of Marshalls and Chevaliers in the Map Room. Lady Knight Swordmarshall Thealia Germain had come to study the map, nodded in satisfaction and dragged her shorter, plumper husband away to bed.

When the door opened Elizabeth scented damp air, not Colorado high and dry air, and wispy mist floated in. It smelled damp. Weather wasn't indicated on the map, and she was most accustomed to animated weather maps. Not in Colorado anymore.

She observed the skirmishes from fence gap to gap ever eastward, raising new golden fenceposts and snapping the electric blue magical barrier into place. The fence itself was powered by the deaths of horrors and people fighting along the border.

Calli and Marrec, wearing black and silver, had left their children sleeping and guarded by the fey-coo-cus to drop by. Calli stared at Elizabeth, murmured. "I dreamt of a woman—but not you. Don't know who." She frowned and shook her head. "We all dream of this woman." Calli sniffed. "Rain's on the way." Studying Elizabeth, Calli said slowly, "In the dreams, the smell is of the sea, the Songs are sea chanties." She shook her head again. "Not you or Bri."

Elizabeth was tired enough to ask, "What is my Song?"

Calli chuckled. "Like I said, I see auras mostly. You and your Song are like sunrise over the Rocky Mountains."

"Thank you," Elizabeth said.

"Koz is fighting," Marrec said.

Elizabeth tensed, someone else to worry about. "Where?"

He pointed to a tiny white shield with a red trident bobbing in the thick of the action, fighting with Alexa's force.

Elizabeth continued to pay close attention to the orange-red shields. Faucon and his people. He was an equal opportunity employer. When she stifled a giggle, she recognized her exhaustion. But she was reluctant to leave, as if she saw history in the making. Surely when the Lladranans destroyed this Dark, Songs would be Sung, stories would be told forever. Lorebooks would be written.

Both Calli and Marrec kissed her cheek before they left.

No one told Elizabeth to leave. All behaved as if she had every right to be there, witnessing the need of the Lladranans, learning the perils of their land.

"Ah!" The small exclamation huffed from a huge Sword-marshall beside her. He strode to the top of the map, stretched out a long arm and said, "We have leagues more of border fence, have connected fenceposts. Too bad we can only build the fence when horrors invade. Only two large stretches to go and our country will be safe from the greater horrors for a piece." His leathery face creased into a ferocious smile. "Then we will *hunt*." He rubbed his hands. "Take the war to the Dark's nest. Destroy it!"

Jerking his head at Elizabeth and toward the door where people filed into a steady rain, he moderated his tone, which had rung with glee and seemed to resound through the very Castle. "Tonight's invasions are ended. Go to bed now, Exotique Medica. The warriors will straggle in depending upon their energy and Power and their volarans' Distance Magic. You'll be needed tomorrow." He was shepherding her out and she glanced back to see the largest bit of red-orange shoot southward, Faucon come to claim dinner in the middle of the night. Her stomach was accustomed to strange meals at strange hours.

"Needed tomorrow," she repeated.

The Swordmarshall took her elbow, hurried with her from the Map Room into the rain and across Temple Ward to the cloisters. "We only lost four, and no more are seriously wounded, or we would have seen healing circles, but there will be minor wounds. There's continuing sickness in the city."

Despite her faint protests, he escorted her to her door, bowed and left. But the night air had awakened her. Her nerves hummed with a anticipation. Faucon Cruess was flying her way.

She turned and descended the tower stairs, out to Temple Ward and saw more than one window of Faucon's suite lit for his homecoming. She was still expected. She heard the rush of the first warriors returning. A moment later, Alexa's grumbling came. "You're as tired as I am. You shouldn't be carrying me."

A swat as if on muscular buttocks. "I'm not tired. Yet," Bastien replied. His quick, wet footfalls sounded from the open door of the Assayer's Office to Elizabeth's right and she faded into the deep shadows of the cloister.

"Damned wild magic black-and-white," Alexa muttered.

When Bastien jogged past, wife over a large shoulder, he said, "Salutations, Elizabeth."

"Salutations, Elizabeth," Alexa said at the same time.

"A good night." Bastien's teeth flashed in a smile. "Good battles," he added with satisfaction. "Good results." Though the rain was falling harder, they appeared only damp. He didn't slow his pace as he entered the keep.

More voices rose from the Landing Field and Elizabeth considered her paths—through the Assayer's Office full of monster parts, God forbid. Or backtracking through the keep then threading a dripping maze, or down to Lower Ward and through the Chevaliers' Horseshoe Close. That was a long walk, but was mostly covered.

As soon as she passed through the gate to Lower Ward she saw two hawks perched on a stone gutter, grooming.

Salutations, Elizabeth, said Sinafinal.

Salutations, Elizabeth, said Tuckerinal.

With a flutter of wings, the feycoocus lifted into the air. *We will accompany you to the Landing Field so you don't get lost.*

Ha. Something in the fey-coo-cus' tones made Elizabeth think the beings didn't trust her to go there on her own.

Faucon gets a lady at last. Tuckerinal craned a look back at her, smirking around his beak.

"We're not staying," Elizabeth protested. But the magical shapeshifters were already flying across the ward. Elizabeth didn't spend any more breath on them, and when she reached the Landing Field, they bulleted into the sky and away.

Again Elizabeth took to the shadows. This time the weary Chevaliers crossing to the stables and Horseshoe Hall didn't discover her or paid her any mind. Nor did the returning Marshall pairs. A few radiated sexual tension as Bastien and Alexa had, but most stumbled wearily through the back door of the Assayer's Office and to their quarters.

She'd kept count of the little markers moving on the map, and soon all but two had returned. Faucon and one of his Chevaliers.

Long minutes later, she heard the tired, irregular beat of volaran wings and two dark shapes landed, separated into men and volarans, the larger supporting the other. Faucon had flown back to help one of his people.

Both winged horses drooped. Faucon's squires rushed from the stables where they'd waited. He waved them to his man, glanced her way. "Help Renny to bed and send for a Castle medica," Faucon ordered. "Let the stablehands tend the volarans."

Elizabeth wanted to volunteer her help, but hesitated. She'd never healed anyone by herself, and no medica had visited the Map Room. They'd be fresh, she wasn't. So she stayed where she was.

The three limped away to Horseshoe Close as the volarans folded bedewed wings and trudged into the stables.

Faucon crossed toward her, eyes gleaming.

"You're here. You stayed up and waited for me." His voice

was rougher than the usual lilt. Desire flamed in his eyes, ignited an answering sensuality in her. There was something about watching a man come to you, focused on you, intent on sex.

Heat sent langour through her limbs, tightened her breasts, her body readying for him.

She had to be the one to break the passion building between them, but she couldn't. She didn't want to. God help her, she was going to take what she wanted.

He stopped, gaze on hers, not a foot from her. Pheromones blazed off him, his aura fiery with passion.

Elizabeth swallowed. This was no sauntering, charming nobleman. This was a man who'd fought and killed monsters, had led men in battle and brought them out. He knew as much about fighting for life and against death as she did. More.

She couldn't move.

Braced, he reached for her hands, took them gently, lifted them, then kissed her cupped palms softly. Did she feel the touch of his tongue? She didn't know. The thought of that had her swaying toward him.

He kissed her, a press of lips on hers and the scent of him, man and stranger, trembled through her. She could hear his Song, loud with the percussion of sexual arousal. Yet there was more—the innate attraction women like her had for him. That was an undertone to all his thoughts and actions. More still, caring. Already, respect. That she yearned for.

His hands were on her, curving around her hips, sliding up to her breasts, and the heat and their Songs thundered in her ears. She wanted this, the lust of the man, the caring, the respect.

He touched her with knowledgable hands, sending her blood pressure high, stimulating a sex drive she'd thought dead.

He wanted her. He knew what she was, of her gift. He *admired* her gift.

Taking both her hands in one solid grip, he held them above her head as he rocked against her, nibbled her neck. "I need. I need," he panted.

She needed, too. Comfort, security, *passion*. Rational thought sizzling away in physical pleasure. "Yes," she said and rose tiptoe to run her tongue along his jaw. He groaned and turned his mouth as she'd wanted him to, and plunged his tongue into her and she tasted him and savored him and let the firestorm of passion rule until she shattered in release moments later.

Faucon came back to himself with a rush, followed by inward cursing. He'd *taken* her, a prized Exotique, with no finesse or tenderness. He opened his mouth to apologize, stopped. Looking down at her flushed face and curved smile, he felt the softness of her yielding body and knew enough about women that an apology might be an insult.

Just seeing her aftermath of pleasure, hearing her humming Song of satisfaction, aroused him again. A quick glance around the Landing Field confirmed that they were alone. Relief trickled through him. A couple of volarans were around, but most had retired to the stable, and volarans were uninterested in human sex unless it affected their flier and volaran status.

Would Elizabeth stay with him for the night, or let him stay with her? In Alexa's tower. He winced. Not optimal circumstances for an affair with an Exotique, in a chamber under Bastien and Alexa. Bastien had never quite forgiven Faucon for trying to claim Alexa. Then Faucon recalled dinner and eased. The night was late, or the morning was early, he'd persuade her to stay with him.

"Faucon?" Elizabeth opened her eyes and he thought he could see the hazel of them even in the dark.

Her wrists pushed against his grip and again he suppressed a curse. He'd pinned her against the wall, with hands and body. Sliding his hands down to her waist, he said, "One moment." Though his sex stirred again with their movements, he needed to show her tenderness more than another bout of mindless passion. No matter how good it had been.

Lifting her from him, he hummed a quick little ditty that most adolescent boys learned for circumstances like these.

She blinked rapidly. "Faucon!" The word was strangled.

Merde! He'd forgotten. Again. That she wouldn't be used to Lladranan ways. Heat crawled up his neck. "A little cleansing and drying spell," he muttered. "For both of us."

"I...see." She snorted. "Or rather *feel*. Very efficient and tidy."

"Ayes." He made sure she was on her feet, then managed his clothes, as did she.

She stood, head tilted, watching him. He brushed a kiss against her lips. Tracing a thumb over her cheek, he stared into her dilated eyes, couldn't fathom her emotions. "I didn't hurt you?" His primary concern.

"No. Ttho." Her smile was wobbly. "It was wonderful. You're a wonderful man."

His fingers drifted over her mouth. "Don't say 'but'. I

want to know you better." He couldn't help the flash of a grin, he felt triumphant. "In all ways." He hesitated. "Dinner awaits us." He dropped his hand.

A little sigh came. "I should think about this."

He wanted to say that she shouldn't, that she should follow her heart.

Taking a step away from her—more difficult than he expected—he offered the crook of his elbow. "Then, lady medica, let me walk you to dinner."

She chuckled, disconcerting him, like her earlier snort. "Ayes," she said. "I've found Lladrana very dangerous. You never know when you'll be accosted, say, on the Landing Field."

He didn't know how to respond. Again he thought an apology might be a misstep. "I can only say that my experiences on the Landing Field have been exquisite." He gave a half bow.

"Oh." She blinked and blinked again. "Ohhh."

"What?"

"I understand you better."

Another grin he couldn't suppress. "Of course you do. A benefit of lovemaking."

"Really?"

"Ayes."

She frowned, and he thought he heard her intricate Song as she considered the matter.

It had stopped raining. Calculating the paths he could take, he opted for the most romantic. "Have you been through the maze?"

"No, I came to the Landing Field by way of Lower Ward and the stables."

He smiled down at her, covered her hand tucked into his arm with his own. "The hedges of the maze are verdant, and the brithenwood tree in the garden flowers early and stays long. The scent is wonderful."

"Won't it be wet?"

"The paths are large enough to accommodate two." Especially since she was smaller than most Lladranan women. He glanced at the sky and the heavy clouds shrouding half the moon. "Though there will be more rain, so we'll walk instead of dally." He kissed the top of her head, smelled the scent of soap and persperation and Elizabeth. Swallowed his yearning. He hoped their meal would be good.

Then he led her into the maze.

"Ohhh," she sighed.

"Diamonds of rain silver in the moonlight, giving life to the new leaves."

She sniffed. "The fragrance *is* lovely."

Yes, her scent still lingered in his nostrils. He hoped he managed to eat and converse before he made love to her again.

Her body relaxed beside him and he realized how tense she'd been. She obviously didn't want to talk about sex or any stronger Song spinning between them. He should slow his wooing down, but his body clambored for more sex, more often. He'd wait and watch and judge the moments with her, and win her.

She was enchanting.

Bri jumped backward to the tower door, yanked. It wouldn't open. Stuck or locked shut. She whirled. More rustling came and black shadows whispered and shifted and s-t-r-e-t-c-h-e-d.

She pulled her dagger.

It laughed in her mind and a creaky wheeze came to her ears.

Something dry and scaly fastened around her wrist, flexed closed and she dropped the knife.

She looked down to see the smallest claw of a bird's foot holding her, trapping her.

"What are you?" she breathed out, and breathing in, caught its scent and magic and lingering evil.

Another chuckle in her mind, then a faint burp.

I am a roc, and I eat the evil. There was the clicking of a beak, the cluck of tongue. *Just finished snacking on bits of monster left behind. Sangvile.*

Bri stiffened. She'd been warned of the sangvile, heard the stories of its rampage.

This was its lair. Now the tower of this place will be my nest. The huge bird angled its head and tapped the ceiling and a large center portion slid open. Cold wind and rain blew in causing the bird to shriek a cry that made Bri's ears ring.

A place of Power that drew me. It tilted its head and Bri saw a gleaming sapphire eye the size of a dinnerplate. The saffron claw dropped from her wrist. *As the place drew you, healer-from-the-land-beyond-the-winds.*

Rain slicked down Bri's face like lost tears.

Or pehaps we drew each other, too. You will nest here, too. Her lips were nearly too cold to answer. "Maybe."

Another, quieter bird-caw of laughter. *Surely.*

It moved to the middle of the room and stepped to the floor above, hopped to the top of the stair tower to the right. Lightning struck behind it and the jeweltoned colors of its plumage dazzled Bri: ruby, emerald, sapphire, gold wing feathers, midnight-blue-black legs, golden head, a body the same color as its wings.

Fantastic.

Lightning and a surreal scene—a bird perched atop a tower crennelation, wings raised.

You should sleep in the room below, where I ate all the sangvile remnants and Sang the place clean, it said, fluffed a huge bush or two that looked torn from their roots, and with a melodious hum, closed the ceiling.

Bri just stood, shivering and cold and damp. Wondered if she was dreaming or if another aspect of this weird place had just hit her over the head. Again. She'd always had a good and flexible imagination, but lately it had been stretched so far out of shape that she didn't know if she'd ever see things right.

"Bri, Bri!" Zeres's irascable voice boomed over the thunder. His heavy, rapid footsteps sounded on the staircase.

"Here," she called weakly, cleared her throat and yelled louder. "Here!"

The door shivered under his strength, jumped open. "Damn stuck door," he grumbled. He looked at her but stood at the threshold, didn't come into the room. "This place stinks of sangvile." His gaze darted around, then his expression eased. "There was one here in Castleton a year back."

"Yes." Bri's voice sounded odd to her ears. "I think it laired here."

He sniffed, sneezed, took a rag from his pants pocket and blew his nose. "Smells like something else, too." He frowned.

"Roc," Bri said faintly.

"Roc!"

The ceiling slid aside and a head thrust down, saffron beak clicked. *You Sing for me?*

Zeres's mouth fell open. He stepped back. Thumps and swears as he missed a couple of steps. He didn't return.

She hurried down.

The ceiling clunked into place. The roc laughed in her mind.

Zeres stood panting, Bri listened to his groans, but knew he wasn't hurt. "Roc." He swore, clumped a few steps down. Cursed again, entered the second level, gave a liquid snort. Limping into the middle of the room, he surveyed it. "Roc." He shook his head. "Not a smidgeon of sangvile in this chamber. Some in the room below, and up there," he jerked his chin up, "but nothing here."

"The roc said it ate the sangvile, then cleaned the room."

Zeres grunted. He shook his head again. "Roc." Lifting his brows, he said, "Something about you Exotiques draws magical creatures. Fey-coo-cus. Volarans. *Rocs*, by the Song." He went up to a window and squinted at it, waited until after the next boom of thunder to speak. "Don't fancy goin' back out into the rain to your pretty little house."

Standing there in the dark, with squares of windows light against the night beyond, cold drips of rain dribbling down her body, one of the windows whining in the wind, Bri agreed.

Muttering under his breath, Zeres stripped off his cloak, spread it on the floor, which the next bolt of lightning showed to be an attractive wooden parquet pattern.

"Girl, get over here and I'll teach you a Song to boost your body heat like a blanket all night."

"The roc said this *is* a place of Power. I feel it, too."

Silence from the corner.

"You were going to teach me. To be honest with me."

"The spell is called Sinedre, a simple refrain."

"This is a place of Power?"

"Okay." He said the English word most Lladranans knew irritably. "Mebbe if I let myself, I'd feel some Power."

"Healing Power," Bri insisted.

"Specifically?"

"Yes. What might cause that?"

"I dunno. Mebbe I'll sleep on it. You want a parta this cloak or not?"

"Wood isn't as cold as stone." Bracing one hand against the wall, Bri pulled off her shoes. Her toes curled. Her socks were damp, too.

"Stone's under the wood."

"The roc's nesting on top of the stair tower. Does that make it a she?"

Zeres grunted, rolled to put his back toward her. "Don't wanna thinka the roc t'night, either."

Bri padded over to him, sat on the cloak and shivered as she felt the warmth of it. Magical cloak. Of course. It was dry, too. "So how does this spell go?"

He Sang and his rich voice so amazed her that she missed the first few words. "Again?"

"You Exotiques are so slow. Child's play for medicas." He Sang again, and Bri could almost see motes of Power gathering around him, encircling him, encasing him, keeping him warm. Her feet felt like blocks of ice. She licked her lips and Sang.

Magic sifted down on her, warmed her like an electric blanket. "Are rocs nocturnal birds?"

Zeres gave a fake snore.

No, whispered in her mind. *We will talk in the morning.*

22

Raine Lindley, once of Best Haven, Connecticut, and now of the Open Mouthed Fish tavern somewhere *else*, scrubbed the iron pot hard. She tried to ignore her distorted image in the dented silver pitcher that was the owner's pride and joy.

She hated seeing even a little of herself, particularly her face. She didn't look younger than her twenty-seven years anymore. Lines had sprouted around her eyes and mouth.

That happened when a person was yanked from one world to another, and didn't know the language, or look like the natives.

She kept dirty. If she washed her hair it showed dark brown instead of black and her skin was whiter than these people had—Lladranans, she'd figured out in the six odd months she'd been here. Nothing she could do to disguise her dark green eyes except keep a hank of hair in front of her face. The locals thought she was from "that filthy city full of foreigners some leagues down south" and didn't have all her wits.

She thought of last night's dream and shuddered. It wasn't one about ships. No, the nightmare held overtones of the greatest mistake of her life.

She was in her Granny Fran's attic staring at The Mirror. The Mirror had fascinated her from childhood, mostly because of the carved gilded frame. That frame didn't look like any she'd ever seen, not stiff flowers and garlands, but graceful curves that reminded her of rolling waves out on the ocean.

Perhaps that's why her great-grandfather had brought it back from his two-week-long trip to France. He'd moved from Boston to Best Haven, Connecticut, and founded the shipbuilding business. Then the Lindleys had prospered.

In the dream, Raine hunched down as if she might step through the frame.

Don't do it. DON'T DO IT! Raine shrieked in her head.

At home The Mirror had haunted her so much that she'd decided to give it to her newly engaged brother. She was transporting it on the new boat she'd designed. The wind had come up with the half-heard singing that had reverberated through her night and day for a week.

When the storm had arisen, it had whirled her small boat, her, and The Mirror all together, then her *through* The Mirror. She'd watched the boat splinter, The Mirror shatter into tiny shards, then had landed in a cold, seething ocean of green. Here.

Not on Earth anywhere.

She tried not to think of home, of her brothers and her father who would be grieving for her. Of her old, incredibly wonderful life she'd been so bored with.

The kitchen door opened. "Well, what do we have here?"

It was Travys. He grinned with broken-toothed hatred. An atavistic fear crawled up her spine. She always dreaded that he might bite her and if he did, her heart would give out.

She'd done nothing to deserve his hatred, but he'd taken an instant dislike to her. Since she was a pot-scrub girl and he was a valued client, she could do nothing but avoid him. She knew instinctively that if she fought with him it would be to the death. He was a big man for a Lladranan, and they were bigger than Earth people.

Always bad luck when he saw her. This was the first time he'd actually come into the kitchen.

He loomed over her, massive and sneering. "Lookin' as ugly and feebleminded as usual." He sniffed. "Stink, too."

He should talk. He reeked of fish guts and some horrible seaweed he chewed. Grabbing her hair, he stared at her.

She quivered and he smiled.

The door swung open again and the dour woman who owned the tavern entered. "Please, Travys. She has work to do, a sink full of pots."

Eyes narrowed, Travys looked at the woman, then back at Raine. He hacked up a gob of phlegm and spit into the sink water, then strolled out.

What was she going to do?

When she'd first awakened on the beach one winter night she'd thought she'd somehow crossed the Atlantic and landed in a backward costal town of France. The language was sort of French.

But that hadn't happened. She spoke a little French and no one could understand her.

It had taken her a full month to understand and believe she was no longer on Earth.

This was the third, and best, place she'd found. The owner of the Open Mouthed Fish gave her food, shelter, clothing, a job. No money—but not many people had hard coin. Travys did. He was the caretaker for the grounds called Seamasters' Market, where fairs were held twice a year. A wealthy man in the one-street village off the pier.

Then there was her sickness. If Raine got more than a couple of miles away from the ocean her strength and energy faded, nausea claimed her stomach and throat. Once she'd pushed herself a few steps too far up a hill and had passed out. She thought rolling back down was the only thing that had saved her. This tavern was built on a pier and she felt almost normal.

She didn't want to put her hands back into the water where the slime of yellow phlegm-spit still floated.

She had no choice.

The tavernkeeper was watching. Forcing her gorge down, not daring to use the rag, Raine flicked the congealed saliva out of the sink. It dribbled down the side of the rough wooden cabinet. Raine rubbed it with her own skirt.

The woman nodded. "Watch yourself," she said, then left, shaking her head and muttering "Half-breed half-wit."

Elizabeth woke before dawn to a man's knowledgeable touch on her breasts, passion sizzling through her. Faucon. He explored her, and she let her own hands roam and stroke and arouse, and they joined and shattered together.

Limply, she stared at him, lying panting with closed eyes. How beautiful he was. He came from a beautiful race, that golden skin, the slight slant of eyes and sculpted features.

Irises that ranged from amber to near black, hair that was black, but held shades of dark red, brown, bronze.

He opened his eyes—brown like bittersweet chocolate. His lips curved. Picking up her fingers he brought them to his lips. "You are thinking. Don't."

"I—" She didn't want to say any of the things she should. *I won't be staying. My life's not here. You're not the man I loved*—and how that would hurt *this* man. A tiny flame of emotion flickered in the depths of her. Perhaps he could be a man she loved. She extinguished it.

He set her hand on his heart—still pumping rapidly after their activity—and stroked her cheek. "Let us live in the moment, Elizabeth. I am Chevalier enough to do that."

Memories of the long and hideous night before flashed back. Four dead in battle, a small casualty of war, but she mourned wasted life. Her entire being fought against wasted life. She hadn't truly *enjoyed* her life, for far too long.

Her muscles were loose, her body well pleasured, but heat rose. She slid her hand down him and liked how his breath caught, how his cheeks tinted red under that beautiful skin and his eyes gleamed. "I think we'll find moments like this often," he said.

Why not? Too many why nots. She wanted more of the expression she found in his eyes when he made love with her, looked at her.

She kissed him again and when he pulled her next to him and she felt the warmth of him and strength of him and smelled the exotic scent of him, she smiled and slept.

Bri grunted as she rose from the floor. She was less sore than the morning before. Since the tower floor was equally hard as that of the tavern, she decided that the lingering magic here somehow cushioned her. Or the simple fact that she was in a place that felt "right" eased her mind as much as the floor made her muscles ache. Though the morning was cold outside, it was pleasant in the wood-paneled room.

She'd rolled from the corner where Zeres still snored. When she stood and shook herself, shock ran through her as she saw she'd slept in the center of a pentacle. Looking around, it was evident that this was a magical workroom. She sniffed. It smelled of old incense, cool morning coming from a broken window, and roc.

"Roc," she called. There was the rumbling of a being fending off waking and huddling into sleep, but nothing else. She decided the roc wasn't a morning person. Neither was she, usually, especially not unless she had a solid seven hours of sleep, but the air in here invigorated her.

She sent a gently questing probe to Elizabeth to reassure and discovered her twin sleeping in a man's arms.

Bri sat down hard on the floor. Shit. Did Elizabeth know what she was doing?

Of course not.

Should Bri say anything to her?

Definitely not.

But Bri bit her lip as her heart twinged. Elizabeth had loved and admired and respected Cassidy. When he'd dumped her, her self-image had taken a blow. Not to mention that she was coming off the end of a *long*, stressful program of study.

Bri wondered who Elizabeth was with and only one name came to mind, Faucon Creusse. His name brought his image and Bri admired Elizabeth's taste. Bri only wished she didn't see heartache for one or both of them at the end of the road.

Elizabeth would never give up her life on Earth for Lladrana, would she?

Bri didn't know. She went to the window and looked out on the green plains rolling to green hills rising in the distance. Lladrana was beautiful. The sound of wings came as a volaran and rider flew past. And fascinating.

But deadly.

The scrape of the door on the lowest level shot anxiety up her spine.

"Bri?" It was Sevair, and she wasn't quite ready to meet him. When she'd realized Elizabeth was wrapped around some guy and loose with the boneless sleep of after-excellent-sex, an image of herself had come to mind. With the very strict and upright Sevair. Of all people.

He couldn't be less like the rock musician, whom she'd thought, once, was perfect for her. A ripple of an idea that Sevair was as thorough and deliberate in his lovemaking as he was in everything else sent warmth down her nerves.

She squashed it. Neither Elizabeth nor she needed the complication of a Lladranan lover.

Absolutely no. She cleared her throat and answered, "Upstairs." More wariness welled. How would the City-masters feel when she told them that she didn't want the pretty town house, preferred this tough old tower in the city wall?

Another scan of the room soothed her. It was beautiful, wooden wainscoting at the bottom, cream-colored finished stone above, windows. Simple, natural material. No fuss. Just to her taste.

Sevair climbed the stairs rapidly, a man in great shape. No, she wouldn't think about the shape of any of him.

"Sangvile." He sucked in a shocked breath on the floor below, raced up. He'd recognized the remnants of the monster?

Then he was in the room, lifting her off her feet, keeping her close as he scanned the room.

These Lladranan men moved *fast*.

He sure was solid. Not a pinch of fat on the man. And he was big, shoulders, length of leg. Hard, too, her fingers on his biceps barely dented the muscle.

"At least you weren't totally alone." He stared at Zeres, who was wheezing and struggling to an elbow.

She stared into Sevair's brown-black eyes. "I, uh." May as well just come straight out with it. Lladranans should understand, shouldn't they? Who the hell knew? With all the events her judgement was totally screwed.

"This place called to me. I like it." She cleared her throat and beamed her brightest smile. "I've found my spot in Castleton."

He didn't slide her down his body, too bad. Plunked her on her feet. He was frowning, but a quick check of his personal Song showed it was calm, if a little irritated.

When he glanced at her from under lowered brows, Bri noted that the fierce look made him even more attractive. Nice.

Rubbing his temples with one large hand, Sevair sighed. "Why should we have thought an Exotique would want what we made for her?" He shook his head. "As unpredictable as a fey-coo-cu."

"It's a lovely house. A beautiful house," Bri assured him. "It's just not for me."

"We'll keep it for you and Elizabeth. Let me look this tower over."

Bri gave a little cough. "There's a roc nesting atop the stair tower."

Sevair stopped examining the room and turned his head slowly to stare at her. He closed his eyes. Opened them. The stare returned. "Of course there is." He flung up his arms in a gesture of surrender, went to door and leaned on the threshold, this time rubbing his whole face.

Then he sent her one last cool glance and tromped down the stairs. His footsteps were hard and steady, like the man, ringing against the stone steps. His disgusted noise floated up along with some loud thumps, probably messing with the broken outside door.

Bri looked at Zeres, but he didn't meet her eyes. "Too early for me."

She tapped a toe. "You are the strangest mixture of coward and hero."

"Ha!" He gathered his cloak, rolled over. "I'm human."

She found Sevair in the dark strip of kitchen in the back of the first floor, surveying the "appliances." Without the spells to keep food hot or cold or whatever, they were simply cabinets.

As she watched, he spread his hand on one and Sang a slow, brittle tune. The cabinet glowed blue for an instant, then subsided. A refrigerator, cold box, Bri deduced.

Then he moved on to the next and a fast, bumpy tune— hot box to keep things warm. Excellent.

When he looked up, beads of sweat showed at his temples. He'd used more Power than he was accustomed to, then. To make the tower better for her. She thought of all the hard work everyone had put into the house and winced inwardly. "*Merci.*"

He grunted, reached for the hobo bag slung across his chest and hanging on his hip, and pulled out two packets. Delicious scents came to her nose. He handed one to her. At least she could eat here, not like yesterday, and alone with Sevair, not a bunch of judging medicas.

Her mouth watered as she removed rough paper from the wrapped food, found a thick pastry pocket. When she bit in, the tang of eggs and crunch of bacon exploded into her mouth. She chewed the first mouthful fast, swallowed. "*Merci.*"

He sent a level gaze at her. "When I realized you weren't in your house, I considered that you'd been out all night again."

He was taking care of her. And laying a guilt trip on her, too. Like her parents would. Her parents! She sent a mental probe zinging toward the Castle. The Circlets weren't there.

Sevair was leaning on the counter, eating, watching her. Nope, nothing like her parents except he was a responsible, caring man.

Don't go there.

Another swallow. "*Merci* again. I was just checking whether Marian and Jaquar are back from—"

"Bossgond's Island. I asked Exotique Alyeka to keep me informed." Strain lines bracketed his mouth. "I don't depend on anyone else."

Alexa. The Lladranans said her name funny, and Sevair had lost a trusted assistant to the Dark.

"You aren't the only one to be betrayed," she found herself saying.

Their eyes met and in that moment they shared hurt. Then he looked away and tidied up his wrapper, took hers and put it in his bag that he lifted off his shoulder and set on the counter.

Hands on lean hips he glanced around the room. "This will need work."

Did she catch a tiny sigh? "You don't have to—"

He raised his brows. "The care of the Exotique for the Cities and Towns is the charge of the heads of the guilds and the Citymasters. We will provide for you. Perhaps Elizabeth will use the house. She won't stay up at the Castle under the Marshalls' thumbs forever. She is a medica, not a Chevalier."

Bri thought of Elizabeth and Faucon. "I wouldn't bet on that."

Sevair narrowed his eyes. "Something else has happened."

Straightening, she nodded. "My sister."

His mouth tightened. "I rarely told secrets on my little sister, either."

"I'm the younger," Bri said, irritated.

His grin flashed.

She lifted her chin. "By two minutes."

With a chuckle he shook his head and left the room.

There was a melodious "caw," the clatter of claws on the street outside, Sevair's gasp.

Bri hurried from the kitchen, past Sevair whose mouth was hanging open as he looked out the door, and into the cul de sac where the roc stood, stretching, preening.

In the small, paved area they stared at each other. The sun had risen, but they were in the shadows. It would be midmorning before direct sunlight touched this place.

Still, the roc seemed to glitter. No, that wasn't quite the word. Neither was glow. It was more as if light was drawn to it and reflected off its feathers to give it a larger than life, more colorful, appearance. Though it was large enough, twice Bri's height for sure, and she and Elizabeth stood five feet eight inches. They were shorter and slimmer than most Lladranans. But the roc...Bri closed her mouth.

She and the roc were the only ones in the small courtyard, but she sensed others watching from safely inside their homes.

I am Nuare.

I am Bri.

It shifted, opened wings longer than its body.

I am female.

Bri swallowed. *Will you be raising your young in the tower?* She liked the place, had slept well there, wanted it for her own, but in a fight between a big alien bird and herself, she figured she'd be running to the pretty house.

I will not lay eggs this year, though I may mate in the autumn.

Something in her mind tone made Bri take a step back. *Ayes?*

This year you Exotiques will fight the Dark. Either you will win, or you will die and the country will be overrun by monsters. I and my kind will leave for another land.

Bri swallowed hard, stood straight. *I do not stay. We, my sister and I, will find the cure for the sickness affecting the people here, but our parents will grieve for us if we do not return.*

The roc clicked her beak, but said nothing. Once again she took a couple of steps and opened her wings.

Sevair cleared his throat. She angled her body so she could see him and keep the roc in view.

He bowed with much elegance and flourishing. "My apologies for interrupting your conversation, Madame Roc. Your lovely Song graces our city. Welcome."

Smooth talker. Bri hadn't expected that.

Nuare preened. *Thank you, He-Who-Shapes-Stone-In-The-Sky.*

Sevair blinked. "Sevair Masif, at your service."

Sevair Massif. I will roost on the tower roof, above the Exotique's nest. Bri, we will fly together later. Now I am hungry and I will hunt. She spiraled beautifully up into the sky, cast them in shadow, then flew over the wall. Bri heard her heart pounding.

"A young, female roc has come to roost in Castleton," Sevair said thoughtfully. "You Exotiques are certainly interesting." He scrutinized the square stone building jutting out at a right angle from the city wall.

"Ronteran's tower. I should have known."

"What? Who?" Bri asked.

Sevair lifted a shoulder, dropped it. "Supposedly resided in by the Circlet who helped found and build Castleton. It is said to be haunted, or cursed." A corner of his mouth quirked up. "Or blessed."

Bri studied the tower in the light. Solid and rectangular, with the small octagonal stair tower on the right, it looked like it would last for several more centuries. Now and then there was a glint of crystal in a stone. Two large, fancy iron brackets held two more roughly spherical crystals.

"Abandoned for a decade," Sevair said. "Such is its lifecycle. Restored, then abandoned." He shrugged. "Sounds like it will be my turn to restore it." He frowned at her. "I'm still not happy about you staying where the sangvile laired." He glanced upward. Nuare was returning with a large branch. "The roc will offer some protection." His lips thinned. "I've heard they like eating remnants of the horrors. Rocs like spiders. She might have found the sangvile particularly tasty."

"Nuare was munching on old sangvile bits when we met."

"Nuare," Sevair breathed the word softly. Stepped closer to Bri, touched her shoulder. "She did not tell me her name. You should remember that names are important here in Lladrana. They can be used against you, Bri."

She opened her mouth, shut it. "Bri is not my real name. It is a shortening."

He nodded. "A nickname. And I would suppose that Elizabeth has a nickname she thinks of herself as."

Bri doubted that Elizabeth had thought of herself as "Beth" for a long time. Well, they both had middle names, too. She tilted her head. "What of you? Is Sevair Masif your full name?"

"Yes, but it is not my childhood nickname. I could be Summoned by the formal name, but not coerced to do anything else since I still think of myself as my young name." His smile was a curve of the lips and sadness in his eyes. "My family is gone. There are precious few who might recall my nickname."

Rustling came from above, echoed a little in the cul de sac. Sevair scanned the small street. "At least the neighborhood is good, if not filled with people of Power. What is it with Exotiques and towers?" grumbled Sevair.

"We don't have them," Bri replied absently.

"What!"

She glanced at him, noted his clothes were already coated with dust and dirt.

"You're an architect." She made a sweeping gesture encompassing the city as well as the tower. "This style of building went out of fashion centuries ago for us. Where we live we don't have towers."

"You tear down the past!"

All too often, but Bri wasn't going to get into that. "The area where we lived belonged to a nomadic people. They didn't build towers." No need to get into American history, either.

"We need the walls and towers for security against the Dark. We have always been conscious of peril."

Bri believed that.

She followed him into the dim room. He studied the door, shaking his head. "It will have to be replaced." He glanced at the pointed arch of the door opening, then the rectangular wooden door, grunted. With ease he picked up the door and set it to one side of the threshold. "We'll get a new one today." His look and smile at her was brief. "Everyone donated their services for the house. They'll do so again."

Bri winced. "I'm sorry about the house, it, um...."

"It just doesn't suit you," Sevair said mildly. "We had hoped..." He shrugged. "A house must suit its owner."

Bri decided not to point out that she wouldn't be owning any property in Lladrana.

Then he stepped into the center of the chamber and did a slow circle, eyes closed. Checking the Song? The ambience of the place? Never in a million years could Bri imagine a U.S. construction worker or straight male architect closing his eyes to *feel* a place. At least not with someone else around. She smiled. Fascinating.

Sevair opened his eyes, nodded. "The roc has been here, cleaned the place up from the sangvile." He walked around the walls, nodded at the carving on the wainscoting. "Very nice. Needs to be cleaned and oiled." He glanced at the floor and Bri noticed that the stone had little crystals in it like the blocks in the outer wall, and there were no chips.

"Good work by Ronteran," Sevair said. He went to the far right back corner, and opened the door of a triangular cabinet that rose the full height of the room. "Toilet and sink," he said, pulled the flush chain and nodded when the plumbing worked. "This might not be too tough or expensive a job," he said and headed up the stairs.

The city alarm bell rang. Sevair stopped, tensed.

Elizabeth's urgent mental voice came to Bri. *Come to the Castle at once. One of the independent Chevaliers was wounded in battle last night and the medicas here have seen nothing like it.*

Like what? Elizabeth wasn't usually so imprecise.

I haven't seen anything like the injury, the sickness, either, she said grimly.

Injury or sickness? Goosebumps rose on Bri's skin, and the hairs on the back of her neck.

Both, Elizabeth said.

"You're needed at the Castle," Sevair said, evidently understanding the pattern of the tolling bell.

We fly! screeched Nuare, sticking her head in the door.

Who was that? Elizabeth asked sharply.

The twist in Bri's gut eased a little. *Wait until you see.*

Come now, Elizabeth ordered, then hesitated. *It's bad. Marian and Jaquar are on the way.*

I'm coming. Bri ran out.

23

Sevair followed, brow knit in concentration. "I'll set everything up with the head of the guilds for work on your tower.
See you later."

Mud had already landed in the cul de sac, lifted again when
she saw Nuare. The volaran's Song shrieked rage and fear.

"Mud!" Sevair called. His brows dipped farther and Bri
could *feel* the Power he sent toward Mud, trying to contact
her mind, merge with it, control the volaran's unruly emotions.

Stupid volaran. I will not eat it, said Nuare. *It is wild
volaran, too spicy.*

"I'm sure that's a great comfort," Bri muttered. Nuare
had hunched down, stuck out her leg for Bri to mount.

I will not eat you, either. Unless the Dark taints you.

Bri put her foot back on the ground. "What!"

Nuare shook her wings. *We must hurry.*

Bri saw a soothing Sevair ambling down the street toward a nervous Mud.

Nuare screeched. Sevair flung himself on Mud and hung on as the volaran zoomed into the sky. Bri figured she no longer had a volaran.

Now! Nuare demanded.

Bri stepped on the outthrust leg, slid onto the roc's back and kept slipping down. This wouldn't work.

Arms around my neck, human!

Adventure was not all it was cracked up to be, didn't match the imagination. But then, most wanted *safe* adventure. Bri threw her arms around Nuare and held on tight.

The roc took off faster and at a steeper angle than Mud.

Of course. I am made for flight, unlike those clumsy horsethings. She turned her head and Bri saw a whirling sapphire eye. Nuare's beak clicked. Bri realized it was supposed to be reassuring. Wasn't.

Good that you smell nice, Nuare said. *Like special Power and strange land. I will not be eating you.*

Uh, do you think you should be going to the Castle?

I have eaten for the day. Castle volarans and Chevaliers and Marshalls who fight the Dark are safe. They must live.

"Okay." Bri let out a breath, inhaled. The roc smelled good, too. "We agree."

Then they landed in Temple Ward, Nuare making a sensation. Elizabeth waved from the cloister outside the keep.

All the volarans in the courtyard launched into the sky, carrying surprised Chevaliers and Marshalls.

Bri controlled her fall off Nuare.

We must practice, said Nuare. *Your grip was too tight. A small rope for you to hold would be good, perhaps a perch for you.* She roughened her feathers and began preening again. *I will hold court here and discuss matters with the Marshalls.*

"Ayes," Bri said. She waved at Nuare and ran across the ward.

For a moment she couldn't attract Elizabeth's attention from the bird. "What's that?"

"Who? A roc." *Her name is Nuare,* she added mentally.

Elizabeth shook her head. "Amazing. Beautiful." She focused on Bri and her expression turned intense and grim. "Come on."

But by the time they reached the healing room, a medica with a strained expression on her face was pulling a cover over a young woman's face.

"No!" Elizabeth cried. "I just left her for a moment."

There were three medicas in the room along with Alexa and the middle-aged woman who led the Chevaliers. All the medicas shook their heads.

"She died as soon as you crossed the threshold of the room," a medica said.

Elizabeth put on her doctor's face and walked up to the corpse, removed the sheet. She glanced at Bri. "Come on, I want to examine the body."

Bri opened her mouth to protest. Shut it. She wasn't used to autopsies. When she'd worked in refugee camps, she'd lost patients, but when they were gone, they were gone. Cause of death was usually pretty clear.

Elizabeth had already set her hands on the body and was frowning in concentration. She, of course, had had a lot of experience with dying, death and autopsies. Bri wasn't going to let her sister down.

Since life had flown from the Chevalier, Bri didn't bother

to place her hands where they'd do the most good, but set them beside Elizabeth's.

"Look inside her," Elizabeth said.

Bri looked.

"See that wisp of gray?" Elizabeth asked.

"Like the frink sickness." A spider web covered the inside of the body, diminishing as they watched, and seemed more spiritual than physical.

"I believe so," Elizabeth said. "But more virulent."

"Something she picked up on the battlefield," Alexa said. "I've spoken to her friends. She was healthy before the battle, has been in the Castle all year so wasn't exposed to the frink sickness. We have no frinkweed here. She took only a minor wound, a small lash of soul-sucker tentacle." Alexa pointed to a suckered welt along the woman's neck. "I've had plenty like this myself. But once she came back from the battle, she went to sleep, she fell ill and feverish and never awoke."

"Check out the wound from the inside," Elizabeth said.

Bri sent her vision to the slight wound, saw a gray slime and a small nodule like a kidney bean.

Elizabeth said, "I would extrapolate that this is a modification of the frink sickness in a more toxic form."

"Sounds right," Bri said. As Elizabeth once more covered the body, Bri stepped away from the table. As experiences went, this hadn't been too bad, though the young Chevalier's pretty face touched her and she grieved for the loss of life.

"The conclusion is that we have an additional danger on the battlefield now," the Chevalier leader said. "A fatal disease. How and why she got it, we don't know." Her lips compressed. "No one else seems to be ill, but I want the medicas to examine *everyone* who was in that battle." She stumped out.

"A good idea," Bri said. She stared at Alexa.

The smaller woman huffed. "Oh, all right."

It took only a hand on Alexa's forehead for Bri to know the woman was at the peak of health.

Alexa sighed. "That's the examination?"

"What, you want more?" Bri asked.

"No. But now I know what's involved, I'll let you check Bastien."

Bri glanced at Elizabeth, managed a smile. "Elizabeth will give Faucon an in-depth examination."

Elizabeth's smile was slight. "He's healthy."

Marian knocked on the wooden doorjamb, then her bright blue gaze went past Bri and Elizabeth to the still form on the table and the auburn-haired Circlet's face folded into sad lines. Her face softened. "I have news of your parents. It's better if I tell you in the Circlets' Suite."

Bri nearly shot from the room, headed toward Marian and Jaquar's suite. She walked backward a little until Marian turned down the corridor and Elizabeth left the room, too, moving with an efficient, determined stride, a doctor's stride.

Marian wouldn't say a word until Bri and Elizabeth were seated with drinks in their hands. Tea, for both of them. It was quickest and easiest, though neither of them took more than a sip. Bri would rather have been pacing the room.

"Tell us," they said in unison, as Jaquar served himself and settled onto a couch with his wife.

"We found your parents exactly where your itinerary noted they would be, at the Buddhist temple." A smile lit

Marian's face. "Your father enjoyed the bell. He was easy to pinpoint. Your mother was close by."

A load of worry released and Bri let it out with a long breath, relaxing in the love seat. Elizabeth, next to her, sighed at the same time.

"They're well," Bri said.

Marian glanced at them, away. "From what I could see, they're better than well. They're wonderful."

"Yes, they are," Elizabeth said crisply. "But they won't be once they discover their beloved daughters have disappeared."

Tension infused Bri again. "Can we get back home before they return?"

"How are you progressing on discovering the cure for the frink sickness?" asked Jaquar, taking the role of bad guy.

Elizabeth held herself stiff and answered. "A third of the Marshalls and Chevaliers have gone to destroy the plants."

"—which may eventually stop the original infection," Jaquar said. "And the Circlets are also working on ways to kill the plants, but that doesn't help those who have already contracted the disease and are dying."

Bri couldn't sit still. She put down her tea with a little clinking of china, stood and circled the room. "So far only we and Zeres can cure the sickness. I *know* there's a way to do this, but I haven't been able to figure it out enough to teach others."

Elizabeth said, "The medicas and I have been studying the disease. It seems to be more of a…non-physical illness. The sickness is not vulnerable to anything any of us have continued to try—vitamins, herbal remedies, regular healings. Medicine. I doubt even antibiotics would help."

"It's a disease caused by the Dark," Jaquar said softly. "Preying upon the light of the Song within us all, using the darkness we all have inside us to spread and kill."

Elizabeth made an unintelligible noise as if she wanted to dispute his words and couldn't. She placed her cup and saucer carefully and quietly on a side table and stood, joining Bri.

Bri stopped her circuit of the room, glared at Jaquar, then Marian. "You won't send us back."

Jaquar raised a hand. "We simply don't have the energy to do so. The Power."

Bri narrowed her eyes. She didn't know if she believed him.

"Perhaps we do," Marian looked at Bri steadily, then to Elizabeth. "We might be able to find the Power, Marshalls and Chevaliers and Citymasters and volarans and all, to return you home. If we bankrupted our sources and left ourselves completely vulnerable to the Dark. Don't think for a minute that the Dark wouldn't sense what was happening and be ready to pounce."

Bri shared a look with Elizabeth, saw the torment she felt reflected in her twin's eyes.

Elizabeth lifted her chin. "Then we must send a message to our parents, for when they return home."

But Marian was shaking her head.

"I've read your book," Bri burst out, heard Elizabeth's same words echo with her own, let her twin go on.

"Marian, the Circlet Bossgond retrieved your PDA. Surely he can send a note."

"Bringing something here, something of a person you have a bloodbond with and who is standing next to you, is completely different from sending an object."

Bri felt a scream well inside her. Horror at the agony they'd put their parents through. Anticipated anguish.

"Then you'll have two very distracted healers," Elizabeth said.

"Surely, you of all people, Marian, should remember how anxious a person can be for someone at home," Bri pleaded.

Marian sighed, leaned against her husband. He took her hands in his. "I knew this conversation would be like this. Bossgond is working on sending objects through the Dimensional Corridor." Her mouth compressed, then she said, "But he will need a secure location."

"My condo!" Elizabeth said.

"Ayes. So you will need to come to Alf island with us to show us the location."

"Then we will," Bri said.

Marian stood. "I'm sorry to disappoint you, but we are trying our best. We will inform you when the time is right for you to take part in our experiment."

Elizabeth and Bri stood, too.

They ARE trying their best, Elizabeth sent Bri, unhappily.

And it might not be enough, Bri admitted. Neither of them liked failure, both of them had experienced it. Bri usually walked away, but Elizabeth had been stuck. How courageous her sister was.

We need to give them an incentive, Bri said.

The idea came to them both at once, Bri saw it in her sister's mind.

Bossgond likes good food, Elizabeth said.

Yes, give them the chocolate cake. Bri didn't think she could look at her father's birthday cake again, let alone eat it. *And it's time to check on the taters.*

Elizabeth turned to Marian and Jaquar, a not quite amused smile on her lips. "You take the cake."

"I beg your pardon?" Marian straightened. Jaquar looked confused.

"We're giving you the chocolate cake."

Marian's eyes widened. She licked her lips and swallowed, gripped Jaquar's hand. "Thank you."

"For Bossgond, too," Bri said.

"Thank you."

Bri forced the next words out of her mouth, at the same time as Elizabeth. "Please help us."

During the next three days Elizabeth established a schedule for herself and Bri that Bri was content to follow. They'd discussed contacting their parents for hours with Marian and Jaquar and the other Exotiques, then they both tried to put it out of their minds. All that could be done was being done, and the sooner they finished their own jobs, the Snap would come and all this might be moot.

On alternate mornings Bri went to the Castle with Zeres, still irascible, and suffered through learning and healing circles with the medicas. Otherwise she stayed in Castleton in the morning and worked with Zeres and his "unconventional" teachings. Since all medical science on Lladrana was strange, Bri had trouble discerning the differences in technique. Elizabeth didn't.

Elizabeth stayed up at the Castle, and, as far as Bri knew, slept in Faucon's bed, or he slept in hers. From the happy glow and sound of her mental thoughts and emotions, he was loving and supportive. Her self-confidence was reviving, and everyone at the Castle thought the affair was a good thing. Bri feared she or Faucon would be hurt, but kept quiet. Her twin was happy and that was the most important thing.

There were no more calls to battle, and the Chevaliers had divided into two camps regarding the strange sickness. One ignored it, like all the other horrors and dangers. The other seemed to dwell on the fact that something they couldn't see to fight might kill them later.

In the afternoons, Elizabeth flew down with Faucon on his volaran and held healing sessions—office hours—at the Castleton house. While they were working, Faucon was seeing to the business of his seaside estates.

Bri and Elizabeth and Faucon and whoever dropped by after the healing, ate early dinners. Visitors included City-masters, guild heads, town and Castle medicas, Circlets, Exotiques, a whole host of interesting people.

Then Faucon and Elizabeth would return to the Marshalls' Castle and Bri would take part in the evening saunter that Castleton folks liked. Or fly with Nuare.

Her second flight hadn't been long, either, just around the pleasant rolling hills and plains near the Castle, but had kept her eyes wide. Calli rigged a harness and seat for Bri that didn't bother Nuare. She knew she had no hope of controlling the big bird. So far her only options had been to deny the bird and herself flight, or to ruffle Nuare's feathers by choosing Mud. At least the roc respected her now. She thought.

Sevair wasn't quite underfoot, but definitely made his presence known. Often he ate with Elizabeth and Faucon and her, giving details of his work on the city hall or the city temple or the city walls, showing plans of new buildings or houses. Or explaining the renovation of Bri's tower to

Faucon. The work on her place—Bri was careful not to call it her home, even in her own mind—proceeded well. Nothing too major was involved except for the garden-level bathing area. That had been so dank and dark that Bri had only gone to the bottom of the stairs, taken one glance and returned to the upper levels. She'd never liked living below ground, always wanted somewhere she could look out over a town.

When Bri had spoken of transferring furniture from the town house, Sevair had nixed the idea. Instead, he'd had the Citymasters turn out their attics and the Castle chief of staff check the storage areas for good, solid furniture of the period when the original Circlet had lived there. Refinishing had taken only a couple of days. When the pieces were delivered Bri made a big deal over them, satisfying the Citymasters. Most didn't understand why she preferred the tower to the lovely house, but were happy that she'd found a place in their city.

And Bri had a housekeeper-maid! That was an unexpected pleasure. A young, large, simple, striped haired woman who liked working for an Exotique, was fascinated by the roc, and thought living "in a room of her very own" on the second floor of the tower was the best thing that ever happened to her. She liked having the small kitchen to herself, too, no one to direct or criticize her. One of the Citymasters had officiously assured Bri that the woman was reliable and a hard worker. As for Bri, the woman's delight at the wonders every new day gave her pleasure.

Then the Exotiques had pressured her into a party, to show her gratitude for the people of Castleton. Bri couldn't say no, and Elizabeth had reacted to the idea with amusement and enthusiasm. Bri *really* couldn't say no then. She invited everyone she'd ever met.

The party was a success. The guests seemed to accept that this living in a city wall tower was just another Exotique quirk and not a specific-to-Bri-oddness. Though she'd always prided herself on her uniqueness, acceptance felt good. She was in such a responsible position and felt for the first time that she should be an example for others. There was pride in that, too, that her gifts were recognized and prized here.

Later, Faucon sat next to Elizabeth and played with her fingers. Only the Exotiques, their men and Koz remained.

Alexa cleared her throat. Everyone looked at her, snuggled in Bastien's lap. It didn't undermine her authority. "We've consulted with the City and Townmasters," she said, and Bri's insides gave a little jump, Sevair stiffened beside her. He crossed his arms. "Is that so? Without me."

Frowning at him, sliding a sly look at Bri, Alexa said, "You've been busy with your own work and affairs and the discussion was all an extrapolation of your ideas." She hopped up and went to the three-foot map of Lladrana that was displayed at an incline on a table against one wall of the room. Large and green, it was animated like the huge battle map up at the Castle.

Alexa gestured everyone to come over. Bastien groaned in mock weariness and rose from the couch. Everyone followed. Bri rose last, Sevair close behind her.

"Show the sickness." Alexa tapped the map.

Large virulent red spots glowed on the map. Bri's stomach contracted. She'd really, really liked that map—now looking at it would never give the same pleasure. Another war map, this one for her, the medica.

"The frink sickness is worse than I'd imagined," Elizabeth said, eyes fixed on the red dots in the cities, the pinkish wash across the north. Her muscles tensed.

The only people who could cure it were Bri and Zeres and maybe herself. Nausea coated her stomach at her helplessness. She was thinking fast, considering, discarding options, wanted to talk fast, spill everything she thought, brainstorm. She'd learned not to do that. "Not a medieval plague, but we're working up to an epidemic. We must train the medicas."

"We've been trying," Bri said.

"Show frinkweed." A web the color of dead gray slugs laced the north, nearly to Castleton in the middle, ragged wisps reaching into the heart of Lladrana. Bri flinched.

Calli traced the lower end of the mountainous spur where she and Marrec lived. "Not here," she let out a breath. "Not near us or ours, thank the Song."

"You Exotiques kill the frinks by your very presence," Sevair said. "As if they can't take your alien Power."

Touching the depression to the southeast of her home, Calli said, "No frinkweed in Volaran Valley, either."

Marrec wrapped his arms around Calli. "We're going to lose more people in the north. Not many villages there anymore, just individual hermits too stupid to move, but there are more of them than I thought." He pointed to the northwest. "Where my old village stood and where we all fought so hard last year is clean." His breathing was uneven. "When this is done, it will be a prime location to live."

"Magnify the north," Bastien said. The top of the map was projected larger, in greater detail. Like Marrec had said, the frinkweed vanished into individual spots. Only three small villages were still inhabited below the towering mountains twice the size of the Rockies.

"Look at the border," Bastien said. "We've been fighting in the mountains all year long. The land with new fenceposts and where the magical forcefield is strong is pretty clear. Alexa's little feet are all over those battlefields." He kissed her hard.

"I've hosted Exotique visitors at both my estates," Faucon smiled, touching the map with a tender finger on a peninsular seaside place and a location in the middle of a curved bay in the south. "Such a great return for simple hospitality."

Marrec cleared his throat. "Don't know that it was simple. I had foods I'd never even heard of before."

Faucon shrugged. "I'm rich." He squeezed Elizabeth and she welcomed the comfort. Then he flung an arm around Bri and hugged her a moment, did the same to the other Coloradan women. "Wealthy in my friends."

"Ayes," Jaquar said. "Our islands have mostly been spared, too. Only the populated ones had frinkweed. Marian and Koz have visited many, so the spread of the frinkweed was halted. No sickness from the frinkweed spores yet, but that may be because of the Power of the Circlets."

"I hope so," Marian said.

Koz said with surprise, "*I* helped stop the spread of frinkweed!"

"Ayes," Jaquar said. He tapped the round island next to where Marian and Jaquar and Bossgond lived. "You bought this island. No frinkweed there now and I'm sure there was. What of your inland estates?"

Stepping closer to the map, Koz said, "Nope, neither of the others is infected either."

"Two?" Jaquar asked.

"My brother the real estate mogul," Marian said. "Nothing around Singer's Abbey, of course. No frinkweed *or* sickness."

"She takes care of her own," Alexa said grudgingly.

"Watch," Jaquar said. "Map, show the destruction of frinkweed." As they watched, a chartreuse green ate up a tentacle of gray. Jaquar's expression was bright with teeth and hard eyes. "We developed an insect that *loves* frinkweed."

"Already?" Marrec asked.

"When you have many personally threatened scholars working on a matter, individually or in groups, you get results," Marian said with satisfaction. Her forehead furrowed. "But there was something...Map display the pattern of the frinkweed only."

Again the deadly net, one thread being unraveled. Clear spots that they'd all listed.

"Troque city on the eastern escarpment has clear spots," Marian said.

"Calli's been to Troque," Marrec said.

"Oh." Marian pointed to a tiny coastal area north of the shared city of Krache on the southern border. "What of this?"

"No frinkweed around Seamasters' Market? That's odd," Faucon said. "There's only isolated patches of frinkweed in the south."

"But Krache has some, and sickness too, I noticed."

Faucon shook his head. "Don't know what caused it, then."

Alexa cleared her throat. "Tea anyone?" She'd gone to the sideboard and was pouring a cup of her own.

Elizabeth met Bri's eyes. *They want something. Here it comes.*

24

Yes, Bri said, then aloud, "You want me to make a round of the cities, don't you?" She held her body easily as she said the words, but Elizabeth knew Bri was scared. Bri traveled on her own timetable and for her own reasons.

"It would be best if Elizabeth went, too," Sevair said tightly.

Faucon slipped an arm around her waist. She didn't lean on him. She wanted to, but didn't. "If Elizabeth goes, I go."

"We need Elizabeth here," Alexa said.

"And…the length of time…," Marian hesitated.

"I'll say it," Alexa said unflinchingly. "I made the rounds, too, when I first came." Her mouth twisted. "'Hey-yah, hey-yah, Come See The Strange Exotique.'"

Bastien swept her up in his arms. "I thought that travel went extremely well."

"You would. Jerk. Put me down."

He slid her down his body, kept an arm around her. Alexa

continued, "We want you to spend several days in each major town, Troque, the Lladranan part of Krache, Coquille on the Coast, a few hours or two in the villages."

"Healing all the time," Elizabeth said stiffly, reached her hand out to her twin. Bri grasped it and Elizabeth felt dismay, loneliness. Glancing around, Elizabeth saw that all the Exotiques' men had a supportive grasp on their women. Bri stood alone.

Sevair hovered nearby, expression serious, eyes watchful as if ready to defend her; did she realize that?

"So she'll need to rest, too," Alexa said.

"Which means I won't be part of the experiment to leave a note for our parents." Bri's aura flared with fearful streaks.

"Perhaps we can arrange for her to come when we're ready," Elizabeth said, squeezing her hand.

Marian gestured to the map which showed the red of sickness again. "We are losing people every day."

Bri flinched, matching Elizabeth.

"When do you want me to start?" Bri asked hoarsely.

"The sooner you go, the sooner you can come back." Elizabeth stepped away from Faucon to hug Bri.

Bri closed her eyes and hugged Elizabeth back. Elizabeth felt the rapid pump of her heart. *Calm.*

Bri breathed deeply and said, "Not tomorrow. The day after."

"Certainly." Sevair put a hand on Bri's shoulder and after one last hug that proved Bri was stronger than Elizabeth remembered, she stepped back.

Sevair said, "It will take me that long to consult with my colleagues who have—"

"—left you out of the loop," Alexa said.

Sevair repeated the phrase. "Left me out of the loop. The circle of discussion and decision." He nodded. "Another good Exotique Terre phrase."

He looked at Bri. "We had planned a trip for our Exotique, but not so soon. When the situation had stabilized."

"Guess they think things have stabilized pretty quickly," Marrec, Calli's husband said, smiled. "When Exotiques aren't stirring circumstances up into an unpredictable froth, they're fixing things quickly." He shook his head. "All a person can say is that with Exotiques around, change is rapid."

"Let's pray so," Elizabeth said, looking at the map again. She hadn't wanted to think of people dying outside Castleton. She wasn't accustomed to thinking of people without doctors or medical help.

It chilled her to the soul. She'd work harder.

The next day Bri packed. Stuffed her solar backpack with two medica outfits. The weather continued to be gray or with weak sunlight, though Colorado was most likely reaching the nineties. She couldn't say that she liked hot weather. On the other hand, her batteries would have certainly taken a lot less time to charge. Denver. Bright sunlight on an average of three hundred days a year. She'd missed that, had tired of gray days, looked forward to returning home.

Elizabeth was subdued at their afternoon session, probably thinking about all the people who were dying without help.

That was a hard emotional concept to accept.

Bri knew her sister had worked through the fact that she couldn't save everyone. That some of her patients would die. She probably hadn't confronted the fact that people in the same country would die because they had no doctors or hospitals near.

Bri'd learned that lesson. Hell, she'd been in some refugee camps where people would die a few tents over because there weren't enough medical—or healing—personnel.

Elizabeth had insisted that the Castle and city medicas work with them, and Zeres, as they healed.

During the healing session, she and Elizabeth tried. The medicas willingly joined the healingstream, worked on the whole body and the crown chakra-chime, saw and understood the deadly gray web. But the Lladranans didn't get it. They could follow and help, but their solo attempts at healing didn't work.

The day went from bad to worse when the Castle alarm sounded and volarans and Chevaliers lifted to face and fight the horrors.

Bri heard Elizabeth's quick gasp, but her sister kept her hands steady on their patient, continued to heal.

Calli and Marrec don't fly, Bri began listing their friends. *Koz does. Alexa and Bastien are not on this rotation.*

Faucon is, Elizabeth said.

Bri thought of speaking, knew Elizabeth was probably analyzing her affair with the man on an hourly basis, and kept her peace.

Since the town and countryfolk knew this was Bri's last day in Castleton, anyone who had the slightest imagining that they'd contracted the frink sickness had come to the surgery. The healers had dealt with several cases of flu, some intestinal disorders, and a migraine, worked until night fell.

As the last patient was sent off, clean of the frink sickness, Faucon strode in.

"We didn't lose anyone on the battlefield, but one of my men has the mutated frink sickness."

"Let's go," said Elizabeth, and ran out to where Faucon's fresh volaran waited.

Mud appeared and Bri mounted; Zeres heaved himself onto the sturdy volaran. Mud could handle two for the short ride.

The rest of the medicas hurried up to the Castle.

Bri followed Elizabeth into the healing chamber, wishing she'd *tried* to pace herself earlier. A couple of medicas stood by. The man's partner, also male, was there as well as the other Exotiques, all worried.

Elizabeth strode to the table, set her hands on the Chevalier. Bri put her palms on his laboring chest. As they had done all day, they linked easily. The web was throughout his body. It would take a tidal wave of healing to clear the sickness. Bri settled into her balance, connected with the healingstream, and began.

Look, Elizabeth said. *A tumor beneath his breastbone.*

Huh, said Bri. It was a solid chunk of gray about an inch in diameter, but it appeared like a miniature brain, with folds and crevasses. The web spun out from it. *Stop the spread, first, as usual.* But the pinpoint of a frinkweed web wasn't nearly as big or as threatening, as this Chevalier battle sickness.

He died under her hands. Bri actually saw a transparent something—his soul?—wisp up from his body and dissipate.

Utter shock hit her so hard her teeth snapped together.

"I'm sorry," Elizabeth was saying. "This new sickness was too well advanced and malignant for us to heal him."

Bri stared at her hands on the unbreathing chest. Her gift had never failed her. Never. Sometimes it had been wobbly. Sometimes, like now apparently, she couldn't help. But she never tried to heal if she knew she couldn't help, just sat and talked and comforted.

But she'd thrown herself into the healingstream, pulled it through her body, used all her own resources, too, and it hadn't been enough.

She should have been able to save him. She knew it. There was some technique or trick that would have healed him. Just doing what she had been all her life wasn't enough, and it should have been.

The other Chevalier wept silently. Elizabeth soothed him with touch and Song, trying to comfort. The loss of a spouse was devastating.

The body convulsed under Bri's palms in a final spasm. Death rattle. Bri jerked away, dazed, to Elizabeth. She'd dealt with this often enough to be able to function.

"We'll take care of him," said a Castle medica, pulling a sheet over his face.

"Appears as if the Dark or the Master knows we can heal the frinkweed disease and has designed something different," Marian said grimly. "It can't be cured by the Exotique medicas, can cause them to doubt themselves, and engender an additional terror into those fighting."

"Excellent analysis," Alexa said.

"An additional horror," Calli said. "Something to take back from the battlefield that eats you inside." She shuddered.

Elizabeth, holding the other Chevalier and leading him from the room, glared back at the Colorado women.

Stumbling to a chair, Bri flexed her fingers. Her hands had failed her.

There was murmuring in the hallway, then Elizabeth returned and came to Bri, putting her hand on Bri's shoulder. *Easy. Alexa's right. It wants us to doubt.*

What am I doing here? I'm a massage therapist! Bri whimpered.

Elizabeth's nails dug into her shoulder. *Stop that! You're a natural healer. Be glad you've helped so many. Helped me.*

Sevair walked in, dressed in elegant flying gear made of strange gray leather. With a little jolt, Bri realized that his tunic and pants were made of soul-sucker skin. "It's time to leave for Troque City."

Bri stared at him blindly. "Leave?" She looked down at her hands that had betrayed her. "I can't leave." Her voice broke. "Not until we figure out why we can't cure this. The Chevaliers need me—"

Sevair's expression went hard. "The Marshalls and the Chevaliers have Elizabeth." He inclined his head to her. "And their own medicas. You are here for the Cities and Towns." He made a sweeping gesture. "People are dying from frink sickness out there. In the other towns and villages, across the land. Your visit will give them hope. Your duty is to us."

Because they were the ones who paid for the Summoning. Bri tasted bitterness.

"He's right," Elizabeth said. "The Circlets and medicas will be researching this new sickness."

"Absolutely for sure," Alexa said, fingering her baton.

"I'll be here," Zeres said heavily. "I'll do what I can. Here and in Castleton while you are away. I can learn from—and help—Elizabeth." His upper lip lifted. "Perhaps other medicas can learn from me."

The other medicas shared an uneasy glance as if disturbed at following Zeres's path, discovering how to cure the frink sickness but surrendering some sanity.

Bri's fisted nails poked into her hands. "I thought we were leaving tomorrow?"

Sevair came to her, lifted her to her feet, and wrapped a plush purple cape around her. "Why waste daylight when we can fly at night? Have a late dinner and rest at a fine inn at Troque—we're visiting the main cities first—then you can begin healing when fresh." He clasped the cape under her chin with a jeweled broach, kind eyes looking down at her. "You're tired. You can rest on the way."

Bri didn't know about that. Or this fine, warm cape. But that wasn't her first concern. "We'll be gone longer than a week?" She still didn't like that idea.

A short nod from Sevair.

"Then I won't get back until after our parents return and find out Elizabeth and I are gone." Her voice rose. She *hated* thinking of that. Their frantic fear.

Sevair's jaw flexed. "I spoke to my colleagues this morning. The Cities and Towns have authorized payment to Circlet Bossgond to find a way of communicating with the Exotique Medicas' parents." One side of his mouth twitched up in a sour smile. "He wasn't cheap."

Alexa drew herself up. "We Exotiques will reimburse you for half. We want this, too. To ease our friends' minds and our own." She shrugged. "Materials for Bossgond's magic spells—"

"*Studies,*" Marian corrected.

Alexa snorted, shrugged. "Whatever. Bossgond uses a lot of dreeth parts." Again she caressed her baton. "We'll provide them. Anything he needs from the horrors. As for you," she pointed a finger at Sevair. "The current Master of the horrors was your man. Consider how he might think. The frinks have been falling for a couple of years, so that was a part of the old Master's plan to demoralize us. But I bet your guy developed this new Chevalier sickness." She twitched as if she felt something between her shoulder blades. "It's bad when you think that you might take something that will kill you slowly and painfully back from battle."

"That's happened for years at home," Elizabeth said. "Bri and I have seen it." She met Bri's gaze, and a tide of love and shared emotions washed between them.

"Yeah, yeah." Alexa rubbed a temple. "But I was a lawyer at home. Didn't fight in stupid wars there."

"I will think on this," Sevair said, biting off the words. "Though I've done little else since Jumme betrayed me. Now it is time for Bri and me to leave."

Bri stuck up her chin. She didn't want to go. She wanted to stay exactly where she was. *She'd* always made her own decisions about when to go or stay.

Elizabeth came over and hugged her hard. "Be safe." So Elizabeth was sure this is what had to be done and therefore it was good. Bri kept hot, futile words from her tongue and mind.

"I still don't know how to ride a volaran well enough for Distance Magic." And that sentence was so odd, so full of Lladranan concepts she shook her head.

"Other Circlets have rented us a flying carriage."

Bri goggled at him.

"They didn't trust security in Castleton." His jaw flexed again. "So it's here in the Landing Field."

Marian sniffed, put her hands on her hips. "As if anyone in Castleton could fly it without knowing the songspell, even if they had the Power." She eyed Sevair. "You're stronger than you appear."

That had him smiling and a slight bow in her direction. "Thank you." He said to Bri, "I've had your clothes packed and your special bag collected." She thought of her solar-paneled backpack, of Tuckerinal. Since Sevair had re-commissioned the safe in the Tower, he knew the passwords. "My things are sitting in the coach?"

"They are secure."

"From the fey-coo-cus?" she asked. "They like to eat electronics…uh, Exotique nuts."

He frowned. "I don't think they've been invited into the coach."

"Knowing who built it, I'd say not," Marian said.

The little spurt of fear had distracted Bri from the greater. She stared at her hands. "I don't know if I can heal."

Yes, you can! It wasn't only her twin saying it. More than stereo resonated in her mind. She blinked and blinked again. Everyone in the room gazed at her, all of them with strong, supportive Songs wrapping around her, lifting her spirits and her confidence. Not one person in the room doubted her.

She stared at them. All her life she'd wanted respect for her gift. Now she had it. She flexed her fingers. Despite all the Power, the healingstream, her twin, even, she'd failed. Might fail again.

Closed her eyes and *listened* to an orchestral piece of blended melodies, all determined to fight the Dark and win with whatever tools they had: baton or spells or healing hands.

Sevair took her hand and her exhaustion lessened. His hand was steady and calloused, as strong and reliable as his Song. She needed that, as a stranger in a strange land, leaving her twin behind.

Elizabeth hugged her again. *You'll do great. And I'll get a message to the folks.*

Bri doubted, but the Songs still bolstered her. She blew out a breath, hugged Elizabeth, opened her eyes and put her hand in Sevair's again. His serious brown gaze reassured her.

She squared her shoulders. "Let's go."

25

The flying coach was an elegant wheelless carriage of green and gold with little medica flags of red with a white cross. Elizabeth had expected something the size and color of a pumpkin.

She watched it rise and zoom away. It was hardly ten feet above the ground before Elizabeth was missing Bri and wishing her twin back. They'd been separated for years and even here hadn't been living together. But lately they'd usually seen each other every day, and that was a pleasure now gone—again.

Elizabeth leaned back against the muscular form of her lover. Faucon held her. If he was near, he was touching her, and that she liked. Cassidy had been hesitant— she stopped that thought. She was *not* going to compare the men. Never mind that she'd never lived in the moment before, always planned. With this affair she was living in the moment. She shivered.

Faucon kissed her hair. "He'll take care of her."

"I know."

"There isn't a man steadier in the world than Sevair Masif."

Elizabeth sighed. "Odd to think of Bri needing someone to take care of her, but I think she does."

"They're a good match." He cleared his throat.

"Don't," Elizabeth said. "Don't mention us or the future."

His muscles tensed a few seconds, then eased. He cleared his throat. "That coach has benches that make into a bed. How do you feel about that?"

Elizabeth snorted. "Sevair would have his hands full if he tried to seduce Bri. *That* I can't see." Exactly. Didn't want to.

But she wanted Faucon. Cowardly of her, to hold so tightly to him, but she didn't want to be alone, especially not this evening.

Night had fallen and those who'd come out to watch Bri leave had drifted away. Faucon's hands slid up to her breasts and Elizabeth hummed in her throat as desire sparked.

Then they were pushed hard, nearly toppled over.

"What!" Faucon steadied them.

A whinny came and a nervous white volaran sidled into view.

Faucon said, "You need to go to the stables." Then he hesitated. "I don't know you."

The volaran took a couple of steps backward.

A little hum sounded in her mind and Elizabeth received an impression of a white five-petaled flower bending to a breeze. From the volaran!

She squinted and met big, shy eyes set in a gentle volaran face. The volaran radiated sweetness. Elizabeth realized that the winged horse was female. They looked at each other, Faucon once again stepping behind her and linking his hands at her waist, leaving her own free.

The flying horse clopped forward, close. She was all white. In the starlight and moonlight her entire body had a silver sheen. Since the volaran wanted her head petted, Elizabeth did so, soft tiny feathers instead of hair. The volaran turned and Elizabeth's fingers trailed across its head and down its neck. Its mane was soft, too.

"I think it wants to be *your* volaran," said Faucon.

Elizabeth stiffened. Faucon stepped away and introduced himself to the volaran. Murmuring easy words, he stroked her from her head to her rump and the volaran made an approving sound, turned her head, and batted her lashes at him! That wrung a chuckle from Elizabeth.

"I love your smile." He smiled back.

The winged horse nickered and Elizabeth sensed it wanted attention from both of them and that made her smile again.

"You, Faucon, are the one who has a smile to melt hearts."

He looked at her, his gaze lingering. "I'm glad you think so." Then he turned back to rub the volaran between her shoulders. "I am not one of those like Calli and Marrec who speaks Equine fluently, and has good telepathic rapport with volarans. My own volaran and I partner well, but I can't understand what this pretty lady is saying."

"Me neither," Elizabeth said.

Once again the visualization of the huge flower waving in the wind came. Faucon met Elizabeth's gaze. "I think that's her name."

Clearing her throat, Elizabeth dipped a small curtsey to the volaran. She held out her hand and the winged horse licked it. Elizabeth laughed. "Lovely one, I am Elizabeth."

The volaran sent a red robe with a white cross on a glowing golden pole that looked like one of the fenceposts that held out the horrors.

"Very strong, very Exotique, very beautiful," Faucon said, lifting Elizabeth's free hand and kissing it.

"*Merci.*" She grasped his hand, looked at the volaran, bright silver against the black and starry night. "I'll call you Starflower?"

The volaran lowered and raised her head.

"Starflower." Elizabeth petted the volaran again.

"She's big enough to carry us both. We could probably catch up with Bri and Sevair," Faucon whispered in her ear. "The coach is slower than a volaran, even with Distance Magic."

The foolishness appealed to Elizabeth. She glanced at the sky, clear and achingly bright and beautiful. A night ride with her lover on a flying horse! What would ever match that? "Ayes," she said.

In a few minutes, Faucon had Starflower equipped with a long saddle and simple reins. He lifted Elizabeth onto the volaran, mounted himself.

"How will we find the coach?" Elizabeth asked.

"Listen, the notes leave a trail." Faucon swept his hand toward the sky.

Elizabeth strained her ears, but heard nothing more than usual. So she peered where she'd last seen the carriage. Concentrating, she saw an iridescent rainbow swath sparkling in the sky, almost lost in the thick starfield. The path was fading. "Let's go!"

So they rose, and this was nothing like the prosaic little hops to Castleton. Now she felt darkness and light envelope her, and Faucon's arm went around her waist. The scent of him and sweet musk of the volaran added spice to the mystery of the night. She settled against him, warmth in the cool air.

They *flew*. The freedom of it blew through her like the evening breeze, lifting her spirits. Magic swirled around her. She was one with the night, the volaran, Faucon.

He didn't talk, nor did the volaran. They were in tune, surrounded by a golden aura.

God, this was wonderful! Laughter rippled from her.

She saw the fancy carriage almost too soon. There was disappointment that they'd be sharing this moment, then came a wild spurt of glee that she'd surprise Bri.

Drawing up to the coach, Faucon yelled with voice and mind, *Hail the coach!*

Elizabeth *felt* the jolt of surprised minds within, then the curtain over the large window vanished, and so did the glass. Bri shrieked with surprise and laughter.

Elizabeth!

Bri!

Bri stuck her torso out of the coach window, screaming with laughter, waving her arms.

Everything in Elizabeth tightened. Bri in a flying coach, off to Somewhere. Herself on the back of a horse with silver wings, flying in the beautiful night with a strong man who adored her behind her, and a winged horse that had come just for her.

She waved at Bri, watched as the two large hands around her twin's waist, steadied, then tugged at her to come in.

"See you later!" Bri screamed.

"Later!" Elizabeth waved back, feeling Faucon's arm around her. Then the volaran turned back.

It was like a fairy tale.

Faucon awoke the next morning, arms wrapped around Elizabeth and smiled. She'd loved the volaran ride. Loved Starflower already.

He dared to hope Elizabeth loved him.

Last night they had sweet, wild sex for a long, long time. She'd given more of herself.

He could only hope that they'd bonded enough or would bond enough to keep her here with him. His arms tightened around her. She murmured and snuggled close.

She didn't say the other man's name.

It had only passed her lips once, and that during one of their lovemaking bouts the first night, and Faucon didn't think she knew she'd said it. The moment had been one of exquisite agony for him. But she hadn't mentioned the man since.

He knew the fool had been stupid enough to let her go, and she knew that Faucon understood she was raw from a heart wound, but they didn't speak of it. He'd been gentle and tender with her.

Faucon, someone whispered in his mind. Ah! That call had wakened him. Glancing at the window, he saw it was full light, past time for him and Elizabeth to be up. He didn't care. His major domo, Broullard, would hold breakfast for them.

But Broullard didn't call him. Frowning, Faucon considered the timbre of the Song. Luthan. A noble Chevalier like himself, a man who lived only a few doors down the hallway, and more, the representative of the Singer.

Faucon, again the murmur. He smelled the sweetness of his woman's body, cherished her against him, thought whether he wanted to answer the man. No.

Yet Faucon, like Luthan, knew of duty. *Ayes?*

I need to speak with you, confidentially. Everyone else has left for the day.

I'll come to your suite shortly. Keep our meeting secret, except—

Please do not tell Elizabeth.

No, she's too new to our world. I don't keep secrets from Broullard.

A sigh from Luthan. *Telling him is fine.* Hesitation. *I need your help. You may have to enlist others.*

Curiosity piqued, as Luthan had probably intended, Faucon said, *I'll be there soon.*

Thank you.

Faucon disentangled himself from Elizabeth, watched her stretch out on the bed. She appeared older than Bri, with more faint lines. He liked that. A mature, womanly lover. From their bonding during sex, he'd gotten impressions of her long and rigorous training to become a medica, harder than here on Lladrana, and that had aged her.

He smiled as he scanned her nude body. She slept raw, and he liked that, too. He'd stopped wearing short trous to bed. As he felt the stirrings of arousal, he turned away, went to the shower and let cool water diminish his ardor. Dressing, he saw it was another gray day. This year had been more gray than sunny and that was a concern. But he didn't let it bother him, just added another layer of clothes.

When he stepped from the bedroom, Broullard bowed and indicated the set table. Faucon smiled at the weathered face of his major domo. They'd been together for years, fought together. Broullard had stepped into his father's shoes when he'd died when Faucon was thirteen. Everything that he knew about being a noble estate owner, a Chevalier, and a man he'd learned from Broullard.

Sniffing, Faucon smelled hot, fresh bread and eggs, knew they'd be prepared exactly as he and Elizabeth preferred. "I'll take my breakfast with me," he said. "Can you prepare the same for Luthan?"

Broullard raised his eyebrows. "Of course."

"Thank you. Luthan mind-spoke me, requested a consultation."

"I would guess that he chafes at the Singer's restrictions," Broullard said. "He's been…restless…for some time."

Faucon hadn't noticed. "Interesting."

A couple of minutes later, Faucon took a loaded tray and walked through the door Broullard held open. "I'll let you know what Luthan says, what he wants."

Broullard nodded.

"Take care of my lady," Faucon said lightly.

"Of course." Broullard smiled. "She's a good woman. Good for you."

Faucon smiled himself, warmed by the approval. "Ayes, she is."

Whistling a Chevalier flying tune, he walked the wide corridor to Luthan's door. The man opened it as Faucon reached it. Faucon was reminded that Luthan and Bastien had lived under the heavy Song of their father for a long time.

Glancing at the sterile sitting room, Faucon clucked his tongue. "I sensed you were hungry, so I brought food." He sighed. "Set the table. You need a major domo, someone like Broullard to take care of you."

"There's only one Broullard," Luthan said, and hurried to put hot pads on the small wooden table for the dishes and Faucon wondered why, the piece of furniture was so scarred it wouldn't have mattered. Broullard had wrapped silverware in napkins and placed them on the tray.

Luthan helped unload the tray, sat and ate and fiddled with his cutlery. He *was* restless. An oddity. The man was usually as calm as a mountain, wasted no motion.

"Thank you for agreeing to come, the confidentiality, this breakfast," Luthan said.

Faucon's brows winged up. "You're welcome." He grinned. "You'll find the food not nearly as expensive as the dinner you paid for last year."

A snort came from the man and his lips curved, too. "Trying to keep you from seducing Alexa. I knew she and my brother would be together, then my ingrate brother goes and gets a fine feast out of it."

Faucon stilled. Luthan's words had been off-hand, but had reminded him all too well that the man had a touch of prophecy.

Faucon put down his fork. "Perhaps the Singer bade you be silent on matters that we, the nobles and Chevaliers and

Marshalls, should know of." A conflict of duties would trouble the man.

"Ayes." Luthan stood, swept a hand over the plates and silverware, Sang a cleansing tune.

Very efficient, not quite polite, and an evident habit that the preoccupied man didn't even notice.

Standing himself, Faucon replaced his possessions back on the tray. He hesitated as he heard the opening and closing of his door down the hall, the strengthening of Elizabeth's Song, then its diminution as she left the building.

Luthan was at the window, watching. "Your woman wears her medica robe well, with authority. I always think of her twin bouncing along like a cheerful puppy. They—" Luthan's hands gripped the window frame until his knuckles whitened. He paled. Faucon froze. The man was having a vision, one of the reasons the Singer, also a prophet, valued him.

Crossing to the window, Faucon laid a hand on Luthan's shoulder. "Can I help?"

Luthan's shoulder heaved under his hand once, twice as the man drew in deep breaths. "No. Thank you."

"And your vision?

"I must think on it." Luthan's voice was sober, with a trace of sadness in it. When he turned and met Faucon's eyes, his gaze was as cool as usual. "Several paths, I believe."

Cold touched Faucon's spine. He didn't doubt that Luthan had seen tragedy. Wanting a reassuring look at Elizabeth, Faucon glanced out the window, but only saw a whisk of red before the door to the keep opposite closed.

So he turned away to find Luthan staring at him, as if weighing him, then Luthan shook his head. "Too many melodies tangling," he muttered. Abruptly, he said, "It's the Seamasters." He stopped, ran a hand through his hair. "I don't know. *She* knows something too, but isn't saying."

"The Singer?" Faucon allowed himself a little sigh. "A strange and difficult elder." He sat in a comfortable chair. "If it's information you want of the Seamasters, you've come to the right person."

"You have seaside estates."

"Ayes. I know the Seamasters, individually and as a group, though I'm not in their counsel. My cousin handles all my sea business except the mercantile trading. Do you want me to ask him about the Seamasters?"

"Yes. No. I don't know."

A skiff of wariness zipped though Faucon. Again, very unlike Luthan. "Have you spoken to Bastien of this?"

Luthan turned squarely to him. "No. I only have *feelings*." Luthan sounded irritated, both at the vagueness and the fact that feelings weren't logical.

"Hunches?" Faucon said.

"Ayes." Luthan's lips narrowed. He closed his eyes.

Faucon waited in silence.

Finally Luthan shook his head, opened his lashes and met Faucon's gaze. "There is something disturbing about the Seamasters. They are hiding something. But it is a relatively old secret." Luthan made a frustrated gesture. "Some moons old, but still affecting," he paused, tilted his head as if listening. "Still affecting Amee's Song."

"And the Singer does not tell you of this secret that she might know." Faucon kept his tone even.

"*Ttho*." Luthan shrugged. "I hinted at the topic, she ignored it."

"Understood. I'll speak with my cousin, my heir. He'll be as discreet as possible."

"Thank you."

Faucon clapped Luthan on the shoulder. "We'll figure this out."

"Please don't tell Elizabeth." Luthan shifted his stance, muttered, "Too much going on."

Raising his brows, Faucon said, "I don't hear how this affects the Exotiques, but I'll say nothing to my lady."

Luthan turned back to the window. Faucon followed his gaze to see Alexa and Bastien volaranback rising to practice battle exercises with a new Chevalier class.

"It affects them all," Luthan muttered. "I don't know how, but it affects them, *us*, all."

26

One night Raine hunched by the fire of the Open Mouthed Fish tavern and listened to tales and old news brought by a traveler to Seamasters' Market. He came from inland, Castleton by "The Castle." She wasn't sure where this was, but knew it was far enough away that she'd never make it on her own.

They spoke of the *others*. That's what she called them, when she thought of them. Which was often, ever since she'd heard of them a couple of weeks before.

She dared think of them in a superstitious whisper. If she said it aloud she might jinx the idea that she was like them. That belief would shrivel up and blow away like that hideous web thing in the older story and leave her hopeless.

She was afraid to hope. Hope was a glittering shard of a sharp mirror. You'd hope, and then it would be ripped from you and you were so much worse off. Hope and despair, a vicious cycle.

There were others like her. She'd heard them called *Exotiques*, women who'd come from another dimension, and from what she could make out, Earth. They were spoken of with respect by all but Travys, and when he sneered he was shut up by the rest.

There was the Swordmarshall, the Circlet, the Volaran partner, and the Medicas. When they were gossiped of, they were all spoken of as being *together*. Stories went that when a person dealt with one, they dealt with all.

Considering that idea was when her heart would start thumping hard and she could hear the tide of her own blood thunder in her ears—because of hope. If she could get to them, contact them somehow, would they welcome her?

Travys swaggered into the Tavern and Raine tensed, faded into the deep shadow of the taproom's corner. It didn't matter. His gaze went straight to her.

She'd frozen too long. He crossed the room with a few strides, lifted a meaty hand. "Why you starin' at your betters, girl? Want a piece of my cock? Well, it ain't got no likin' for half-breed trash like you." His heavy arm swung down.

Pain! But she'd ducked in time. The blow only grazed her cheek. Good luck, then. Not as bad a bruise as the last two times. She didn't fight back, not when he always hit her in public and no one protested. He'd kill her if she fought.

She ran into the kitchen, now off limits to all customers, and began washing a stack of pots. Not looking at the gleaming pitcher that might show her battered cheek. As she set the crude pot on the drainer and reached for another, she faced facts.

She'd have to leave. It had been a while since she last tried. Maybe she'd acclimated by now and the sickness wouldn't claim her this time. Maybe she could walk inland more than a few miles. Maybe she wouldn't be tied to the sea and this tavern on the pier. At least she could follow the coast, but so far this was the best place she'd found to keep the sickness at bay.

She'd wanted to stay and hear more about the *others*, ask about them where people might actually answer off-hand and truthfully.

Not now.

She fumbled to plan an escape. The timing would be tricky. To stay as long as she could, but not so long that she didn't survive Travys.

The first couple of days passed and Elizabeth was kept busy with minor injuries and classes—with the medicas and Calli, who taught her and Starflower volaran partnering. To her chagrin, but secret relief, the townspeople didn't expect her to keep the afternoon surgery office hours in Castleton. Nor did the city folk come to the Castle with the frink disease. Despite the fact that she'd healed the sickness, it was always with Bri. Doubt niggled at Elizabeth whether she could do it on her own. She just didn't have the verve Bri did, throwing herself into that healingstream.

Elizabeth spoke with Bri every day by crystal ball. The other cities were keeping her busy, and Bri looked… subdued. Elizabeth could only imagine what it felt like to be seeing a portion of an epidemic, healing only for a few hours, knowing that before you came and after you left, people would die.

As for the Castle, no more battle alarms came. That concerned everyone, as if the Master was brewing up even more nastiness. Elizabeth fervently hoped the fact that they'd been unable to cure the sickness hadn't reached the Master's ears.

Most of her time outside of work, she spent with Faucon, learning magic, or flying, or making love. The man was a fabulous lover. She deliberately lived in the moment. She learned he was a rich man, born to title and wealth and privilege, much more than most. He could command resources, and when the Marshalls asked for his help, he gave it generously. Usually he'd do paperwork in the evenings with her in his rooms; he kept up a good correspondence with his cousin who handled his northern estate. She wrote reports on each patient, and kept notes regarding Lladranan healing for herself. She also endeavored to get down some basic medical information about germs, bacteria, viri, and other issues, translating them into Lladranan terms for her teachers.

Zeres, Bri's mentor, came up to the Castle only once and irritated all the medicas so that they didn't welcome him again.

Finally, on the fourth day, the doorharp sounded just after breakfast, followed by a knock. When Marian entered, Elizabeth's heart thumped hard in her chest. "It's time?"

Marian inclined her head. "Bossgond's ready to experiment by sending something through the dimensional corridor to your condo. Despite your directions, we've been unable to locate it on our own. Marian shrugged. "It's been years since I lived in Denver and my geography is no longer precise."

"Let me change into flying gear and I'll be right with you." Elizabeth hurried into the bedroom and stripped off her formal medica robes. The day was cool and she finally settled on Chevalier leathers instead of the traveling medica costume.

"Can you fly on your volaran clear to the islands by yourself?" asked Marian.

"She certainly can," Faucon said. "But I'm going, too."

"Bossgond is slightly reformed," Marian said, "but he still doesn't like visitors."

Faucon opened a desk drawer. "I wouldn't dream of arriving without a host gift. Would Bossgond like a vial of jerir?"

Marian said drily, "I'm sure he'd find a use for such a valuable item."

Faucon bowed.

A few minutes later Faucon's squires had helped her saddle Starflower and all four of them were off. Her heart picked up beat. Her first long flight, and to the sea! She could hardly wait to use Distance Magic, the spells that shortened the time spent on a journey, spells Sung by both volaran and human. She yearned to see the geography of the maps that she'd become so familiar with.

The sky was pearly gray, with coal-colored clouds billowing in the distant north. The west, toward the sea, appeared clearer with wisps of silver-lined clouds.

Though she didn't really speak Equine to Starflower, the volaran was sweet tempered enough to take direction well. They flew southwest, Faucon on her left, not quite within reach, but reassuring nonetheless. He'd fought in many battles and he and his volaran knew how to rescue a falling comrade. Not that she wanted to think about that.

To her right was Jaquar, Marian's husband. Both he and his volaran were large. As a weather Circlet, he commanded air. He, too, could catch her, magically, if she fell. Behind her was Marian. Elizabeth had some doubts whether the Exotique woman was trained enough to help her, but she kept that to herself.

A half hour into the flight, Jaquar gave the order to initiate Distance Magic. Elizabeth felt the brush of minds on her own, inhaled, then Sang. She heard the others Sing the few couplets too.

A not quite translucent bubble surrounded her. She got dizzy if she looked at the ground. With each sweep of her wings, Starflower covered more than was natural to a volaran. The rolling hills gave way to green plains, then grassy dunes, then the island-studded Brisay Sea.

Too bad Bri is so far away, Faucon said.

Elizabeth gritted her teeth. She didn't want to do this alone. Too bad, was right. Soon they were spiraling down to the largest island of the chain, Alf Island, which always belonged to the premier Circlet of the age, currently Bossgond, Marian's mentor.

Marian's volaran picked up speed until she came next to Elizabeth and pointed down. *The towers I raised as my last test!*

Elizabeth goggled. She'd read Marian's book, so she should have expected Tower Bridge from London, but it was different. No bridge, just the towers, connected by a walkway. Before she could get a good look, they'd landed close to a tall round tower, of the ubiquitous gray stone. Elizabeth slid off Starflower and Faucon took Starflower's reins, gestured to the rest of the volarans who moved around him. He bowed to the short, bony man in the doorway. "Salutations, Circlet Bossgond. I will care for the volarans."

The old man just gave a loud snort, turned and went into the tower.

"Oh, dear," Marian said, frowning. "Not a good sign."

Elizabeth didn't like the sound of that. Faucon gave her a kiss and she clung for an instant before following Marian and Jaquar. This journey was probably tame compared to what Bri was enduring, but Elizabeth had qualms.

Their parents. That was the bottom line. Trying to spare them grief by transporting something from here to Earth.

As they climbed the inside stairs that circled the tower, Marian spoke to Bossgond, then threw words over her shoulder. "You're sure your parents will check your condo if you don't return."

"Yes. Of course. They both have keys."

Marian cleared her throat. "Ah, when is the mortgage payment?"

Beneath her breath, Elizabeth said, "Too bad you didn't ask that before you jerked us away." She was cold. Her hand was trembling on the stair rail. Aloud she said, "I have automatic withdrawal for most of my bills. I'll be fine."

"That's good."

They finally reached a large circular room, covered in shelves crammed full of strange objects, with a few windows high in the wall. There was a grouping of several fat pillows on a thick pad of colorfully patterned rugs in the middle of the room, a conversation pit. The most riveting item was a huge brass telescope with a multitude of gears and levers pointed at many mirrors. Elizabeth just stared until the man, about her height, which made him short, came up and got in her face. "Come along. No time to waste. This task is *not* easy." He examined her up and down, then moved away. "Would have liked to have seen the set," he muttered.

Elizabeth followed.

He gestured to the eyepiece of the telescope. "It is fixed on your city, but Marian could not locate your abode." He harumphed. "Not good enough directions."

Marian stiffened, folded her hands. Jaquar slanted a sardonic look at the old man, put his hand on Marian's shoulder.

After one last glance around, Elizabeth bent to look into the telescope. Colfax Avenue sprang into life, cars trundling along. She caught her breath. It appeared completely alien.

People wore shorts and T-shirts, the sun was harsh, she could almost see heat waves rising from concrete and asphalt. Not at all like the cool Lladranan weather.

A bony finger poked her side. "The sooner you indicate your home, the sooner I can get my experiments under-way. I understood that there is a time limit." The old man's voice held a rasp, but like most Lladranans' of Power, it was compelling.

"My parents will be returning home at the end of the week. I doubt they'll even wait a full day before trying to contact us."

"Oh, dear," Marian whispered again.

Elizabeth didn't like the sound of that. Wiping her damp palms on the bottom of her tunic, she tried to move the tele-scope. It didn't budge.

"This way." Bossgond's fingers set hers on a gear. "Is the perspective acceptable?"

Clearing her throat, Elizabeth said, "For the moment. We will, ah, be able to see my apartment itself?"

"We have zoom features," Bossgond said

"Uh-huh." Elizabeth slowly turned the large gear; it moved easily under her fingers. She located the capitol building, moved the view until she found Denver Major, followed the streets until she reached her building. "How do we get inside?"

"You are there?" The old Circlet was eager.

"Yes. Ayes."

Bossgond nudged her away, glanced in, hummed, went to the end of the telescope and flipped a lens. "There, try that."

Elizabeth looked, the parking garage, her car. She could see into the elevator shaft, followed it to her floor, saw other apartments, focused on her own. A lump came to her throat. *Her* home. The shabby furniture, the deep blue rug, the wide windows looking out toward the mountains. How she missed that view!

To her complete astonishment, someone walked into view. Cassidy Jones. Her mouth dropped open. What was *he* doing there? He must have kept an extra key.

As she watched, he looked around, rubbed his face, an action he only used when he was completely stressed. He looked haggard. His lips moved a little. He was talking to himself! He stalked over to her landline phone, picked it up, punched the read-out button repeatedly. Then he shoved the phone down and put both his hands to his face, rocked a little.

She stumbled back, her hand jogging the telescope to point at the ceiling.

"What happened?" Marian asked.

Elizabeth just shook her head in disbelief. "My ex fiancé

is there. He's a doctor at Denver Major. Something must have come up." She found she was hyperventilating and regulated her breath. "It looked like he already knows that I'm, we're, missing. I can't guess how soon he'll tell my parents."

Bossgond glared at her. "My experiments are best conducted when the target location is empty."

Elizabeth murmured an absent apology, staring at the telescope, torn, yearning for another look. She only wanted to see her place again, not Cassidy.

"I have the coordinates now," Bossgond said. "Go away."

Elizabeth wetted her lips. "Will you be able to send a message through?"

The older man ignored her. Bad sign.

"Our parents will worry. A lot."

Faucon walked through the door. Elizabeth checked his expression. She couldn't tell how long he'd been there. As they'd begun to land, he'd grown quieter, his Song uneasy. He didn't want her here.

Elizabeth shook her head, trying to align the two men in her mind—her past, her present so entirely different. She couldn't. All her emotions jumbled together. The love and time and goals she'd shared with Cassidy.

The beautiful man before her in this strange land, making it bearable, who held out his hand to her. She wobbled a smile. "Just a minute." Swallowing hard, she turned back to Bossgond and the other Circlets. "We must send some message to our parents. Please, let me show you their house."

Bossgond hummed again. "A good idea." He flipped back the lens. Elizabeth, knowing she wouldn't be viewing her apartment or Cassidy again, felt a flare of mixed emotions, grief, longing, hurt, fear. Controlling her breathing, she squinted through the eyepiece, found Cheesman Park, the home she grew up in, stepped aside and waved Bossgond to the telescope.

He looked. "This house?"

"Yes."

Again he flipped the lens. Scowled. "Odd looking furniture."

"My living room was mostly books," Marian murmured. "That's the only place he's seen."

Elizabeth glanced into the telescope. Her insides squeezed as she saw the family room, the matching recliners and large-screen TV and electronics. "Our home," she choked. Too painful. She didn't want to feel. Didn't want to think. Didn't want to analyze any feelings. She went to Faucon.

The first couple of days of Bri's journey were…interesting. The inn at Troque and the savvy merchant Citymasters were a more sophisticated lot, probably due to the proximity of the City States. Though down a huge escarpment wasn't exactly what Bri called close. Still, the view was fabulous, something she'd never contemplated, and the falls of the river were as large and impressive as Niagra.

Outwardly courteous, the Citymasters had lines by eyes and mouth that didn't relax until Bri did the Healing Hands Show. Then they became downright friendly, confiding that many who discovered they had the frink sickness had simply jumped off the escarpment, appalling Bri. Yes, this place was different.

After the visit to Troque, they went down the eastern

boundary of Lladrana, the escarpment, visiting small communities not even on the map. Here people stared at Bri, some actually ran from her and two of the diseased refused to let her touch them. Bri had read Alexa's book, but she'd said little of her "goodwill trip" so the volume was no help. By the fifth day, Bri hated the traveling. Wondered how she'd ever had itchy feet. But that was then, on Earth, and this was now, on Lladrana. At home someone usually knew English, or French, or Spanish. Here she had to listen *hard* to figure out accents; more, she spent time listening to personal Songs.

The flying coach was boring. Good for sleeping, for eating, but not much else. Hard to look at the view unless she hung out of it, and Sevair disapproved.

He disapproved of a lot—of her wanting to sleep late, wander the town, meet other people than the City and Townmasters. So he irritated her.

But she saw the sick and the wounded and the scared, and sometimes their emotions overwhelmed her. She flung herself into the healingstream and it was different wherever she went, sometimes Powerful, sometimes close to the trickle she'd felt on Earth. Sevair was always there, providing food, support, making excuses when she couldn't face one more person. So she was glad he was with her. She actually relied on him.

The dichotomy was enough to wrench her.

She watched him. How he stood and moved, how his quiet confidence reassured. How he raised spirits by being open and answering any questions, patient of those he'd heard a thousand times. How was the fight against the frinkweed proceeding? What of the sickness itself? The northern boundary? The horrors?

The latter were spoken by the southerners as mythic legends, few having seen even trophies of the monsters. At each town he handed the mayor a crystal ball provided by Castleton to keep in touch. This was seen as a great bounty. This trip was knitting the cities and towns of Lladrana together as never before.

Occasionally the coach stopped at some noble estates. Then Sevair was stiff and punctilious and Bri found herself smoothing waters. When they were at a Castle, her status was considered far higher than his.

They skirted the Singer's Abbey and headed for Krache. That city was larger and more bustling. A major seaport, it was shared with the southern country of Shud, which ignored Lladrana's "strange" problems. They stayed at a walled mansion, with guards for Sevair, Bri and the coach. Her patients were fewer, the citizens hard-eyed and less inclined to believe in Power. Only the highest ranked had the silver mark of Power at one or both temples. Bri suspected some of the guild people colored their hair to downplay it. Bri's own purple streaks had faded.

Krache was also the most diverse. Bri might have been able to pass for a foreigner if she was foolish enough to run away in this dangerous place. It was Krache where she'd had a long conversation with Elizabeth and found out about Cassidy visiting her sister's apartment and the lack of progress in contacting their parents.

Elizabeth's voice had held an odd note when speaking of Cassidy, and once more Bri said nothing. She wouldn't give any advice unless asked. As for her parents, she couldn't think of them, anticipate their pain, or she'd go crazy.

She sat in the moon and starlight on the step of the

magical carriage. Being with the vehicle that would take her back to Castleton and Elizabeth soothed her. Though if she screamed loud and long in her mind Nuare, Mud or the whole contingent of Exotiques might come rescue her. But she couldn't leave the towns without hope. Her shoulders hunched against the weariness of the day. Lately she'd healed mostly children, a couple of elderly women, two teenagers. The sickness, like the frinks, were less harmful the further south. She rubbed her arms, covered in the undershirt and the three-quarter-length medica tunic. South in Lladrana didn't mean warm.

Authoritative bootsteps rang across the courtyard of the inn, passed the two guards who gave her a little privacy. She didn't have to raise her head to know it was Sevair, didn't look up until the polished-to-meet-and-greet boots were nearly touching her own broken-in leather ones.

His expression was grave. Reaching down, he took her hands, unlinked her tight grip. "Come, Bri, it's time you sleep."

She couldn't stop a great sigh from escaping, like all her lost steam that had kept her chugging along. She rose when he pulled on her hands, then didn't know who moved, whether she stepped into his arms, or he paced forward. Didn't matter. His head lowered, angled and her lips tingled. She knew she'd been waiting for the press of his lips on hers.

The kiss started out tender, gentle, as soft as his mouth. She set her hands on his shoulders, wide and strong, felt herself flattened against his frame, muscles as hard as his own stonework. Warmer, more wonderful. If—when—this man stripped he'd be better than any statue of masculinity.

Her weariness was lost in a rush of intoxicating passion.

She opened her mouth and he explored with thorough and probing tongue. His taste was all she'd expected. His flavor was earthy, mint and man, a little gritty and that fascinated her, almost like sharp liquor—brandy maybe. Just as heady. Unexpected depths to this reliable and sturdy man.

He felt wonderful. Solid. Strong, with just that teasing wisp of wild passion that drew her.

She surrendered to herself, her needs, her desires, wrapped her arms tightly around his neck, nibbled at his lips, gloried in his stone-hard erection against her stomach. Oh, *yeah*!

He peeled her arms from his neck and stepped back. She staggered, her mind whirled with the excitement coursing through her, was plunked back on the carriage step. Panted.

"I am a cautious man." His voice was thick, she had to run the words through her dazzled mind twice before she understood them. She wet her lips. Yeah. Cautious, but there was something more under that quiet exterior.

He watched her, not bothering to hide his arousal, his face impassive. She knew how affected he was—in the thumping of her heart, she heard his, the racing and ragged pace of his Song. She blinked and realized he expected some answer. Running her tongue along her teeth, the taste of him sending a quiver to her core, she cleared her throat and spoke precisely. "It's obvious you're a cautious man."

"You are returning to Exotique Terre."

27

Bri gathered her wits. Earth. Home. Her parents, her future. She stood straight as her past and future plans clashed with present wants. Meeting his gaze, his widened pupils still showing his passion, she said, "Yes. I am."

He nodded. "I've had enough people leave me in my life."

His parents and sister? They'd died and the man was dealing with abandonment issues. She couldn't say that she blamed him. She was surprised that he realized he had such feelings. "I understand," she croaked.

"So," he said deliberately, "you will know that if we have sex and sleep together it will not be a casual affair."

"It won't be casual on my part either." Casual sex was rare for her. She heard the warning in his tone. Not a casual affair, but not a deep connection of the heart, either. Something she always had a problem with. Her problem. "It may be short but I'll give you all I can."

He was holding out his hand again, cool and steady as could be, showing her his control even as his pants jutted in an interesting manner. She tossed her no-longer-purple-streaked-hair. She could match him, put her fingers in his. Immediately his Song was in stereo, hell, it felt like it was in her head, her veins, her center.

She studied him as they walked back to their guest rooms. This guy was dangerous. This guy might possibly make her forget her once and future plans. If he decided that he seriously wanted her, she could be in trouble.

Two afternoons later, Elizabeth stood in the cool cloister outside the Castle keep and sweated. Bri was due "soon," but some patients couldn't wait. The sickness would kill them shortly. According to the Marshalls "soon" was today, tomorrow, the next day, maybe even next week. No one could give Elizabeth a definite time and that irritated.

Five people with frink sickness lay on pallets, ready for her healing hands. The gift Bri had always told Elizabeth she had. Which she'd used with little success on Earth, but had achieved great results here on Lladrana. With Bri.

Elizabeth would be performing before a critical audience scrutinizing her every move. She set her jaw and ignored them—the medicas and the Marshalls and the Chevaliers and most especially the townsfolk radiating worry. Bri had endeared herself to them with all her quirkiness, and the people who had brought Elizabeth here didn't have much faith in her alone.

These were her clients! Living in the Castle she'd forgotten that. Most of the time she'd kept herself in a nice little enclave, as usual. Foolish to chide herself now. Bri wasn't here and she was and patients needed her. Her healing gift.

She took a deep breath and let it out slowly, checking her own chakras as she'd been taught. Almost second nature to her now, but she'd *never* done it at home as part of her regular medical training. She hadn't been this nervous since the first years of med school, either.

The first time she was using her healing gift alone in Lladrana. Breathe in deeply, slowly let it out. She *had* practiced breath control on Earth—many of her friends had.

She'd already checked the patients as a doctor. There might be some herbs she could recommend, but she was all too aware that even on Earth she couldn't have cured them. Treat each symptom, and somewhere down the line of that treatment they'd die.

This patient was a young man, a farmer with compromised organs. He had a film over his eyes, a coating on his tongue, moaned when she touched his abdomen. His breath was shallow, his heartbeat too rapid.

A shifting of feet came and she knew she'd hesitated too long. Nothing to do but trust her intuition, her gift. And pray.

She placed her left hand on his throat, her right on his lower abdomen. Another deep breath, then she opened herself. She knew Bri had the image of a healingstream. When they worked together, Elizabeth was swallowed by a flood. For herself, healing wasn't water, a rushing river, but fire. Heat and light she drew from around her, the crackling of a wildfire in her head. Her hands grew warm, and she sent cleansing, bright fire that lit but did not sear down her tingling fingers. Moving her hands along her patient's body, she sought the cobwebs inside him, shriveling them to black, to dust, to tiny motes that were attacked by his own white blood cells, defeated.

She stepped back, and as the snapping of the fire inside her mind quieted, she heard murmurs, ignored them. Blinking, she cleared her eyes, saw the sharp fascination on the medicas' faces, almost smiled. *Felt* the pride and support of Faucon. Her gaze met his and he nodded. He'd had no doubt of her skill.

All of her life, no one had had complete confidence in her gift except Bri. Elizabeth herself had doubted, time and again, others hadn't known. They might have suspected, felt the aura of her energy when she tried her gift in desperate times, wondered what she might be doing, figured nothing could be done to save some patients. But Elizabeth *had* helped. Looking back, she understood there had been a couple of lives she had saved.

Her fingers curled, sending energy back up her nerve endings, giving her tiny shocks of renewal. She kept the Power safe from harming anyone, took cleansing breaths, moved on to the next. Her heart jolted. It was a Castle soldier, a young woman she recognized. The fire in Elizabeth burned hotter. Anger. Anger that this disease had been deliberately sent against the Lladranans. Fury that something evil loved death and dying more than the spark of life.

The soldier whimpered, looked up with suffering eyes. Elizabeth stroked her forehead, left her hand there, put her other hand on the jut of the woman's hip. This time Elizabeth went deeper, into the bone marrow, into her own mind. Further. The flame of her danced until she thought it leapt into the the earth of Amee, giving and receiving, beyond the planet, into the heart of space itself, connecting with starfire. Her marrow burned, and she sent the healing energy from her fingertips into the soldier, swept away the sickness in a sheet of rushing flame.

Stepped back a pace, panting, wiping her arm across her forehead. Marian was there with a bota of cool, clear water, holding it to her mouth, squirting it inside. Elizabeth's head felt light and she settled into her balance. No time for dizziness. Despite that, she felt strong, Powerful.

Her twin would fling herself into a healingstream, a rush of energy she thought of as a river. Finally, Elizabeth knew that image would never work for her. She channeled the energy of the stars.

"Very impressive," Marian said.

"Thank you." Elizabeth allowed herself a faint smile. She knew, now, what Marian had felt when she had come into her Power, raised her tower, became a Circlet. Elizabeth had crossed the barrier of self, found limitless Power. After a last swallow of water, she turned to her next patient, a girl about seven, thin and pale. Elizabeth tucked away compassion, which could only impede her, and studied the sickness, the disease that lived just under the skin.

Hands on throat and groin, Elizabeth let the flames flash through her, slid the energy into the child's body, crackling under her skin, radiating through her, searching out the dark cobwebs, frying them, killing them. When she stepped back, she was smiling fiercely.

She leaned over and propped her hands on her legs, gulping in air. Not a position she would ever have taken in the halls of Denver Major Hospital, where doctors strode with dignity and arrogance. A couple of medicas looked at her askance. Tough. Healing was hard work and took energy. She'd rather pant and sweat and move on, than retreat to a bench in the shade of the cloister for a little break to keep her dignity intact, as a medica's soothing voice urged.

The fullness of the Song—and now she could hear the sparkle and crack of it, the rhythm more of drums than of melody—and Power from her gift was finally inside her. Maybe she could find dignity later. Now she had work to do.

She straightened, rolled her shoulders, rubbed her hands together and wasn't too surprised to see a fountain of sparks. People withdrew a pace. Except Marian. Elizabeth turned her head to see the other woman's smile.

Marian shrugged. "I'm fire, too."

Elizabeth heard a clang of understanding, as if the silver gong had gone off next to her ear. Slowly she swivelled her head to look at the other Exotiques. They all represented the ancient four elements. Alexa, earth. Calli, air. Bri was water. Herself fire, too.

"We'll need spirit, too, to untie the weapon knot, the final destruction spell. The last of us Summoned, for the Singer, the Song—spirit," Marian said.

Elizabeth shook her head to rattle some sense back into it. "I'll take your word on that." With small steps she moved to her next patient, an old man. The tips of his fingers and toes were white—there the spiderwebs lived in him, in his arteries and veins, down to the tiniest capillary. She'd clean them out.

She would have liked to position one hand on his heart and curl one around his toes, but she didn't have the arm span. She glanced at the chief Castle medica, Jolie, who could help. "Can you stand at his feet and warm them?" Jolie would be better at the feet anyway, she knew all foot pressure points.

A frown knit between Jolie's brows. The medica took the

man's feet. "I don't think I can help you, Elizabeth. I can't link well with you without others." Jolie blew a breath out. "You and your sister access so much of the Song…."

"Just do your best," Elizabeth said. At least she'd been saying those words to herself and others all through medical training, so that was familiar.

She set her hand on the old man's navel, felt an immediate connection, and an immediate draw of fire from beyond herself. Then the tug of that healing energy down to his feet. Jolie had joined her, massaged the man's feet with strong fingers, broke up cobwebs with little bursts of Power, and with caring. Jolie lifted her voice in Song, and the energy she drew from the sky and the earth and the sun and the humidity of the air washed through the man.

The melody caught Elizabeth. She hadn't begun to fashion healing Songs. It was all she could do to open herself to the Power and direct it. Couldn't hurt to hum. She discovered she was holding notes that corresponded to the chakras, fine-tuned them for her patient. She punched up a scale that would help him heal, saw her hands fire with flaming green light, and opened herself to the bright starfire energy.

It *whooshed* through her, prickling her fingers, into the man. He arched, yelped. Elizabeth clamped down on the flow, narrowed it to a laser. She visualized the arterial system and she sent the light, the heat, the flame through him. Again and again she met wisps and clots of gray cobweb energy, fired it, destroyed it. Now in control, she opened the floodgate a little wider, let the push of the Power, the hum of the Song send healing force through his arteries, veins, capillaries.

Jolie Sang louder. Elizabeth spared her a glance, saw she sweated. Jolie smiled, and her Song held thanks. Then Jolie let go and the backwash sped through the man's body, spreading into muscle and sinew, repairing as well as destroying the disease. A little of Jolie's Power smacked at Elizabeth. She gritted her teeth, took it, checked her patient and raised stinging hands.

This time Faucon's strong arm was behind her, supporting her and she let herself sag slightly into him, feeling his satisfaction, knowing his pride in her.

Cassidy had been proud of her, before he'd seen her use her gift.

Stop it! What was *wrong* with her? Since she'd seen Cassidy again, she'd been comparing the two men. So wrong. Why couldn't she just accept her affair with Faucon and the respect and affection and sexual desire they shared? Why did she continually have to pick everything apart?

The fire was affecting her emotions, licking at her, amplifying negative feelings. She shook her hands out, stamped her feet.

"Water." Marian held the bota up to Elizabeth's lips again, and the residual overburn of the fire was banished as she drank deeply, then she turned her head away and wet her lips. She smiled up at Faucon, nodded thanks at Marian. "I need a little protein boost," she said.

Faucon waved and Broullard strode up with a small box. He opened it. Sweetcheese, antremay, lay there, looking like baked brie. Bri would have snatched at it and stuffed it in her mouth. Elizabeth wished for juice with an addition of wheatgrass.

Nevertheless, she took a pre-cut wedge up and bit into

it, letting flakes of the pastry fall to her bosom. The treat was fabulous. All thoughts of mango juice with wheatgrass faded from her mind as the taste of the naturally sweet cheese lay on her tongue. She ate two slices in undignified haste, swigged from the bottle Marian handed her and drank deep.

Her head cleared, she could almost feel her cells plump in rehydration. She dipped in her pocket for a clean handkerchief and wiped her mouth, her hands, brushed the crumbs from the slight shelf of her breasts. She caught Faucon's gaze and saw a promise…that they'd both eat more sweetcheese later. The notes of his personal Song twined around her, tender, and she sighed.

"Thank you Jolie, Marian, Faucon and Broullard." She spread a smile among them.

"Can you go on?" asked a female Citymaster. "We have one more. My sister," she whispered.

Elizabeth had very little energy, though she'd snagged some as it had rushed through her like fire eating dead weeds, the Power was only enough to heal, to keep herself going. Her brain, her nerves, felt fried, as if using more would damage her.

Four. She'd only been able to heal four. Fewer than the number of cases being discovered every day. In Castleton. They *had* to find a treatment for this sickness, and a cure.

Elizabeth was beginning to believe everything she'd read in the lorebooks, others had told her. She and Bri would *not* be called home until they figured this out. She bit her lip. They had to find a way, and fast.

She went to her last patient and stroked the middle-aged woman's face, wiping away perspiration, sending a tiny amount of Power to boost the patient's. This woman was fighting the sickness hard. Elizabeth could feel her exhaustion, her will to stay alive, to thrive. She was also a woman of Power, with the touch of silver-turning-to-gold at both temples.

But Elizabeth didn't want to leave this woman overnight, treating her only with herbs. Didn't want to subject her family to the worry. She wasn't sure of her limits here, but had learned to push them back home.

She met the Citymaster's eyes. "I will do as much healing as I can of your sister now, and finish later. I don't want to burn out my Power, nor do I want my control to deteriorate so far that the healing Power and Song could hurt your sister."

"Wise," said the woman lying before her in a raspy voice. She clutched her intertwined hands over her heart, as if pressing against a hard ache.

Elizabeth let out a quiet breath. *"Merci."*

The sisters smiled at her. "We are not young and demanding." The Citymaster's lips curved. "We are older and *sometimes* commanding, but not in this."

Their acceptance of her limitations—everyone's limitations—eased Elizabeth's mind.

She shook out her arms and legs, drank more water and laid her hands on the woman.

Just then, the alarm clanged. Elizabeth stiffened, but it wasn't the call to battle. Faucon grinned at her, turned and stepped into the courtyard, shaded his eyes. "It's the flying carriage. I believe your sister has returned."

Bri spoke to Elizabeth mentally. *I'll be right there. We'll land in the courtyard.*

Something in her tone alerted Elizabeth. *You've slept with Sevair.*

Amusement and affection rode on the next wave of love. *Not quite. We're considering it. Lots of sexual tension adding a nice buzz to life. We're both glad to be back.*

Then the coach was there in the courtyard, hovering like a silent helicopter, settling down without disturbing dust.

Bri flung open the door, hopped out and hurried over. Though her step had as much bounce in it as ever, faint lines etched around her eyes. Elizabeth stepped to her and they hugged hard.

Energy surged between them. Water and Fire, and though they should have clashed, they mingled, providing strength to each other, as always.

Wow, what zing! Something new? Bri squeezed harder, and Elizabeth chuckled.

I don't do the healingstream. I do the starfire.

Ah! The fire of the stars instead of the stream of energy from the space between them. Bri sounded pleased. Then images of the other cities and towns flowed to Elizabeth—dark images of death and dying and helplessness. After one last squeeze, she released Bri and they turned to scan the patient.

Usually five a week here, said Elizabeth. *I know that doesn't sound like much…*

Worse and better elsewhere, depending on the location. Five fatalities a week is not good. I tried to teach the medicas, but it didn't work. Bri's smile twisted. *Hell, I tried to teach anyone with a glimmer of silver or gold at their temples.*

We'll figure out a way, Elizabeth said, and returned to her patient, whose hand was being held by Sevair Masif. He was talking in a low-key way, distracting her. The patient's sister, a colleague of Sevair's, had relaxed. Excellent.

"Let's get to it," Bri said briskly and Elizabeth's smile widened.

Bri stepped into Sevair's personal space, nudged him, teasing. He gave her an intense look and slow smile. Elizabeth blinked. She hadn't seen that particular smile.

He patted the sick woman's hand, took her sister's arm and led her a few paces away, joining a clump of townspeople. Everyone appeared relieved to see him and gathered around. Now that Elizabeth noticed, they no longer looked at her with anything but approval. Inner tension eased. She was accustomed to being approved. That these folk had doubted her skills and preferred Bri's had been like a splinter.

Elizabeth joined Bri at the healing table. Bri had placed her hands on the woman's head and heart. Elizabeth put hers on the woman's solar plexus—the energy that corresponded with fire, and laid her hand over Bri's on the heart.

They all breathed together, though the patient's was unsteady and cut short from pain.

Then Bri connected with her source and the river of energy opened. This time it didn't sweep Elizabeth away. This time she didn't fight to stay afloat, struggle to a calmer eddy to plant her feet and siphon off some of Bri's energy to heal. This time she watched it surge by.

One deep inhalation, and she *reached* for her own source of Power, the snapping, electric current of starfire. It whipped through her, to her fingers, warmed their connection, penetrated the woman's skin and bathed her in the sweet cleansing of controlled fire—light and heat.

Bri laughed.

Elizabeth's fire sank to the middle of Bri's river, providing a tight core of energy.

"Hmm," Bri hummed, then narrowed her own stream of Power. It wasn't quite as controlled as Elizabeth's and she smiled.

They worked together to clear the patient's heart, repair tears, revitalize it. Elizabeth healed the circulatory system, Bri the nervous system. Reenergized herself, Elizabeth was able to slide into detachment, watch the process. Bri's and her Power *didn't* conflict as the ancient elements of water and fire were supposed to. Because they were from the same source.

Both she and Bri visualized the depths of space. They tapped into the underlying pattern of the universe. Each built their own image of the energy. Bri thought of and sought the energy of black holes, of the darkness between stars. Elizabeth imagined the blaze of a solar flare, a starpoint.

What would people of other "elements" see? Air: the solar wind? Earth: the coalescence of mass into the formation of planets?

She didn't know. If she hadn't been so awed by what was happening, she'd have been amused at considering antique concepts rationally. As odd as the four old "humors" the body was made of—blood, yellow bile, black bile and phlegm. Or the four temperaments—choleric, melancholic, sanguine, phlegmatic. But concepts were constructs for the human mind. She understood that now.

Then Bri's froth of enthusiasm at healing, doing her *destined* work, her joy that Elizabeth had found her Power, had joined her fully as a partner, hooked Elizabeth's emotions. Once again, she was wholly *there*, experiencing the heat and flaming of her hands, the flow of energy from *somewhere else* through her body, the destruction of evil that lived as a disease.

In tune, they examined the woman from crown to toes—and Elizabeth gained admiration for Bri's knowledge of anatomy.

Massage therapists know the body as well as doctors, not to mention acupuncture, acupressure points and chakra energies, Bri said.

Elizabeth nodded.

Now to withdraw, watch. Instead of narrowing the conduit which would increase the force of the Power, Bri widened her focus, letting her river gentle. Elizabeth followed suit, letting her starfire dissipate into the huge surround of space.

Keep some for yourself, Bri said. *I gave you some of my energy to jump-start yours. Take some from your own source now to keep you going, though I can see you're through for the day. We can only be vessels for the Power so long.*

"Ayes," Elizabeth said. She let the last shower of starfire spark through her like fading fireworks, then cut her connection.

They turned to each other, hugged.

"You were fantastic, Elizabeth."

"Thank you, Bri. I understand better now."

Another touch added when Faucon placed his hand on Elizabeth's nape, another element illuminated with aura and Song—air, Faucon was air, and his tenderness was close to her heart.

Elizabeth sensed when Sevair's fingers twined with Bri's,

adding the last, slow rolling of Earth. Her shoulders eased, lowered.

"Awe full," Sevair said thickly voiced. "To see you two work together."

Dropping her arms from Bri, Elizabeth blinked her eyes to see Sevair the staid kissing Bri's ear. Faucon nipped at her own and had a flick of passion zipping through her.

Bri smiled, put her hand on her abdomen. "I'm starving. Let's eat." She glanced at Faucon. "In town. Sevair can tell you the best inn."

"I *know* the best inn," Faucon said.

The watching medicas moved forward. A couple supported a swaying Jolie. Elizabeth frowned. "Jolie, didn't you take some Power from the healing energy?"

Jolie slowly shook her head. "I could feel you're the Power from both of you, but could not link. We have never been able to do so. We can draw from Mother Amee, but she is so stricken we do not like to use her Power."

Elizabeth met Bri's eyes. *The medicas didn't have a proper image or construct for human minds of the pattern of the universe.*

Hope surged through her, matching Bri's wonder. Now she *knew,* she could teach them. She was sure of it.

They'd teach the others how to find the energy. Then to cure the frink sickness.

She'd done it, not Bri with the healing hands, a mind more accepting of the Lladranan's ways. Elizabeth, who'd been scrambling hard to learn, pretending she knew what she was doing. She with the medical training.

Pride burst through her. She stood tall and looked around Temple Ward. People met her eyes and ducked their heads in acknowledgment.

Bri said, *We'll talk later about teaching the medicas. I could NOT get images or explanations through people's heads. You can.* She didn't sound resentful, but grateful.

"We'll talk later," Elizabeth said aloud. "I need to discuss this with my sister, but *we can now train you to cure the frink sickness!*"

28

The news ran through the audience like a shockwave. For a moment Elizabeth thought that they might be mobbed.

"The Exotique Medicas are tired." Sevair stared at individuals who'd taken involuntary steps forward.

With feigned casualness, Faucon scanned the crowd, played with Elizabeth's fingers. "I'm hungry."

People broke into clumps to discuss Elizabeth's announcement, Sevair moved to supervise those tending the recovering sick, relatives from Castleton. From the energy Elizabeth had sent through them, she thought they should be bouncing to their feet, charging out of Temple ward.

"It doesn't work that way," Bri said softly, though Elizabeth knew it from observation. "My patients have told me their bodies feel different, but they aren't quite sure how. Their minds are used to their bodies feeling a certain way and can't process the information that they are different for a while."

"Muscle memory?"

Bri shrugged. "Body and mind memory?"

"All is under control," Sevair said with satisfaction as he watched the former patients helped from the courtyard to the next, and the gate beyond where coaches waited to take them home.

"They want their own beds," Faucon said.

"We'll fly," said Sevair, walking over to Mud.

"Ayes!" Faucon said, and let out a piercing whistle.

Come, Elizabeth called to Starflower. She whinnied in delight, trotted from the stable and joined Faucon's volaran in the short hop from the Landing Field to Temple Ward.

"Guildhall Inn," Sevair said.

Bri blinked. "Of course the best inn would be attached to the place where the townmasters and guild masters congregate."

"Of course," Sevair said. "And the chef has a new dish he is introducing tonight." He paused. "Called, I'm told, Fries of the Potato. Very simple: potato, hot oil and salt." His aura pulsed with a lighter, teasing hue. Then what he said sank in and saliva pooled.

"Fries," she breathed.

The word resonated through her mind, through Bri's mind, then snagged the attention of Marian and Alexa who were talking to Marshalls near the Temple.

"Fries!" Alexa screamed. Her head swivelled. "Where?"

"Fries," Marian whispered reverently, swallowed.

I like these fries, Tuckerinal said. He pranced in grayhound form to Sevair. With a doggy grin, he assured Sinafinal, who trotted beside him, *You will like fries, too.*

Alexa had heard that. She shot from the group and only waved a hand at the protest, ran up to Sevair, skidded to a stop and put her hands on her hips. Looking up at him with narrowed eyes, she said, "Fries. From potatoes?"

His gaze warmed with amusement. "Indeed. At Guildhall Inn."

She licked her lips. "I'm invited, right?"

He raised his eyebrows. "Of course." He bowed and raised his voice. "The Guildhall Inn would be honored to have all the Exotiques dine. In fact, they are expecting you."

"Fries, already?" Marian snagged her husband's arm.

"Some from the proper bag of frying potatoes," Sevair said, "but the farmers' guild has found potatoes are prolific." Now he grinned. "With a little nudge from Power."

"I bet they have," Alexa said.

"Better watch out," Marian mounted her volaran, as did Jaquar, whose Song held amusement and curiosity. "We don't want a kudzu situation here."

"Kudzu?" Jaquar asked.

All the women frowned. "A too-prolific plant that has turned into a menace."

"Potatoes are being grown in contained beds," Sevair said.

"Too bad that didn't happen with the frinks," Marian said.

Just that easily the optimism of the evening faded. Sevair's face went blank, but Elizabeth saw the deep blue of disappointment.

Marian winced. "Sorry."

Alexa elbowed Marian. "Not your smoothest lately, kiddo."

"Kiddo" translated to Lladranan as "thoughtless youngster."

But Alexa beamed at them all, ran and jumped onto her large volaran, obviously using Power for both the spring and landing. "Come on, there's a plate of fries with my name on it waiting, right?" She stared at Sevair.

"Right."

Then she swore, pointed at two small specks in the distance. "Those sly folks. Calli and Marrec have already left. They'll beat us all there!"

Laughter bubbled up in Elizabeth. She knew how to teach the medicas to cure the frink sickness! A victory equal to earning her medical degree. She would help save a land! Around her was the friendship and fellowship from people she valued. She hugged Faucon hard. He looked surprised, grinned, lifted an eyebrow at Sevair. "You can put me in touch with the head of the farmers' guild. I'll invest in these 'potatoes,' be the first to have them on my land."

"Too late," Sevair said. "I purchased a small estate between Marian's island and Alexa's place." He looked at Faucon. "Near your own home holding. Potatoes are already growing there."

Bri's mouth fell open. Shock flashed through Elizabeth. Sevair was planning ahead, as if he expected Bri to stay. As if he thought Elizabeth would, too, at Faucon's. Her stomach tightened, and she shared an uneasy glance with Bri. For once she had good advice for her twin. *Live in the moment.*

Bri switched her gaze from Sevair and Mud to Elizabeth.

Elizabeth said, *I'm learning that lesson. Enjoy the moment.*

Yesss, hissed a voice. Nuare alit, startling the volarans into the sky until only Elizabeth and Bri were still on the ground. *A good idea. Now come, both of you. I, too, would like to try these "fries."* She stuck out a leg for them to mount, but she had no tack, no reins or perch.

Bri smiled with nearly her usual sunniness. "Good advice, and we'll not be the last there." She got onto Nuare, held out her hand. "Hang on tight. It's going to be a wild ride!"

An understatement. Laughter tore from Elizabeth at the roc's speed. They landed before everyone except Calli and Marrec.

The fries were devoured in minutes, accompanied by burgers. Happy murmurs came from other diners.

Alexa lifted a glass of iced tea in a toast. "To the Exotique Medica twins, Elizabeth and Bri, heroines of the hour."

And so French fries were renamed. Lladrana knew them as "Twin Fries."

The next afternoon at the Castleton house, before the regular surgery, Elizabeth opened the door to medicas. They came from within easy flying distance to gather in the dining room. Other representatives were there, all the Exotiques and their men. Every crystal ball in town was in the room with her, organized by Sevair. A televised lecture, how nice.

She wasn't really nervous, had performed often enough under pressure. When she coughed, the dining room packed with red and white tunics fell silent. Bri sat near her, grinning with pride, and that was better support than anything she'd had in her career.

"We have discovered why we Exotique Medicas can heal the frink sickness and you have been unable to. We will teach you this. More, we will teach you to tap into the greatest Power you will ever know." Good grief, she was beginning to sound like a self-help seminar. She straightened, gave them her best intimidating professional smile. "This is the truth."

Zeres coughed.

"Zeres, of course, has learned this lesson, but has been unable to explain it," Elizabeth said.

Bri interrupted, "I haven't been able to put it into words myself, didn't figure out the essential aspect needed for such healing." She beamed again at Elizabeth.

"Our civilizations are very different in some ways," Elizabeth said quietly. She scanned the room, making sure everyone was paying attention. "Our particular society has gone into space." She waved a hand. "Off planet, to our moon. We've sent machines into space to see the universe and return images."

She took a breath and waited for the awed comments to fade, looked at Zeres. "Tell me, when you link to your great Power flow, do you see the blackness of space? Stars—great globes of fire, and your sun?"

From the way Bri was wriggling on her seat, Elizabeth already knew the answer.

Brows knit, Zeres said, "Ayes." He gazed at her, spread his hands. "A huge darkness, raging balls of fire that would sear me to ashes in an instant."

"Space, the sun, the universe," Elizabeth said. "It is vast, and though the skies here on Amee are filled with many more stars than on Earth, the darkness between the stars is greater than one can imagine comfortably." Her voice went quiet. "Our people have been to space and are accustomed to the images and ideas. Yours are not. Yet." She reached to the table and sipped water, took the time to meet each person's eyes. "Bri and I and Zeres can teach you how to think of space and the universe. How to connect with the Power flow. Using that flow you can burn out the frink sickness in a patient."

"Burn out?" asked a medica.

Elizabeth smiled. "Of the four elements, I am fire."

Encouraging nods came. She said, "Bri is water and feels a healing stream."

"I feel a cold wind rushing through me." Zeres shivered.

"There would be the heaviness of a mass descending through a person, perhaps," offered another medica.

"Ayes," Elizabeth said. "We will teach you today. Then you can go and teach others." She held out her hand and Bri hopped to her feet and linked fingers, raised their hands over their heads.

"We will win!" Bri said.

Applause broke out. Elizabeth felt heat in her cheeks, but inclined her torso a little. Bri did a boogie.

A moment later, Luthan, representative for the Singer, pushed away from the wall where he'd leaned with arms crossed. "This is a great step indeed."

Elizabeth tensed, managed a tight smile. "But?"

He gathered the gazes of those around them. "It is not enough to teach the medicas how to heal. We need to find something the common people can administer for themselves."

Elizabeth's mind flipped through medicines, antibiotics,

herbal remedies. Her link with Bri told her that her twin was thinking along the line of meditation techniques, personal faith healing. They shook their heads together.

"I'm sorry." Luthan inclined his head. "That is the Singer's prophecy. Each person must know the cure. This does not address the Chevaliers' Sickness, since you have been unable to cure that."

Man, that's twice we've been riding high and had a downer, lately, Bri said. "Thank you," she said stiffly.

"I am sorry," he repeated. "This is good progress. I must report to the Singer." He left.

There was a snuffle and a sob. Everyone turned to see one of the medicas at the table holding her head in her hands. Elizabeth didn't know her. She looked up, face puffy with tears. "I am the only medica for three villages," she said thickly. "I have had to stand by and watch my people die. My relatives die. No matter what I did, drawing on Amee's Power herself, I could not heal my friends and family. I've been helpless." She stood, walked unsteadily to the twins, threw her arms around them. "This is a great, great boon."

"Ayes!"

"Ayes!" The medicas' cheerful shouts soothed Elizabeth.

"Wonderful," Marian said. "Congratulations." She wiped her eyes with her handkerchief.

Bri choked, sniffed, said, "The sooner we teach you, the sooner you can go home and heal."

The sessions went well. Elizabeth and Bri first worked with Zeres and three others, stabilizing the man's vision, teaching him how to accept and control his Power. The other medicas took longer, but by the time evening fell, the weary but enthusiastic medicas were winging away to spread the word.

Alexa, Marian and Calli linked with Elizabeth and Bri in the last set, the twins nearly staggered by their Power. It was a real experience, trying to control the differing magic. Alexa the warrior, used to being a part of a battlefield healing team; Marian more detached, more interested in the how and why; Calli, eager to learn so she could tell the volarans, her people. The other three Colorado women easily understood the concepts and images. When they were done, they sagged in silence, hugged and left almost silently; they'd shared thoughts and feelings enough.

"What with what Luthan said, looks like the Snap isn't coming tonight," Bri said shakily.

Elizabeth stared at her twin blankly. She hadn't considered that. "Guess not."

"Mom and Dad will be back home tomorrow."

"I know." Elizabeth frowned. "Didn't Marian have a hopeful glow to her?"

"Yeah, maybe." Then Bri gasped.

"What is it?" Elizabeth demanded.

But Bri was giggling a little hysterically and holding out her forearm. On the tender skin underneath her wrist, a line of five colorful tattoos ran up her arm. Starting with a golden caduceus near her wrist bracelet lines, then a red shield with a white cross, a green baton topped with orange flames, a black volaran, a book with a lightning bolt. "We've bonded." She pointed to the caduceus. "I think that's you."

"I didn't feel anything." Elizabeth glared at her own arm. A fancy brown patterned hand was under her wrist, then all the others, with the book first, the baton, the volaran. "I don't have the shield."

Bri peered at Elizabeth's arm, her own, sighed. "I think

that's Zeres." She touched the brown tracery of a hand. "I like that one for me. Like a henna pattern on a hand. I've had mine done like that occasionally."

"Bonded." Elizabeth could barely force the word from suddenly chill lips.

Bri met her eyes, spoke the shared thought. "This doesn't mean that we're staying here, does it?"

Elizabeth's teeth clenched. "Not if it means forsaking our parents."

Tears welled in Bri's eyes. "No, not if it means leaving Dad and Mom."

Bri went home to her tower after Elizabeth flew to the Castle. The guild masters had been busy when she was gone, finishing up the restoration and furnishings. It now showed a rich, eclectic style. She touched the carved newel post of the stairs, a roc, gazed at the dark jewel-toned carpets that suited her exactly. They'd learned her style.

She'd bonded with the other women during the healing sessions. She supposed she should be glad she didn't have a roc and a volaran and other medicas, too. Shoot. Despite everything, she didn't think she could stay.

She was on her bed, staring up at the gold-embroidered maroon canopy, when the doorharp sounded. Knew it was Sevair. Didn't know what to say.

He came in anyway, trod the stairs with even footfalls, entered her bedroom and sat down next to her.

She didn't look at him, mutely held out her arm. From the corner of her eye she saw a flash of surprise and pleasure, then he schooled his expression. In a rare gesture, he lifted her hand to his lips, kissed her palm tenderly. All the sexual tension building in her over the days with this man surged through her. Her body wanted his. Her heart wanted the slow smile he saved for her. Her mind wanted to run away, go home to Denver and her parents.

"I'd like to show you something," he said.

"What?"

"Not here in the tower. It's a beautiful evening. The sun is setting."

"Everyone's on the streets, then. I don't know if I can face them. They'll all want to talk about today."

He kissed her forehead and she liked the sweet press of his lips. Too much. "We'll go by back streets. You like our narrow passages." His mouth pressed gently to hers. "Come with me."

She could have grabbed him and pulled him down into bed—desire was rising in her. But it wasn't fair to use him. She wanted neither of them to use each other. His fingers brushed her face. He'd stay and torment her with tender touches and that would lead to other things, lovely things, but something she was unsure whether was good. So she sat up.

"Come with me," he repeated and she put her hand in his.

29

Sevair took Bri's hand. Her fingers linked with his. He could hear the melody of her Song, quieter than before. Yet there was an underlying lilt of passion that had him tugging her from the bed. Quick hearty sex wasn't what he wanted. Not entirely.

They were out of the bedroom quickly. Good. "Follow me." He'd planned this carefully, of course, so he had a light wrap for both of them waiting on a bench. But the evening was warm enough that they wouldn't need them. The weather had been so uncertain, he'd played it safe. As always.

When he opened the door to the evening glow his heart thumped harder. He wasn't playing it safe with Bri.

His emotions had been tangled around her from the beginning, when she and her sister had responded to the Summoning, two shining beings. At the time she'd been afraid, yet she'd used her Power to heal the boy, the rest of his people. Gratitude and relief had filled him, that they'd done right in paying for and participating in the Summoning. He'd had trouble keeping his mind on the welfare of his charges, had only wanted to turn and watch the women. Did one of them have *purple* streaks in her hair? What did that signify?

The sight of her the next morning in a flimsy shirt and tights, bedroom attire, had stirred more than his loins. His heart had jumped, too. She'd looked…fresh. He'd held her in his arms on the volaran trip to town and had listened to her Song and had never wanted to let her go.

Events had moved fast since then, and to his surprise, he'd stepped forward to block Faucon's interest in her, and Koz's, and any other man's. Been possessive, even when he knew Bri should not be distracted with…caring.

Even when she said she wouldn't stay, would return *home*. She didn't consider Lladrana her home. Didn't think she'd remain and make a home here, like the other Exotiques.

He was taking the greatest risk of his life trying to tie this independent and mercurial woman to him, to Lladrana. He was leaving himself vulnerable to being abandoned again.

They'd left the square and had walked through the public gardens full of brilliant summer flowers catching the low rays of the sun, looking more like stained glass than living blooms. They strolled along Guildhall Boulevard. He'd walked this path so often that his feet had carried him the right way. But he certainly hadn't been charming on the way. Others were out, but were respecting his body language and Song and not approaching.

"Sevair?" She looked up with raised brows. He'd been silent too long.

Her hand was tucked into the corner of his arm. When

had that happened? He'd been holding her hand. Her fingers had escaped him and were around his elbow where they could fall away so easily.

She'd distracted him, as usual, so he wasn't following his plan.

He put his free hand on hers, stopped and turned toward her. "You were…magnificent…today."

She sent him an odd look. "It was Elizabeth's show. She was the one who figured this out."

"Elizabeth was the one who deduced this portion of the problem," he said.

Bri's eyes widened and he saw weight come into them, perhaps even an anticipatory fear. He ground his teeth—he wanted to compliment her, tell her how much he valued her. He was going about this all wrong! Better to have kept his mouth shut.

She sighed deeply. "There are more tasks."

He was guiltily glad all their problems hadn't been solved, that no Snap would come to whisk Bri away from him too soon.

Again he took her hand and raised it to his lips. "I have every confidence in you." Stiltedly, he added, "I am sorry that you can't leave Lladrana."

"No, you're not," she said flatly.

"I'm sorry you're worried about your parents." Turning her to face him, he went with the complete truth. "I want you in every possible way."

When she didn't answer, he wondered if he'd been clear. She wasn't Elizabeth, who'd slept with a Lladranan man and knew nuances of the language.

"I want you, too," she muttered.

He let out a breath he hadn't known he'd been holding, glad she could admit it. Taking her other hand, he brushed his lips against hers.

She looked shocked. "In public?"

A lift and a fall of his shoulder. He didn't care what others saw, speculated upon. Not in this. He said none of the things racing in his head, expressed none of the feelings beating through his heart. He didn't want her to know how determined he was to have her. To keep her.

Letting one of her hands escape, he began to walk, all too aware of her fingers in his, that Powerful, small hand clasped in his. Like the first morning they'd spent together, he listened to her Song.

It was different.

The realization jolted, and lifted his spirits, the wings of hope, that perhaps, perhaps, she might stay.

If he asked her if she wanted to stay, she'd deny it. Such a contrary woman. But not foolish or feckless.

He couldn't walk in silence while he considered the change in her Song. A daring idea came to him, and he freed his Song, directed it to her, showed all of himself.

She stumbled and he righted her, slowed the pace and kept on strolling.

Her Song had reacted to his, rising high. Her cheeks flushed and her palm grew damp against his. He smiled, settled his own Song, kept it strong and steady, and analyzed hers.

It was more ebullient.

He blinked. *More!* How could that be? Her lifeforce must have been low, her energy depleted when they'd Summoned her, and events had drained her more than she revealed.

Could he *ever* keep up with her? He set his shoulders and his Song reflected intense determination.

She glanced at him, a little wary.

She should be. He wouldn't let her abandon him easily.

There were other changes in her Song, had been others, now that he compared it over time. There had been a loosening of a tight, minor key melody, anxiety perhaps. She'd have been anxious after the Summoning, then settled in. Now worry tightened that portion of the Song again and he didn't like it.

"Where are we going?" she asked.

He smiled slowly and she glanced away. He said, "You don't like the walk or the music?"

Pink smoothed over her cheeks, fascinating. He squeezed her fingers.

"Seeing and being seen. Not doing any business tonight," she said.

"Perhaps I do conduct a little business during the after-dinner walks. I hadn't thought of it much."

"Because business is duty and you would never shirk your duty."

"True," he said lightly, wrapped her in his Song. "But this walk has nothing of business and duty."

She glanced at him, eyes wide and fathomless. Thinking non-Lladranan thoughts when he wanted her concentrated on him. He lifted her hand to his lips and kissed it.

"You're smothering me with that Song of yours," she said softly.

"No, I'm not. You're free to listen or to shield yourself."

"I don't like to be smothered, controlled. Live up to expectations," she said sulkily.

"Who could control you, such a free spirit?"

Her eyebrows lowered. "Are you mocking me?"

"Teasing perhaps. Don't you say I am too serious?"

"You have a lot to be serious about."

"You're not going to divert me with duty, Bri. Walking with you and listening to your Song, sharing my Song with you, has been nothing but pleasure." He chuckled. "But I take my pleasures seriously, too. Here we are." They stood in a small side door to the guildhall. He hummed the pass-spell he'd created and *heard* the rhythms of it again, felt its beat like a hammer against stone.

When they entered it was to light. Bri looked up at the ceiling window five stories above them. The rest of the small room was shadowed. A switchback stairway lay ahead.

He shut the door and turned and pressed her against it. No, he didn't mind kissing her in public, easy kisses, but what he wanted was more and deeper. For that he wanted privacy so he could savor her. He moved in, his mouth finding her soft lips, tasting her, connecting Song to Song.

Sensations flooded him as he'd never allowed. He needed the taste and touch of this woman. Infinitely intriguing. It was the last thought he had before he succumbed to passion and pleasure and desire roared in his ears.

Then he was being firmly pushed away—with Power more than her hands against his chest. She smiled up at him. "You wanted to show me the side entry to the guildhall?"

His eyes narrowed even as his body pulsed with need. She was flushed, and her Song held arousal, her heartbeat fluttered fast in her throat. She wasn't rejecting him, exactly.

She was…wary. Wouldn't be controlled by her own passion, let alone another's. A chuckle rumbled deep in his throat. By the time he was finished with her, she'd be bound to him and Lladrana by a million tiny chains she hadn't noticed him forging.

He suppressed the fiery demands of his body, the impatient desire tumbling through his veins. His pants were tight, his fingers shaking, heat slid through him. He ignored it, brushed a barely-purple strand of hair away from her face. Her skin was much lighter than his. He could see her easily in the dim light.

His hands were around her upper arms, he slid his palms down to her fingers—her limp fingers—squeezed them briefly and kept her left hand clasped in his own as he turned to the stairs. "Up." The word came out rough.

"I can tell you are," she muttered.

He roared with laughter. Catching her close with one arm, he lifted her off her feet and whirled around in exuberance. *He loved her*. He knew it, it burst through him, but he was canny enough not to say it.

He set her feet on the second step of the staircase, released her, patted her bottom, did *not* let his hand linger on the supple firmness. "Up."

She glanced at him over her shoulder, a baffled look on her face. "I'm not going to be ravished in your office, am I?"

He wanted to, oh, yes, the blood pounded through him, swelling his shaft. But now was not the time. Perhaps later, maybe even later tonight, but not now. Her defenses were too high.

"No," he said. His office was in his parents' house. "We're going all the way up. To the rooftop."

Her eyes widened with curiosity, another treat, good. He jerked his chin up. "Go."

She turned and ascended the stairs. He had to fist his hands to keep them from the sweet sway of her ass. His vision dimmed a little as his body surged once more.

The stairs were wide; his former master, the architect of the building, was perspicacious in that. No twisting, narrow staircases for the guildhall, leave that for Castles and warriors. This was a solid building of the merchant class. Up they went, with skylights well placed to show them the way. At the top landing, she waited for him, head tilted as if she was considering his strategy and forming her own.

Sevair smiled. The lady was spontaneous, more used to abandoning a plan when a new idea came along than sticking to it. He was just the opposite.

"I don't know that I like that smile," she said.

"Just admiring you," he replied lightly, unlocked the broad oak door and swung it open. "Let's admire the view, one of my favorites. I'd like to share it with you."

She went out onto the stone walkway around the tiled roof. The parapet came to his waist, higher on her. She turned toward the setting sun and gasped. "It's a beautiful sight."

"Yes." As he'd anticipated, the sunlight gilded the city, showing orderly streets, verdant parks. The walls, too, looked golden, then the green and gentle hills.

"I don't know that I've ever seen a more beautiful land, and I've been to many." She breathed deeply, smiled. "Nice, clean air, too."

"What?"

Her smile flicked on and off her face, wistful. "The wonders of our world come with a cost. Our air is not clean."

How could you have unclean air? He thought of the horrors, how their stench, physical and spiritual, befouled the air. How frinks fell with the rain. Surely they left a smudge, too.

But the romantic mood he was trying to create was in danger. She'd turned north to the towering mountains with the everlasting snow gleaming on their peaks, appearing pristine.

Putting an arm around her waist, he moved her more to the west, to the brilliant sunset streaming golds and reds and oranges, a touch of light purple. "Watch the sun set over the city." He pointed. "Your tower." Her body lost the droop of depression and set with her usual optimism and vitality. Her Song lilted.

"My tower," she said, satisfaction and pride in her tone.

He'd done a good job on repointing the stones in the days before their trip. The concrete made the small building look whiter, now creamy in the light. A beat of affection for the tower made him blink, as if he'd become attached to the structure as well as his love who lived within. He stilled. Something had changed within him beyond falling in love with his lady. He'd finally let the last of his grief for his lost family go because he was focused more on the future than the past. He'd forgiven them for leaving him. Now he could move away from their house and find his own place. The tower?

As they watched, the roc rose from her nest and streaked into the sky, more brilliant than the sunset as rays flashed on her gleaming rainbow hues, a myth, a legend. She Sang and the wondrous sound wafted to them. The people walking below stopped to listen.

Sevair's arm tightened around Bri's waist. "You have given a blessing to our city. Thank you."

Bri chuckled. "She was here before I came."

"She was here because she knew you were coming," he said. He kissed her temple. "Thank you. She reminds us of all the lovely things in our lives, adds a touch of wonder and magic." He held Bri as they watched the day fade and the colors of the sunset mute into soft blue and heather. Then darkness fell and the brilliance of the night was upon them with the rich velvet of blue-black sky and shining abundance of stars.

He whispered a kiss on her head. She sighed, leaned into him, as if appreciating how solid and steady he was. He knew those traits exasperated her when she wanted to fly high and wild like the roc. But those characteristics would lure her back to the nest that he'd craft for her, the life he'd craft for them that they'd share. He could give her these quiet moments of pleasure, and an infinite tenderness along with his love. He could give her wild passion.

When they left the guildhall, she took him to her bed. Joining with her went beyond his imaginings. Through her he felt that touch of the universe she'd shown others. Even better than the touch of the stars were her soft moans, her quick and nibbling kisses that fired his blood until all he desired was to show her ecstasy. When she cried out and clutched at him, said his name, he thought no other moment of his life had been so good.

He'd do anything to keep her.

30

The sex had been too damn good. Bri had never made love with such a detailed and methodical man before, and he'd applied those qualities to their lovemaking. Simply driven her out of her mind. He proved tough and full of endurance, too. She was a bit sore and used a splash of the healing star-stream to ease discomfort.

It *had* been lovemaking. They'd gone beyond sex into emotional closeness, caring. He'd whispered his secret name to her, urged her to use it, *Vere.* She couldn't wait to share loving with him again, even though she wondered whether she could block feelings for him. She should. Definitely. Because she still intended to go home and make a new life, surrounded by family, encouraged by the support of her parents.

She checked her arm and was glad there was no symbol of his, nor had Elizabeth had one from Faucon. Bri didn't speak of the matter to Elizabeth and though her twin was aware of what happened, she didn't ask Bri about Sevair. Elizabeth wasn't one to often hide from a problem, but she was doing a good job of it now. As was Bri.

Bri understood Lladranan much better, people's Songs were clearer, the healing went better, faster.

Their parents had returned home and no word had come from Bossgond about a successful message being sent. Worse, the lull between battles had ended, with three incursions between that day and the next. When the battles were done a Chevalier would sicken and die in hours, painfully. No cure had been found for that disease, and everyone feared that it would spread. Morale was low, the Exotiques showing the most strain.

The next several days wound Bri's and Elizabeth's nerves tight. No word about their parents. The alarm claxon rang daily. Much to the disapproval of Zeres, Nuare, and Sevair, Bri felt the need to be close to Elizabeth and moved back to the Castle and shared the tower room with her. Elizabeth herself spent most nights with Faucon. Elizabeth's features became tight and drawn. She looked worse than when she'd been an intern.

Bri went through the days like a zombie, false smile twitching on her lips when someone smiled at her. Polite but withdrawn. Only when she snatched an hour of sex with Sevair or flew with Nuare could she forget that her parents were desperate. She and Elizabeth became closer. With that came the echoing Song of their grieving parents that they could sense across dimensions.

They kept the afternoon office hours, and Bri lingered to sit with Zeres and listen to his tales of times past. He'd moved into a tavern close to the inn, Bri's stipend paying for his room and board. He seemed to be drinking less. Unlike everyone else, he didn't expect her to socialize with him, talk or pretend to be happy.

Finally, finally, Marian requested Bri and Elizabeth come to Bossgond's island. Faucon and Sevair insisted on coming, too.

Soon they were confronting the old stick of a man who was the most Powerful Sorcerer in Lladrana. He let Marian do the talking. "Paper hasn't worked. When messages were inserted into the Dimensional Corridor, they were just blown away. Who knows where they went?" She met their gazes in turn. "You must understand that we just can't lob objects in there. Who knows what will happen!" She glanced at her husband. "Neither Jaquar nor myself can control the winds in the Dimensional Corridor from here." She added stiffly, "We don't have the time or the means to enter the corridor ourselves without calling on a full circle of the Tower Community. Resources are at a premium."

"Have you seen them!" Bri demanded, glared at the scrawny old geezer. He glanced away.

Elizabeth gripped Bri's hand hard.

"They…are not doing well." Marian swallowed, met Bri's eyes, then turned to Elizabeth. "They seem to think you've been kidnapped and they'll receive a ransom note."

"We aren't rich, but we're well connected," Elizabeth said. "Most notably to Judge Trenton Philbert III. You've met him."

Marian winced. "After Alexa went missing."

"He won't be pleased we're gone." Bri showed her teeth. "He's our father's best friend, an honorary uncle."

Bossgond uncrossed his arms, spoke for the first time. "Hostile."

"Ayes. *Yes!*" Bri said. She pulled her hand from Elizabeth's to slap it onto her chest. "You see what the loss of us is doing to them. Well, we *feel* it. Our parents. Daddy... Mommy...."

Sevair stepped up behind her, drew her into his arms. She couldn't deny him, liked his support and touch, was torn.

Faucon slipped an arm around Elizabeth's waist. She'd gone pale. No one spoke for a full minute. Then Marian said, "We know this is hard."

"Should have considered that before you Summoned us."

Marian send a glance to Jaquar. He said smoothly, "The Song reaches those who are best for the task, and who might stay. We did not specifically know who you were."

Bri just snorted.

Marian inhaled, let her breath out slowly. "We *are* working on a solution. Trying our best." She hesitated.

"What?" Bri demanded.

"If you're still emotionally connected—"

"Oh, we are," Elizabeth said as Bri laughed harshly.

"Then perhaps you can be hypnotized to send them a message emotionally..."

Elizabeth opened her mouth, ready to reject. Bri squeezed her twin's hand. "We'll try anything."

"Yes," Elizabeth agreed.

So they were settled into the softly carpeted and pillowed conversation pit. Faucon and Sevair were banished from the room so the twins could concentrate. Marian, Jaquar and Bossgond sat at equidistant points around them. The twins half reclined, half sat on the pillows. Excellent feather pillows, Bri thought hazily as the Circlets Sang.

To her amazement, and Elizabeth's equal surprise, a foot-long hamster was positioned so they could easily see him. Tuckerinal. *Look into my eyes*, he said.

Bri did. They swirled with colors, not as rich and sparkling as Nuare's, but fully as Powerful. That was the last thing Bri was aware of until she found a portion of herself in the Dimensional Corridor, with Elizabeth floating beside her. Her parents were sitting on the couch in the living room holding hands.

Bri bit her lip at the sight of them, exhausted, with lined faces. They cuddled in each other's arms, turning to each other for comfort. Her eyes stung. Facing adversity together, as always.

Oh, look at them, Elizabeth choked.

Nodding, Bri said, *Let's do it. We only have to convince them that we are safe in an unusual place.*

Huh, Elizabeth said.

So they did. Bri knew she'd never projected an idea so hard in her life.

Her father shifted, tilted his head. "Did you hear that?"

"No," their mother said too quickly.

Concentrate on Dad, Bri said, again sending a stream of thought, of *feeling* toward him, knew Elizabeth did the same.

After a moment or two, their father whispered, "I have the strangest feeling that they are safe."

"No!" their mother said. "Don't do this to me, Perce."

"They're safe." He held her tight. "They're not here, but they're safe."

"How can you say that?"

His expression turned stubborn. "I just know. We won't be receiving any ransom notes."

"I don't believe you."

"And I believe in God and miracles."

That shut her up.

But it wouldn't for long, Bri knew. Her mother's intellect always overbore her father's vague feelings.

Then mist whirled in front of the portal and she felt a tug and a clunk as she fell back into her body.

Elizabeth sat up first, shoved hair from her face. She looked around and her gaze fastened on Faucon. When she held out her hand, he came and pulled her up and into his arms.

Sevair stared at Bri. She wriggled her fingers to him in a wave. He took that as an invitation to follow Faucon's example. Bri let herself lean against him.

"Did it work?" Bossgond demanded.

"*Ttho.*" Tuckerinal answered. "Not good enough."

"Not enough to banish doubt," Elizabeth said thickly.

Marian sighed, gazed at Jaquar, then Bossgond.

The old Circlet paced the circumference of the room, rubbing his chin. Stopped in front of Bri and Elizabeth. "We have one last alternative."

"We'll do anything," Elizabeth said again. Bri was glad her twin had taken over the speaking for them.

"It may be that you must be in the corridor itself to communicate with someone on Earth. Since the Snap hasn't come and you are not fully of Lladrana yet, we can try to insert you into the space between dimensions, for a message only. Would you be willing to do that?"

Bri hadn't realized until then that her cold hands had twined once more with Elizabeth's chill fingers. They spoke as one. "Yes."

"It will take a while for me to set this up," Bossgond said. He seemed less ornery and more interested.

"How long?" asked Elizabeth.

"A week. The procedure will demand drugs and a ritual."

Bri said, "We'll do it."

Bossgond nodded.

Marian said, "Very well." A faint smile curved her lips as she looked past them to Sevair and Faucon. "Requirements for the ritual are no solid food, no sex for the next week."

Sevair said, "I'm perfectly capable of sleeping with Bri and not making love with her."

Bri stared up at him. His jaw was set.

"You're moving back into your tower in Castleton where Nuare and I can take care of you."

She didn't have the energy to argue, and he felt so good against her that she agreed.

"I, too, can only sleep with Elizabeth," Faucon had said silkily when Sevair had made his pronouncement at Bossgond's tower. "And I have been taking good care of her for some time now." Faucon had run his hand down Elizabeth's spine, sending a little warmth, a little Power to ease her muscles. He *had* taken good care of her.

Of course, she'd given him, emotionally and physically, all she was capable of. Now and then she had the lowering thought that that wasn't much, wasn't enough, was far less than he deserved.

His will had proven as steely as his sword, as hard as a certain part of his body when they were in bed together. They'd had trouble sleeping, but had held each other. He'd been called to battle a couple of times and then Elizabeth didn't sleep at all.

Her own determination to follow Marian's rules were

strong. Strong enough that Elizabeth could dismiss her body's ache for sex. As for food…she stuck to liquids, and her old standby, a raw egg in orange juice, both of which Faucon provided. She also sipped on starfire. Every time she healed, every time they attempted to heal the Chevalier's disease, she took a little Power for herself.

All their efforts to cure that sickness had been futile. Elizabeth shuddered when the battle alarm rang, knowing Bri did the same. If they could have hidden from the noise they would have.

Today she had a bad feeling. The claxon had shrilled during breakfast, and she forced herself to drink. Faucon flinched. He wasn't on rotation. He'd lost another of his Chevaliers to the sickness. If it hadn't been for her, she thought he'd fly to each battle like many leaders who fielded Chevalier teams, instead of keeping to the schedule. That she *was* preventing him from fighting was a guilty gratitude in her. A notion that somehow she was saving his life. Irrational but true.

Then the alarm clanged that the battle was over and they eased.

For a half hour.

Telepathic screaming and the bugling of terrified volarans hit her. The screams were Alexa's. *Elizabeth, help. Help!*

She shot from her seat and to the Landing Field taking whole flights of stairs at a time and landing softly… hurrying magic.

Alexa screaming. Disaster. Doom.

Oh, God. Oh, God. Oh, God. Elizabeth! shrieked Marian hysterically. That was even worse.

Bri! Marian and Elizabeth cried in unison.

Bri yelled back, *I'm on my way. Nuare brings me and Zeres.*

Elizabeth didn't argue, but zoomed through the maze, pulled along by the linked Power of the other Exotiques. Calli was crying softly. Elizabeth burst out onto the Landing Field, shouting herself as she saw a clump of impenetrable backs and wings. "Make way!" She plunged forward, and beings were shoved from her path as she fell into focused emergency-room mode.

Koz was lying in a flat net on the ground, his left leg nearly torn from his body, gray faced and with blood trickling from a head wound. Adrenaline dumped into her, and all her years of medical training clicked into place.

"He's *dying*!" Marian screeched, holding the leg in place, draining herself of Power and energy and all her strength, sending it to her brother.

As Elizabeth kicked a fold of the net aside, her Song quested along his body. His femoral artery had been torn but repaired, by his team or the Shield he'd worked with or himself. Or all three.

"Why is he *here*? Why didn't you set up healing circles on the field after the battle! He's lost blood. He's lost energy, coming here." Elizabeth knelt, reached for him.

Alexa wept. "Because we *lost* Partis and Thealia." Alexa wrapped her arms around herself and rocked. "They and their volarans fell. Partis always led the healing groups. We lost another new Marshall pair. No one…we couldn't…we didn't…" Alexa halted. "Our team is shattered."

Elizabeth spared her a glance, saw a shiny red burn covering half her face. The half without the scar had tears dribbling down her cheek. Some of her hair was gone. She was buried in grief. Her mentor gone, and her mentor's partner, the man whose voice had called every Exotique to Lladrana.

As always, Elizabeth spared only an instant for a flash of her own grief at the loss of the gentle Shieldmarshall and his fearsome wife, then she blocked her emotions and those screaming from the other Exotiques. Definitely not the optimal atmosphere for surgery.

Bri appeared dazed, shook her head, sent her emotions away, too. Elizabeth smiled grimly. She'd learned her professional distance from doctors in the emergency rooms of hospitals. Bri from health care workers in refugee camps.

One last stray thought—the Marshall team was torn. Alexa would have to be the one who mended it.

Other medicas joined them.

"We will have to take his leg," Jolie said.

Marian wailed, pressed harder on the leg they'd aligned.

"No," Elizabeth said. "See to Swordmarshall Alexa's hurts. I place her in your care."

Jolie frowned but moved away. Elizabeth upped her flow of starfire into Koz. It was only keeping him alive, not healing him. Knitting his muscle sinews, tendons, arteries and veins together would be a massive undertaking. Elizabeth refused to fail.

Time to see just how much starfire she could pull. She drew on the Power. Human and volaran auras sparkled, Songs filled her. The rhythm of the planet Amee itself throbbed through her, renewing her strength with such Power she had to keep her mind knife-keen to stay conscious. She began to work cell by cell until she could do more.

Nuare's dark shadow draped them in cool shade. People gasped, volarans whinnied.

"Easy." Bastien's voice trembled. "Calli, I need your help with the volarans."

Marian's knuckles turned white over Calli's hand. "Andrew. Koz, needs it more."

Calli said, "I can do both. Send calm to the volarans and you." And she did. "Elizabeth, can we link with you? Five of us would be mighty strong."

"More than five," Bri said, placing her hand on Elizabeth's. "Nuare and Zeres are here, too. They can help. Calli can link with Koz's volaran—"

"He's hurt, too." Calli's voice caught.

"Then we'll link with him and heal him, too," Bri said. "Link with those of the herd who will help. Marian, can you connect with Jaquar?"

"He's on his way from the island, Bossgond, too."

"So we'll have Circlets joining us, and Chevaliers." Bri raised her voice. "Listen!" Her words echoed around the Castle. Quiet blanketed the place. "I want every Chevalier and volaran hurt in the battle to join in the healing circle, the most Powerful unharmed on each side of those injured, then we will connect."

"That can't work, alternating unharmed and healthy," Jolie muttered, shocked.

"It *will* work," Bri said.

"I haven't seen a healing circle like this since Parteger Island," Faucon murmured, placing a trembling, savaged volaran—Koz's volaran—on Bastien's free side. Bastien had one arm around Alexa's shoulder. The volaran folded to the ground and Bastien tangled his hand in its mane. Faucon did the same on the opposite side. Jerked at the force of the energy cycling up and down their line.

"You've never seen a healing circle like this." Bri's smile was so strong and fierce it twitched Elizabeth's lips up too. "We are the Exotique Medicas. We will show you how."

"We need to close this circle," Jolie said.

"Yes, for the moment." Again Bri's voice rang out. "When others arrive, they will add to the circle. Luthan, I want you to be the gate-point. You will open and close the circle with new additions, connecting them to the person before you."

"Always the end of the chain when you open," Elizabeth said.

"Right."

"Ayes," said Luthan and he began ordering hurt and whole.

A shaken Marwey, clothes ripped open along her side showing a long, acidic scratch, took Bri's other hand. Both Bri's and Marwey's hands were brought down to Koz's wounded leg. The leg first, then the head. He moaned. Bri opened herself and a river of Power flowed through them all, leaving more than Elizabeth gasping.

You're fixing Koz. Joy lit Bri's tone. *Good work.*

I AM a doctor.

Yes, you are, and we will rely on all our skill to heal this leg. Marian?

Will he die? Marian gibbered.

No, Elizabeth and Bri said at the same time.

He will not lose his leg, either, Elizabeth said. *Though he will have damage to it. I suggest a new career.*

Definitely, Bri said, *especially with his head wound. We don't want him to harm that again.*

Playtime's over, said Alexa with forced insouciance. She seemed to hear the echo of her own words and stifled a sob.

Elizabeth let Bri regulate the Power, keep it even and strong. Steadying as each new person or winged horse was added to the circle, pushing it through the injured, healing them and flushing their bodies with her healing starstream.

A beautiful, melodious chant rose and fell around Elizabeth, suffused her. Letting her mind and fingers mend Koz, she listened, heard a lovely masculine voice, looked up to see Calli's Marrec Singing. Before her eyes, strands of black turned to silver over his temples.

Power.

What we are doing not only heals, Elizabeth sent to the circle, to Alexa, *it is making us more Powerful.* She could feel her own scalp tingle, hair raise, understood that she'd be another with a streak of silver. *The Marshalls' team might be fragmented for the moment, but when it returns it will be stronger than ever. Chevaliers, too.*

Bri Sang, her voice low but tuneful. Her hair looked the same, brown, purple streaks gone. No silver. Bri smiled, tears running down her face. Elizabeth blinked, but her eyes were dry. No way was she going to cry in the operating room.

Bri sent down the circle, *We Sing and sorrow is shared, comfort is shared.*

Every few minutes someone else joined. Elizabeth felt the sparkling youth of a young female volaran and her dam, became aware of the auras and the Songs of others already connected. The steady strength of Sevair Masif, the whispering wind of the roc, Nuare, Luthan's clear tones.

Faucon, Powerful and true.

All the while she mended capillaries, twined muscle together, reknit sinew like a surgeon, and Bri healed beside her.

Jolie's soprano spiraled high in counterpoint. *So beautiful*. She, too, wept.

Luthan opened the circle, Power diminished.

Then surged, swamping Elizabeth, letting her mind dissolve into instinct. She faltered. Bri was there with her, sending the excess energy into Koz, brushing his brain with slight Power.

Fascinating, came in a dry, observant tone. Elizabeth didn't have the vision to see, but she recognized Bossgond.

Plugged into a whole different energy, Bri said.

I do not like these Exotique phrases, Bossgond grumbled. He'd bloodbonded with Marian—he had an idea of the concept.

A lightening of spirit flowed around the circle.

Elizabeth never knew how long it took, the healing of Koz enough so that he'd live, mend on his own, then pinpointing other hurts: Alexa's burn, Marwey's slice. When Luthan finally wrapped up the Song, the day was still a few hours away from sunset. Sometime during the circle, they'd all sat. It was the strangest medical experience Elizabeth had ever had.

Many fell over.

With a grunt, Bastien stood, wobbled a little, scooped up Alexa. "Going to bed," he said thickly. No one had the energy to comment. Marrec stood and gestured to the commander of the Castle soldiers who had stayed alert and away from the circle. "Can you help us take Koz to—"

"Our suite," Marian said loudly. "The Tower Community's Suite in the Castle."

"He's going to love that," Marrec grunted.

Marian ignored him, stood and swayed with regal grace,

put her hands on her hips. "He's staying with us until he's completely well."

Now Jaquar grunted, and with fisted gestures, gathered wind. Elizabeth thought her mouth fell open as she saw Koz rise from the net, cradled on an invisible gurney of air.

Sevair pulled Bri up, kept her within his arms. His feet were planted solidly. He wouldn't fall.

A medica apprentice hurried up, biting his lip. "Exotique Medicas," he said hoarsely, cleared his voice and gathered himself. "As ordered, I checked on every Chevalier. I found the Chevalier with the Dark sickness dead in his rooms."

Elizabeth looked around blindly, glance sliding over other wounded. "He wasn't here?"

"No. He carried not the slightest injury, but shows the symptoms of one who has died from the disease." The apprentice looked a little nauseated himself.

"No injury, something new." Bri sounded punch drunk.

Elizabeth drew sparks from the starfire. So much easier than working through the exhaustion she'd experienced as an intern. She put a hand on the apprentice's shoulder. "Show me."

"He is dead. No hope."

That echoed around the Castle, too.

31

The next day those of the Castle mourned. And they Sang. The air was filled with Song. Bri and Elizabeth were included in all the formalities and, like everyone else, wore their best clothes. Lady Knight Swordmarshall Thealia Germain's and Shieldmarshall Partis Germain's grown children had come, the oldest a middle-aged man who appeared resigned. Alexa made no effort to hide her tears.

Bri was uncomfortably aware that Alexa had lost two sets of friends: the other Marshall pair had died in their first fight.

Since bodies sank into the ground of Amee, there were only possessions left of those who'd fallen. In the great temple, Bri and Elizabeth watched as the Marshalls' armsmaster unfolded the cloth case that held the batons and returned four dull-looking ones to empty pockets. The simple ceremony had tears prickling behind Bri's eyes.

Late the next morning Bri attended a briefing for the

first time in the large Marshalls' council chamber in the Castle keep. Sevair came too. She was glad to have his solid, quiet presence.

Alexa sat on three pillows at the head of the long, scarred but polished table. Her intricately carved chair was nearly thronelike and showed a banner and sword on the back. Bastien sat at her left hand in a chair marked with a shield. The rest of the Marshalls, sixteen pairs, sat in chairs marked with a sword or shield. Bri had heard that two Chevalier pairs were testing for Marshall over the next few days.

The Chevalier representative, a middle-aged woman, sat in a chair with a carved flying volaran at the top. Calli and Marrec were seated next to her. Marian was in the Tower Community's chair shown by a Castle, Jaquar beside her, and Luthan Vauxveau in the chair with a singing woman.

Elizabeth sat in one with the outline of a town hall, gazed at Bri and Sevair, then stood. Sevair waved her back down with a slight curve on his lips. "Unusual that we of the City and Towns have more than one representative here, but not unprecedented." He motioned to Bri and she saw that there were two chairs with cottages carved on them. Faucon was on the other side of Elizabeth.

Bri slipped into her place, Sevair did the same. They were the last to arrive. Even Zeres and the city medicas were there, sitting along the edge of the room with their Castle colleagues. From the shifting going on in their ranks, Bri got the idea that this was new to them, too. A full complement of medical people, interesting but not unexpected.

People crowded the wooden-paneled chamber with windows showing baton insets of stained glass. All were quiet, intense.

Bastien stood. "This meeting has come to order. Let us Sing." Song lifted, seemed to penetrate the gloomy keep walls into the gray day. The prayer rose, speaking of dedication to Amee, the fight against the Dark, and asked for blessings. Bri *thought* she felt a little pulse of an answer, a warming of the soles of her toes where they met the floor, didn't know for sure. She shared a quizzical glance with Elizabeth. What the others felt, she didn't know.

The meeting proceeded, Bastien following some sort of agenda, one of the female Shieldmarshalls, the archivist, Bri thought, keeping notes…by tapping a piece of paper with her finger. Nice trick if you could do it.

Arms were tallied, spell weapons discussed, the frinkweed destruction shown on a map. At least that was proceeding well. Then the Chevalier sickness was brought up.

Everyone turned to Bri and Elizabeth with palpable interest and no accusation.

Following an idea that had stirred in the pool of her mind the night before, Bri stood up. The quiet intensified. "It's time medicas fly with the Marshalls and Chevaliers to battle."

Immediate and loud protest. She raised a hand and her voice. "Not simply us, Elizabeth and me, but others, too."

"We will not allow this." Bastien's expression was as commanding as his voice. "You are our hope. We cannot let you fly to every battle."

"Just one battle, then," Bri said. "To see if we can understand how a Chevalier is infected." She turned and looked at the seated line of medicas behind her. "To develop a team to fly with the warriors." Some of the men and a couple of the women nodded, determined eagerness in their gaze.

Bri's breath silently sighed out of her. She'd *felt* that there might be some who'd wanted to help on the battlefield.

Her glance swept them. "If you wish to assist the Marshalls and Chevaliers on the field, let me know." She saw fearful faces. "If you don't, no disrespect to you." She held out a hand and Elizabeth stood up and linked fingers. Bri felt surprised pride from her twin. "We don't want to fracture the medical society further." She held out her other hand to Zeres. He blinked and slowly rose, took it. "We *do* want to emphasize that a different way of healing should not be shunned." She gave Zeres's fingers a little squeeze. "It might just mean that a person is ahead of his time."

Turning back to Bastien, she said into the quiet room, "I believe we must do this to understand what is happening, to try to prevent it, or learn how to cure the sickness. We've explored every other way."

Alexa joined her husband. "I've been chosen the new Lady Knight Marshall." A slight smile flickered over her face. "The first time ever that there have been two women in a row. I agree with Bastien and with Bri. Let the Exotique Medicas come once to see how the battle fares. We Marshalls haven't been hidebound to our Lorebooks for a while and we would welcome on-the-scene medicas. However, the medicas must have volaran partnering training for battle. Calli, can you do that?"

"Ayes," Calli said. Her forehead furrowed. "I must judge how this'll work. Marrec and I will fly to the next battle, too."

"I don't like this," Bastien muttered. "Four Exotiques on the battlefield. Asking for trouble." He stared at Marian. "Under no circumstances will you be allowed to go."

She nodded. "I agree one of us needs to remain safe."

"No one except Bri and Elizabeth will stay together," Alexa said. "Calli, you and Marrec will *not* dress in your colors. Medicas, you will not wear red and white." Alexa smiled again and it was a little wider. "Camouflage for you. Soulsucker leathers, maybe. They blend best with the countryside."

"Listen!" Bastien raised hands and Sang. Bri's tongue thickened in her mouth, the edges of her mind fizzed and her fingertips tingled under the silencing spell. Dazed, she listened to his chant. None here could communicate of this to anyone else, could not speak within the hearing of outsiders.

Then they were all dismissed. All the Exotiques and their men lingered. When everyone else was gone, Bastien closed the door.

Marian sucked in and blew out a breath, then said, "Bossgond and Jaquar and I have discussed your problem." She frowned as she studied Elizabeth, then looked at Bri. "You were magnificent when you established the healing circle. But your Songs are uneven. You worry about your parents and it stresses you."

Bri shot her a sour look. "You think?"

"I thought we'd made the matter clear that we would be distressed if our parents were worried about us," Elizabeth said.

"Point is…" Alexa tried and failed to hitch a hip onto the table that was too high for her. Bastien picked her up and set her on it. She smiled at him and went on, "None of us can afford distractions. Not now and not in the crucial months to come." She gestured to Bri and Elizabeth.

"You got a problem—" she waved to the rest of the Exotiques "—we have a problem. So..." Now she stared at Marian. "Fix it."

Nodding, Marian said, "I can tell that you've followed all the necessary requirements for the ritual. So we're moving up the schedule. If you're agreeable to spending the day in solitude on Bossgond's island, we'll try to reach your parents tonight." Marian grimaced. "They've been going to bed early."

Bri sagged. Sevair put a strong arm around her waist. "That's good."

"It hasn't been easy restraining myself," Faucon said lightly, brushing Elizabeth's cheek with his finger. "Let's go make arrangements."

"Excellent idea," Marian said, and they filed out.

Sevair's iron grip on Bri's wrist radiated temper. They stayed. He kicked the door shut, muttered a locking spell and Bri knew her impulsiveness had landed her in trouble again. She had also decided that she didn't like the room. Lots of negative energy. Much of it from the man beside her.

"You must be mad," Sevair said through gritted teeth. His hands clamped around her upper arms and he lifted her from her feet. She'd never seen him so angry—pale under his golden skin, mouth thinned tight into a narrow line.

"Don't call me mad." She wet her lips. She didn't mind being eccentric, New Age, different, but she'd never been— hardly ever been—out of her mind.

He plunked her onto her feet. She glared up at him. "It's time medicas go to the battlefield."

"Let them go. You stay here."

Eyeing him, she did a quick pace around the council table. "We need to determine the cause of this sickness."

Robin D. Owens

"Let someone else do that."

She stopped, put her hands on her hips. "It's our responsibility. The Exotique Medicas. You understand all about responsibility."

Jaw clenched, he turned away.

Bri continued. "We can't just stay here and watch people die. I can't do it." Her breath caught and she hated that. She steadied her voice. "We have to take action!"

He swung back, hands fisted at his sides. "You've tried to heal every single Chevalier, no matter how tired you were."

"Tried!"

"Elizabeth and you have done autopsies."

Bri rubbed her temples, sure the silver would be sprouting any minute and wouldn't that surprise everyone if she got home. *When* they got home. Elizabeth already had a swatch over her right ear. "We tried pulling the tumor and its tendrils from a living body. Elizabeth even kept one poor woman alive after her soul had gone, as she tried to surgically remove the mass." Bri had bowed out of that experiment. Most of the medicas had thought the invasive procedure an abomination. Zeres had assisted Elizabeth. Since then, Bri's medica friend and Elizabeth had gotten along just fine.

Bri tugged at her hair, brought it around to look. Still brown. "There must be an answer on the battlefield." She sucked in a breath. "And the new Marshall team needs all the help it can get."

"You haven't done this on Exotique Terre," Sevair snarled.

Stiffening, Bri said, "I'm not trained in military medicine. But I can organize health care workers and the sick in refugee camps, and Elizabeth is an emergency-room doctor. We can put a battlefield medica team together and train them. I think some of the men have been itching to do this for years, just couldn't go against tradition." She glanced at Sevair. He was still tight-lipped, seething. Standing her ground, she lowered into her balance. Nothing would move her on this. "I don't think Faucon will make this much trouble for Elizabeth."

"He's a warrior, and you can bet everything you own that he'll have an extra team of his Chevaliers protecting her alone."

"Protecting me, too." Bri jutted her chin.

"Ayes. If you stay near her." Sevair's lip curled. "When do you ever stay in one place if not constrained?" Finally spitting out what was really bothering him, she was sure. In two strides he was standing toe-to-toe.

"I'm sorry if my wanting to return home hurts you. But you knew all along—"

He kissed her. Hard and hurting and wanting. She heard all from him, felt all. Tough muscles, warm heart, Sevair. She loved the tensile strength of him, his working-man's muscles. Then he set her down again. Met her gaze with an intense one of his own. "There's nothing to do but go to battle with you."

Fear spurted through her. "No! You're not a Chevalier."

"You're not going alone." His jaw clenched, relaxed. He touched a big-bladed knife at his hip. "I can fight." After one last sizzling look he headed for the door. "I'll be going to that Circlet's island with you, too. Where you go, I go. Faucon isn't the only one who must organize for an absence. I'll talk to someone about the battlefield. Luthan, I think."

Then he was gone and her heart thumped hard and she wondered what she had done by being responsible.

* * *

Night had fallen and Bri was twitchy. She and Elizabeth held hands and stood in the middle of a candlelit pentagram. Despite that fact, everything seemed sharp and distinct, the other Exotiques, their men, Sevair, Faucon, all surrounding her. Having Sevair here added to her nerves. She yearned to see her parents, yet also thought it was his steadiness that kept her calm. He was letting no hint of his own emotions disrupt the circle. Bri met Elizabeth's eyes.

Sevair cares for you, Elizabeth said.

And Faucon cares for you. We're going to leave some cracked hearts when we return home.

Ayes, Elizabeth said, and Bri didn't think her twin realized she'd spoken in Lladranan.

"Let us begin," Bossgond intoned.

Elizabeth quivered like a too tautly strung door harp beside Bri. Probably she had a better idea of what they'd face in the Dimensional Corridor.

Song rose around them. Bri hadn't listened to her music player for days, and that odd thought had her nearly giggling. Elizabeth sent her an incredulous look. The Song brought pale blue light that caged them, then the room faded away and a shadowy door appeared in the tube of light. The door opened.

Before she could say anything, they were shot into a...space. Bri had read of the awful winds of the Dimensional Corridor, but she felt nothing. Elizabeth, holding so tightly to her hand that Bri's finger bones scraped together, pointed.

In front of them lay their parents, twined around each other in bed, appearing exhausted in the moonlight, sleeping. Tears sprang to Bri's eyes. She couldn't bear to look at them.

Now! screamed Elizabeth into her mind.

Bri scowled at her, then heard it. A sound like the ringing of their parents' phone. Bossgond and Marian and Jaquar.

Daddy, she whispered, and felt a push, a pull and she was connected to deep, slow images of the sleeping mind of her father.

More ringing.

Answer the phone, Daddy, Bri prompted.

32

Bri, baby, is that you? Even in sleep hope leapt in their father. He pulled Bri's mother closer as if wanting to share good news.

Yes, Daddy, it's me, Bri. Brigid idjit. She'd *hated* that childhood name. She remembered the carefully crafted script. *I'm so sorry we couldn't get through earlier. One of my friends who runs a refugee camp needed some immediate help. Daddy, people are dying.* That wasn't in the script, stupid! *I convinced Elizabeth to come with me. She's a wonder.*

Bri? he asked groggily.

But Bri turned to Elizabeth.

Hi, Dad, Elizabeth said breezily. *Just wanted to let you know everything was ok. Bri and I have been sick that we couldn't reach you earlier. Communication with the States isn't easy.*

Understatement.

Can you put Mom on?

Bri felt her mother's thoughts stir.

Hi, Mom, Elizabeth said.

My Elizabethie! Tears dribbled from under their mother's eyelashes.

Elizabeth gave a choked laugh. *Yes.*

Their mother sniffed. *Where are you?*

Africa, a refugee camp. We'll be back soon. Only temporarily. Elizabeth's mind-voice faltered, broke. *Just calling to say we're all right.*

Thank God, thank God, my girls are safe.

Yes, Elizabeth said. *Here's Bri.*

The link with her mother was strong and sure now. God, how she loved her parents! *Hi, Mom. We didn't mean to worry you.*

Bri, you never do. A bit of a scold.

Elizabeth and I are safe, we'll be fine, back soon. I love you.

Then Bri could feel, touch, hear everyone, Elizabeth, her Dad, her Mom. Their love meshed them together. *I love you, Mom. I love you, Dad.* She was losing it so she shut up, waited for the all important words.

We love you, their mother said. *I love you, Elizabeth. I love you, Bri. Be safe.*

You, too, Elizabeth said. *I love you, Mom. I love you, Dad.*

We love you. I love you, Bri, I love you, Elizabeth. Their father's tones were warm.

Sleep, and remember, Bri and Elizabeth said together, and that particular phrase was the spell's end, backed by all the Power of those in Lladrana.

Everything went dark. Still. Then a tremendous boom rattled her bones and she and Elizabeth were back in Bossgond's tower, hugging each other and weeping.

* * *

They'd spent the night in Marian's tower. Never in her wildest dreams had Bri ever thought that she'd sleep in London's Tower Bridge. But she wasn't in London, was sure Tower Bridge didn't have a lovely teal-appointed guest suite, and with Sevair there, she didn't do much sleeping. She'd been an emotional mess and he'd carried her all the way from Bossgond's tower to Marian's, passing the low buildings of the Circlets' school on the way. The sex, of course, had been magnificent. He'd been urgent, he'd been tender, he'd been strong. And she'd responded to him, let her passions reign, touched him and kissed him and caressed him until all she heard was his moans and not any sounds of the corridor or Earth beyond. Then they climbed to ecstasy and fell from the peak and shattered together.

When Bri saw Elizabeth at breakfast at Bossgond's she figured that Elizabeth and Faucon had had as athletic a night as she. The other Exotiques all had a glow to them and the men appeared supremely satisfied.

The food was great, but didn't hold Bossgond's interest. They were eating in his round tower room where the intricate brass telescope was and he fiddled with it all during the time the others were eating.

"Ah!" he finally said. "Your parents are awake and discussing your telephone call." He sent a wrinkle-faced smirk over a bony shoulder at them. "They wish they'd asked for more details."

"Naturally," Jaquar said, putting jam on toast.

Bossgond turned back to the telescope, grunted with surprise.

"What?" asked Marian, Bri, and Elizabeth all together.

"They are using that communication device to call someone," Bossgond said.

Bri shared a glance with Marian.

"Ca-see-dee," Bossgond reported.

Elizabeth's eyes widened. She almost dropped her fork.

After a moment, Bossgond said, "A man who has also been worried about you. I do not entirely understand the Eeng-lish. But there is a…project?"

"That man has been trouble since we first met him," Bri muttered. Elizabeth wasn't looking at Faucon. "As for projects, plenty of them. I should have signed up for nursing school, but that probably didn't ring any bells for him. Elizabeth?"

Elizabeth finished chewing her syrup-covered waffle and replied, "I'm sure there's paperwork I would have submitted for my position at Denver Major." She put down her silverware and rubbed her eyes, looked at Marian. "I'm supposed to take up my first hospital job in under two weeks. This could ruin my career."

The air pulsed with emotions. Everyone in the room wanted to convince them to stay. No one said anything. Bossgond had turned away from the telescope and studied them, rocking on his heels.

Jaquar coughed. "Luthan sent word that the Singer has revealed a new prophecy regarding the Exotique Medicas."

Bri set down her orange juice so hard it slopped. Now everyone's attention was focused on Jaquar. Marian appeared serene. She already knew, probably as soon as Jaquar, the bond between them was that intimate. Bri didn't know whether to envy or fear that sort of bond.

"Go on," Elizabeth said steadily.

"The Chevalier sickness and whether the Exotique Medicas stay or go will be resolved in two weeks."

Before Sevair placed his knife on the table, Bri saw his fingers tremble. It gave her a pang.

"The Singer has a good forecast rate?" Elizabeth asked, her voice a little high.

"Ninety-seven percent," Marian said.

"Then it will be finished. Fine. Good." Now Elizabeth sounded stilted.

"Any more detail to that prediction?" Faucon asked casually. His fingers clenched around his fork.

"Not that Luthan said, and, I think, not that the Singer told him. Some friction there. Luthan's not a man to follow others blindly."

Bastien snorted in his ale, spoke for the first time. He'd been concentrating on his food. "Not my brother."

"All over in two weeks," Bri said, disliking that her voice rose. Facing life-altering decisions and changes again so soon. Pushed around by fate. She wasn't ready. How could she prepare except by thinking about things she didn't want to?

"You might consider the prediction that way." Jaquar smiled charmingly.

"Or you might think of it as a deadline," Marian said.

That afternoon, after Elizabeth had left to catch up on Castleton's healing, Faucon went down the hall to Luthan's door and strummed the harp.

"Come," said Luthan.

Faucon wasn't surprised to see Sevair. He nodded to the

Citymaster. "I'd like to speak with you, Luthan, about the Exotique Medicas' safety in the upcoming battle."

"We'll talk shortly about the battle," Luthan said. "First, I understand that you made a quick trip to your cousin's. What did he say about the Seamasters?"

Faucon hesitated.

Luthan said, "I think the Citymaster should know. In fact, I believe it's time we talk to selected people."

"The Exotiques."

"Ayes."

Faucon raised a hand. When he spoke his voice was rougher than he liked. "I also want to know about any predictions regarding my lady." He nodded to Sevair. "I'm sure Sevair would appreciate some indication about the future of his lady, too."

Luthan deliberately looked aside, toward the window and the sunless day beyond, not catching either man's gaze, though they both stared at him. "I would rather not say anything," he replied softly. "The future is still in flux."

He sent Faucon a glance, did the same with Sevair. "The Snap is a very strange phenomenon. More often than not, an Exotique's decision to stay or go happens in that instant, not before." He smile wryly. "Exotiques' futures are notoriously difficult to predict." There was a short pause. "Sometimes I experience glimpses of the future, years in advance. I knew there was a great chance of my father falling in battle last year. I knew Thealia and Partis would not live to see the final outcome of the fight with the Dark—and that ultimate resolution is still very much unknown to me, too." He shrugged. "But when I try to look even a week into the future of *any* Exotique, nothing happens. So, please, either of you, do not ask me again."

"Agreed," Sevair gritted out.

Sighing, Faucon said, "I won't, upon my word of honor."

"Let events progress as they will." Luthan spread his hands.

"About the Seamasters," Sevair pressed.

Faucon shifted and the others knew he'd be giving important news. "The Seamasters have not been forthcoming—"

"A secretive lot," Sevair said.

"—but my cousin has been able to piece together a very interesting story."

"Ayes?" asked Luthan.

"It seems that the Seamasters have listened to the tales of Summonings and Exotiques with considering and discerning ears." Faucon took a seat on a sofa. It was too hard to be comfortable. "The Seamasters, being the thrifty souls that they are, and suspicious of the Marshalls and their authority, decided to try a Summoning of their own. Last winter solstice at their biannual gathering at Seamasters' Market."

Both Sevair and Luthan gazed at him with wide-eyed astonishment. Gratifying.

Faucon coughed for emphasis. "Needless to say, they failed."

Luthan swore, low and long and Faucon stared at *him*. He'd never heard Luthan, the perfect gentleman, curse.

"By the sweet Song," Sevair finally said.

"Fools," Luthan bit off, the least of the names he'd called the Seamasters. He rolled his shoulders, then as if he couldn't continue to remain seated, he stood and paced toward the window. A great deal of window-looking going on today. Panes of glass. To the outside. To the future. To the past of the winter solstice.

"Stupid merde-begotten fools," Luthan said. He whirled from the window, scowling. "Equinox and Solstice times may be fine for regular rituals, but a Summoning!" He shook his head, hard, as if trying to get beyond the notion of the Seamasters' stupidity. "They could at least have consulted Bossgond to find out when Exotique Terre was most open to Lladrana."

"Bossgond's consultations are expensive and the Seamasters' cheap," Faucon said simply.

"Truly idiotic," Sevair said. He shook his head. "We City-masters didn't like the amount of zhiv we had to pay to the Marshalls for the Summoning, and we discussed the matter of parting with the money long and hard. But we weren't stupid enough or prideful enough to think that we could work as a team to bring an Exotique to Lladrana by ourselves."

"Many seafolk work as a team on their fishing vessels," Faucon pointed out.

Sevair gave him a tough look. His words were crisp. "The guild leaders? Do they still go out on their ships? Do they work with their inferiors or their equals? How often do they work as a team with their equals?"

"All good questions," Luthan said. "All which should have been considered. Whether they were, we'll never know. At least this answers a few questions."

"Such as?"

Shrugging, Luthan said, "The Singer has been dropping hints about the Seamasters. Wondering aloud whether they pursued some important endeavor, or whether they would. Whether they often reported to the Marshalls."

Faucon grunted. "They haven't had a representative at Marshall Council meetings for years. They would occasionally ask me what happened here at the Castle, but I think they usually spoke to my cousin about information I passed on. Third hand." He snorted.

Luthan's brows lowered. "Also, the Exotiques have occasionally mentioned dreams they've had of a woman. When Elizabeth and Bri arrived the others didn't recognize either of them as this dream lady. Probably the prospective Exotique of the Seamasters." Luthan paced to the window and back, hands clasped behind him, then he shot Faucon a glance. "To invade the Dark's nest we will need a ship like Lladrana has never seen."

Faucon raised his hands. "Don't look at me. My brain was wrung dry just designing my yacht. I couldn't begin to build a ship that would take Exotiques and Marshalls and Chevaliers and volarans to the Dark's volcano home." As he heard his words and realized their impact, fear came that the ultimate battle would cost the lives of those he loved. One or all of the Exotiques. Elizabeth. How could he allow her to fight the horrible Dark One itself? A woman who healed? Far, far worse than just experiencing one battle safely from the sidelines. Perhaps it would be better if she returned to Exotique Terre, at least then he'd know she was safe. But he wanted her so.

Again he stooped to clearing his throat for attention. "Now let's talk about this battle." They spent the rest of the afternoon with several bottles of ale, thrashing out a good plan to keep the medicas safe on the field of war.

33

The alarm claxon rang midmorning on the second day. Bri jerked and dropped the cup of tea she'd been drinking. It shattered in a thousand pieces on the stone floor of her living room, leaving a sticky residue she didn't have time to clean up.

Her housekeeper-maid dropped something with a clatter in the kitchen and stumbled in, excited. "I'm s'posed to help you dress for battle. Just like a real body servant or squire." She clumped hurriedly over the mess as she flung open the door and raced up the stairs to Bri's bedroom

Bri's nerves jittered and she put a hand to her stomach. Suddenly this flying to battle thing seemed like a really, really bad idea.

"Ready!" her maid caroled down.

So Bri trudged up the stairs to her bedroom. Her battle gear lay on the chest.

A few minutes later she wore surprisingly thin and

Powerful chain mail under her icky soul-sucker skin tunic. Her tights had been replaced with "bespelled protective pants," also the weirdly textured soul-sucker. She had a knit cap on her head, then a clunky helmet. It had been a while since she'd worn anything but the red and white of the medica. This wasn't an improvement.

Her maid swatted her on the behind. "Go."

Bri stared at her in surprise until the serving woman lowered her eyes, smiled weakly. "I saw some squires do that."

"We don't," Bri said, sounding like Elizabeth.

"Ttho, Lady."

"We clean up the messes in the living room and kitchen."

"Ayes, Lady."

But "Go!" and not "Think!" seemed to be the word of the hour. Bri turned and ran outside, settling herself on the roc. Sevair would fly on Mud.

We fly to battle.

Then Nuare was angling steeply, rising high into the sky. There was a thunderous clap of her wings on the down-stroke, the whirl of blue sky and white clouds and shafts of yellow sunlight in broken stained glass around Bri for a minute, then the world settled again.

"Wha—?"

Roc Distance Magic. Those clumsy horses will be another half hour. Since we are here I will show you the border. That blue line below is Power keeping horrors and the Dark from invading. The yellow glows are fenceposts.

Bri had read of this, seen 3D magical images, watched the occasional battle in the Map Room. She still stared at the awesome sight. "Lower!"

Nuare obligingly dropped, skimmed the border just above the fenceposts, circled one. *This was the first, set by Alyeka.*

"Then we're near Prevoy's Point. In the middle of Lladrana." Bri focused on calling up a mental map.

Ayes. All the fenceposts to the west have been replaced. There are still gaps to the east. Old ones burn out and fail, but new ones are there, too. Wherever the monsters have invaded over the last year.

The new fenceposts, tall as telephone poles, glowed brightly, almost hurting Bri's eyes. Some were golden, the others bright yellow.

The golden ones are those raised by Exotiques. Alyeka or Calli.

Bri hadn't been aware that Calli had made any, but they were directly north of Calli and Marrec's estate, so that made sense.

More thunder from Nuare's wings, another spatial discontinuity, and Bri saw that they were farther east. In the distance to the south was the low oval that was Volaran Valley, to the southeast the shadow of the great escarpment.

The mountains to her left, the north, were massive and intimidating, much larger than any she'd ever seen. It was late June and peaks glistened a deep and icy white. The snow never melted. Wonderful, fabulous, and the area was so dangerous from the horrors that people had abandoned homes and villages. Even with the borders safe, she didn't think humans would return to stay until the Dark was finished.

Bri knew people who'd moved to Denver, who'd grown up there, who never wanted to live outside the mountains.

What had this done to that sort? Where had they gone? Had they stayed in Lladrana? Did they sicken and die of grief? Too much thinking of sickening and dying. But she was flying to a battle after all.

There is the breach in the border. The horrors have already crossed.

They were certainly in Lladrana, pouring from a narrow canyon onto a plain with grass and scrub brush. Seeing the ugly things lumbering over the green land, deep hatred and protectiveness welled in Bri. There were yellow-spined slayers; thick-black-furred renders with long curving claws flashing in the sun like steel; soul-suckers, gray and tentacled and somehow slithery. She was glad her leathers didn't touch her skin.

This wasn't a small invasion of a dozen. This was hundreds.

34

Whoops and shrieked battle cries split the quiet. An arrow of Marshalls and Chevaliers dived. All the Marshalls and two-thirds of the Chevaliers were called to this battle.

Bri caught her breath at their absolute courage.

You said the medicas are to stay west and center of any battle, ayes?

"Ayes." She saw a smaller contingent, heard Elizabeth on Starflower but didn't see her since she was surrounded by all three of Faucon's teams. Mud trumpeted to Bri.

Luthan was standing as an overseer for unusual situations. With four Exotiques on the field—two rank novices, there were bound to be unusual situations.

Work to be done. Even as she asked Nuare to turn she saw a pair of Chevaliers go down, their bodies sink into Amee. Cries of human pain mixed with the dying screams of monsters.

She didn't know how she could stand it. But she would. She gritted her teeth. Nuare landed in an area with rocky boulders and tree brush. Elizabeth was organizing the four young, volunteer male medicas. "You're best at triage." She pointed to the one with the shortest hair.

"Here's Bri," Faucon said, hauled Elizabeth up for a hard kiss, then set her on her feet and leaped to his mount. "Stay. I'll be back if you need me." He flung up a hand. "First team with me!" Off he flew.

The burliest two medicas followed in his wake, ready to bring wounded to the camp.

Mud watched everything with an anxious gaze, but Sevair was with her, keeping her calm. The man radiated control, keeping Bri from a panic attack, too. Probably siphoning away fear from everyone else in the small medica unit, all first-time battle participants. Volaran-back, Luthan hovered around the camp.

Before the space was fully organized, the first wounded were brought in. Then all Bri thought of was work fast and heal, a huge lump in her throat. Why had she thought she'd have time to watch the battlefield? Foolish.

We are watching, Nuare said. *Luthan and I. I will find the evil seed—my eyes are sharper than puny human and volaran eyes. Sevair is watching you.*

A pair of Chevaliers died as Bri and Elizabeth worked over them. The medicas lost another. Sweat dripped in Bri's eyes as she fought death, won. Seven times. Being here, on site, they had seven in the recovery area. She was already wrung out. Took the bota she wore full of energizing herb tea and drank.

There was a slight lull. Elizabeth joined Bri to stare at the field where horrors and Marshalls and Chevaliers clashed. Screams. Warcries. Weapons meeting flesh or monster hide or monster claws, teeth, spines.

"Terrible," Elizabeth said. She was pale and the scent of lavender came from her, a herbal cleansing spell for when she perspired. Bri figured she was equally fragrant.

Elizabeth took the bota from Bri, swigged, her gaze fastened on their medicas, flying low over the field, searching for the injured. "I could never be a battlefield medica."

"Me neither." Bri glanced at Nuare who glided a few feet away. The bird's eyes were whirling and her beak and claws coated in monster fluid.

Luthan and Sevair were close.

There! Nuare yelled in her mind, screeched aloud.

"What!" shouted Bri and Elizabeth together.

A strange soul-sucker, not the same as the others. Mutant.

"Sounds like the Master's been busy," Bri snapped, craned to see it. "Which soul-sucker?"

The one with the rougher skin.

"Rougher skin's all that distinguishes him?" Elizabeth asked.

"That's enough if Nuare can pinpoint the monster. Maybe the Master only has one. It takes a while to create horrors."

It has already inserted the evil seed into a victim through a slayer's spine wound.

"What!" Bri said in unison with Elizabeth.

Nuare dipped her head, pointed a claw. *Over there.*

They both swung to see Faucon leading his team against a cluster of renders and slayers and one soul-sucker.

Elizabeth's blood froze. Her heart pounded and her breath stopped. Nothing all morning was as terrible as this.

Like all morning, she couldn't hesitate. "No!" she shrieked, ran. Swerved to miss Bri's tackle and leave her on the ground scrambling to catch up.

"Can you kill the mutant soul-sucker?" Bri shouted.

Nuare bulleted forward. *Ayesss.*

"Please, not Faucon," Elizabeth prayed as she ran. A man and volaran blocked her. "Don't get in my way!" she yelled, ready to use any Power, all Power, to reach Faucon. Luthan shot out a brawny arm. Hoping he meant to help, she grabbed it, was swung onto his stallion. "Faucon," she gasped.

"I know," he said.

Wait! Power amplified Sevair's mental voice. People checked. *The Master is here. I can sense him. If you kill the mutant soul-sucker, or when you kill all the horrors, he will leave. We want him.*

There were only two knots of monsters left, both surrounded. Nuare swooped down on the mutant soul-sucker, snatched it up, smacked it against a boulder. *It is dazed but alive.* The roc sped to where Calli and Marrec were checking volarans. Nuare dropped its prey.

Luthan used the mental broadcast band next, calmly, incisively. *Faucon, you and your teams report to the medica unit now! Any with slayer spine wounds may be the next sickness victim. Sevair, find the Master. Divert him. Marshalls and Chevaliers split to confine the horrors. Toy with them until I give word we have the Master.*

They were flying close to Faucon's teams. Elizabeth's gaze fixed on her lover, scanned his armor, looking for wounds. Nothing on his neck. His face was whole, but his expression grim. She saw him stare at the man at his right. The one showing a split shoulder seam of dreeth dragon leather, and a round acidic hole in his upper arm.

Faucon's major domo. The man who was like a father to him. Broullard.

Trusting Mud, Sevair closed his eyes, tilted his head, searching for the warped personal Song of a man he'd once known well. Familiar but not. It had taken nearly the length of the whole battle for the Song filtering through his brain to make sense. Sevair swung Mud toward a mass of heavy brush.

Then Nuare was beside him, and Sevair controlled Mud's instinctive fear of the roc.

Nuare clicked her beak and projected her thoughts. *He is here watching. He has another diseased-sprout and an "eye."*

"Eye?" Sevair said, flying high.

Eye. A small Powerful pebble to be implanted in someone. To see and report back to the Master and the Dark.

"That could explain some things," Luthan said, joining them. His volaran ignored Nuare. "Like every time our Exotique Medicas try something new, the Dark wards the next Chevalier seed against such a procedure. Surely one or several of their solutions should have worked."

"Huh," Sevair said. Pure glee rocked through him. "He was my assistant. I *trusted* him and he betrayed me. Now he'll pay."

"Wait!" Luthan circled until he was face to face with Sevair. "What if we implant this 'eye' on *him*? If we send it back and keep a link with it, we may learn what's going on."

Sevair grinned. "I like that. We'll do it. More suffering than a fast death."

Luthan matched his smile, nodded. "And I like a man who thinks on his feet, makes quick decisions. Can you draw his attention so we can plant our own eye?"

"Ayes," Sevair said with harsh satisfaction. He and Mud landed, and he told her to stay. He used Power to glide over the ground, to bend branches away from him. If he'd wanted to question and kill the man, he'd have unsheathed his knife and come from behind. He rushed forward and grabbed him. "Got you!"

The Dark's servant was monstrous, no longer a man. But he'd been a secretary, helping with city business and architectural plans. Sevair had worked with stone and hammer for decades.

After a brief struggle, Sevair had his ex-journeyman's thick throat between his hands. He squeezed. Even a monster's eyes bulged, and they flashed with fear, which was gratifying.

"I think I owe you something for all your good service," Sevair said and tightened his grip, wondering how much he could damage the thing. "Perhaps I should give you to the roc. You know a roc now lives in Castleton, don't you? Likes to eat sangviles. You ever send more and we'll bring in a fleet of rocs. This particular roc might like Master-flesh too."

As Nuare's shadow fell over them, the Master shuddered.

The huge bird dipped, rose. *As easy as filleting fish, to open a small slice in his scalp. You have distracted him well,* Nuare said. *I put the "eye" in his scalp. He will not notice it.*

Since the man's hair seemed crawling with vermin, Sevair didn't think so either.

We'll check, he returned with relish. *I'll shake him and you can see whether it falls off.* He did so.

The eye remains, Nuare said.

Let him go, Luthan said. *You're killing him. We want him alive so the "eye" can see. Let him escape.*

Sevair lessened his grip just slightly on the man-horror's throat. Turning his head at thrashing bushes, Sevair said, "Luthan is that you? Does the Singer want this one? I don't know that she's ever interrogated a Master with one of her Songquests. Might be interesting to see what sort of shape he's in afterwards, eh?"

Luthan crashed through the brush. The man-thing-Master flung himself away from Sevair. Cloth ripped and he was gone, disappearing in a stench of smoke.

"Well done. I think he soiled himself, my friend." Luthan clapped Sevair on the shoulder, then continued quietly. "It was the right thing to do. If we killed him we would not have been able to understand the Dark, in all its alien impenetrably. He will translate the entity's actions for us when he instructs the horrors. And a more competent Master might have arisen." Luthan lifted his head and gazed beyond Sevair into the past or a future-that-never-was. Then Luthan looked east. "The border is very close to being complete, only a few holes. Some weak points, but we can leave and invade the Dark's nest soon, Song willing."

But while they'd been handling the Master, they, too, had been distracted.

A woman shrieked. Bri or Elizabeth. The men whipped around, plunged through broken branches of scrub, just in time to see a dreeth materializing above the medical station and plummet down, wickedly sharp beak primed to stab.

* * *

The dreeth was diving straight toward her! Elizabeth flung herself aside, fell, scrambled. Fire flamed from the dinosaur-bird's mouth, singeing grass, her hair. She rolled, crawled. A pair of female Marshalls stopped the dreeth. They fought, slashing at head and wings and horrible claws.

Too close, too close, too close.

The thing opened its mouth, fire spewed. One of the woman-volaran pair was simply incinerated. The other screamed, she and the volaran fell. She'd put her sword in the dreeth's wing and as they plunged, it came down, too.

Then Bri was there. Patting her all over. "Are you okay? Elizabeth? Elizabeth!"

"I…" Her voice was scared down to her gut.

The Marshall! She forced her weak legs to stand, her knees and ankles to move. She was running to the dreeth, frantically looking for the woman and volaran.

Gone. A dark depression in the ground showed where they'd hit and died. Shadowy batons rose to mark the Marshalls' passing; the real ones lay dull. The women and volarans had sunk into the soil so soon. Or was it hours? Time passed so oddly.

Then Bri was screaming, waving a long dagger, shooting toward the thrashing dreeth. "You tried to kill my *twin*!"

Chevaliers and Marshalls around the monster moved aside for Bri. What was the *matter* with them? Didn't they see she wasn't made for this sort of life? Yelling words even Elizabeth couldn't understand, Bri stabbed the dreeth. Its truck-sized head jerked, swiped at her.

Sevair jumped on the horror's neck. A horrible snap. He

had a hammer and hit the skull. His knife sawed the neck, severed it. The dreeth shuddered and the blood pumping from a foot stump stopped.

Sevair glared at Bri, blood shimmering on his knife blade and his hammer. Because of her he'd used his cherished tool to kill. Fierce triumph glinted in his eyes.

"I will fight for you, Bri. I will always fight for you."

It was a promise as much as a statement. Almost a threat.

Elizabeth shook so she could hardly walk, but heard her name called over and over again. Faucon. Broullard. She'd been looking for a net to carry Broullard. His best chance was at the Castle, where Zeres and the medicas could form a circle. Again. Must *not* be futile.

The Marshalls' circle was broken again, with the loss of another old pair. It couldn't be mended until they dealt with their raw grief.

To Elizabeth's surprise, Bri was organizing the medicas— none of them had died, thank God—though a wildness showed in her eyes.

Faucon supported Broullard. Everything had happened so quickly. Broullard's hand tightened around Faucon's as he made to put him aside.

Elizabeth shook her head. Since she wanted to keep on shaking it "NO!," fold onto the ground and cry, she straightened her spine and walked to them.

Bri was talking to the roc, pointing to a net.

Carry a net. Nuare snapped her beak in dislike.

"Please! Just this once!"

Nuare turned a baleful eye on Bri. *I have helped much this day.*

"Yes, but he's important to my sister's mate."

Elizabeth wavered toward them, spoke through cold lips. "Please, lady roc."

Nuare snorted. *Very well. You ride, your twin rides me. We will go FAST! Use Distance Magic. Be there quick.*

But Bri had already thrown her arms around Elizabeth, gave her a quick hug, gave her energy, Power. Bri's dagger was back in its sheath and she was focused on healing.

As Elizabeth should be. She managed a jerky bow to Nuare. "Thank you," she said. Put a hand on Faucon's shoulder, giving and receiving comfort.

"Let's go!" Bri said, and tugged on Elizabeth's hand to an already harnessed Nuare. When had that happened? Things were happening too quickly for Elizabeth to even *see*. She'd have take hold of herself. She was a doctor, goddammit, trained for emergencies, clear thinking.

But that was in the hospitals of Earth. She kept her back turned from the battlefield as she climbed onto the roc. Battlefields were not for her.

To Bri, everything moved *fast*—her heart pumped quickly, her breathing was nearly panting, and Nuare zoomed. When they reached the Castle, it was ready for them, doors held wide and strong soldiers to take Broullard and run through the keep to the healing room.

The bed was clean and Broullard was placed gently on it. Bri and Elizabeth set their hands on him. The tumor was already large. Gray tendrils strangled his organs. Bri and Elizabeth connected with the medica circle and Sang.

This was their battlefield and they fought valiantly, shrank the mass from fist sized to a lima bean, snapped the threads with starfire, drowned them. Still they lost.

"Broullard." Bri barely recognized Faucon's voice. "My friend, my father. Stay."

Broullard fought, too, like the excellent Chevalier he was. But he was slipping into death.

"Anything!" Faucon shouted. "Spare no Power. I will give anything that he might live."

Beside her, Zeres tensed.

No, she sent to him, but he didn't reply. Faucon could restore Zeres's fortune. Zeres himself was gaining respect every day. *No!*

He didn't listen.

Zeres gathered Power, took all the excess in the circle. *Sang.* Flung himself into space and embraced the vision of the universe, the stars exploding around him. The gray tendrils shriveled, the bean diminished to a new pea.

Everyone pushed Power into Zeres. Then he plucked the mass away from where it nestled near Broullard's heart. With too much force. Broullard died. The deadly seed broke open, a hideous black wormlike thing darting out, latching onto Zeres's energy, lodged in him, unfurled more tendrils.

He had given his all to destroy it, had nothing within him to battle it.

Bri focused the circle on Zeres. Threw herself into the healing starstream, opened herself to the huge force between the stars. Lost control and tumbled around in the Power she'd called as if she'd swum into a riptide. She gasped, floundered, struggled to control it so she could heal. She grabbed the healing starstream, planted her feet in the river, and *fought*.

She used *everything*. Everything she felt instinctively about healing with her hands, every tiny drop of knowledge from

404

Robin D. Owens

alternative medicine, every smidgeon of western medicine. All she'd learned on Lladrana of chimes and chakras.

Sought out the evil gray threads of death, broke them again and again as they created a web. They reformed.

Once more the kernel of evil pulsed gray next to a red-beating heart, poisonous beyond what they'd seen.

She fought and she fought. Got nowhere. The web tendrils would reform, the fatal seed send out more feelers.

Only one thing to do, and she prayed and Sang that this would kill it. She cradled the thing in her energy. Then she withdrew from the healing circle and submerged herself in the raw Power of the healingstream. Shot out into the universe with the kernel.

Zeres came with her. Hovered near. Seemed to look at the stars and the galaxies and the space between them. "Wondrous," he sighed. *If I'd only known to tune my own chimes to the real Song.* He died.

35

Bri returned to Lladrana with a thump. Collapsed. Knew she'd failed.

She'd taken the evil into herself, could feel the pealike kernel.

She had the sickness. Now she and her twin *must* find a cure if she was to survive.

Sevair's arms lifted her and cradled her. He was wearing the impassive stone mask he used to cover desperate emotion. He loved her and she— She'd lost.

Elizabeth's expression also disappeared behind a cool, distant, doctor mask, though her eyes met Bri's and begged for reassurance that all was fine.

Bri closed her eyes.

And saw her parents, clinging together, worried about their daughters, then laughing in relief when they got the "phone call." How they'd grieve, and everything in her ached.

She couldn't go home. If the Snap happened, she couldn't go. Nothing on Earth would heal this, would it?

Maybe it would, maybe Mother Earth would sense the wrongness and scourge it from Bri. Yet that didn't sound possible.

If she stayed, would she trap Elizabeth, too? She couldn't see Elizabeth leaving a sick twin. So Bri would have taken both children from her parents. Awful, awful, awful.

As the darkness of exhaustion settled over her like a shroud, Bri knew she'd fight. Elizabeth would fight. Eventually, when they had to disclose the sickness to others, they would fight, too.

Would she bring the entire Exotique team—more— down?

The Dark would have definitely won.

Bri felt cold. She *was* cold, her hands, her skin, her lips. Cold inside, too. From panic fear more than the effects of the terrible seed inside her.

Sevair swung her up and took her outside to the Landing Field where Mud awaited. The bright summer sun didn't warm her, nor did it abate the new shock of the Castle folk in losing two more Marshalls.

The passage of air with sweet smells and Sevair's arms didn't warm her. Nor did his concern or that of her housekeeper-maid. Bri was tucked into bed. Hot tea was provided and Sevair remained, chafing her hands, ready to stay beside her all day if she wished.

She wanted to unburden her fears to someone, but contrarily didn't want to speak of the sickness, as if talking about it would make it true. After a swallow of tea that seemed weak and cool, she set it on the bedside table. "You should return to your work. Give a report to the city and townmasters," she said.

He shrugged. "They'll already have heard the news."

Curving her lips, she said, "I'm fine. Just in shock."

"The battlefield is no place for you." He squeezed her hands until she squeaked, apologized and did a circuit of the room. Not looking at her, he said, "Promise me you won't insist on fighting again."

"I promise I won't fly onto a battlefield to fight horrors again. I should be up at the Castle debriefing and working with the medica team."

"You are exactly where you should be." He sat beside her again, took her hands. She didn't know how long she could mask her complete and utter fear from him, control herself, so she lifted his hands to her lips, kissed them and saw surprise bloom in his eyes, and let them go. "Go to work, Sevair."

He scowled, studied her face, then nodded. "Very well."

She thought he sounded relieved. How much did he really care for her? What of those dramatic words he'd said to her after he'd killed the dreeth? "Go," she said, and lowered her eyelashes. She kept them open the merest crack because she didn't want to be in the dark.

He kissed her brow. "I'll go." He hesitated, spoke very gently. "We carried Zeres back here and placed him in the square, where Amee blessed him by taking him."

How selfish of her, to think of herself and not the old, funny man who'd helped her so. And now that she did she was overwhelmed by feeling—grief, fear, desperation. She scrambled around for the handkerchief she kept under her pillow, mopped at her face, kept her head averted. "Thank you very much."

"You're welcome. I'll carve a plaque for him." A brief touch on her hair and Sevair walked to the door. "Tonight we'll have soup and freshly baked bread."

"Yum," Bri said with only a little waver in her voice. Soup wouldn't cure this mess. "Can you send the housekeeper away? Tell her to go visit friends? I want some privacy."

She felt his gaze on her, heard the little spikes in his Song. How much was the kernel affecting *her* Song already? Was he sensitive enough to hear any changes? Of course he was. "I'm not used to servants. I like being alone." Some rare times, but this was one of them. If she wasn't alone she would spew fear and desperation all over someone.

The floorboards creaked as he returned, another soothing stroke of her head, another kiss on her temple.

"I'll tell your servant to go," he said. Then he was gone and she was tired and very scared and alone. How much time did she have? She was an Exotique, and Powerful, and a medica, so that might slow the disease down. Who knew? If she took a nap, would she ever wake up?

Her eyelids grew heavy. The last image she had was of Sevair and how he'd looked when he said he'd fight for her. Knew he would. But this was something she'd have to beat alone. Healer, heal thyself. If she had the time. If she had the chance. If she had the strength.

When she awoke, Nuare was looking at her with a tough and considering eye. *You have the evil sickness inside you.*

Bri felt all the blood drain from her head. She pushed

herself from bed and onto her feet, ignoring the sweep of dizziness. "You're in my bedroom." She saw the floor-to-ceiling window open.

A click of the beak.

Of course that was obvious, but Bri was trying to come to grasp with her fate. She straightened. "You said once you'd kill me if I had the taint of evil. Are you going to kill me?"

Nuare's eyes widened. She blinked, tilted her head. *No.*

Breath whooshed from Bri. She was still facing very hard facts, but having a friend kill her didn't seem to be in her immediate future.

Watching her slyly, Nuare picked up a claw and cleaned it with her sharp beak. *Now you will have to pay attention to that which is around you and learn.*

You can't cure me, then? Bri's throat was too closed to speak, and the quick leap of hope plunged.

No. Blinking again, Nuare said. *I could rid you of the nut and the web from it, rip it from you, but it would kill you.*

Bri coughed. "That's the general result."

You did well today. All of your fighting. Continue to fight. Nuare walked over to the long, open casement window. Without another word, the roc shot into the sky and away.

Bri staggered back to bed and curled onto it. This fear was horrible, but she didn't know how to make it go away. She had to face the facts, though, and she had to have help if she was going to destroy this thing.

Much as she hated to, it was time to tell Elizabeth.

Elizabeth!

Hmm? Her sister's answer was absent. *I would have thought you'd be up here at the Castle,* Elizabeth said. *The Assayer and his journeymen and I are dissecting the mutant*

soul-sucker. From the looks of it, this may be a very compli-
cated construct of a monster, not easily duplicated.

That's good. Elizabeth, can you come to Castleton, please?
I need you.

Ayes, I'll be there in a bit.

Elizabeth, I need you now! Then she just let go. Allowed
the hysterical shriek bubbling through her out, into the
tower, echoing through her mind.

I'm coming!

Curling into a tight ball—as if she could deflect danger
that way when it was already inside her!—Bri shoved her
fist against her lips and tried to think through terror.

Now she was stronger—no, more rested, she could
already feel the sickness sapping her strength—she reached
for the healingstream. It flooded her, and the little tendril
stopped growing, but was not defeated.

Then Elizabeth was pounding up the stairs. *What is it?*

Bri straightened, looked into her sister's eyes. "I have
the sickness."

"No!" Elizabeth said.

"Yes, and I can't stop it."

Color drained from Elizabeth's face. With trembling hands
she examined Bri's eyes, took her pulse, checked her heart.

Then they were linked together and scrutinizing Bri's
body and the evil kernel with the sprouting tendril.

Elizabeth breathed deeply. "Calm," she said and Bri knew
she meant it for herself, too.

"All right, together we link to your healingstream,"
Elizabeth said.

Bri had lost the rush of her source, had closed the door, and
now fumbled for the healingstream as never before. Elizabeth

summoned her starfire and Bri felt its heat inside her, cleansing her. Bri added her healingstream to batter the kernel.

Nothing affected it.

"A shield," Elizabeth said. Sweat trickled down her temples. "Let's encase it in a forcefield. We can do that."

They couldn't destroy it. Bri heard the hysterical gibbering in the back of her mind, locked it down. Following Elizabeth's lead, she surrounded the seed with pressure to keep it from growing. Elizabeth's starfire and Power enveloped it first, then Bri added hers.

Then they sat and stared at each other. Bri said the words neither wanted to acknowledge. "It won't stay that small forever." She put a fist to her chest. "I can feel it struggling to grow. What are we going to do?"

Elizabeth's gaze was as fearful as her own. "I don't know." She pressed her lips together, then spoke. "We'll find a way to kill it."

Bri shrugged. "I don't think we can."

Waving her hands, Elizabeth said, "How did you get it?"

Confession time. "When we attempted to heal Zeres, I tried to take his sickness as my own."

"Empathic healing. Our gift hasn't ever worked like that," Elizabeth's words were sharp bullets.

"I know. But…but…it was one thing we hadn't tried, and Zeres had almost destroyed Broullard's…"

"This goes back to Broullard!" Elizabeth rubbed her temples. "It's been a hideous day. One of the worst of my life. Faucon's grieving, the Castle people are grieving, you're grieving."

Bri guessed they weren't mentioning the awful battle. "You're grieving."

Elizabeth swallowed. "I lost my emotional distance for sure."

"Happens occasionally."

"Yes."

"Zeres didn't deserve to have that horrible thing inside him."

Elizabeth went to the basin of water and dipped her hankie and washed. "Neither do you. Neither do I. The question is, what are we going to do about it?"

"We've trained medicas, but we never found a cure—a vaccine or pill people could take."

"Don't you think I know that!" Elizabeth snapped. Bri could almost see her grabbing for her professionalism. Her back rose and fell with deep breaths, then she turned. "Natural organisms—bacteria, viri, yes, our culture has found ways to destroy them, 'cure' patients. But evil? The Dark? How can we find a cure for that? A 'good' pill?" She came and sat down on the bed, put her arm around Bri. "It's as if the Dark can't mutate living organisms, can't have this sickness be contagious. A boon for us."

"Right." Bri licked her dry lips. "I've been wondering about the Snap," she said softly.

Elizabeth stiffened.

"If the Snap comes, how can we return home with this thing in me?" Bri whispered, touching between her breasts.

"We can't." Elizabeth's voice was unsteady, then she repeated the words more strongly. "We can't. Earth can't provide a cure for this disease. If it could have I'd have convinced someone to send us back and return with a medical miracle."

Bri's fingers tightened around Elizabeth's. "I can't take this back home. Who knows what would happen? It doesn't seem to be contagious here, but who knows whether it would be there?"

"I am not taking any bit of the Dark to Earth. Never!" Elizabeth said.

"So I've stranded us here." Bri swallowed.

Elizabeth hunched a shoulder, but her lips trembled. "We have a choice. We will 'choose' to stay. Our lives can be good here. And we will find a cure for that tumor inside you." She sniffed, straightened her spine, which reminded Bri not to slouch and she did the same.

"Finding a cure for the frink sickness and this disease, that we can give to individuals, is our task," Bri said, her mouth twisted. "And I'm the one to do it, find the cure for myself, teach others, regular people."

"Yes."

"I don't want anyone to know for a while," Bri mumbled, letting her head drop.

Elizabeth hugged her. "No. We'll keep this to ourselves as long as we can."

"Not even the girls."

"Not even the girls," Elizabeth assured.

Bri's thoughts circled around. *What the hell are we going to do?*

"Find a cure. We *can* do that," Elizabeth said. Bri flushed. She hadn't meant her thoughts to be so loud. "We can't let negative thinking or fear stop us." Elizabeth took her arm from Bri, linked fingers, squeezed. "That's advice that has been given to me more than once by a very wise woman."

"Very stupid woman sometimes."

"No more of that! We can't afford it. We *will* find a cure."

Bri hoped so. Her life depended upon it.

"Besides," Elizabeth said with forced cheerfulness, "Luthan said everything would be resolved in a few days." Her smile faded as if she'd listened to her own words, found them wanting.

Sounded like a death sentence to Bri, then quashed the little nasty thought and hoped it didn't live in the back of her mind as the Dark lived in her body.

36

The longer Bri waited for Sevair, the antsier she got. She tried reading Lladranan medical texts. They still didn't help. Evening faded and she didn't walk.

So she paced the room and looked out the windows toward the park where her medica house was, where Zeres's body had been sucked into the ground, all neat and tidy, and did anyone else in the whole world think that was strange and gruesome?

Her mind went 'round and 'round. Couldn't bear the thought that she'd die and Sevair would wake with a corpse beside him, or see her die. This whole horrible mess brought out the meanest and lowest of herself and her stupidity.

She didn't think she could tell him, either. Surely it would be best if she broke off the affair. Save him hurt. Save her strength.

If the seed could travel through her bond with Zeres, it could do the same between her and Sevair. Anyone else.

Elizabeth!

Don't panic. I already thought of that.

You did? Are you sure you know what I'm thinking?

Ayes. I've been monitoring you. You think I could get it. But I can shield myself from it. Not let it in me.

Bri let her weak knees take her to the floor, crossed her legs, bent over and put her forehead on the floor, felt small, vague waves of comfort from the planet.

Thank you.

You're welcome. I have a grieving man to comfort. We WILL overcome this, Bri.

Okay. Faucon's lucky to have you. I'm lucky to have you.

Ayes, Elizabeth said.

Bri let the link with her twin fade.

Elizabeth could protect herself, but what of Sevair? Did he really love her? It had sounded like it that morning. But that had been in the heat of battle. He'd never said the words.

She was obesessed with the idea that she'd pass the sickness to him, or, even worse, that she'd split it somehow and they both would die. She couldn't bear that. She had to tell him the affair was over.

She had to clean up her life. Make sure if she did die, it was with her affairs in order. She looked around the tower. Someone would move in again. Maybe. Or would her death confirm it was a bad luck place?

Dammit! She was being so morbid. Where was Sevair anyway? It was full dark and she'd wanted to do this in the golden sunshine of the daylight. Or at least when the sun was up.

Negativity. She was nothing but a mass of negativity. She

rubbed her breastbone where the kernel hunkered, soon to break that forcefield and sprout. When it did, would it explode with tendrils and kill her quickly?

What was wrong with her? How come she couldn't shake this? She'd been in tight situations before, wondered if she'd live to the sunrise as the refugee camps were invaded.

The tumor was working on her. Fear. Depression. Negativity.

Evil.

She'd be a wonderful person to be around if she continued to give in to negativity.

If she was on Earth, what would she do? Give someone a good massage. Koz.

No. She didn't trust herself to work alone. Yoga. Meditation. Yes. Salute to the Sun sounded good.

Since the bath downstairs still wasn't finished, she showered, then went up on the roof. Nuare wasn't in her nest. Bri watched for Sevair and counted her blessings. She should write some affirmations down and repeat them ad nauseam to fight the fear and negativity. She had tools.

Blessings. Nuare wasn't going to kill her. Elizabeth was with her and would be working on the problem. She had emotional support from the whole city and Castle, if she cared to use it.

Then Sevair came within sight, looked up and raised a hand of greeting. She had a man who loved her, maybe. But whom she had to send away. That hurt more than the evil growing inside her.

A few minutes later—too soon, why hadn't she practiced what she'd wanted to say?—Sevair entered the rooftop with a tray. The scents of chicken soup and her favorite freshly baked bread, rosemary sea salt, wafted to her. She felt empty.

He walked toward her, smiling. Too bad. Get it over, quick and clean and blunt and *done*.

"Sevair, I want you to go and not come back. Our affair is over." She shrugged. "Elizabeth and I only have a few days left on Lladrana and I want to spend them up at the Castle, working with her."

He dropped the tray. The thick pottery bowls bounced over the small rim onto the rooftop, broke. Chicken soup went everywhere. The bread lay in grit.

All expression fled his face until it was as stiff as one of his own chiselled sculptures. He retreated to the other side of the roof.

His Song was stricken silent. His hands flexed, fisted. He stared at her for two long moments.

"Please leave." Her voice cracked.

He drew in a ragged breath, another. Shuddered. Then he advanced on her. His eyes burned with angry determination.

"I won't let you do this, dismiss me or our love." His gaze narrowed, his Song rose or sank beyond her hearing. "Something's wrong." Striding over, he lifted her by her upper arms, let her feet dangle as he scrutinized her. Meeting his gaze was one of the hardest thing she'd ever done. She didn't think she'd disguised her fear and misery.

He cocked his head as if listening to her Song, to *their* Song, still holding her high without apparent effort. "A beat is missing. A few notes." He shook her gently, aware of his great strength as she hadn't been. Not that he wasn't as strong emotionally. Stronger than she.

Words tumbled from her. "I've got the sickness. I can't cure it, neither can Elizabeth. I'm dying."

"No." It was a whisper, then a roar. "No!"

"Ayes."

A harder shake, then he set her gently on her feet and stepped back, hands fisted. His eyes looked wild now and his Song cacophonous with fear. "Then you will just have to learn to vanquish this sickness once and for all," he said. "I'm not having you dying on me."

She managed a watery chuckle. "I'll do my best to survive."

"You *will* survive." He paced the tower roof, avoiding the mess. A lot of that going around today. "I will *not* let you go. I will do everything in my Power to keep you." He sucked in a great breath, hissed it out. "Even if I must move to Exotique Terre with you, I will be with you."

She staggered a few steps backward to the wall, leaned on the cool stone, stunned. "But your country, your world… "

He made a dismissive gesture and her mouth fell open. "You are more important." Who would have thought it? The most steady, responsible, practical man she'd ever known ready to cast aside everything for…love.

But underneath that she heard the subtones of his Song, the subtext of his words. *I will not be abandoned again.* Not give up everything for love but from fear? Wouldn't it be easier for him to close his heart and step away? He didn't. Of course he wouldn't, as stubborn as his own rough rock.

Gaze locked on hers, he untied his belt pouch, opened it and poured some triangular clicking things into his hand. He took her fist, caressed her fingers open, palm up. "The reason I am so late. The Assayer was…busy."

"You were at the autopsy of the mutant soul-sucker."

"Ayes. But I wanted these for you."

"No gifts."

"You haven't let me give you anything but my labor on this tower. Because you think it will bind us together? Too late." He sifted a few of the triangles to her. They felt like bone.

"Dreeth teeth? *Yuuck*."

"We killed a dreeth together. If we can do that, we can do anything." He repeated the words he'd used only this morning of this eternal day. "I will fight for you, Bri. I will always fight for you." With the utmost gentleness he curled her fingers loosely over the three jaggedly sharp teeth. "Tell me how to fight with you."

"I'm afraid our bond will transfer the kernel to you."

"Let me take it from you." He was too intense.

Her heart jumped in her chest. "No!"

His eyes were wild.

"I'm afraid it will split and lodge in us both," she confessed.

He prowled toward her. "Then we will fight it together. Live or die, together."

"*Merde!* I don't want that. That is *not* romantic, Masif."

"I can be romantic." He swept her into his arms, carried her to the stair tower.

Nuare swooped down and swallowed the loaf of bread in one gulp, suctioned up some soup. Closed one eye in a wink at Bri.

Letting herself press her face against him, draw in his scent, she mumbled, "No sex. I don't want to transfer the mass during sex."

He laughed. Laughed! Jiggled her a little as they went down the stairs. "Not sex. Loving. We make love." He kissed the top of her head. "We are bound strongly enough that the evil could come through our touch."

She was afraid he was right.

Bri suffered wild mood swings over the next couple of days, sometimes affecting Elizabeth. But Sevair was rock solid, an anchor for them. She could barely believe how tough he was, though the strain of pretending she was fine showed on him, too. Like Elizabeth, more strands at his temples turned silver.

Both Bri and Elizabeth redoubled their efforts, reading Lorebooks, questioning Circlets, researching, studying. Bri missed Zeres, who would have been another anchor in the storm battering her, the old and canny man. He'd have had a different view on all this, the empathic healing thing. She wished *he'd* left notes about that. Surely he'd tried it.

Everything else seemed to be going very well. No invasions by the Dark horrors. The Marshalls learned through the spy eye Nuare had placed in the Master that the reason was they'd shaken up the monster-human.

Bri withdrew from the afternoon sessions to "supervise" the healing of other city medicas of the frink disease. Their training was spreading, not only other medicas coming to learn, but medicas teaching each other.

The frinkweed itself was close to being eradicated.

The Marshalls trained day and night, reforging their team. Bri was reluctantly relieved that Alexa was kept too busy to discover something was wrong with the twins. Calli was equally involved in her children and bringing a new

Chevalier class up to speed. Koz's injuries meant he couldn't fight anymore and he'd decided to learn mirror magic. Marian hovered over him and watched as he strived to establish links between Lladrana and Earth. Bri's and Elizabeth's and Sevair's pretense was accepted.

Elizabeth hadn't told Faucon. He was taking the loss of a father figure hard, as anyone would. So Elizabeth was comforting him, too.

Sooner than they expected, they had a message from Koz. During dinner Bri was having with Sevair, Elizabeth contacted Bri mentally. *Did you hear from Koz?"*

A note saying you'd discuss something with me. Bri hadn't had the energy or the curiosity to contact her twin. That was getting harder and harder. As hard as believing they'd whip this sickness, as hard as putting on a smiling mask.

Just as we've been working hard on curing you. Elizabeth's thoughts scattered, realigned. *He's been learning mirror magic. Apparently it's a much different magical system than Bossgond's Dimensional Corridor processes. Koz believes he can put a mirror into my apartment.* An undertone of wistfulness shadowed Elizabeth's mental voice. *We may even get audio and visual capabilities.*

That's wonderful. Bri meant it, just didn't have a lot of juice to say it.

He wants to experiment tonight. Wants us to be there.

Bossgond's island. Ttho.

No, he already has some sort of location mirror to lock onto my apartment." A mental shrug. *I have no idea how it works.*

Sounds good. Bri hated the night. Hated sleep, even with Sevair's arms around her. Even after lovemaking.

He won't be here until very late.

That didn't bother Bri. *Still fine with me. When?*

There was a little hesitation. *Would you spend the night with me here in my tower suite?*

Bri sniffled. *I'd love to.*

I want to be near you, just tonight. Sisters. Twins.

Me, too.

So Bri explained to a scowling Sevair that it was a twins-only night together. He didn't like it and that actually cheered Bri. The man was not too good to be true. They argued with some heat before he remembered her condition and grudgingly gave way. She kissed him, grabbed her solar backpack and all her remaining goodies and flew with Mud to Castleton.

They ate chocolate—Elizabeth still had more than Bri—took turns listening to Bri's music player, sang silly songs and did a few gentle dances together.

It was late, near 2:00 a.m., when Koz strummed the doorharp and knocked. The door opened and Elizabeth saw him. "Finally," she grumbled. She and Bri had been dozing on the love seat, tilting toward each other.

Koz smiled. "That's a lovely sight."

"Huh," Bri stood and stretched, a little too pale. Elizabeth's heart squeezed. She hoped Koz wouldn't notice.

But Bri had a diversion ready. She reached into her pack and pulled out gold-foiled candies. "Want some chocolate?"

Koz's eyes sharpened, his teeth gleamed in a smile and Elizabeth realized the light had dimmed in the room—after she and Bri had stopped speaking and fallen asleep. "Lights." The room brightened. Bri grunted.

A chocolate nugget disappeared in Koz's mouth.

"Have you got the stuff?" Bri said, then giggled, not quite the usual Bri giggle, but Koz shouldn't notice that. "I always like saying that."

Elizabeth relaxed at Bri's cheerful tone. Bri was feeling upbeat. This would all be easier.

"Brilliant," Elizabeth said, looking expectantly at Koz.

He didn't answer, merely opened a belt pouch and brought out a thick wad of velvet which he put on the nearby dining room table and began to carefully unfold.

"Koz?" Bri asked.

"Enjoying chocolate here," he mumbled thickly and Elizabeth understood he was letting the candy melt in his mouth, not chomping it down, demonstrating patience and sensuality. Too bad neither of them had fallen for him. He deserved a good woman.

A minute later two hand-sized mirrors were revealed.

Koz swallowed, gave a little moan, shook his head, sighed. "Don't know if I'll ever ask for that again. The taste buds aren't used to it and that makes the experience all the more intense. When that candy's gone, it's gone." He grimaced, a corner of his mouth lifted. "Like the nuts by the way. Thanks."

Touching one of the mirrors, Bri cocked her head at Koz. "I didn't think they made magic mirrors so small."

"*They* don't. I do." He grinned, tucked his thumbs into his belt. "Revolutionized the process—which is progressing fast and cutting edge for this culture, don't think anyone understands that. Good people, mirror magicians." Nodding at the mirrors, he said, "Think of them as cell phones. One for each of you. They'll tune to your personal Song as you use them."

Elizabeth picked up the other. It reflected her face and the room darkly.

"It's not a real mirror," Bri said.

"Of course it is," Koz said. "It just doesn't show what's around you, but is linked to a different place."

"My place?" Elizabeth asked.

"How do we activate it?" Bri asked.

"Bossgond can occasionally transfer an object to and from Earth." Koz waved a hand. "It depends on the cycles of the Dimensional Corridor, which is shifting by the way, soon to close between here and there."

"We know." Elizabeth couldn't keep the sharpness from her tone. That had been mentioned in the Exotique Lorebooks, but no one had spoken of it to her or Bri.

"Right," Koz said. "Bossgond's the only Circlet who knows the cycles, but the Singer knows, too. *She* was the one to tell the Marshalls the day to Summon Alexa. Anyway, Bossgond got a large magical mirror into your empty apartment. He says empty is easier and best, though he tried several times. That's the first. If it works, we'll try to put one in your folks' place."

"Oh." Bri sat down all the way to the floor. She cupped the mirror in her hands, held it close to her chest.

Elizabeth's knees felt weak and her eyes watered. Koz took her hand, eased her and himself to the floor, too, with him between Bri and her. He pulled Bri's hands gently away so the surface of the mirror could be seen by all of them, gestured for Elizabeth to angle her mirror the same.

"Let's see if it works." He was tense. "Tap the mirror and say 'abracadabra.'"

37

"Abracadabra!" Elizabeth looked at him.

"What? You wanted 'open sesame'?" He lifted and dropped a shoulder. "They're my mirrors. I wanted something easy for us, the Exotiques, to remember but hard for the Lladranans." Another shoulder twitch. "Security measure."

"Good idea," Elizabeth approved.

"Colorado time's a couple of hours behind us, so your apartment will be empty. All to the good."

"It will be dark, how will we know—" Bri started.

"Abracadabra," Elizabeth said.

But her apartment wasn't dark. The glow of the lamp on her desk in her living room cast soft light. Elizabeth's breath caught at the rush of affection for all her old, familiar things. Another life. Another lifetime ago.

"I didn't think you left that light on," Bri said.

A man groaned.

It wasn't Koz.

"We have audio, too," Koz whispered proudly.

Cassidy Jones sank down into the desk chair. He riffled the pages of Elizabeth's open desktop calendar, as if he'd done it time and again. He propped his head in his hands, despairing.

"Cassidy!" Bri hissed softly.

"Him again," Elizabeth muttered. But her chest tightened.

"He looks bad," Koz said in normal tones.

"Can he hear us?"

"Safety feature, for not causing folk to think they're insane," Koz said. "You have to tap the mirror and say, 'Testing. Testing. Testing.'"

"Will someone be able to see us, too?"

"That's the idea, though of course we haven't tried the audio or visual. Gonna take guts on the other side to try that. Looks like you ripped him hard," Koz said.

"You have it wrong," Elizabeth said coolly. "He dumped me and ripped me hard."

"Guy got the guts to accept voices from the air?" Koz asked.

"He couldn't even believe in my gift for healing and he's a doctor and *saw* how I helped. Of course not. I don't want to talk to him, anyway. Damn man, in *my* apartment."

Cassidy moaned again, whispered, "Where *are* you, Elizabeth? I've checked all Bri's flaky friends and the refugee camps. You aren't with Doctors Without Borders or Hospital Ship Hope."

The three in Lladrana stilled.

"Uh-oh, trouble," Koz said.

"He's talking to himself," Bri said. "The great Cassidy Jones. Not like him."

"I have contacts with all the international groups. Where

are you, Elizabeth?" He stalked to the mirror. "This is new, a present from your parents? Suits you." His mouth turned down. "I can almost *feel* you, Elizabeth." He shook his head. "I was such a fool."

"Sounds like the man has had this conversation with himself before," Koz said. "Sure you don't want to try to contact him?"

"I'm sure," Elizabeth said.

"Would he be cruel enough to tell Dad and Mom?" Bri turned wide eyes on Elizabeth.

Elizabeth shook her head. "No, he loves them. He won't tell them." She looked at Koz, "How do we disengage?"

"Tap the mirror and say 'signing off.'"

"Signing off." Elizabeth touched the mirror, watched it fade into darkness, waited for Bri to do the same.

Her twin stared into the mirror. "I wouldn't have thought it of him. Who knew?" She shrugged, tapped the mirror. "Signing off."

Koz rose easily to his feet and went to the door. He bowed, expression serious. "The mirror magicians and I worked hard on these mirrors. It isn't Circlet Power like Bossgond's interdimensional magic. We've initiated a link with Earth through your apartment, and intend to send one to your parents' house. Or maybe we send it to your place and have you 'call' them again and take it to their home. You'll be able to see and talk to them even after the Dimensional Corridor shifts and the portals between our worlds close. Think of *that* when considering your futures." Another bow and he was slipping out the door.

Elizabeth met Bri's gaze. Koz had meant the little talk to be about the Snap, their choices. That was far outside the orbit of their concerns right now. The only fate they cared about was whether Bri would live or die.

Carefully, Elizabeth put the mirror in its sleeve. Bri's eyes were wide and staring. Elizabeth could feel her being sucked into despair. She wouldn't let that happen. She wouldn't accept that her twin sister would die. Not possible.

So she put her arms around Bri and kept her safe through the rest of the dark hours of the night. And prayed.

Bri waited until she knew Sevair had gone to work before she flew back to her tower. She stopped at her bedroom threshold, staring at a plump, foot-long hamster snoozing on the broad ledge of her windowsill.

A little surge of delight, some fizz of Power, when she saw the magical being. The fey-coo-cus had been absent from the Castle scene for a while.

When he saw her he rose to his haunches and clasped pink-claw-tipped paws together. His Song, a mixture of classical Earth music and lilting Lladranan notes, pulsed with deep yearning. A tingle ran down Bri's spine.

The baby needs good nuts to grow well.

Bri stared. "Baby."

Tuckerinal thrust out his hamster chest. It looked more like his belly. *I am a father.*

She grappled with the thought for a minute, caught him staring hungrily at her backpack. Good thing she hadn't left it. "Um, can't the Circlets make it good nuts?" Knowing that group, they'd be making atom balls and whatever like mad to feed the new fey-coo-cu and see the results.

Not the same. The baby needs EARTH nuts, since it is half-Earth.

She clutched the backpack to her chest. The evil sprout inside her burned. She refused to let it dictate her life.

Look appealing, Tuck said, and Bri got a jolt when she realized he was speaking to a small shimmer of air beside him. A pinwheel of sparkling rainbow color coalesced and spun rapidly until she looked away. When she looked back, there was a pale pink kitten, half the size of Tuckerinal. It lay curled on the windowsill, then opened blue eyes at her and gave a tiny mew. *Hel-lo.*

You see, sh-he does not speak English well.

"Maybe because it's a baby."

Sh-he is not an it. Sh-he has not chosen sh-he's sex yet.

"Oh."

The kitten stretched. Clumps of long pink Persian hair were mixed with short hair that seemed to be turning calico: orange, white and black. Bri took a step back.

Tuckerinal clapped his little paws together, grabbing her attention again. *Sh-he needs nuts.*

"That would be my extra PDA batteries."

And the camera.

She put her hands over the pocket holding the camera, protecting it. "No. Not the camera."

And memory, too. He raised his nose, pointed at her backpack. *You have memory in the yummy bag.*

"I suppose you'd like me to give you this." The strap was making indentations on her hands. She didn't relax her grip.

Squealing, Tuckerinal jumped up and down, his hamster mouth opening in what could be a smile. "Oh, ayes!"

"Not going to happen. I need it to power the camera."

Another mew, this one sounding pitiful. Bri glanced at the

kitten. It was now wholly short-haired and calico, with two big splotches of black over its eyes. She pressed her lips tightly together. It looked like a kitten she'd had as a girl. The cat had lived to old age and passed away sleeping in the sun. Ever after, Bri had always wanted to slide into death that way. Seemed she was going to fade agonizingly instead, unless she and Elizabeth found a way to prevent it.

Maybe these creatures could help. Magical shape-shifters. Feeling weak with hope, she walked to the bed and sat on it, stared at the creatures. Everything she had was worth her life. "What do you know of the disease?"

Tuckerinal squeaked sadly. *Only what all know. And that you have the sickness.*

Bri decided to reply mentally, since her throat was dry. *We don't want anyone else to know that. It is important.*

He made a bow, and it appeared only slightly silly. *We have honored your wishes.*

The kitten hopped from the ledge to land on the bed, rolled and rolled, making Bri smile. It tumbled close and she scooped it up, heard dancing windchimes and felt a little zing. The deep ache in her bones vanished for a split second. Interesting.

Gently, she set the kitten aside. Held out her arms to Tuckerinal.

He waddled to the ledge, hopped down, rolled once, scuttled to Bri. She picked him up. He was lighter than he looked, weighed less than a groundhog-hamster-whatever should have. She held him, warm and full of that effervescent feycoocu energy, banishing her sickness for a moment as she smudged his Song, drained him for a moment. She placed him on the bed.

Something about you and the baby stops the sickness in me.

Good. Learned enough to give the baby nuts? He looked at the small puff of fur. *Kitten didn't move her, try puppy.*

Bri snorted with laughter that became a yelp when Tuckerinal nipped her hand.

How many nuts do you have?

You thought I had, what, two?

Four.

I have more. She wasn't about to enumerate them, but she'd added a memory card to her PDA, and carried extra batteries and memory for her music pod and even more for the digital camera.

A little noise came and Bri glanced over to see a pale pink puppy all long ears and stubby tail, mouth open, tiny tongue lolling, grinning at her.

She sighed.

So did Tuckerinal. *Sh-he likes pink. Sinafinal and I don't know why. We believe she has spent too much time in Alexa's dreams.*

Alexa dreamed in pink? The whole thing made no sense. Bri stood and walked to the wall paneled in exquisitely carved wood. *You promised not to eat any of my nuts. Baby must promise, too.*

Baby will promise not to eat any nuts you do not give sh-he.

The little feycoocu wriggled with joy. *Nuts! Nuts! Nuts! Nuts from Tuck-er-in-al's land!*

Which made Bri wonder if baby got to chose a name, too, or whether sh-he had a name they weren't telling Bri. Names were power, here. She wondered if the Dark had a name.

No, Tuckerinal answered her thoughts. *The Dark does not have a name, but the new Master does. You should remind Sevair and the others of that.*

Bri made a mental note to do so. She opened the safe and looked into the dim stone square. How much should she give them? How much did the baby need? How much did *she* need? Last night was the only time she'd listened to tunes lately. The Lladranans prized music so, that she'd thought when she left she'd give Sevair—her bones ached more. Wearied her. She yearned for Denver, missed her parents desperately. The thought of never seeing them again was unbearable. She was sliding into love with Sevair. And all that was moot if she died.

She sorted through her stuff. The PDA had appointments that had already passed, addresses of people who one minute were bright in her memory, then next dim as if she'd left them far behind. All backed up on her laptop. She weighed the PDA in her hand. A good, solid piece of technology. She'd gone with an off-brand for a big screen to read ebooks. She only had four on there now, light pieces she'd downloaded for the trip. There were a few tunes, nothing she couldn't live without.

Her hand closed around the padded sleeve tightly. It should be a very good "nut" for the baby feycoocu. As long as she was feeding it, she should feed it well. She scooped out the extra batteries and memory for the PDA, for the music pod. She touched the camera, left it, and the memory. Left her solar-paneled backpack. The feycoocus could have them if….

Slapping the door to the safe shut, she locked it with a mental password and twist of tune and went back to the bed, set the feast in front of the puppy. Sh-he dived in, burbling as it ate plastic casing and all.

Bri's fingers touched stiff foil and she remembered the cat medicine. She popped two. It hadn't helped but who knew?

Tuckerinal turned over one of the batteries as if it were something interesting, but his desire for it had faded. He'd been hungry on behalf of his child.

"Is this enough for sh-he to thrive and prosper?"

The hamster hesitated, sighed, inclined his head. "Ayes." His mouth opened and closed. "Since you have helped me I will say that you must not work so hard to find the answer that will come to you if you allow it."

Bri wrapped her arms around herself. "There's hope, then."

"There's always hope. Good hunting."

The outside tower door slammed below. Sevair grumbled, *We are wanted at the Castle for another damn meeting.*

When she turned back to the bed it was empty of all nuts and magical beings.

38

Luthan stood in front of the whole contingent of the Castle—Marshalls, Nobles, Chevaliers, Soldiers and Support Staff. He seemed easy with the fact that every eye was upon him, Elizabeth thought. A natural leader.

Ttho, Alexa whispered in Elizabeth's mind. *A man always conscious that as a child someone was always watching him and reporting to his father, and his father was judging him.*

Elizabeth winced.

All the Exotiques were there, sitting together. Their auras held a blue-green tinge of Earth under their personal colorful layers. Elizabeth shared this with Bri as they linked hands. Bri sent back the intricacy of Song between them, the notes of folk tunes that they all shared. Songs they recognized from each other but didn't personally have. All knit them close. They had more in common with each other than any Lladranan, except for the men, who were learning to understand them.

Luthan's face was stern, but his expression naturally fell into those lines and from the general joshing and loud talk going on among the company, no one felt this was a serious meeting. But Bastien's muscles were rigid as he watched his brother, a smile on his animated face that hadn't moved since he'd walked into the room.

Luthan clapped once and the room fell silent. Elizabeth had seen Command Presence before—the stance, the manner, the one sound that ordered a room. He paced from one side of the room to the other, then back to the middle, garnering everyone's attention, but Elizabeth met Bri's eyes, the man was nervous, and not about addressing this company.

"Amee is in danger of dying," Luthan said.

The silence deepened with utter shock, with terror.

"As everyone knows, the rains and cold lasted far into summer instead of ending with spring. Amee has expended some of the heat of her core, some of her great Power, to warm the land and our country and keep our seasons more natural." A mass shudder went through the crowd.

Sevair stood. "We would rather not—"

"Please sit, Citymaster. It is done, and Amee is stubborn about this. Those of Lladrana need her support and she is giving it. Because…" He stopped. Elizabeth thought she'd never heard such an absence of sound. Seen such a flaring of aura, bright enough to light the hall. Bri rubbed her ears. When she focused, Elizabeth heard the screeching of fearful souls.

"Quiet," Luthan said, and the mental tunes stopped,

though the personal Songs were charged with seething energy.

"The Singer and I believe Amee used her Power so our country would be strong and ready to free her from the Dark. That the battle in the fall will be decisive. That if we fail, if our Exotiques fail, Amee will die."

Bri's hands flew to her throat. *Oh, man,* she whispered in Elizabeth's mind, in the minds of all the girls. *Nothing like a little pressure.*

"So be aware that we fight not only for Lladrana, but for Amee herself." The skin over Luthan's face tightened to show good bones and steel determination. "Make every blow against the Dark count. An expedition to the Dark's island nest *will* take place and must not fail, even if we all must give our lives. Those of you who wish to go, test your skills. *When* we win, we will free Amee from a leech which has fastened upon her for eons, and she will survive and prosper. It is for that result that Amee spent her Power to make our summer less cold."

He swept the room with a probing glance and Elizabeth knew he saw her, measured her, as he saw and weighed each person. Definitely a natural leader.

"One last word. Cherish our Exotiques, because they will lead the way. They have sacrificed their old lives on their strong Exotique Terre to fight for Lladrana. Protect them, for they are our hope and our symbols."

Everyone turned to look at the group of alien women.

Bastien had pulled Alexa into his lap, shielding her with his body.

A blank check, Bri said mentally to Elizabeth. *Why do I wish I didn't get it?* But if she could have cashed it in for the knowledge of how to cure her sickness she would have. Negativity again. She tried for a joke. *Why do I have the feeling that I will never be able to go to the bathroom alone again?* Not that Elizabeth or Sevair left her alone much.

"Later this month we'll choose the invasion force," Luthan said.

Faucon shifted and murmured so only their group could hear. "What of a ship?"

Then Luthan continued, "One last matter. The Singer believes there was a great magical ritual during the shortest day, but has seen no results." From his ironic tone, Elizabeth was sure that the Singer wasn't sharing any more information than what Luthan had pried out of her.

"I have consulted—"

"A ritual by the Dark!" someone cried hysterically.

"No, this was a Lladranan ritual." He raised a hand. "Not of an evil bent. Had that been so, the Singer would certainly have notified the Marshalls to handle the problem. As I was saying, I believe this was a Summoning ritual by the Seamasters that failed. Be aware that in the future, great rituals may very well sap the Power of us all and refrain. The Seamasters have been so notified. You are dismissed."

The alarm claxon screamed.

"The Dark sensing our great emotions, sending horrors," Luthan shouted over the siren and the noise of bodies rushing from the room to fight. "Let it sense our unity, too."

The incursion was small and easily handled with no casualties. No Chevalier returned with the sickness.

As soon as that glad news was verified, Bri collapsed.

* * *

When Bri woke in the keep's healing room, terror inundated her. So many Chevaliers she'd tried to heal here, so many had died. She realized immediately that Elizabeth had told the others what was happening. She heard the pair-songs of the Exotiques and their men. Her twin. Faucon. Sevair.

She was dying. Elizabeth was with her and would be doing just as she had done, trying to take the sickness into herself to heal it.

Her body hurt so that she let herself fall into the healing-stream and allowed it to carry her away. She floated in space, the source of the healingstream, her Power, feeling like a mote of the universe, captured in a bubble perhaps. Being distant from pain and emotion, she realized that she was a fraud.

She'd always cherished her gift, always linked to it, directed it, controlled it. She was more of a control freak than her sister. When Brigid Elizabeth Drystan didn't like something, she ran away. She took life on her own terms. All this time when she'd been telling others to let go, to surrender to the healingstream, *she* hadn't surrendered. She'd linked to that flood of Power between stars and manipulated it, but had not let it manipulate her.

She had to really *change* if she was going to save her own life and Elizabeth's. She recalled Zeres's thoughts, his wonder, his epiphany. *If I'd only known to tune my own chimes to the real Song.* Tune herself to the Song. Understand her own Song and what notes of the Universe she echoed.

So she listened, root chakra C, but other more subtle notes that held other senses, Bri's C also had the cadence of the patter of rain...so it went, analyzing her own Song, that which made her unique, *hearing* it in the Universe around her...that small pulse from that galaxy there, that wisp of solar flare from that particular star. How odd.

How wondrous.

When she knew herself, and her Song, she opened herself to the Universe and let it take her. She floated in serenity. She coalesced. The sprout inside her withered and died.

She opened her eyes and saw vivid and rich colors around her, lovely textures: the deep red of Elizabeth's damask medica robe, the creamy tunic underneath, the polished satin wood of the walls. The brilliant sunlight shining through pointed windows.

Someone was sobbing. Since the sound was in her mind and blood as well as outside her ears, she knew it was Elizabeth. Bri moved her head slightly to see her twin held in Luthan's steely grasp. On each of Elizabeth's shoulders was a feycoocu, also restraining her. Luthan was repeating something over and over as if trying to impress it upon Elizabeth. Good luck.

"Losing one is terrible enough. We cannot let you try to save her. She would take you, and perhaps the other Exotiques and their mates and children, others we *cannot* spare."

Bri blinked as, during the third go-round, the words made sense. She couldn't see the men and women ranged beyond Elizabeth, but could hear their lovely Songs, singly and in pairs. A great spring of delight filled her. The other Earth women had always said they'd stand by each other, and they'd been ready and willing to link with Elizabeth and pour Power and energy into her to heal Bri.

Her mouth was dry. She swallowed and swallowed again to wet her tongue enough for words. She thought of the last bit of chocolate she had in her pack and saliva pooled. She tried to speak. A tiny cough emerged.

Everyone froze, all their Songs pitched higher.

Elizabeth put a fist to her mouth, met Bri's eyes.

Bri must not have floated around in the healing stream for eternity after all, perhaps only the eternity that comprised each moment of living.

"I," she whispered.

Everyone came closer to hear, so she decided to shout it with her mind as well as propelling words with breath.

I healed my own self! She smiled and her lips cracked and the pain was almost sweet. She lived, which was good, because she still had many, many things she wanted to do, to learn, to love.

"I healed my own self," she said, louder. "And I can teach other people to do the same."

"How? *How!*" sobbed Elizabeth.

Bri thought a minute, ideas swam. "Um, adjust my vibrations to the space-time-dimensional continuum?"

"Tune yourself to the music of the spheres," Elizabeth said softly.

"Ayes."

The big red bird feycoocus hopped on Bri. One walked down her body—Tuckerinal. Sinafinal stared her in the eyes.

She speaks truly! A long, melodious warble rose from Sinafinal. *She has learned how to stop the frinkweed sickness and the Chevalier seed sickness!*

A great shout tore from many throats. Luthan released

Elizabeth and the feycoocus circled around the ceiling of the room, Singing joyfully and with tones outside the range of human hearing.

All the Exotiques surged forward, formed a healing circle and sent her energy and Power—and love. She hadn't realized until that moment how much all these people actually cared for her. As soon as she struggled to sit, Sevair's arm was behind her. The flow of love from him added to the rest, simply overwhelmed her. Perhaps it was also the aftermath of tuning her Song to the spacestream or letting the Universe's Song permeate her body, whatever, but she burst into tears.

Sevair slid to sit on the table, lifted and placed her across his lap. Elizabeth gave her a handkerchief.

"It's gone." Bri stretched the arm not clutching Sevair wide. "It's gone and I'm healed and it was beautiful and I love you all." She'd gained strength and energy from them all.

A couple of men shuffled their feet.

The chief Castle medica took her wrist and sent a probe through her that she felt in every nerve. "The sickness has been vanquished." Jolie's eyes were dark and steady. "You will have to teach us how to do that."

Bri nodded. "Yes, I can." She smiled at Elizabeth who was letting big tears roll silently down her cheeks. "If I can't find the words, Elizabeth will help me, but I know how to find the *feeling* and I'm sure I can show others how to do so, too, even the most average Lladranan."

Alexa let out a big sigh. "That's good, excellent."

The medica said steadily, "You will teach us so we can also spread this technique."

"The Circlets, too," Marian said. Her brow creased. "A few young people with healing gifts have approached us for training."

"When the need is so great the Song provides," Jaquar said.

Her burst of energy drained, now Bri felt as if a bulldozer had flattened her, and sleepy. "I'll start tomorrow."

Sevair lifted her with that ease that always sent a thrill through her. "I'll take her to our tower."

And when he let her sink into the soft feather bed and he joined her, uncaring of the jubilant rumors already spreading through Castleton and people milling in the cul de sac, she turned in bliss to sleep in his arms.

Her deep and heavy slumber was roused by desperate wailing. How *had* Elizabeth made it through her internship? Bri couldn't imagine doing the same.

Sevair was up and moving and soothing by the time Bri cracked her eyelids to see streams of sunlight painting bright transient squares throughout the room. Before she could do more than stretch, Sevair was back at the door, wearing his carved-in-stone expression of utter seriousness.

"What is it?" Bri asked.

"A stricken Chevalier flew in from patrolling the northern boundary."

As she dressed, Bri muttered, "The Dark is learning what works just as we are; it made another soul-sucker, mutated the disease."

"Yes." Sevair crossed the room, took her hand and kissed it. "But you know how to vanquish this plague once and for all. Destruction can never triumph over survival. Good always has an edge over Dark just because it *is* good."

She was glad that he believed that simplistic philosophy. Finding herself smiling, she chuckled. She was glad she believed it herself. Sevair dropped her hand to hold her tight. Though outwardly as solid as ever, she felt his inner quivering.

"Too close." His murmur was rough. "Your death was too close. Let me hold you, know you are healthy again."

She hugged him, rested against him until he reluctantly dropped his arms.

Downstairs she found a young man wearing ragged leathers pale and hunched on the settle. He rose and stood stiffly when he realized she was there, as if he was even more distressed that she discovered him in a private moment of despair. "My pairling is dying," he said starkly. "Up at the Castle. They are doing the best they can, but he—" His hands flexed uselessly. "Lady, they say you battled the illness in your own body and won, that you can teach others to do the same."

Bri nodded. Mud's whinny came from the cul de sac. "Let's go."

The man's smile was wan. "I walked down."

"Then we'll meet you there," Bri said.

"I'll run back," he said.

A few minutes later Bri strode into the lush main healing room of the Castle. She didn't like it anymore. She hoped this would be the last time she used it.

A team of medicas were keeping another young man alive, and from their Songs, Bri knew they were professionally compassionate but detached. He was more an experiment for them, to see how Bri could cure him, than a person. They barely knew his name.

She stepped up to the dais holding the ornate healing table with Elizabeth.

"Let me help, listen, *watch*," Elizabeth demanded.

"Sure," Bri said, "but let me *teach*. Take his feet."

Elizabeth did as she asked and curved warm-aured hands around the man's feet.

Bri *reached*. It wasn't the healingstream as she knew it, but an outside force that she hooked up to, opened a portal, determined the flow she needed.

Now it felt as though the innate creative force of the Universe permeated her body. She wasn't a conduit, a manipulator, she was one with the source.

Link with me, she told the young man. *Listen, feel!* She showed him space.

Elizabeth said, *You've done it. You've taken a Lladranan out to the Universe.*

This is what surrounds Amee. She altered the point of view and showed him his green-blue world floating in space, circling a bright sun, with a large moon in turn revolving around it.

So vast, he said weakly, and Bri knew she was losing him.

No! Look at the light.

Too much dark.

No! There are motes of light even in the darkness between suns and stars and galaxies. Find them, LISTEN.

More light than dark. I...I hear my Song! He sounded exalted. *There are notes of it in the wind of the true Song of All!*

The music of the spheres, Elizabeth murmured.

Yes! Bri shouted,

Ayes! agreed the young man.

Find your Song in the Song of All, the music of the spheres, Bri said. *Tune yourself to it.* Shifting slightly, a little embarrassed, she advised, *Surrender yourself to it—the light and music of the Universe as reflected in you.*

To her utter amazement, he went limp, and she *saw!* A sphere of—music incarnate? light and music? sound?—something coalesce and penetrate his chest. Without any Power from her it burst inside him and filled him, and vanquished all touch of the Dark.

Bri and Elizabeth folded onto the ground from sheer awe.

Maybe it's better not to be linked with the patient when that happens, Elizabeth said drily, turning her head to stare at Bri. *When the bubble bursts.*

Probably true, Bri said, still too limp to stand. *But I'm glad I saw it once.*

39

Bri ate first, stuffing her face with an order of the Marshalls' Dining Room's premier delicacy, Mickey Potatoes. Life was good. She was surrounded by babbling people and that was good too.

Sevair and Faucon had mysteriously disappeared. Bri figured it was because all the Exotiques were moving as a group.

Alexa had offered the seclusion of the Marshalls' Baths to relax in, the Exotiques and Bri and Elizabeth had taken her up on it. After a fun and wild time, they'd retired to Elizabeth's suite for a nap.

Hours later, Bri woke, checked herself out mentally and danced with joy to find herself clean and healthy and feeling fine. Elizabeth shook her shoulder and smiled.

"What?"

"We've been invited to a picnic in the Brithenwood Garden."

Bri stretched. "More food. Excellent."

"I think so. Faucon has the best food."

"Good man."

"Ayes."

Bri dressed in cream-colored gown and red damask overgowns Elizabeth looked the same.

The doorharp sounded. Sevair and Faucon led them through the maze to the Brithenwood Garden and Bri's nerves started twinging. *I'm getting a weird feeling about this,* she sent to Elizabeth.

Elizabeth didn't reply. Her face had frozen into a mask Bri had seen on rare occasions when she was thinking too hard, all her cylinders revving. The men didn't seem to notice.

Sevair did reply. "Calm, Bri."

She snuck a glance at him from the corner of her eyes. Had he *heard* her? On her personal telepathic line to her twin! Was he that sensitive to her?

He caught her gaze with an intense one of his own, and everything inside her stilled. A Big Decision was coming her way.

Elizabeth's palms sprang with sweat, matching the dampness of Faucon's. *What the hell was she going to do?* She knew when a proposal was coming. She'd been through that before, nerves and sheer delight.

"It's a beautiful evening," Faucon said, his tone only carrying a little strain, his aura erratic.

Sevair said nothing at all.

"Ayes," Elizabeth said. She inhaled, smiled. "The brithenwood tree still scents the air, though we're into summer."

"It's the bark and leaves," Sevair said. They'd reached the door to the garden and he made to pull it open. It stuck. He yanked on it and it came off its top two hinges. A muscle flexed in his jaw. "I'll have someone see to this."

Bri snorted a nervous laugh.

Faucon ducked under the low lintel first, glanced around, ever the warrior, checking security. Elizabeth hesitated and he pulled her through, whirled her into his arms for a quick kiss, flashed the grin she loved. His eyes twinkled as he stood staidly beside her when Bri and Sevair entered.

Elizabeth's heart pounded.

Lifting her hand to his lips, Faucon said, "Please sit." He released her hand and his chest rose as he took a big breath. "Ayes, the scent is wonderful." He eyed the garden, wild and colorful. "Lovely." Looked at her. "Lovelier."

Bri separated her fingers from Sevair's, walked to the bench circling the brithenwood tree. Elizabeth found herself rolling her eyes at her twin, an anxious habit she'd thought she'd mastered in middle school. Nerves betrayed a person. They sat side by side on the bench around the tree, thighs touching so they were connected.

The men shared a look, then Faucon's eyebrows lifted and a half-smile played on his lips. He drew a small oblong box from his belt pouch and Elizabeth saw the slight tremble of his fingers. He was as tense as she. That should have reassured her. It didn't. What was she going to do?

Sevair cleared his throat. He had a little box, elegantly carved of stone so thin it was nearly translucent.

"Oh, my," Bri said.

Faucon's box looked like carved ivory. Elizabeth wasn't sure she'd ever seen ivory outside a museum.

"Pairbond with me in a *coeur de chain*," Sevair said, and slid the top off his box, showing it to Bri.

"Pairbond with me in a *coeur de chain*," Faucon said, and lifted the lid and offered the box to Elizabeth.

She stared at the wickedly sharp small silver knife, lifted her shocked stare to Bri, who was panting.

"Knives!" Bri squeaked. "What happened to rings?"

Sevair angled the box to examine the little knife gleaming against a nest of gray velvet. "It's a beautiful knife for the ritual. My friends made it especially for you. See the little medica symbols and your healing hand glyph?"

Faucon smiled, sent a reassuring glance to Elizabeth. "You want a ring? A ring will be forthcoming."

"Rings shouldn't be worn by working people. They can get caught on all sorts of things. I've known people who have lost fingers because of rings," Sevair said.

A bubble of uneasy laughter erupted from Bri. "Oh, yeah, that's romantic. We're both medicas, we know what fingers ripped off look like." Her hand snaked out and grabbed Elizabeth's.

Everything changed.

A clap of thunder and shimmer of bright rainbow colors encased them.

"No!" yelled the men, reached for them.

But the Snap had come.

Elizabeth and Bri were whisked into the tunnel between dimensions. The wind slowed from hurricane to a steady breeze. They linked both hands, wanting to be closer because they thought they'd be torn apart.

Despite multiple readings of the Exotiques' books and personal descriptions, Elizabeth wasn't prepared. They were actually *in* the corridor, not flashing between the dimensions as they'd done when they were Summoned. Dread seized her. That wasn't a good sign, was it?

It's like Marian's experience. A real corridor with portals, Bri said. Since she'd said it, it seemed to solidify around them. They were facing the Earth side, past on their left, beyond Bri, future to Elizabeth's right.

They hung between worlds.

Directly in front of them the portal opened on Elizabeth's high-rise condo. Shocked exclamations came from the three people there, staring at them. Her mother, her father.

Cassidy Jones.

Oh. My. God.

Decision time, Bri said grimly. *We can't hang around here forever.*

They shuddered.

Elizabeth couldn't think. She seethed with a knotted mass of emotions. Fighting the wind, she looked back at the closing portal on the Lladrana side of the corridor and Faucon's grief-stricken face. She loved him, didn't she?

"Elizabeth, Elizabeth!" cried Cassidy. His face twisted in anguish, his arms open for her, pleading. "Come to me. I was stupid and arrogant and cowardly. Come to me!"

She loved him. Too. More?

And he loved her. She could feel that, see it in the splashing desperate colors of his aura, yearning for her.

Another glance at Faucon. His Song was muffled, his aura dimmer. He loved her, but not as much as Cassidy. Didn't need her as much as Cassidy. Never shared her goals and her life as much as Cassidy.

But Faucon respected and admired her—and Cassidy?

Cassidy flung himself at the portal. It looked as if he hit a wall. "Or I'll come to you. I was wrong, all wrong. You're such an amazing person, such an incredible physician with something *special* I could never match. Stupid, arrogant, cowardly," he repeated, as if he'd said it to himself like a mantra since she'd left. His fingers clenched to fists and bloodied as he hit the portal wall to reach her. He, a surgeon who'd ever been careful of his hands.

She stared at her old love.

"I love you," he shrieked. In front of her parents, her sister, the other two men.

She loved Cassidy. God help her, she still loved him deeply.

The scab on her emotions ripped away and she seethed with them. Cassidy. To her shame and dismay, she realized she'd never stopped loving him. Faucon had been a safe love for her, gentle, attractive, respectful. Cassidy had been her passionate, dangerous love, igniting tumultuous emotions. Despite all her outer control, she wanted that kind of love.

Faucon deserved that kind of love, too. One she couldn't give him. One he didn't feel for her.

As Bri deserved the love she'd found with Sevair.

Her love for Faucon—rebound love?—tore from her like a tumbleweed and vanished in the corridor. She faced Earth and home. She yearned for her parents, her old life that she'd worked so hard for.

"Bri," she said, then stopped. She didn't have the words, would never have the words to say goodbye to her twin.

But Bri was focused on something else. The open portal to Earth and the shocked look of their parents who obviously saw them. *They could come through!* Bri whispered in

Elizabeth's mind. *They see us. They KNOW. And I bet they heard those chimes and gongs, too. Mom had the two sacks of spuds!* She stretched out an arm, yearning in every line of her body.

A second of communication among all the members of the family, like a group hug. The love they shared, the bonds that would never be broken. Then their mother stepped back. Tears flowing, sliding down her face, she shook her head.

Their father had stepped forward, but his arm was around the waist of his wife. He hesitated, then joined her.

"No!" Bri cried. "No, come."

"Bri," Elizabeth said. "I have to go back. I love Cassidy!"

"I thought you loved Faucon."

"Rebound love," Elizabeth said.

"Shit. No." Bri's free hand clutched the material of her robe over her heart. "No."

"You belong here on Lladrana. Let me go!"

Bri's grip tightened on her hand. "No."

"Yes. Cassidy," she whispered. But he seemed to hear.

"I love you," he yelled again. "I was so wrong!"

The wind had picked up around them, pushing at Elizabeth more than Bri. Elizabeth swallowed hard and faced her sister. The love and knowledge on Bri's face matched her own. "You belong on Lladrana." She raised her voice. "You fit there like you never did on Earth." *Don't make this so hard, like always.*

I won't. I can't hold on to you and pull you back. Or go with you. That would poison us. I love you. She turned to their parents. "I love you!"

This was goodbye. They'd never see each other in person again.

With strength she rarely demonstrated, Bri pulled Elizabeth from the winds and into her arms. Hugged her tight, tight, tight. "I love you."

"I love you," Elizabeth said.

Bri's voice broke. "Later," she said, as she always did when her itchy feet had her leaving.

Then Elizabeth was free and a moment later, she'd landed in her own living room, plush carpet under her feet.

"Oh, Mom. Oh, Dad!" She flung herself into their arms, and their familiar scents enveloped her and she burst into tears. But this was not the time for tears. She wanted to spill everything like Dorothy back from Oz.

She stepped back, whipped a handkerchief from her medica gown pocket—one that smelled like brithenwood—and wiped her eyes and blew her nose. Then she met her parents' eyes, and Cassidy's, lifted her chin.

"I have a gift." She tucked away her hankie and raised her palms. "A wonderful gift of healing hands." She gulped, stuttered a bit before she spit out the next. "I never thought people would accept me if they knew what I was really like."

"Oh, darling." Her mother hugged her again. "We always knew."

Elizabeth snuffled. "I suppose so."

"We'll always love you," said her father.

"I'll be discreet, but I'm not going to hide my gift anymore. I may use it and that will reflect on us all. We all may be called weird."

Her father shrugged, smiled his dear, lopsided smile. "I'm the Dean of Anthropology at a major university. I'm supposed to be weird."

Cassidy stepped toward her, radiating intensity. "I love you. I'll always love you, no matter what. I was a stupid jerk. Arrogant and cowardly."

"Yes, you were," Elizabeth's mother said crisply.

Her father choked. Elizabeth whirled.

The portal to the dimensional corridor still gaped open. Bri hung in the winds, her hair flying out from her head, her Song so strong and beautiful it kept her in place. Beyond her, other portals to Lladrana were opening. The Brithenwood Garden, the two men. The other man she'd loved. She couldn't bear the thought of the hurt she was giving him, the sight of his shadow.

"I left a good man back in Lladrana," she said unsteadily.

Cassidy grabbed and kissed her and his tongue and taste was in her mouth and his body radiated heat that warmed her and ignited the firestorm she always felt with him and she was *home*.

"I love you, Mommy. I love you, Daddy!" Bri shouted and watched the portal to Earth fade. Elizabeth was kissing Cassidy with a hunger that couldn't be mistaken. Her life was there.

Bri's wasn't. She belonged to Sevair, and Lladrana, and Amee. They accepted her for who she was.

The decision made, the wind shrieked around her, shot her toward a bright square that was closing. Elizabeth's condo had a magic mirror. Bri had to hang on to that knowledge, even as her throat clogged with tears.

She *snapped* back to Lladrana, to the springy ground of the Brithenwood Garden. Sevair's strong arms caught her close. His heart thumped fast. His body was hard. His Song beautiful and mind filling and wild. She held on tight, hugged him, then turned her head so she could breathe.

She met Faucon's gaze. His eyes were hard and desperate, wounded. His face went expressionless. He turned on his heel and left. Oh, God! Bri knew how he hurt.

How she hurt. No more parents or twin. Not in this world.

"I love you, Bri," Sevair murmured in her ear. He didn't let her go. His melody and hers joined, twined together, harmonized.

"I love you, too," she said, and all the love inside her ached.

40

Faucon didn't stumble away from the garden. He wanted to. But he'd been too damn well trained for that. He marched from the garden and Sevair embracing Bri. Opened the door, ducked through, and closed it behind him without looking at them.

Elizabeth was gone. Had not loved him enough to stay, to abandon that career she'd worked so hard and long for. To forsake those parents whom he'd glimpsed, love for their daughters radiant on their faces.

Those were good reasons to return to Exotique Terre, Earth, but didn't help the ripping inside him.

She'd chosen another man. That thought was as bitter as brine in a wound. The ivory box and bonding knife passed down through his family for centuries dragged in his belt pouch like a heavy stone. He'd wanted to fling it away, never see it again, but he hadn't done so, of course.

Now he stood in the maze and was glad that high hedges

shielded him, though they reminded him of that first night he'd made love with Elizabeth.

"Faucon."

He flinched, saw Luthan in his white leathers round the corner of the path from the keep. "I'm sorry," Luthan said.

Faucon didn't move. For one of the few times in his life he was unsure where he wanted to go and what he wanted to do. The keep? Other Exotiques. Elizabeth's rooms. No. The Landing Field and fly away? Tempting.

"You saw this future, didn't you?" His voice didn't sound the way it should. Not melodious. Brittle.

"I saw several futures regarding the Snap. Both twins go. Both stay. Bri stays, Elizabeth goes. Elizabeth stays, Bri leaves." Luthan waved a hand.

Faucon didn't bother to sort out those shadings. His mind wasn't working. He was all hurt. He'd loved Elizabeth.

"Tell me, is a woman *ever* going to love me for myself like I love her!" Anguish wrenched from him. Luthan froze beside him, and Faucon realized his heartfelt plea had been said at the wrong time to the wrong person. Slowly he turned his head. Yes, the man was in that far-seeing, Song spiking, strange trance of prophecy.

Faucon waited, unable to stop what he'd put in motion. Torn. He wanted the answer with desperate hope. He never wanted to hear a truthful answer on the subject because a negative might be a killing blow.

Luthan made a strangling noise, turned his head and their gazes clashed. Luthan's eyes had turned silver!

"Ayes," Luthan said. "Ayes. You will have a love and she will have you. But in the end you may rue. For with great love there can be great loss." He laughed hollowly, his shoulders hunching like an old man's. "The same for me." His head turned again and his gaze went to the pathway to the keep.

Faucon spun, tensed, hand on his sword.

"You, too, Koz," Luthan croaked. "You'll have a love like that, too."

The large man stepped from the shadows. His lips twitched up in more grimace than grin. "Thanks for nothing," he said. Since it didn't make sense, Faucon figured it was an Exotique Terre saying. He never wanted to hear anything like that again.

"What happened?" Koz asked. "Everyone heard the Snap come."

"Bri stayed. With Sevair Masif. Elizabeth returned...."

"...home," Koz said softly. "She returned to the place that is home in her heart. To the life that is right for her."

A growl issued from Faucon and he didn't stop it, let it rip from him. He leapt at Koz and Koz held on to him. Luthan put an iron arm around him, too. For a moment the other men shared his sorrow, then Faucon stepped away.

He didn't care what Luthan had said about future love and grief. That didn't concern him now, wouldn't for a long, long time, if ever. He didn't feel like risking his heart again.

Bri woke to snoring. Sevair was sprawled in her bed— their bed? One of his arms was outflung, the other was around her, hand on her breast.

Huh.

Memories returned with a sweet, horrible ache.

She was never going back to Earth. She was stuck here in Lladrana, on Amee. A little voice of panic screamed in the back of her mind.

Already she could feel the difference of being Bri-After-The-Snap. Earth's Song was but a lingering kiss of blessing, Amee's Song welled through her quietly, not strong. That was why she was here. To free the planet from the Dark.

Which would mean she'd be in that last battle at the Dark's nest, loosing the spellknot. A shiver went through her and Sevair mumbled, drew her close.

But Bri wanted to torture herself. No, just wanted to make sure Elizabeth's mirror was working, both their mirrors were working. She'd have to move all Elizabeth's Lladranan things here, especially the hand mirror. That flipped the sadness switch on again and tears backed behind Bri's eyes. She didn't turn to Sevair, but slid from his arms, tiptoed to the door and down one floor to her den-home-office. There she went to the beautiful desk she'd moved from the house—and what was going to happen to the house, now? Opened the drawer and removed the magic mirror from the silk sleeve Koz had made.

It was dark. She held it in her hand. Wondering. Not daring, but hoping. "Abracadabra," she whispered.

Sunshine from the skylight bathed Elizabeth's living room. Later than Bri thought, then. Bri tilted the mirror, saw the tangle of naked bodies on the floor and a strangled sound caught in her throat. She stared. Cassidy covered most of Elizabeth.

He had a fine back and butt, though looked as if he'd lost weight. Served him right.

Okay. Don't be a peeping Thomasina. Put the mirror away. Obviously the mirror worked, visual at least, from her side. She snickered. Then she looked down at herself and realized she was nude, too. Well, that might have been an all-around awkward conversation.

"Signing off." Her knees went weak, she sank into the desk chair, felt the velvet on her bare bottom. Would have taken her a while to work up to handcrafted furniture in Colorado. She wiggled a little. Yeah, the velvet was excellent. Gray velvet, Sevair's color. She smiled.

She stroked the satin wood of the desktop, traced the pretty inlay of woods. Yes, this would have been far out of her price range in Colorado. She might never have had enough money to buy museum-quality furnishings. The best of the best. The colorful tatts on her left wrist caught her eye. The colors were brilliant, now. Elizabeth's caduceus. Zeres' shield, faded. Alexa's jade baton, Calli's volaran, Marian's book.

Bri would be adding Sevair's hammer. Tingles slipped along every nerve. Good thing she was sitting down. A thought snagged and she grabbed the mirror again. Had she seen...? "Abracadabra." She focused on Elizabeth's inner arm, her left. Yes! Not as bright as Bri's, of course, and they might fade even more with time, but Bri didn't think Elizabeth's bonding tatts would ever vanish. That comforted her a little. She swallowed. No, she'd never see Elizabeth again, but, the Song willing, they wouldn't be out of touch for the rest of their lives.

The length of Bri's life might only be a few months. If that was so, she'd better go back up and pounce on the man in her bedroom.

One last thing.

She and Elizabeth had wanted a mirror in their parents' home. Bossgond had sent another large mirror for that purpose through to Elizabeth's place. Their parents had been there last night, during the Snap—and what a blessing that had been, to see them one more time.

So her folks would have taken their mirror home and activated it. Any one of the Drystans would have done that under the circumstances.

What had been the spell word for that one? Open sesame? Open sez me? Alakazam? Mirror, mirror on the wall? They'd joked about it. Bri scrabbled in the drawer for the bit of paper Koz had given her, found it, smoothed it from a crumpled state.

"Laugh." It said.

Laugh. That was *stupid*.

How could she laugh under these circumstances? Bri muttered "fuck," under her breath. She settled herself, tried to think of something humorous, touched the mirror. And recalled the startled wonder of seeing Elizabeth flying on her volaran outside the coach window, hair and clothes wild, face rapturous, screaming with laughter at her.

Bri laughed.

Her mirror cleared, showed the book-lined family room where they'd celebrated her father's birthday so very long ago. The night they'd been Summoned to Lladrana.

The room was empty, and from the view, the mirror hung over the fireplace, easy to see the whole room.

Breath blew from Bri. She tried to recollect the day or date, but couldn't. Elizabeth's day timer would be in her tower suite and turned to the proper day, previous ones marked off.

She'd get Elizabeth's stuff. Soon. And take up the habit of knowing when it was on Earth—just to be able to look in on holidays, if nothing else.

Her face was wet with tears. If this was a work day, and it probably was, her parents would be gone by now. She glanced at the clock, flipped the image in her mind. Seven-thirty. She'd just missed them.

How she would have loved to have been there when Elizabeth explained everything that had happened!

Pictures! She hopped up, hurried over to the safe and opened it, took out some of the prints. Her and Elizabeth in their medica robes. Temple Ward of the Castle. Sevair. Volarans.

Her mirror wasn't big enough to handle them all. So she picked the one of Sevair.

"Abracadabra." To Elizabeth first. Bri turned the pic over, placed it on the mirror, said a sticky spell.

There! She felt better. She could share.

A little cough echoed in her mind.

You should have given them a picture of me, Nuare said.

I don't think—

I am in the cul de sac. You could image me and your tower for your family.

A good idea. Bri flung on some clothes, got her pack from the window ledge where it was charging her camera.

She ran down the cool stone steps and flung open the door. There was Nuare, preening. She snapped a shot, three, then lowered the camera. "You look better in the sunlight."

True. Then Nuare rocked back on her feet and opened her wings.

Bri knew an offer for a hug when she saw one. She ran to the large bird, was enfolded.

I am glad you didn't leave. I would have mourned.

Bri stuttered, "Thank you." Then wept.

After a couple of minutes, Bri became aware of soft breast feathers sticking to her face, tickling her nose. She sniffed.

"Bri! Bri! Bridgid Elizabeth!" Sevair's fearful roar reached them. "No. She didn't go. She stayed with me. Not a nightmare." He ran from the tower buck naked, plucked her from Nuare, lifted her to sizzle a kiss on her lips. Holding her up against him with one arm, he brushed her hair from her face with a trembling hand. "You're here. You're with me. You're mine."

"Ayes," Bri managed. It was good to feel his arms, stopped the anxiety lingering in the back of her mind.

Ayes, she is Amee's, said Nuare smugly.

"Giving the neighbors a show," Bri said.

"I don't care," he mumbled into her hair, but belying his words, he backed inside and slammed the front door shut with Power.

Murmuring soothing reassurances to himself and her, he carried her back up into the bedroom, then stood near the bed and went to the dresser.

"I love you," Sevair said. He stared at her.

Well, she was here, and with him. "I love you, too."

He came back with the little box that held the small, fancy knife. Bri's throat closed again. A lot of that happening this morning. Last night. The whole damn time. Too many huge decisions driven by huge emotions. Or vice versa. And her mind was chittering.

Setting a strong hand on her shoulder, he gave a push and her knees obligingly buckled and she was back to sitting on the bed.

"Please pairbond with me, in a *coeur de chain*."

Bri avoided looking at the open box and the knife. Her breath came fast. "That's the really big deal, right? The if-I-die-you-die thing."

He sat beside her, took her hand. His fingers were steady, hers trembled. "Ayes," he said.

She met his gaze, equally steady, very determined. "I don't know if I can." Her breaths became pants.

His strong hand flattened above her breasts. "Breathe slowly. The ritual doesn't hurt."

"I read about a bloodbond in Marian's lorebook, and the *coeur de chain* in Calli's. I don't think I can."

"You can do anything."

She peeked at him. He looked the same, utterly confident of himself and of her. Wow.

"You accepted the Song inside you, taught others, me, to do the same."

"You weren't sick!"

His solemn face broke into a laughing grin. "During loving."

"Oh." She felt better now he wasn't so serious, bit her lip.

"Watch." He put a hand over his heart, closed his eyes. When he pulled his hand out, the image of a bubble came with it.

Bri stared. He'd obviously worked on it. It wasn't a clear bubble, no. It was a round sphere that looked like thin stone—layers and layers of stone carved in moveable balls, like those she'd seen as souvenirs in Chinatowns the world over. She found her tongue. "Wow."

But a little crease was between his brows. "There's a roughness here—"

"No! Do not mess with that right now in front of me. I'm glad you're One With The Universe, but I don't need proof."

He chuckled again, stared at her. "You showed us all how to do this, make a sphere of our Song tuned to the universe."

"Yes."

"It's no wonder I love you." He offered the box and knife.

"Can you put that away, it makes me nervous," Bri said.

He let it sink back into his chest. "I can see that. Let's consider this matter rationally."

"Huh."

"I love you." He leaned over and pressed a kiss on her lips. Waited, again with the patient look.

"I love you," she admitted.

"Good."

"You returned here to Amee, to Lladrana, to me after the Snap." His voice was rich with satisfaction.

"Ayes."

"I want to live here with you, in this wonderful tower." She eyed him. He looked sincere. His Song sounded sincere.

"Okay."

"Do you want me to live with you?" he prodded.

"Ayes." No hesitation there.

"Good." His hand enveloped hers. "We've established the fact that we love each other and want to live together. Our Songs have already entwined in a pairbond—"

"That should be enough. Living together, loving each other. Certainly enough for now."

"I want it all," he said.

She was flapping her hands. "This bloodbond, mind, heart, soul thing. It's too much, I think. We don't have stuff like that on Earth."

"Perhaps you only need a little time," he said indulgently.

"Maybe." She wasn't so sure.

A squeeze of the hand, another tender kiss. "Just leave all the arrangements to me."

Irritation snaked through her. "You think you know me better than I know myself."

"Ayes, I do." He stood, pulled her up, took her mouth until she melted against him. Then he stepped away. "I must work. I'll take care of everything. All you need to do is show up."

"When?"

"When you're ready. I'll give you a week or two to settle." He smiled. "And I'll make sure the other Exotiques bring you."

"I don't know that I like this."

One of his dark brows raised. "If you would prefer to plan the ritual…."

She crossed her arms, stuck out her chin. "I'm not sure."

Another brief kiss on her forehead. "I am." He tapped her heart with his forefinger. "And you are, here." On that last word, he left the room.

41

What had she done! Bri kept the cheerful smile on as she closed the door of the house on her last patient the next afternoon.

The people in the class on Aligning Your Song with the Music of the Spheres—a New Age title if she'd ever heard one—had been nearly wild with enthusiasm. Everyone had heard of the Snap. How Elizabeth had left and Bri had stayed, and Bri was the recipient of effusive gratitude.

She hadn't had a minute to herself all day. She, who'd ordered her life exactly how she wanted it for as long as she could remember.

Not to mention the Exotiques had sent a note down saying that there'd be a Girls Night In at Calli's suite this evening. The Future of Lladrana would be discussed as well as men. That meant the invasion of the Dark's nest and that final ritual spell—untying the weapon knot.

She wanted to run, but where? She was well and truly stuck. Here in an alternate dimension.

She sank onto the floor of the entryway and crossed her legs and brought her head low to the floor. A hiding-thinking position she'd developed when stressed to the max.

It had seemed to be the right thing to do at the time, but she was way beyond second thoughts now, coming up on hundredth.

She'd followed her heart, her gut, her own damn Song. But like every other certainty in her life, this had vanished. Now it was her head that said she was right to do what she'd done, and currently her gut said run, run, RUN.

The door opened and closed. Sevair's Song enveloped her. Strong, steady. She resented it. What happened to Bri who was the free spirit?

"Ah, I suspected this would happen."

Smug, too. He was strong and steady and *smug.*

His large hands settled around her waist, lifted her. *Bri, beloved.*

She flinched.

You are not trapped. You are free to go anywhere. Nuare will take you.

"Oh, yeah, that's great. Free to go anywhere in a world I don't know." She let her feet down, but still couldn't reach the floor. She didn't meet his eyes. He toted her into the parlor, set her down and she watched as he opened a wall safe she didn't know was there, disguised by paneling.

He took out a clinking leather pouch. Then he went to the table and spilled out…gold and silver and jewels. "This would last you a lifetime anywhere on Amee," he said. He scooped the valuables back into the pouch and handed it to her. "Running money."

She set her mouth and lifted her chin. His expression was serious, as usual. "*Merci.*"

"It was supposed to make you feel better."

Pressing a hand to her heart, she said, "I forsook everything I knew. Everything I was in the past." She was just beginning to understand the ramifications. They didn't even have ice cream, did they?

"We need you," he said. He put the pouch down, took her hands. "*I* need you. I will cherish you."

Her breathing slowed; the anxiety attack backed off.

"I love you," he said.

"I love you, too." Solid, steady. He'd get her through this if she let him.

She couldn't run anymore, even if she wanted to. Now she had to trust herself and this man and her new life. "But I think I moved too fast."

He inclined his head. "You weren't given much choice."

Quiet fell between them. She wanted him to say that he wouldn't press for the pairbonding thing.

He didn't.

Over the next week and a half all the Castle and Castleton were busy implementing the training of ordinary people to link with their pattern in the universe. It wasn't easy, but all Lladranans cherished the Song and were willing to try anything to beat the illness. A recognition and connection with the Music of the Spheres, a legacy of Elizabeth's, was a concept the people could accept. As well as the idea of a stronger, reciprocal bond with their home planet.

If this had been the States, everyone would have been in big, big trouble. Bri left the town square to stroll home, which, oddity of oddities, would also become Sevair's home. Time for him to leave the house of his family, though he'd dealt with that abandonment issue. Her heart twinged as she thought of the pain she'd put him through. Relatively short, but intense none the less.

On impulse, she stopped in at the Nom de Nom. Sevair was probably already home by now. She tried not to think about a ritual bonding, soul-melding ceremony with Sevair, because panic nibbled at her nerves. She didn't want to run away. Not really. And her feet didn't itch. Even if they did and she did run away, where would she run *to* on Amee?

But it was hard sticking it out when she thought of being completely and totally committed to Sevair.

So she'd moved from running away to avoidance. Hey, a step up in coping strategies. She told herself that she'd be ready when the ritual came, somehow, and believed it. Sometimes.

It was odd not to see Koz lounging against the counter, but now that he'd become a mirror magician, he hung with a different crowd in a different part of town.

Chevaliers looked up at her entrance, smiles lit their faces and Bri sniffed back tears. She'd miss Elizabeth and her parents forever, but she'd found her own place in a different world. She whipped out her camera and took a flash shot. Elizabeth would like seeing this. With a little tinkering by Koz, all the images could be sent home—no!—back to Earth.

She slipped the camera into her bag, a new leather healthy back bag that had been a gift from Sevair, and scanned those before her. They looked wearier, worn, thinner, and tougher than when she'd taken that first step inside this tavern. The month and a half had been hard on them. Bloodier battles, greater losses, the fear and anxiety that each would be the next one to fall to the Dark's evil sickness.

Sevair's ex-assistant had much to answer for. Suppressed fury roiled within her. She'd make him pay.

She walked to the Exotiques' booth and found Faucon drinking in the shadowy corner, watching her. Oh, man! She closed her eyes for a moment, braced herself.

He scowled when she joined him. Instead of taking the bench across from him, she slid in next to him. His eyes looked bleary, his clothes rumpled. His Song lingered in the low register, sad. She rose a little and kissed his cheek, feeling stubble.

"Go away," he said.

"No. I want you to continue to be a good friend."

"Seeing you hurts me."

That hurt, so her voice was rough. "Sorry, but I don't entirely believe that. You, more than anyone, always saw us as different."

"Yes, but memory fades." His mouth stretched in an unamused grin. He patted his heart. "I hope. You're all who is left of her."

Bri sniffed. "Elizabeth would have given you gifts."

He raised his cup and drank. "Ayes. But she did not find pleasure in mine. Perhaps that was my mistake. I didn't know her well enough. Didn't have time to."

Bri laid a hand over his. "You made no mistakes. It just wasn't meant to be." How stupid she felt uttering such banalities. "Lladrana wasn't for her. She had too much waiting for her at home, a career she'd worked very hard and very long for, our parents." Her voice trembled.

He turned his hand over, squeezed her fingers, then looked aside. "And that other man. I believe she thought of him, sometimes, when she was with me, or tried to make me him. She just didn't know it, and neither did I." He stood abruptly, swayed a little. "No offense, but I'm leaving."

He nudged at her and she reluctantly slid out of the booth, but blocked his way, curving her hands around his face. "You're a little drunk. I can take that away."

"Please don't." He picked her up and set her aside, took a couple of careful steps. Another twisted smile from him. "Unlike those machines in your and Elizabeth's minds, volarans don't need to be steered home."

His heartache wasn't easing. Faucon had stuck it out nearly two weeks, but being in the Castle, in Castleton, wasn't helping. Alexa had forbidden him to fly to battle and fight and his teams and volarans were obeying her.

Bri and Sevair spent more time at the Castle. Sevair was coordinating a *coeur de chain* ceremony between Bri and himself and between Bastien and Alexa, that Bri was willfully blind to. Bri herself worked smoothly with the Castle medicas.

Faucon had moved his quarters to a suite in Horseshoe Hall, and remained mostly in Lower Ward, or in the stables. Being around the volarans helped.

Seeing Bri at the Nom de Nom had been the last straw, Faucon decided as he and his volaran set down in the Landing Field. He'd grab a few things, then go home. Let his cousins wrestle with him, the women pamper him, work with the tough Seamasters on their problems.

I am sad, too. Starflower said, trotting up. It was the first time he'd ever heard Equine clearly and Faucon wished he had not. His emotions nearly overwhelmed him. He thought only the clenching of his jaw kept him in control. So that was how one spoke with volarans, with emotions. He slid off his mount and leaned against him. Then Faucon looked at Elizabeth's volaran, blinking slowly, keeping his eyes to the slight breeze so they would stay dry.

Sad, Starflower had said. His heart was *broken.* Damned if he'd ever trust it to another Exotique. When three had rejected him, he should have known that the Song did not have such a lady for him.

Now he hurt worse than he ever remembered. Starflower's head drooped. He took one step, two. Flung his arm around her neck and buried his head against her. The wind hadn't done its job.

"You should take her with you," Bastien said quietly. "She'll pine with us, even Calli, but you comfort her."

Faucon didn't ask how Bastien knew of his decision, didn't want to think about that. Starflower's emotions washed over him, blended with his. Knowing he was not alone with this pain helped. A stupid idea to him, but true all the same.

"I see that you've finally allowed your mind's pathways to open and can now learn volaran," Bastien continued.

Faucon didn't care, didn't reply.

"Partner with Blossom-Greeting-The-First-Warm-Spring-Wind. You can learn together what a real flier-volaran relationship is like. Your war volaran will thank her."

He felt Bastien move, heard the man croon to Star—Blossom? Windblossom?—and the high notes of the volaran's mental sobbing eased. As she relaxed under Bastien's touch, her calming emotions let Faucon settle. Sharing the worst of her sorrow alleviated his own.

Raine stared down at Travys, bleeding from his head, curled on the ground near the pilings of the pier.

Her breath came in pants. Her fingers trembled so that the rock fell from her hand.

Blood thundered in her ears. Doubling over, she braced her arms on her thighs, took longer breaths, tried to think. He'd lust for revenge.

She had to leave, now!

No one would protect her. He had status and money.

She was nobody. No one would care if she died. He could kill her and lie about it. Or he'd just make her disappear. She was only a pot-girl after all, and one who spoke Lladranan with an accent and looked odd. A half-breed half-wit.

No one would believe her if she'd said she was an Exotique. Everyone knew the Marshalls Summoned *them* in The Castle.

She'd be beaten. Would be beaten anyway for hurting Travys. Or worse. She blinked slowly, studying him. He'd fallen into the deep shadows beneath the pier. Lucky. His chest went in and out.

She had to leave, and now, before the man came to. No reason to return to the tavern. She had nothing there—not even the tattered blanket was hers. Her Earth clothes had long since disintegrated.

Late afternoon, evening coming. Get a move on! So she turned and let the northward pull she'd felt lately lead her.

No one knew her mind or character, either. They wouldn't be able to think like her and follow her, if they bothered.

With one last glance at Travys, she began her journey. He'd follow her. She was an obsession of his, God help her. She didn't know why. But he'd be finished playing with her. Now he'd kill her.

She'd prepared the only way she could, traded sex with the local cobbler for good shoes.

She walked and she walked, on the coast as long as possible, and fell into a stupor where she dreamt of ships. Ever since she'd landed on this world, ship designs had haunted her, even more than when she'd been part of the family yacht-building business. She tripped over a rock in the beach and snorted.

She'd been so dissatisfied with her father and brothers and their insistence on tradition and wooden vessels! How she'd wanted to push the boundaries—make twin hulls, using the newest metal alloys.

A few days here and those dreams had shattered like spume on rocks. Now dreams came of building a massive ship, the like no fisherman or Seamaster of this world had ever seen.

The narrow strip of sand disappeared and the coast became rocky. Raine walked in the sea, feet numbed, until she realized the tide was coming in. She struggled up to solid ground.

The smell of baking bread lured her. Even though she had no zhiv to buy any. Could she possibly find the baker, just hold out her hand? Look pitiful? That last sure wouldn't be hard to do. These people were mostly like everyone else, surely someone would have a charitable bent.

With a last breath of salty air, she turned to a rough path toward the town. It took her only a half hour to reach the square, and she found the streets fairly deserted as people ate dinner. The people she met glanced at her, then away. Her mouth twisted at that. How often had she done the same thing when she saw homeless beggars on Earth?

Her strength failed, as it always did, when she was forced inland, away from the sea. Wobbling on shaky legs, she headed for the town square, surrounded by buildings. She'd learned from experience it would be warmer there. The square was usually cobbled and had a fountain or pump in the middle. Proximity to water helped her land-sickness.

As she prowled the square she realized that it had been market day. On the cobblestones she found a couple of moldy vegetables, a stalk of turning broccoli, and the heel of a burnt loaf of bread. She washed what she could in the fountain.

Gauging the sun and direction, she found the best corner of the buildings on the square for sleeping. She drew into it, ate fast and greedily. She'd stay just for a little while.

She was dozing when the volaran found her.

One minute she was asleep, the next a soft whuffle came and sweet breath, and a scent she'd smelled before but couldn't put a name to.

A bright image of a five-petaled white flower in a spring sky flashed before her mental eye.

I am Blossom-Greeting-The-First-Warm-Spring-Wind, said a quiet voice. A mental voice.

Raine blinked grit from her eyes, stared at the horsey face. Touched its soft nose. A tongue came out and licked her palm. That would have been disgusting half a year ago, but ranked far down on the repulse-o-meter now. In fact, it was comforting.

She'd heard of the winged horses. Most people spoke of them reverantly. But she didn't really believe this vision. "Who?" she croaked with both voice and mind. Her mind voice was definitely clearer.

Blossom-Greeting-The-First-Warm-Spring-Wind. YOUR volaran, Exotique of the Sea.

She'd been called an Exotique! This being knew what she was. Her heart started beating fast and hard. Her mouth was drier than ever.

She could see in Blossom's eyes that the flying horse knew of the *others*.

Finally, finally, this was the beginning of the end of her ordeal. Hope flooded her. She couldn't breathe. Her shoulders were shaking too much. She was crying! Crying hard and holding herself.

A man's bootheels snapped on the town square's cobblestones. He saw Blossom and shouted at them. Something about the guy roused all Raine's instincts for evil. He was another one like Travys. Someone who'd enjoy tormenting her, killing her. Might like to do the same with a stray volaran.

Mount! demanded Blossom with a mental image of Raine leaping gracefully onto the winged horse's back.

Raine had never been on a horse in her life. She grabbed the mane, scrambled with her feet. Heard the volaran grunt. She was still half-on half-off when the flying steed rose into the sky. Her scream of terror was muffled by solid horse—volaran—flesh.

Go! Raine cried mentally. *Fly!* She didn't have the nerve to sit up, settled herself along the wide back, hands hurting from a tight grip on the silky mane. The volaran flew low, legs tucked up as they glided over the houses.

North, Raine said when her fear subsided enough to squeeze a thought in.

North is good. To Faucon, Blossom said.

As soon as she cleared the town, the volaran headed northeast. Raine's vision dimmed. Her limbs trembled. "No!" she shouted, but it was too late. Darkness fell. Hard.

She awoke with sand in her mouth and spit it out, found herself on a beach. There was no volaran in sight, and no town.

Hope and despair, a vicious circle. She wiped her face on her arm. She knew she'd dreamt the whole episode.

42

Bri dreamt of a woman. She was scared, hurt, running. It reminded her of the night she'd left the rock star. She woke with a shudder and let her heart slow. Sevair lay beside her, breathing evenly, radiating heat. It wasn't late, but they'd had a full day, and she'd begun to adjust to Sevair's schedule of up at dawn. And they'd jumped each other as soon as he'd come home and actually ended up in bed.

She set a hand on his back and felt more connected. Their Songs *were* merging.

She hadn't had an anxiety attack for two days, but she'd been pretending that she was just on the other side of the globe from home, not cut off completely. She thought her inner child was buying it so far. Maybe.

Sevair rolled to her, reached for her, drew her into strong arms. He was aroused, ready, and that sexy song and the scent of him had her own arousal speeding through her. She didn't want to think anymore. Didn't want to feel stupid, childish panic.

Her hands touched, stroked. He groaned and that pleased her. Equal. They'd be equal. He, Lladrana, were not assimilating her, they were allowing her to go the way she'd always wanted.

He thrust into her and thought vanished in her body's needs. "Bond with me," he murmured in a dark, sensual voice as his hands slid under her bottom, raised her up.

She let passion take her, let her Song spiral high and join with his, and hoped the panic wouldn't return.

Faucon, brooding that night on the top of his Castle, heard a volaran's mental call. He'd begun to communicate better with his mounts in the past couple of days. Calli would be proud of him. Calli...his mouth turned down. Another Exotique who was not meant for him.

He hadn't realized he could experience so much pain and still live.

Faucon, come. You MUST come, now! It was Starflower, Elizabeth's volaran. No. Elizabeth hadn't stayed, so the volaran was partnered with no one.

Faucon, help! The volaran shouted, forming easy Equine.

The sigh was more groan than a exhalation of breath. His very bones ached as if the malaise of his heart affected his whole body. But he was Hauteur Faucon Creusse, nobleman, master of several estates. Responsible for many people and volarans. He could not ignore a call for help.

He pushed away from the battlement. Night had fallen and he couldn't see anything except the white line of seafoam breaking against rocks in the distance.

Hurrying through his home, he noted that his people still watched him with concern. Impatiently, he wished they'd just let him be. At the door, his new valet held out a short, light flying cape. Never breaking stride, Faucon took it from his hand and whirled it on as the footmen swung open the door. Broullard wouldn't have allowed him to sulk so long, or kept quiet about Faucon's moods, but Broullard was gone. Another grief.

Starflower circled the courtyard, showing nerves and impatience. Probably wasn't wise for them both to be in such an irritable mood while they flew, but Faucon had no inclination to soothe her fidgets. He doubted his own distress would fade soon.

At the side of the stone steps, she stopped in front of him. *Come, now!* So he leapt on her and she angled upward. Grief was replaced by sheer terror as his hands scrabbled for reins, a hackamore, *something*. No tack. He entwined his fingers in her soft mane and held on tight and prayed. He hadn't flown with a volaran bareback since—never.

They didn't fly high, nor did she request help with Distance Magic, so they weren't flying far. They kept to the coastline that changed from the small smooth beaches between rocky coves to long beaches and dunes as they flew south. They were almost at the point where they'd be over open sea. He didn't want to do that with no tack. He leaned close to her neck. He wouldn't let her lose him.

The moon had risen and was large and full and bright, low to the water. An exquisite sight, but it reminded him that he and Elizabeth had made love under the last full moon. Anger spurted through him. Why did his first thoughts always have to be of Elizabeth? Time to place her

Song firmly into the past. Stop brooding. Stop mourning. Live life and believe in the future.

Then they were over the sea and Faucon Sang prayers for long minutes.

Finally Starflower lowered to the ground, landing gently. Faucon saw a figure walking toward them. Her Song hit him hard.

Exotique. How could this be? He gasped. He knew all the Exotiques well. This wasn't any of them. He stared at the scrawny woman slowly shambling toward them, head down, as if she didn't realize they were there. As if lifting her foot for each step was an effort.

Everything inside him squeezed at the knowledge that she would be nothing but trouble. Complicate his life. By the Song, he was sick of Exotiques!

She stopped, raised her head and he saw that her skin showed patches of dark and light, as if she'd tried to disguise herself. With dirt, he supposed. Her hair was to her shoulders and looked like a solid mat, dark—he couldn't tell if it would be any strange color like the other Exotiques.

He sat tall on the volaran. "Salutations," he called.

She stood still.

Let me go to her, Starflower said. *She knows me. I found her earlier tonight. She has been in Lladrana for months.*

There was only one explanation. "The Seamasters didn't fail in their Summoning like they thought they had," he whispered. Sighing, he slid off the volaran.

Truth.

Faucon watched as Starflower trotted forward until she was within arm reach of the woman. Then the volaran stretched out her neck, lifted her wings as if to show them for admiration. It was a strong person who could ignore a volaran's advances. The woman raised her hand tentatively, but had to take a couple of steps toward her, toward Faucon, to touch Starflower.

Come get her. She is weak and does not walk well. She needs to be taken to the Marshalls' Castle.

"Perhaps I should call them to come and pick her up." The wind was flowing toward Starflower, and volarans had good ears. He had no doubt the steed would hear him.

Starflower snorted. Stamped. The woman stumbled back. The volaran crooned.

Come, it will rain later and there is no town nearby.

"Gentian is only a few miles," he said. She'd probably come from there.

She cannot walk so far.

Since the woman was swaying on her feet, Faucon reluctantly agreed.

Aren't you curious about her?

"Not enough to touch another Exotique."

Starflower tensed. *Alarms ring at the Castle.*

His gut clenched. What was he doing here, indulging his emotions? Lladranans still had battles to fight and win, the Dark to defeat. Best focus on that. But he could do nothing right now without Starflower.

The Marshalls and the Chevaliers are occupied. You are here for her.

His turn to snort. Grumbling, he walked toward the woman and volaran. Gave this strange Exotique his briefest bow. He felt the instinctive slide of attraction and ignored it, for once not thinking at all how he would charm and impress her. Over that affliction, thank the Song.

"Salutations," he repeated brusquely. She didn't turn her head but eyed him. "We should go. Rain's coming. Do you fly?"

She only continued to stroke Starflower's silky hide.

A rocky point of land rose ahead of them. They were coming up on the last easy path up the incline

"Ttho," she said, her voice husky. A little curl of sexual interest teased his groin. *Merde!*

"I don't ride," she said. Her accent was strange—all the Exotiques had varying accents, but a commonality, too. Her underlying tongue was different, reminded him more of how the Singer spoke the Exotique language.

By. The. Song.

The more he looked at this woman, the more it became obvious that she had not been treated well. Not like the other Exotiques. There was a bruise on her swollen cheek, something dark and crusty under her fingernails. Blood?

He didn't want to think about it. He drew out a practiced smile, bowed again, a little deeper.

Her eyes glittered some color he didn't think was brown or black, but were set deeply and surrounded by dark smudges.

Then he took her arm and walked inland.

"Ttho!" She jerked her arm away. "Not again. I still feel sick." Not only was her underlying accent different, her words were overlaid with the thickness of rough southern fisher-tongue.

Impatience gnawed at him. "We have to go. My duty lies elsewhere, and rain is coming." Again he gripped her arm and nearly dragged her up the path.

She doubled over and clutched her belly, screaming, flailed an arm to fight. But she was half-starved and sick and weak.

It hurts her if she goes too far from the sea. Starflower tramped nervously in the sand. *And she has had a hard day.*

Faucon gave the volaran a disbelieving stare.

The woman turned her head aside and retched. Not much came out of her.

The volaran lifted her head, met his gaze and repeated herself. *It hurts her if she goes too far from the sea.*

Snorting, ready to prove Starflower wrong, Faucon walked toward the lap of waves that was the tide going out. The woman relaxed beside him. *"Merci."* It was spoken so quietly that he didn't know if she whispered it or the word insinuated itself into his mind.

She was pitiful, with none of the strength and sparkling Power and confidence of the other Exotiques. He clenched his jaw. Why was *he* the person who had to deal with this?

Because you live by the sea.

Wonderful. He ground his teeth. She smelled, too, not awful, just…odd. Brine, woman, Exotique. His grip loosened. Whatever she was, she was ill. Could it be the frinkweed sickness? The thought stopped his breath.

The Dark has not touched her, Starflower said.

Faucon gazed at the flying horse.

Starflower sidled. *I would know. We all knew when Bri was touched.*

"Hmm," he said.

The woman moaned, began to shiver. She was too thin, and so was what she wore. He could see her ribs, more dark marks against her fair skin. *"Merde!"*

She flinched, drew in a shuddering breath and struck out. He thought she meant it for his eye. He ducked. She clipped him on the ear and it stung. She struggled again.

"Quiet!"

She didn't listen, raked his cheek with short, broken nails encrusted with who knew what. He spun her around, trapped her arms to her body. "Easy," he soothed, trying to keep exasperation out of his voice, his Song. He had not handled this right. She was sick. She was frightened. And what in the pit of the Dark was she doing in such a state?

The Seamasters had botched their Summoning at midwinter. They hadn't even known they'd succeeded in bringing an Exotique over.

When he'd heard they'd tried a Summoning, he should have sent searchers around Seamasters' Market, but hadn't. No one had. Everyone had believed the Seamasters when they said they'd failed.

Error upon error upon error.

She stood still for a moment, then twisted. Her heels struck back, but his boots were thick.

He freed her. She stumbled away, not looking at him, avoiding Starflower, too.

He followed. "I'm Faucon Creusse, a noble and Chevalier."

She said nothing, shambled faster. She didn't move with the grace of the other Exotiques. Could he be wrong? Perhaps she was a woman from a different land, unusual, but not unknown. His estate was in the south, after all, near Krache, and Song knew all sorts landed and stayed in Krache.

"I want to help you."

She snuffled, kept staggering away. *You lie.*

Faucon winced.

"You all lie." She had a certain tone in her voice that made him think of Alexa. Stopping, he concentrated on her Song. *That* was strong, held notes of Power, rhythms associated with the sea. But her melody was missing several beats, or he couldn't hear them. His heart squeezed. They always got to his heart first—why was that? Why couldn't this attraction go straight to his groin so he could shove it aside, or satisfy it as easily as Elizabeth had done.

He strolled behind the woman. He didn't want to be here, do this, know her. "I feel obligated to help you. That's the truth. I will not go away, *Exotique*."

She made a keening noise and wrapped her arms around herself and picked up her pitiful pace. "You will kill me. You are like the others who hate me and will kill me."

He stopped. Exotique, yes. Which meant that some were innately repulsed as well as attracted. He hadn't thought about that much. Luthan was the only one Faucon knew who had the affliction, and Luthan was the most honorable man on Amee.

Bruises on her skin, anger sparked inside him. No matter who she was, she did not deserve that. He caught up with her. Stuck his hands in his pockets, kept pace on her right, with the sea to their left. It was easy to match steps with her. Like all Exotiques, she was smaller than he, shorter. Marian was the tallest, the most voluptuous, and this woman didn't have her height, was perhaps as tall as Elizabeth had been. In far worse shape. Faucon didn't know how much weight she usually carried, but she was skin and bones now.

"I am Faucon Creusse, a Chevalier," he said again mildly. He gestured to Starflower, who was munching seagrass. The volaran ignored him. "Don't you know of Chevaliers?"

"Not much."

"You came in midwinter, Summoned by the Seamasters. They didn't want to pay zhiv to the Marshalls to bring you through the Dimensional Corridor properly. The Seamasters thought they failed and said nothing."

She just kept walking, though he sensed she listened.

"Am I right? How long have you been here?" he demanded. "How did you come?"

She flinched.

This time his sigh came out like a sigh. "We are walking north. Tell me where you want to go and I will take you."

Her hands curved into claws. Faucon took a pace away, gave her more room, let her feel less threatened. They walked for a couple of moments in silence. She snuck quick glances from under matted and ragged hair. He kept his hands in his pockets.

"I fell through a mirror," she mumbled.

That gave him pause. The Singer, again. Maybe. Koz had told him the Singer practiced mirror magic. The thought of Koz made Faucon smile. Just the man to win this one. "Come with me," he soothed. "I promise you food and a warm bed and safety."

Tears dribbled down her face. "I can't," she sobbed. "I can't leave the sea."

"I have a dock house." A fancy to protect his yacht. "Or you can sleep on the yacht."

"Yacht?"

"It's a large boat of—"

"I know what a yacht is. I design ships."

It all fell together in his mind like rippling chimes. The assault against the Dark would need a special ship to carry

Marshalls and Chevaliers and volarans. Amee had seen to that, had prodded the Seamasters' pride to Summon this woman.

He shook his head. The how didn't matter as much as the fact that she was needed here. In Lladrana. A true Exotique. And his charge. Again he felt the tug of his blood toward her.

He set his jaw. Not this time.

It took him a long while, until the moon began setting, disappearing behind the ocean waves, before he could convince Raine—her name was Raine Lindley—to fly with him.

And though he'd tried to project an ease at that flight, he thought he'd dream of flying double with a novice without tack over the open sea forever.

43

Thrills ran up and down Raine's spine as she watched the waves under them during the lovely flight across the sea. The volaran felt solid and comforting. Sang somehow in Raine's mind. Or maybe Raine heard a Song from her. That happened to her now and then—she heard Songs.

She thought it happened to Lladranans more often, another reason she'd been considered lacking.

The sexy noble Chevalier didn't like her. Fine by Raine, especially since she'd spent a little time in his gruff and irritated company and he hadn't hurt her. He wasn't like Travys.

She didn't know how much she could trust him, but him helping her while he was irritated was a good sign. As if he was an honorable man. Honorable. It wasn't something she'd thought about on Earth. There she might have called him a decent guy.

Perspectives changed.

An honorable man was a treasure.

The large setting moon was orange and gleamed in the sea. They called it a sea and not an ocean, and spoke of many islands, but she hadn't seen a map. She fell into a half-sleep and images of a ship sailing an ocean flitted through her mind. It would have to be a big ship, she knew that. To carry….

The tiny jolt of their landing, and the man's arms behind her falling away, taking warmth, roused her. She blinked at him as he stood next to the volaran. A sheen of sweat showed on his face, and she became aware of his masculine scent.

Blossom arched her neck and whuffled at his hair. *Well done.*

Raine thought so, too. She stroked Blossom's neck and shoulders. "*Merci*, Blossom."

"Blossom," the guy muttered.

He grabbed Raine by the waist and swung her up into his arms with a matter-of-factness that spoke of expediency and no romantic urge. He turned around and Raine caught her breath at the beauty of the yacht at the end of a sturdy well-kept dock. The ship was painted white and pristine, its lines sleek and eminently seaworthy. She could improve on the design a little to make it faster…

Faucon grunted. "Get the door, please."

Raine was craning her neck to keep the boat in view and the door to a cottage was before her. She reached down and turned the knob. As they walked in, lights came on and she found herself blinking again. "How did that happen?"

Raising his brows, he touched his temple, which showed a streak of silver. "Power," he said, and she knew that meant "magic." She swallowed. She wasn't with the fisherfolk anymore, and concepts she'd heard of—"streaks of Power," "Power at both temples," "just a few hairs of Power" suddenly made sense.

Eyeing her, he said, "There's a fresh-water bath over there." He gestured to the right. "I hope this suits you."

She was dazzled. The wooden floors were clean and polished to a gleam. There were chairs with cushions! Knit throws, rag rugs. "*Merci.*"

"I'll take care of Starflower."

"Who?"

Me, whinnied Blossom. *That's what they called me.*

"Oh," Raine said. "Blossom Greeting the Spring Wind. Blossom."

"Ayes," he said shortly. His bow was just as brusque. "Catch up on your sleep. You look like you need to. Sleep late. I intend to do so."

Translated, she looked like hell and he didn't want to be bothered with her in the morning.

"There should be food in the kitchen," he said. "I'll talk to my housekeeper and confirm, and will send down more supplies tomorrow." He gave her the once-over again. "Clothes. We must have something to fit you. There should be bathrobes in the closet. Good night." Then he was gone, striding out of view.

Raine went to the threshold and looked to her right, inland, and not to the ship across the dock and to her left. Her mouth fell open as she saw lights from the huge bulk of a looming Castle, a black shadow against the night sky.

Then she stepped back into the cottage and closed the door. There was only one flimsy lock. The nobleman didn't think anyone would violate his property. Raine shrugged and locked it, headed to the bathroom, opened that door to see a large turquoise rectangular tub sunk into the ground with a wooden ledge. Another wisp of old conversation came to mind, "them nobles take their bathing serious like." She guessed so. How glad she was to see that!

She turned on the faucets, moaned when hot water poured through the brass. Tears leaked from her eyes. She wiped her running nose with a corner of her apron that she ripped from her. The fabric gave all too easily, as did the rest of her clothes. Rags. All of them. She'd never have to wear them again.

She bathed and shuddered with weeping. Hope filled her.

Faucon strode to his Castle from the boathouse, muttering under his breath about strange women, then actually *listened* to himself. This is what happened when you got deeply involved with Exotiques. He'd noticed it before in their men. They talked to themselves. Sometimes not even in Lladranan. Once he'd yearned, then enjoyed being a part of that exclusive group. No more.

No more, indeed. There was another Exotique sitting down there in his boathouse, and he was responsible for her. He stopped grumbling and clenched his jaw instead. He hated that he had a sick and confused Exotique on his hands. Hated that his body reacted to her, hated that he more than pitied her. He respected her for her grit and determination. She must be tough to survive in the docktowns for months as an alien.

When he reached his home, he left instructions with the

night captain for his housekeeper to provide food and clothing for the Exotique during the day and his medica to see her. Perhaps he should leave that to Bri. He sent a quick search for a Song.

Jaquar wasn't at the Castle, and Sevair...damn himself for a coward, but Faucon didn't want to contact Sevair or Bri yet.

Tomorrow.

He sank into a well-padded leather easy chair and rubbed his hands over his face. There was much to do. Informing everyone of a new Exotique meant dealing with the Marshalls and the Chevaliers in a council meeting. That might be best. He could imagine the ructions of the other Exotiques when they discovered one of their own had been misused.

Confronting the Seamasters about a Summoning that had gone terribly wrong. How much did they know of their lost Exotique? Would they seek to claim her? Harm her? They certainly hadn't protected her.

Dealing with the sick Exotique herself. Yes, he'd have to contact Bri first thing in the morning.

That recalled him to *her* task, to build a ship. He wrote another note for his housekeeper to have a drafting table, tools, paper and parchment sent down to the cottage.

Exhaustion settled on him and he welcomed it. He hadn't been sleeping well. Tonight, with all the surprises of the day, should be better. His eyelids went closed and his muscles felt heavy, so he let himself slip into memory-dulling sleep.

Travys rocked to his hands and knees. Shook his pounding, painful head. Rain splattered against the wood of the pier above him, swept in on the night breeze and smacked him with cold drops. Staggering to his feet, he leaned against the piling of the pier and touched his head. Felt blood.

Rage surged through him and he trembled with it. Bared his teeth. The fucking bitch had tried to kill him. Then his violent anger turned to glee. Now *he* could kill *her*. No one could deny him. His hands flexed and fisted, released.

He could taste the pleasure of beating her to death. She'd pay for what she'd done to him. For what she was, a half-breed, half-wit. He'd squeeze the life from her throat, silence that strangely pitched atonal Song that nearly drove him mad. No, strangling her was too fast. Too easy.

He'd break every bone in her body and enjoy her pain, see it in her eyes, listen to her beg. Ah. Ayes.

His head came up and he sniffed the air, tested the tavern above him. It was full of people but not one of them was pot-girl. Slowly he turned, and caught her scent.

North. She'd gone north, perhaps even over the bay. He shrugged, working kinks from his shoulders. He knew people who'd lend him a boat to cross the water. When he stepped from the pier, the rain stopped. A good sign.

Raine woke in dawn's gray light, and knew at once where she was. That nobleman's dockhouse. Her body sunk in a soft feather bed, a down comforter of silk so fine that it caught on the ragged cracks of her rough hands when she tried to pull it up. The linens smelled good. *She* smelled good.

She'd had a bath, used fluffy towels to dry and stumbled into this wonderful bed. She stretched luxuriously. Warm. Finally warm.

Testing her sickness, her inner compass told her she was on land, next to the sea, as she'd remembered. All right, then.

Compared to the past six months, she was downright fabulous. Her body ached with bruises and unaccustomed walking—flying!—the day before, but she wasn't curled and cramped in a corner of the Open Mouthed Fish under a tattered blanket. She wasn't expected to get up right now and do another cleaning of the kitchen and the taproom. That in itself was sheer luxury.

She let her muscles loosen and didn't wake again until there was a knock on the bedroom door. This time memory was a little slow, as if she'd slept too well or too long. She was used to no privacy and noise around her all the time.

The door opened and a solid, middle-aged woman came in carrying a pile of folded clothes. Raine's eyes widened. She knew Lladranans loved colorful clothes, but the people she'd lived among had only worn color for feast days. These clothes were bright. The woman herself wore a blinding red dress over an orange underskirt of a quality Raine had never seen on Lladrana.

She dipped a curtsey to Raine. "Salutations. I'm Lydia, the Creusse housekeeper." Then said over her shoulder, "Bring breakfast for the Exotique."

"Salutations," Raine croaked. "I'm Raine Lindley."

The housekeeper nodded, but curiosity lit her eyes. "We won't stay long, or bother you while you work. Here are some clothes. We've stocked the kitchen, and the men have arranged the drafting table and instruments in the living room. Is that acceptable?" She eyed Raine and laid out a tunic and skirt of blue, put the rest of the clothes in a wardrobe.

"Urgh," Raine said, scrunching back until she was supported by the headboard, pulling the covers to her chin. She focused on the rapid Lladranan in a different accent. So people had been speaking slowly to her. Well, hell. She was less ready to be out in the world beyond the Open Mouthed Fish than she'd thought. Try to catch up, woman!

"Drafting table?" she murmured.

"For the ship." The housekeeper's mouth pursed in disapproval. "That was all I was informed of. That you were here and would be designing The Ship that will take the invasion force to the Dark's nest."

She was a lot more informed than Raine. Several of those concepts had just whizzed right by her. Invasion force. Dark's nest. "Um, Faucon," she said.

The housekeeper's face softened. "He's had it rough lately. That Elizabeth and Snap of your land weren't good for him." Her voice was accusatory, her Song sharpened. "Reminds me." She waved and two other women came in. Maids, Raine guessed, but they were as far above her as a pot girl as the moon was the Earth. Dressed well, walked gracefully, fine hair and skin and hands. One brought in a tray of eggs and toast with strips of bacon that had Raine's mouth watering. The other held a stack of three books.

"Here," Lydia shook out what looked like a bed-jacket garment like Raine's Granny Fran had once used. It was bright red and smelled of lavender. With competent movements that managed to preserve Raine's modesty, the housekeeper tucked her into it. Talk about efficient.

"Breakfast." She took the tray from the maid and placed it on Raine's lap. "We'll leave you now, but if you have any wishes, just use the horn." She bustled back out with the wide-eyed maids before Raine could find words, but not before her stomach gave a serious rumble.

"Eat up!" Lydia chirped. In a moment a door closed and Raine sensed she was alone.

She stared at the food, the clothes, the furnishings of the room. So much opulence! She'd finally landed in a place where people might give her a chance.

Breakfast in bed. She didn't think so. She slipped from the bed—remembered too late it was a little higher than Earth beds as she thunked a few inches to the floor—and took the tray through the living room to the kitchen. The drafting table in the corner of the living room looked good, but she wanted food!

She ate. No, she gobbled. Tastes she'd only experienced in dreams exploded in her mouth. She moaned at the simple crunchiness of crisp bacon. She'd once read that cross-culturally on Earth, bacon was considered to be a smell associated with the wealthy. She understood that now. She hadn't seen bacon, or ham or any other part of pig for six months, and she'd rarely eaten pork before then. For a moment she wondered how her stomach would handle such rich fare. It didn't stop her from shoveling buttered toast in her mouth.

When she was done, she washed the dishes automatically, though the soap wasn't a scent that she recognized—lots less harsh on her hands than at the tavern. Then she went back to the bedroom and opened the drawers where the housekeeper had put undergarments. She pulled out fine lingerie like long underwear—chemise and leggings—then she dressed in the blue tunic and skirt. They fit.

Raine sauntered into the living room, checked out the

drafting table, noted that the stand was made of wood, not metal, and played with it until she had it raised and angled just right. A cabinet had been added, which contained feather pens, ink, straightedges, protractors and other tools. Sheets of paper and parchment lay atop the cabinet. Her rescuer had an agenda.

Hell, from what she'd understood about the previous Summonings, the whole damn planet, literally, had an agenda. Nibbling her lower lip, a habit that probably made her look stupid and hadn't helped her in the past, she went back into the bedroom and looked at the books.

They weren't in English and she didn't know how to read Lladranan. A flush heated her neck. How could she have learned how to read! But she opened one at random, saw the picture of a blue-eyed blonde and her breath came a little quick. No way could this woman be from Lladrana. She flipped through the volume, studying the pictures of a Castle and volarans. As she riffled the pages, more pictures flashed before her, and when a 3-D image of a fire-breathing monster popped out at her she dropped the book and let it stay on the floor.

She was breathing fast again, eyed the other books with extreme caution. Yes, *they* wanted something from her, and she got the idea that designing and building a ship was the least of it. As far as she was concerned, she'd already paid her dues.

Don't think of that, or the past. Go open the door and stand in the sunlight, feel its warmth, loiter for a few minutes. Precious little free time in the past six months.

She strode to the door, realizing that her posture had improved. She no longer walked as if ready for a blow.

Then she flung open the door and let the midmorning sunlight in, stepped out onto the landing that led to the dock.

Travys attacked her.

He grabbed her in a bear hug from the side. She sank low, flung herself with his momentum, and they both crashed to the ground. She kicked and pounded and freed herself and jumped up and hobbled fast with a hurt body to the door.

He was faster than she recalled—she didn't get the door closed. She retreated and looked for a weapon.

The man would kill her.

But not if she took care of him first.

44

Faucon woke and his standard morning rush of sorrow mingled with irritation at the thought of the new Exotique. Progress. He showered, ate the breakfast set on the warming mat in his sitting room, then reluctantly decided he could avoid his duty no longer. He walked down to his den.

He didn't want to call Alexa, or Marian. Really didn't want to call Bri. That notion was like a splinter in his heart. But she was the best medica in Lladrana and he had a sick Exotique woman. He tapped a beat on his crystal ball.

Bri's face filled the small one she held at eye level. "Faucon?" She sounded startled. For the first time he noticed that she didn't seem so cheerful either. Shadows were under and in her eyes. She'd lost a sister, her whole family. But he didn't want to be reasonable.

Bracing, he said, "I have some news. Sit down."

Her eyes widened. She nodded. "You aren't sick, are you?"

"No." He rubbed his jaw. He was not handling this smoothly. Perhaps he should have taken time to gather his thoughts. He didn't know why he felt the pressure of time, but he did.

"I'm ready," Bri said.

"I've got a very sick woman here," he said baldly. "Another Exotique, Summoned months ago, I think by the Seamasters. They said they'd tried a Summoning and failed. Apparently not. To give them credit, I don't think they knew they succeeded."

Her mouth opened, closed, opened. Emotions too fast to read, too Exotique, flashed across her face. "Does she have the frink disease?" she asked in a focused, clipped tone that reminded him too much of her sister. He wished Bri still had purple streaks in her hair, that it was shorter.

"No. She is malnourished, has been ill-treated." He was equally abrupt. "She can't be moved far from the seashore without experiencing great pain."

"I'll contact the Castle medicas immediately for information, also Alexa and Marian. We'll be there in an hour."

That was pressing Distance Magic hard, but he nodded. She was already moving, calling for Sevair and the roc and volarans.

He said, "I will speak with Alexa and Marian."

"No need, I've sent them word telepathically."

"Fine," he said between gritted teeth. "But—" Screaming hit his mind. *Raine!* Already he knew the tone of her. She was fighting for her life. He knew it, cursed, sped down to the boathouse. He'd been no better than the Seamasters, had left her unprotected. He prayed he wouldn't be too late.

Her keening went on and on in his head, above the thundering of his heart, the heaving of his lungs. Power, fear, pushed him along until his feet barely touched the ground. He *felt* the smash of a fist against her face, tasted blood that washed into her mouth, yelled himself.

The door to the boathouse was splintered, half off its hinges. Now he heard half sobs, half cries, animalistic sounds of a fight, roars of a wounded man.

Then the male voice stopped.

He shot into the room to see Raine pounding a table leg onto the limp man's head, brutal features showing deep runnels from raking fingernails. She saw Faucon, launched herself at him, a wild thing pushed too far.

He caught her, grabbed her hands, brought her close. She struggled and they fell on the man. Faucon rolled, wincing as broken china and glass cut his back through his shirt.

"It's all right. All right!"

"Let me go!"

"Don't hit me and I will."

A trace of reason appeared in her eyes. She made a strangled noise, went limp. He rose and she crawled away from the man, fast, to a corner of the room.

It hurt Faucon to see that.

Then she huddled and watched him from wide eyes the color of the deep ocean—dark green and fascinating.

He threw off the thought, stood himself, and looked down at the man. He seemed to have two head wounds.

"Is he alive?" Raine's voice was thin. "What will you do to me if he dies?"

Faucon brushed off his dreeth leather pants, flexed his back and felt pain and the stickiness of blood and wished he'd worn his dreeth leather tunic. He stared down at the man and let the curses come. "He's alive and a freak. A man who is instinctively repulsed by Exotiques. There are some people like that, about one in fifty." He could *feel* the brush of her Power, how it slipped along his skin, the spellbinding but broken notes of her Song. He met her eyes. "There are some like me who are instinctively attracted to Exotiques." He snorted. "I'm getting over that."

She shrank into her corner, but said, "Yeah, right, I could see the attraction."

He hunched an irritable shoulder. "I'm getting over that." Then he toed the body of the rough fisherman. "As for this one, he tried to kill you, a valuable Exotique, which our country, our very planet, needs. He'll get what he deserves."

"Yeah, right," she said again, mouth turning down.

But he caught her glance, willed her to believe him. "I'll make sure of it, I promise you." Then he smiled thinly. "If the other Exotiques get their hands on him, his life won't be worth living. Better that he hopes the Seamasters judge him."

"He works for them," she said. "Travys. He's the caretaker of the fairgrounds, Seamasters' Market."

"Ah." With that information more clicked into place. "You know something."

He gave her a charming, superficial smile. "I know many things. And we will talk." He prodded the man again, but he didn't stir. "After I have this piece of scum removed."

Faucon went to the door where his housekeeper hovered, along with several of his home Chevaliers. "Get the mistress carpenter and bring her here to fix the door." He stepped aside for three of his men to take the piece of *merde* to a locked basement room under the far tower of his Castle. He ordered three others—females—to stay and guard.

When he turned back to the woman, she'd barricaded herself in the kitchen, with the upended table across the door. She stood holding a long, sharp kitchen knife. He sighed. "I'm not going to hurt you."

"Doesn't look as if you are going to help me, either."

His face stiffened; he could feel his expression chill. He inclined his torso in a straight, formal bow. "I did not protect you as I should have. You have my regrets and my apologies." He gestured to the door. "Many of my best Chevaliers are female. Do you want a guard with you here in the cottage?"

She considered him. "Ttho."

"Very well. I have spoken with Bri, the Exotique Medica, at Castleton and she has alerted the other Exotiques, their men, and probably all the important personages of the Castle, as to your existence. They will be here shortly. Do you wish me to wait with you until they come?"

"Ttho."

"Do you have any more questions?"

"Ttho."

Frowning, he studied her, but he couldn't read her. Was she as tough as she seemed? She didn't appear as if she was going into shock, but…He shook his head. She didn't want him here and he didn't want to stay. Duty had been fulfilled, though recompense for her injury remained outstanding.

Another bow in her direction. "I will go and wait for the Exotiques, and work to resolve the matter of how you were Summoned and no one knew."

"Just line up your thoughts," she said. "You know."

He'd guessed, but wanted to confirm the details. With a last look in her direction that he hoped didn't show his distaste, he left.

Raine's knees gave way and she sat down hard on the floor. She didn't feel it. Adrenaline was still racing through her body. But now the man was gone she began to shake. She should move, but she simply couldn't gather the wits and energy to do so. Awful to know that she'd come to the end of her strength, while she was in the power of this nobleman. He could hurt her so much more than Travys, if he cared.

She sniffed. That song and dance about being attracted to her. Was that a pitiful lie or what? She put her head on her knees and tried to pretend she wasn't trapped.

Bri arrived no more than fifteen minutes later. The first Faucon knew of her presence was when she rapped briefly on his study door and walked in. He dropped his pen. "How did you get here so soon?"

"I rode the roc. She has better Distance Magic than the volarans."

"Ah, of course."

She lifted a bag made from the dreeth she'd helped kill. A twinge of pain went through him. Elizabeth had designed that bag, said it was traditional medica equipment on Exotique Terre. She'd never used hers, which he'd given her. She hadn't taken it home. So she probably had nothing to remember him by. Just as well since she was with another man. The taste of bitter ashes coated his mouth. "I'll take you to the new one." He was up and around the desk and striding away, Power pushing his steps. "The sooner you treat her and arrange for her to go to the Castle, the sooner you all will be gone."

"Gee, Faucon, thanks for the lovely welcome."

Heat rose to the back of his neck. He hadn't ever been so rude in his own home in all of his life. "Excuse me," he said stiffly. "Come this way, please." He headed through the Castle.

Bri caught up with him. "I'm sorry. I know that you still hurt. So do I." Her tone was short.

"Exotiques have been more pain than pleasure for me, that's certain," he said. "I would appreciate it greatly if you took her back to the Castle as soon as possible."

"Who's *her*? What's her name? You did—" Bri stopped abruptly. She was more than a little irritable, too. Two people mourning or something more? Not his concern.

He didn't *want* it to be his concern, didn't want to remember that he cared for Elizabeth's twin and had thought of her as the sibling he'd never had. Once. He mastered his unaccustomed temper and tried a smile. Was fairly sure it didn't look sincere. "Her name is Raine Lindley."

Raine Lindley. The new Exotique's name echoed. Then he understood Bri had sent it to the other Exotiques.

"Everyone's following. We'll have a council here, then take her to the Castle."

He stopped to give her a brief, insincere bow. "*Merci.*"

As they walked outside, she made a surprised noise and said, "You aren't housing her in your home?"

Another comment that hit him on the raw. He sent Bri

a long, cool look. "I told you she couldn't be moved from the seashore."

"I didn't think you meant it literally."

"I did. She's at the boathouse." He resumed his rapid pace.

They walked down the stone path from his castle to the dock and the small one-story cottage set at a right angle to the dock. Carpenters were already replacing the door as guards stood by.

"What happened here?" Bri asked.

"One of those who have a repulsion has been stalking her. He found her here."

"You—"

He raised a palm to cut her off. "I didn't know. I only found her last night. She hasn't been forthcoming with me. Can we save this conversation until later? The lady needs your care." With a gesture more brisk than elegant, he waved her into the cottage before him.

Raine was still barricaded behind the table in the kitchen, staring at them with big eyes and a large knife in her hand.

"OhmyGod." Bri said, in English. Faucon hated that he still had the dregs of that language inside him from the love-making with Elizabeth.

The knife lowered.

"Full light," Bri said.

Raine blinked as the crystals in the beams brightened. She looked terrible. Very thin, visible bruises all over her face and arms, torn clothing. Bri stared at her, then glanced at him.

Another short bow. "I'll leave you alone." He was glad to do that. He hesitated, then sent mentally, *I hear that we still have this link between us.* The mental Song that connected the Exotiques and their men. Another hurt. *I have guards in place. Come back up to the Castle when you are done.*

I'm sorry. I miss her, too, Bri said.

He turned on his heel and left.

Bri had treated abuse victims and refugees before. She walked over to a table in the sitting-dining room and put her bag down on it, pulled up a chair and sat. In English, she said, "I'm Bri Drystan, late of Denver, came here a few weeks ago. I'm a medica, a healer."

"You're one of *them.* One of the *others.*"

"Yes. They call us Exotiques."

The knife clattered to the floor. The woman began rocking herself, weeping.

Bri approached slowly, but Raine didn't look at her, not even when Bri climbed over the table, righted it and slid the knife into a block. She sat down, then put her arms around the previously unknown Exotique, who clung to her and sobbed.

There was a brief knock on the outer door jamb and Bri looked up to see a large woman wearing a tool belt watching with interest and sympathy. She ducked her head. "Just wanted to let you ladies know that the door is back on. Solid. Hauteur Cruess has left guards."

"*Merci,*" Bri said.

With another nod, the carpenter closed the door, tested it, and left.

Bri found herself stroking thick, damaged dark brown hair. "That's right," she said. "Let it all out. I can't imagine how rough it's been for you."

The woman pulled back, grabbed a rag and blew her

nose, stood, and moved near the door. "No, you can't." Bitterness laced her tones. Bri listened to her Song. More than her hair was damaged. But Bri had dealt with disadvantaged people hating those better off before, too. She rose.

"Please don't dislike me because I've had it easier. There are only five of us here, and we need to stick together."

"Then why didn't you come for me *before*?" Anguish now.

Bri raised both her hands. "We didn't know you were here." She took in a breath, blew it out. "We were all Summoned in a big ritual ceremony by the Marshalls. They planned for us to come. Prepared for us for a month. I don't— we don't, the Marshalls don't—know how you came here."

"To Lladrana," the woman said flatly.

"Ayes, Lladrana."

Raine jerked her chin in the direction of the Castle. "He knows."

"He?"

"The slick guy, Faucon." She said his name as if it were a swear word.

"He has an idea he's checking out." Bri considered the description, of all she knew of the man. "Slick" was a good word for him, but so was "honest." She shook her head. "He didn't know you were here."

"Maybe. Maybe not. But he's got the right idea." The other put a hand between breasts. "I feel it here."

Bri let her lips curve slightly, in sympathy at having to rely on feelings instead of facts. She tapped her right ear with two fingers. "Don't you mean that you *hear* it?"

Raine's face crumpled. She stumbled to the chair Bri had vacated and sat, rocking a little again. Bri walked up to her, stood close, within the personal space of an American woman—though she didn't think the other one came from Colorado. Her accent spoke of east coast. "Let me help." She opened her bag, saw the other eyeing her warily, drew out a stack of handkerchiefs. "They don't have tissues."

Raine took one of the fine linen cloths and pressed it between her hands, as if savoring the texture. Then she mopped her eyes and blew her nose. "Just as well," she said thickly. "Don't need any more trees cut down."

"I agree." Bri studied the woman. "Now let's see about those bruises. What hurts the most?"

Raine lifted her tunic and chemise and Bri sucked in her breath as she saw the dark purple-black over the ribs. She'd been lucky they hadn't broken but surely one or more must be cracked. She looked up to meet the other's eyes. "You must have a high pain threshold."

"I've developed one."

Bri noticed the tension in her own shoulders, relaxed. Okay, take a step back in this little dance. "I'm Bri Drystan from Denver, Colorado," she said again and offered her hand.

"Raine Lindley of Best Haven, Connecticut." She stared at Bri, but Bri kept her gaze steady, sympathetic, her hand out. Raine slipped chapped fingers into Bri's and a bright and whirling rainbow enveloped her. A long, lovely, mournful melody, speaking of wind and water and the sparkle of the sun on ocean waves spun between them. Bri let go. "You're water."

"What?"

Bri smiled. "The Power we have resonates with one element more than others. You're water."

Blinking, Raine said, "I guess. I build ships."

"I'm water, too. I heal people." Stepping forward, she slid her hands under Raine's blouse, found the tender ribs, called the healingstream, a little push of lovely Power.

Raine gasped.

"Better?" Bri asked.

But Raine had lifted her top, and stared at her ribs. "It's gone."

"I heal people," Bri repeated, thought of Raine's words. "You build ships. Of course that's why you're here."

Rain sniffed. "You just figuring that out? Slick knows that, too."

Bri smiled. "I'm from Colorado. All the rest of us are." She touched Raine's cheek, sent healing to it, watched green flames dance as Raine's bruise faded. "Most women from Colorado don't think about building boats."

"Family tradition," Raine said. She ran her fingers through her hair, smiled humorlessly. "I didn't want to stick with the old plans. I wanted new, to build different hulls, use metallic alloys. I wanted twenty-first-century cutting edge." She looked around her. "Guess not."

45

A couple of hours later, Raine sat in a cushioned deck chair with the rest of the Exotiques clustered around her. The chairs were set in a circle on a grassy terrace overlooking a cliff that plunged to the ocean. Faucon's dock was on a tiny crescent of beach between the cliff to the north and a lower, rocky shore to the south. The path to his Castle rose steeply.

Four men also stood or lounged or sat nearby. She'd been briefly introduced to them, but didn't recall their names.

She wasn't comfortable. She wouldn't be able to fight all these people and run away. She suspected if she escaped, they'd come hunting for her.

The women hadn't gushed, but they seemed to think she'd accept them immediately and be friends. Ha.

Raine didn't like the bitter resentment she held toward them and their easier lives, but couldn't seem to shake it off.

Calli, the blond horsewoman—Volaran Exotique—met

Raine's stare. "We didn't have it *that* easy," she said. "All of us faced death in fulfilling our task on Lladrana."

"We've been in mortal peril," said Marian, the voluptuous redheaded scholar, nearly at the same time. She sat next to Raine—ostensibly to answer any questions—and nudged the stack of three books with her foot toward Raine. They were the same bindings as the books she'd been given in the morning, but these were in English. The top one read, "The Lorebook of Calli Torcher, Chevalier and Volaran Exotique."

"We'll help however we can," Calli said.

"What you went through sucks." Alexa's eyes were hard. She fingered her baton. "I had to fight and kill a guy like that once. As soon as I got here, actually."

Raine just stared at her, decided that she was telling the truth, but wasn't sure what to say.

"We haven't been stalked or attacked since then," Marian said. "Those with the revulsion reflex usually stay out of our way."

Faucon walked into view, accompanied by a man in white Chevalier leathers and a couple of other men with a roll to their walks that Raine understood to be wealthy Seamasters. Alexa, the little one with white hair, came over and stood beside Raine, putting a hand on her shoulder.

"In fact," Alexa said, "Luthan—the man in white and the representative of the Singer and my brother-in-law—has the repulsion thing and it distresses him." Alexa squeezed Raine's tense shoulder. "Watch how a real man deals with it."

Raine sat straight, stared at the tall man in white. He nodded to her politely, but when he was a few yards from her, he stopped, and a shudder passed through his body. Then he continued on and was formally introduced. He took Raine's hand and bowed over it, didn't drop it with haste, then moved a couple of steps away.

"That's it?" Raine muttered from a corner of her mouth.

Another squeeze from Alexa. "That's it. That's all he ever shows. And in a couple of months he will know you well and the instinctive-revulsion-thing will wear off."

Scrutinizing Luthan's handsome face with the silver mark of Power at his temples, Raine noted his impassive expression, his cool gaze. She *sensed* his emotional withdrawal. More, she heard the ramping up of his heartbeat and strident notes in his Song. But he showed no outward indications that her presence affected him. He met her eyes, his own polite.

"An honorable man is a treasure," she said.

He blinked. His lips curved slightly. "Thank you." He was sincere. Raine was *hearing* Songs much clearer than she had before. Probably because these people were Powerful. She'd heard how magic touched people at the left or right temples and made streaks of silver—gold for the old. But this was the first time she'd seen it.

The delegation from the Seamasters had greeted the Exotiques' men first, with sideways glances at the women. It was easy for Raine to know they worked on the water by the look in their eyes and the way they carried themselves. There was a short thin man and a big burly one, both honed tough by their life.

Marian stood, and everyone else followed. Even though none of them were actually touching, Bri could feel the energy and emotion cycling through them, uniting them. Alexa's fury was driving the link.

Interesting, not like other men in different walks of life, Marian sent. *Don't antagonize them,* she cautioned Alexa.

But Alexa had withdrawn her baton from her sheath and the end flared with flames.

Too late, Calli said.

Raine felt a little more secure that the people around her would take her part.

"Let's sit," Faucon said smoothly and Alexa reluctantly went back to her chair, scowling at the Seamasters. "Refreshments will be here shortly. I know all your tastes except Raine's. What will you have, lady?" His smile was quick and superficial. "Tea, mead, ale, whiskey, brandy?"

The memory of the alcohol stench permeating the Opened Mouth Fish tavern and many of its patrons tickled her nose, though that place sure hadn't had good whiskey or brandy. Raine didn't know if she could choke down alcohol.

"Orange juice for Raine," Bri said.

"Done," Faucon said. He took a tiny horn-shaped thing from his belt and spoke into it. Raine recalled a couple more of the horns in the cottage. So that's what they were for.

Everyone sat. No one appeared casual or relaxed.

Alexa leaned forward, glare locked on the Seamasters. "Tell us about this failed Summoning last Winter's Eve."

The burly man's eyes widened at that. "You know it was Winter's Eve?"

"At the Seamasters Market Gathering," Faucon said, stretching out his legs. "My cousin's wife was having a child. Convenient for you," Faucon continued smoothly. "Since you knew my cousin would report anything out of the ordinary to me, and I would most certainly inform the Marshalls that you had done a Summoning."

"Wouldn't have mattered if your cousin had been there if we'd succeeded," muttered the burly guy. "Weren't going behind everyone's back, exactly."

The thin man's nose twitched as he stared at Raine. "A puny and pitiful thing we Summoned."

"Perhaps because you did the Summoning incorrectly," Marian said. She radiated fierceness, but Raine didn't know whether it was on her behalf or the irritation at sloppy work.

"In order to acclimate to Lladrana, Exotiques must be attuned to Amee by the gong and chimes, which are sent to them for several weeks," Alexa said. "That's why the Marshalls always Summoned them."

"One more thing the Marshalls failed to share with the Seamasters," the thin man sneered.

Calli sat straight, said, "Wanted to do it on the cheap, didn't you?" The English phrase translated perfectly into Lladranan.

Alexa met the thin Seamaster's gaze coolly. "It is apparent that you Seamasters only decided to Summon someone *after* it was successful. Which means that I, Marian, and probably Calli were already here. *You had only to ask for the information.* We Marshalls and Chevaliers would have let you use the great Temple at the Castle. Would have helped. Fee negotiable." She bit her words off. "You failed." Her nostrils flared as she sucked in a big breath, nailed the thin guy with her hot glare. "You call Raine pitiful."

Raine flinched, knowing everyone here thought of her that way and it was a blow to her ego. Not that her ego was more than the size of a pea lately.

"So she is, since she had no one to help or protect her. Obviously your Summoning circle didn't work well as a team. Some of you must not have really wanted to Summon her. You didn't look for her."

"She didn't come into the circle!" the burly one protested. "How were we to know she came at all?"

Marian spoke again. "That's what the chimes are for. But you didn't know that. What did you do, just half-heartedly perform a Summoning, hang around for a few minutes, then disperse to your fair? A good Summoning takes three hours. Idiots." The last was only half under her breath.

"You didn't even look for her," Calli repeated.

"Then kept the whole thing secret," Marian added.

"Didn't tell us what happened until we asked. Then just said your Summoning failed so we didn't know Raine might have arrived." Alexa stood. "No details so we might figure out what actually happened." She stared at the two men sitting stiffly in their chairs. "I don't know that I can forgive you for that." Then she took in a long breath and Raine saw her settle herself. "Since you don't value her and we do, she is ours. We'll gift her and take care of her. She'll will have nothing to do with you. All we want from you is information so we can correct her health," Alexa said and had the burly man shifting in his seat, looking uncomfortable.

The short man stood, was large enough by Earth standards, and Alexa short enough, for him to tower over her. "You can have her, and welcome." He spared a disdainful glance at Raine. "Shows no sign Power to me. A dud."

Alexa bared her teeth. "I was called that once."

Bad phrasing on the Seamaster's end. Raine was beginning to enjoy herself.

Faucon stepped between them, Alexa at his back. He nodded at the women. "Ladies." He aimed a look at the big seaman who slowly stood. "Gentlemen. Why don't I get every detail from the Seamasters in my study and keep tempers cool."

"I'll help," Marian's man said. He was a Sorcerer, a Circlet Raine had heard them called, but he didn't look weak, though his smile was more sincerely charming than Faucon's. "I have questions."

Raine bet he did. He looked the sort to have endless questions.

The short man snorted as if he'd had the same thought.

"I also know the components of a Summoning exactly, so I'll be able to postulate what went wrong." Now there was an undertone of steel in his tone.

Little guy turned on his heel and walked away. He met the serving woman carrying a tray and snatched a short glass of whiskey from it and continued in the direction of Faucon's Castle.

The big man nodded to Raine. "Sorry," he said, and took off after his companion.

"Sorry!" Alexa hissed, not bothering to lower her voice. "They put you through hell and that's all they can say. One effing word. 'Sorry.'"

"Tea's coming for you," Faucon said, soothing, nodded to Marian's man. "Let's go." They followed the Seamasters. When they reached the server, both men took brandy snifters.

"Good job, ladies." Alexa's man uncoiled from his chair. He walked up to her, picked her up and kissed her hard on the mouth, put her down.

Then he sauntered over to Raine. "I'm Bastien Vauxveau and pleased to meet you." He held out a large hand. His callouses were different from a seaman's, Raine noted, realized they were from holding a sword. She thought about bobbing a curtsey, decided against it. Everyone here thought she was an equal—she'd act it. "Pleased to meet you." She put her hand in his, felt a wild buzz that stunned her.

Saw the blow to her chin too late.

It could have been worse. Much, much worse. Staring down at Raine, Bri felt her heart wring at the miserable shape she was in. Scrawny and malnourished, neglected and abused.

Everyone rushed around them, getting a carrier sling ready for Raine before she woke up from Bastien's carefully calculated blow sizzling with Wild Magic. Neither Bri nor anyone else wanted to re-enforce the unnatural sleep. They could hope the poor woman was tired enough to stay asleep after she recovered from the shock, but didn't know that for sure. Didn't know exactly how Distance Magic—any additional Power—would affect her. They had to get her to the Castle and the great Temple before she awoke.

It was pretty damn evident that she hadn't been near a person of more than average Power in all the months since she'd been improperly Summoned. If she had, that one would have noticed Raine's own latent Power.

So Bri sat beside the new Exotique on the lush grass of Faucon's lawn and kept a hand on her chest, monitoring her vitals. It was one of those there-but-for-the-grace-of-God-go-I moments. This could have happened to her. And more than Raine's plight touched her heart. She stared at the woman and knew that Raine still had to perform her own task, suffer through the Snap. Bri could only hope that the toughest part of Raine's time in Lladrana was past her, and Bri wouldn't make odds on the woman staying.

Since Elizabeth had left, Bri thought it had been borne upon the Lladranans how lucky they'd been in Alexa and Marian and Calli. True, the Song would naturally Summon those who could stay—and how wonderful and strange it had been that the whole Drystan family might have crossed over to the different dimension—but so far most of the Exotiques had stuck.

Marian joined them, sinking gracefully to the ground. She stroked back Raine's hair. "Poor thing."

"We'd better watch that—in our words and thoughts," Bri said. "No one wants pity for very long."

"True." Marian met Bri's gaze. "Everything will be ready in a couple of minutes. They're improving on the makeshift net that brought Koz and Broullard home from battle."

Bri snorted. "You'd think that that would have been done a while back."

Marian inclined her head. "You'd think. If Circlets had been involved, it would have been."

Bri sighed, glanced at the two volarans Calli had chosen to carry Raine and the half-real, mostly bespelled net lying on the ground between them. Alexa and Calli were working together to get the task done. "The Marshalls have been pre-occupied with rebuilding their team."

"Understandable." Marian hesitated. "You looked sad."

"I was thinking of all that Raine still has to experience."

"Maybe designing and building a ship won't be too dangerous."

"I was hoping that, too. Wondering if she'd stay after the Snap. I can't recall what portion of the Exotiques Summoned do."

"Three-quarters stay. One-quarter leave."

Bri shifted in the grass. "That means we might be safe." She shook her head. "I don't see Raine staying. Not right now."

"We can only hope to persuade her."

"Right. And if we don't, two more will need to be Summoned, not one. Maybe more."

"Let's hope not. We're running out of time." Once more Marian hesitated. Looked down at Raine and blinked, swallowed, licked her lips. "If I'm right, she's the descendant of the last Exotique before Alexa."

Bri prodded her brain for details. "Came for the Singer, right? To teach her English?"

Marian nodded. "Ayes, Thomas Lindley stayed two weeks."

"The Singer's a quick study." Bri rolled her shoulders. She'd heard enough about the woman to know she didn't want to meet her. There was something else…"Didn't the Singer and her Friends Summon that guy?"

Again Marian nodded. "Through mirror magic."

Raine twitched under Bri's hand. Her patient's slow exhale held a hint of a moan. "Mirror magic," Bri said.

"That's right."

Despite not wanting to upset the delicate balance of the spell on Raine, Bri couldn't help herself from sending a wave of comfort and healing to Raine and was pleased when the woman sank deeper into sleep. Marian was observing the new Exotique. Bri said, "Mirror magic rang a note for Raine. Think she's for Koz?"

Marian shrugged. "Maybe. Falling in love and pairbonding tends to keep a person here." She sent a pointed look to Bri.

"Yeah." Bri's heart gave a little leap as she saw Sevair striding across the lawn toward them. She *did* love him. Her life would be so much less without him, and his love. Her inner child's panic at being trapped went down a notch.

Alexa said, frowning, "The net's ready. Good enough for now, but I'd like to commission the Circlets to make another." Her lips thinned before she said, "We'll probably need it again, should have such a thing in our arsenal."

"More like my arsenal," Bri said, narrowed her eyes to see and *hear* the net. "I could maybe coat it with healing spells."

Alexa said, "That would be great."

Sevair smiled and the day seemed brighter. "I've been told that I'm the best man to move her." Pride emanated from him. He was finding his place in the rhythm of the other Exotiques' men.

He squatted, set his hands near Raine's back and thighs. Brow knit in concentration, he used his Power to gently lift her a few inches so he could slide his arms under her. Strong, steady, solid—Bri's mantra about her love. Of course he would be the right man to move Raine.

No wild Power like Bastien's Song that might rouse her, or curiosity from Jaquar, or attraction from Faucon. Marrec might have done, but Bri thought Sevair had more experience in moving heavy items gently. Not that Raine looked very heavy.

As she rose, Bri let her hand drop away from Raine. They made a little procession to the net where Calli stood with the two interested volarans.

"I notice the Seamasters aren't here to help Raine," Bri said, not keeping anger from her tone.

Marian said, "They're still in the Castle consulting with Faucon. I'm pretty sure that at least one Seamaster should be part of the ritual at the Marshalls' Castle to complete the Summoning spell. Faucon's convincing them they owe Raine that."

Bri snorted. "And so much more. What do you think of their comment that the Marshalls should send out instructions for Summoning?"

"Their accusations that we were delinquent, do you mean?" Marian answered. Fire kindled in her eyes. "It's the Circlets' responsibility to disseminate information, even though the Marshalls usually do the Summoning."

"So?" Bri raised her brows.

Marian's mouth tightened. "I don't like keeping information secret, but distributing instructions for a Summoning might be asking for trouble. You need a very close team for a Summoning and other precise factors as well."

"Like the gong and the chimes," Calli said.

"And the chant length and wording and timing," Marian said. "The Seamasters botched the job because they were ill-prepared and sloppy." She gave a little shudder. "See what happened—a good and Powerful woman coming through the Dimensional Corridor and no one knowing. Worse could happen."

That kept them all quiet as they arranged Raine and made sure she was secure and supported by the net.

"Well, it's gonna be moot in a few months anyway," Alexa said, mounting her volaran. "The Dimensional Corridor is closing."

"To Earth," Marian said.

They stared at her. She shrugged. "There have been two other worlds Summonings have pulled from, in the ancient past."

Calli broke the silence. "We need to take care of *this* Exotique."

Bri heard the horsewoman speak mentally in Equine to the volarans as she vaulted onto her steed. "Besides, the last Exotique from Earth will be for the Singer. I doubt she needs any help Summoning someone."

"Probably doesn't think she needs anyone," Alexa muttered. "Too bad. We take care of our own. *We* should Summon the next, all of us and the Marshalls and Chevaliers and Circlets and Citymasters."

"Ayes," Marian said. "We should." Another little sigh. "I noted that you left out the Seamasters."

Alexa's expression hardened. "They opted out themselves."

"I'm sure one of Raine's tasks is to integrate them into the rest of the culture, like we've done with the others. We all have a common cause, after all, and we may need the Seamasters when we sail to the north to invade the Dark's nest."

Bri sucked in a quick breath and straightened her spine.

"If we need Seamasters, we'll have Faucon set up a circle of those we can trust," Alexa said.

"Thus fragmenting that particular segment of society further," Marian pointed out.

Alexa tugged her gauntlets onto her hands, squinted with irritation at Marian. "Why are you playing Devil's advocate?"

"Because if Raine's task is to integrate the Seamasters as well as design and build the ship, she's going to need all our support and not our antagonism against them."

"They deserve our antagonism. They hurt one of ours." Alexa stared at Raine, shook her head. "She *is* one of us, ours." For Alexa, that was the last word. Her volaran shot into the sky and away northeast toward the Castle.

46

Raine woke to hideous pain of a thousand needles piercing her body. A shriek tore from her raw throat. Her sweaty hands were grasped on both sides, the left by Bri, the right by Alexa, and the pain diminished. She was hauled to her feet and only then realized that she'd been lying on cool, hard stone.

Marian linked hands with Alexa and the pain was shared again. Calli took Bri's hand and Raine's head cleared further, enough to grit her teeth and bear it, stop the screams ripping from her. She stood in a huge, circular building with high windows, some of stained glass, some clear. Around her a large circle of people linked hands—the Marshalls in color-coded pairs, those who wore flying leathers—Chevaliers. Middle-class townspeople were there too—she recognized Bri's serious husband; Circlets stood in long velvet robes with bands of precious metal and jewels around their foreheads.

And those who wore clothes that showed they worked

on the ocean—Seamasters. Those who had originally Summoned her, torn her from her world. There weren't many of them, four, at what might be the compass points. They looked as grim as she felt.

The thin guy was nowhere to be seen, but the big guy caught her eye and ducked his head. Then there was a man who resembled Faucon—a cousin? A third, older, bent man with shrewd eyes and a hard jaw. Looked as if he might have come out of retirement. The fourth was middle-aged, but had lost a hand and wore a hook.

Raine couldn't see Faucon, but knew he was there.

The man in white leathers who'd shaken with revulsion upon meeting her but had not attacked, raised his voice in Song. The others Sang too, chanted. The Exotiques' men. Even Alexa and Marian and Calli Sang. Bri hummed.

What's going on? she asked the other Earth women, jolted a little when she realized she'd sent them words with her *mind* as well as muttering them.

You weren't Summoned properly. Marian's mental voice was laden with disapproval. *You must be attuned to Amee by the gong and chimes. That way you will come into your full Power.*

And the pain will go away, Bri said.

And you will be able to fly anywhere in Lladrana, Calli said. *Blossom wants to fly with you.*

Raine glanced at Bri and saw a drop of sweat bead at her temple and trickle down her cheek. She was dressed in a deep blue-green gown, more sapphire than emerald. Each of the others also wore a gown—Marian's flame red, Alexa's the brown of rich loam, Calli's a cloudless sky blue.

Raine herself wore white cloth that shimmered with many colors like possibilities.

Brace yourself, Alexa said. *We're coming to the end of the first verse. The rest of us will let go of your hands a bar before the end. You will have to endure the pain yourself.*

Or just succumb, Calli said. *We will still be here inside the pentacle with you.*

They were in a pentacle? Now that Calli mentioned it, Raine saw the flaming lines of neon blue. She didn't like this, any of it, but figured like the rest of her life the past six months, it would have to be survived.

The chant rose, perfect and beautiful, one rhythm pulsing like her heart, secondary voices breathing in time with her. Or she was with them. Magic. Power.

Bri and Alexa let go of her hands and the needles were back in force, piercing her flesh. She fell to the floor, writhing, sweat instantly coating her body. She didn't have the breath or the energy to scream. Agony was all.

Chimes rippled and the pain tugged through her, faded a moment. The gong rang and the note reverberated through her; her limbs thrashed.

Her ears popped and the Song coming from many throats surrounded her, beautiful. The pain *was* less. Bri and Alexa took her hands, lifted her again. She became aware of the smooth stone under her bare feet, the marble walls, the beams with Power crystals overhead, the sunlight in the windows.

Is it almost over? she asked the women linked with her, standing with her, becoming her friends.

Two more times, Marian said.

A wave of empathic sympathy came from the other Exotiques. The sweat that had been drying on Raine's body slicked again. She gritted her teeth and concentrated on the Song. Some of the transitions were not quite smooth.

We lost Partis and Thealia, the lead Marshalls, who led all the Summonings before. Alexa answered her thought with quiet grief. *Luthan is leading now, mentally linked with the Singer, whom he represents. But before we Summon the last we will need a stronger Singing pair.*

Luthan was the man in white leathers, the honorable treasure of a man. He had controlled his revulsion of her. Having experienced Travys, Raine could respect the man. He met her gaze with grave regard, inclined his head. Now that she *listened* she could hear Songs better, nuances better, even see auras a bit. Luthan's shone bright with integrity. She nodded back.

There were two other male voices adding depth and Power. Cocking her head she sought out the next one, found him—Calli's man. Marrec? He smiled at her, reassuring, letting her know that not only the women stood with her, but all those in the circle wished her well, wanted her here.

End of verse coming up, Alexa warned. She squeezed Raine's hand and some of *her* memories flashed. Alexa had been attacked when Summoned, both by a monster and one of the repulsed ones. Raine turned her head, locked gazes with Alexa. Then the women released her hands and a massive pressure gripped Raine, crushing breath from her. She landed on her knees. More pain shot through her. Chimes rose and fell, the gong sounded. Raine panted.

This time when Bri and Alexa grabbed her hands, she got her feet under her and pushed up.

You are doing very well, Marian said with warm approval that eased Raine's stinging pride that so many witnessed her weakness.

Not weak at all, said Calli, and from that woman Raine saw that she, too, had been damaged before her Summoning, had collapsed with pain.

The chant got louder and not from the force of breath, but of Power shared and resonating. Harmonies and tones melded together in an intricate weave of melody and magic. Power was audible now, and nearly visible as darkly glowing threads. Luthan, Marrec, both men with extraordinary voices. Raine heard a lilt rolling through the melody giving it a different twist, a little something extra. Another man. Raine looked around. Bastien, Alexa's man, one of the rare, brilliant black-and-whites, winked at her. Raised his brows as if asking her forgiveness for his blow.

She found her lips curving and smiled back. He made a show of a sigh of relief.

He's a love, Alexa said, grinning.

Bastien winked at Alexa, too.

Yes, the chant, the Song was as deep and Powerful as an ocean swell, pulling at her, preparing her? Attuning her to the land, more, to the sea.

The women around her were single, pure, major chords. Raine pulled knowledge from Bri—chakra tones, embodying energy and Power of the elements.

But there was one last throbbing rhythm that she needed to follow, to find. A harmony that wasn't as aurally exquisite as Luthan's and Marrec's voices, not as unusual as Bastien's lilt, or as rock steady and solid as Sevair Masif's beat, but which called to her more.

She sank into herself, listened with more than her mind, flowed with the surge of her blood.

Behind her.

She turned gently, the other women pinwheeling slowly around her, until she could see him, though she knew his voice and his Song before she caught sight of him.

Faucon.

Their gazes locked.

Yes. His was the Song she wanted, that provided her with everything—strength, wonder, comfort.

Fascinating man.

She heard the verse coming to an end, and dropped Bri's and Alexa's hands. Let the pain wash over her like an old aching bruise. Endured it. Stood tall.

The chimes rang and this time they were fizzing in her blood, down every nerve. She trembled.

The gong sounded and all her mind was the tone of it. Her body arched.

She kept her gaze on Faucon, gasped as Power swept through her and around her and expanded to the sky and the earth, the wind and the wave.

Pain was banished. Her gown turned deep emerald with a dark blue shimmer.

Faucon was still there with her, mouth tight, unwilling.

She didn't care. She felt incredible.

Fabulous Song.

Over the next few days Bri spent more time at the Castle than in the town, helping Raine settle into Elizabeth's old suite, one floor below Alexa in her tower. Learning Raine preferred dark chocolate, Bri had given Raine the last of Elizabeth's stash, thinking it might comfort her.

Bri accompanied Raine to her first few lessons in Power, something that came easily to her now and brought a radiance to her face, straightened her hunched defensive posture into the confidence she must have had before.

There were short introductory meetings with the Marshalls and Chevaliers, and more casual evening gatherings that included meals. Alexa had a very different style of leadership than the lost Thealia.

Faucon had returned to his seaside estate to travel to other coastal towns with his cousin, ostensibly to speak individually to the Seamasters.

Koz and the rest of them had learned that a mirror had been pivotal in Raine's Summoning, and that she was indeed the descendant of Thomas Lindley, the man who had been the Singer's teacher and lover. Who had taken a mirror from Lladrana home to Earth somehow. Or the Singer had transported the mirror to Earth and to Thomas.

These deductions had fired Calli and Marrec's irritation; everyone concluded that the Singer *had* somehow primed the crystal in Calli's mountain to show Lladrana when she was a child, and later bring her through. They all suspected she had help on Earth.

Sevair spent the nights in Bri's bed and the sex was wonderful. When they spoke, it was of daily happenings, or the additional renovations Sevair wanted to make to their tower, or the fact that the couple next door had been persuaded to move away to a new house in the southern part of the city. Their old, smaller, square two-story building would eventually be Bri's new office and surgery space. Or they'd talk of life plans, after the Dark was defeated. Bri got the idea that Sevair was gently accustoming her to the fact that she'd have to face the final battle with the Dark, with five other women to help her. Despite all their plans, she might not survive that battle. Sevair did not speak of the bloodbonding thing, but Bri knew he hadn't given up those particular plans.

One evening she'd spent a full hour talking to her parents, Elizabeth and a wide-eyed Cassidy. Sevair, using Elizabeth's retuned mirror, had been introduced and stayed several minutes, then excused himself.

Elizabeth glowed. Cassidy kept his fingers linked with hers, or his arm possessively around her waist. *He* was the one who detailed the plans for a huge wedding on the autumnal equinox. Watching him closely, Bri was of the opinion that he'd never let Elizabeth go, never stray, always would support her. A knot of worry eased in Bri. They looked in love and happy.

When she felt she'd burst into tears, she reluctantly signed off, though her father had insisted on a weekly family talk. How Bri missed touching them, hugging them, though the knowledge that they were well and thriving comforted her.

She still felt trapped.

Raine didn't like the Marshalls' Castle. It was a city in itself, bounded by high stone walls. Every couple of hours or so someone would knock on her door. To meet her or talk with her or check up on her. The Exotique women, Circlets, Chevaliers, Marshalls. Even Luthan of the repulsion and the white leathers came, though she thought that was to overcome his instinctive reaction around her. While she admired him for it, he wasn't easy company. Faucon didn't come, hadn't stayed after her Summoning ritual.

She had, of course, been provided with paper and parchment, drafting tools and table to design The Ship. The Ship. People already called it that. Capital letters. The Ship. They'd already accepted that she could plan and build it. She was still figuring out what it needed to be designed *for*. To carry Exotiques, some Marshalls and Chevaliers, for an assault on the Dark's nest. She shuddered at that. But she wasn't sure of the size of the invasion force, and thought that they'd need to carry food and weapons, and surely needed space for volarans.

She had maps and strange hard-copy visuals from Calli's and her volaran's minds. She had no clue how such a ship was supposed to be powered. Magic Power? She was sure that wasn't the energy source of most boats. She'd have heard during those horrible months at the Open Mouthed Fish.

The Seamasters weren't much help. Mired in failure and guilt and pride, none stayed after the ceremony. But for her to design and build a ship, she'd need their knowledge. So she'd have to make the first move, ensure that they knew she forgave them. To be sincere in that would take a while.

So there was really only one answer to her needs. Faucon. He was intelligent enough and knowledgeable enough about the sea and Chevaliers and the Dark's nest to help her. He could also be a liaison between her and the Seamasters. But she felt this Castle wasn't the place to work with him.

An odd sound came at her door and Raine hesitated in opening it. She'd read the Exotique Lorebooks, knew danger could lurk beyond a door. Then strumming came from the door harp, but since it also sounded in her mind, she didn't think that it was truly physical. She stepped away from the door. "Who is it?" And why were none of her pesky visitors around when she needed them?

Sinafinal and Tuckerinal, came to her mind. The feycoo-cus. She knew their names from the Lorebooks written in English, had been told that their real identities weren't mentioned in most Lladranan Lorebooks. But she hadn't been introduced. They'd been absent lately.

We will never harm you, Raine Emma Lindley.

That raised gooseflesh on her arms. She remembered that Alexa had said they'd known her full name when no one else had.

They were magical beings. Knew a lot. Didn't reveal all. "Did you know I'd been Summoned?" Her voice came out hostile. She didn't care.

Ttho. We didn't. There was a high whine. *We bring someone to meet you.*

That was a standard saying of people at her door the past few days. "You can't come in unless I invite you, right?"

Two sighs. *Ttho.*

These were the magical shape-shifting beings. She wondered what form they'd taken. The books and other women had talked about many.

Staying on her side of the threshold—did reading those vampire books pay off or what—she swung the door out and open.

Two swans and a little ball of fluff with eyes and sharp beak and feet, not *quite* a bird, stared up at her.

They didn't appear threatening, but their Power was strong, their melodies beautiful. She hesitated, gave in. "Come in."

Merci, came two strong voices and a teeny one.

They flew in, settled on her bed.

I am Sinafinal, said the one with a darker orange beak.

I am Tuckerinal, said the other.

This is our child, Enerin. Isn't she beautiful?

She was.

She likes your Song the best of all in the Castle.

Raine's throat tightened.

The little being fluffed her feathers, and squeaked.

She would like to be your companion when she is older.

Someone of her own on Lladrana. An image came of Faucon, but now that Raine had heard his story, she thought that even if they worked together, he'd keep any relationship impersonal.

"I'd take them up on it," Bri said from the still open door. "Pretty cute."

Ayes, said Sinafinal.

Yes, said Tuckerinal.

Ay-yes, said Enerin.

The baby set up a cheeping, flapped her wings. Raine went over and picked her up. She was soft and downy and her eyes appeared dark blue. Raine lifted her to study her better.

Pret-ty Song. Pret-ty Song, the little one hummed.

"Yours is pretty, too."

Louder humming. Then Enerin's sharp beak pecked Raine hard. "Youch!" She dropped the bird, but Enerin hovered in the air, her wings blurring like a hummingbird's. She darted in and sipped the droplet of blood from Raine's hand.

Decided and done. We will go now, said Sinafinal. She flew from the room, followed by Tuckerinal and Enerin.

"Let me see." Bri shut the door behind the trio, strode in, scowling. "These Lladranans and their bloodbonds."

Raine's stomach clutched as she realized Bri was right. The healer took Raine's hands and examined the puncture, touched a finger to the small wound. A flash of flaming green warmth and the skin was whole again.

"Extraordinary," Raine said over the lump in her throat.

Bri smiled. "Yeah." She smoothed her thumb over Raine's hand. "But it will leave a scar." Shaking her head, she said, "I can't do anything about that."

Raine liked Bri the best of all the Exotiques. Mostly because she was the newest, and learning of the land and people just like Raine. Less intimidating. And they both naturally resonated with the element of water.

The medica glanced around the suite, stared at some ship models the Marshalls had retrieved from storage and took a chair. "I have a proposition for you."

Raine smirked. "Colorado woman, you know nothing of ships."

A chuckle from Bri, then a shake of the head. "Very true, though I think I've been on more boats and ships than the other Exotiques during my travels. But that wasn't what I came to talk about. Before Elizabeth and I were Summoned, the Castleton Citymasters earmarked a house and furnished it for us." As far as Raine could tell, only Bri and Sevair were easy with discussing Elizabeth. Everyone else hardly mentioned the other twin. In considering that, Raine didn't hear the actual proposition. "Come again?" she asked.

"Sevair and I live in a tower built into Castleton city wall. The house stands empty." Bri spread her hands. "It's not my style, but I think it would suit you." Bri's Song intensified and Raine sensed that Bri *wanted* Raine to take the house, that Raine deserved it after all she'd gone through.

Bri said, "The Lladranans are perfectly serious when they say that they'll give us—you—a rich estate. Something by the coast for you, maybe." Bri shrugged. "Sevair and I have some land in addition to the tower. But the house in Castleton is mine and I'd like you to have it. Or live in it until you find something else you like better." Bri studied her. "But I think the traditional style would suit you fine. Very elegant."

Raine swallowed. "Thank you."

"We can move you there tomorrow morning," Bri said.

Raine opened her mouth to remind Bri that she was doing the bloodbond thing with Sevair the next morning, recalled that everyone seemed to think it would be best if Bri was blissfully unaware of the ceremony. As if she'd bolt. Eyeing Bri, Raine thought that Sevair and the rest might be wise in springing this on her. Bri struck her as someone who was hard to pin down.

Raine smiled.

Bri narrowed her eyes.

"I'll be there a little before dawn," Raine said.

"You must be crazy!"

"I'm going to do a flyover of the coast tomorrow," Raine improvised. "See how far north I can get in a day, check out the currents and regular fishing lanes. Need a very early start."

"Oh." Bri grimaced. "Okay." Her expression brightened a little and she stood. "I'll let the servers know that we'll need a hearty breakfast in the house. They keep whining that they don't have enough to do. But, really, the place is completely furnished." She flashed a smile. "There *is* one purple room."

For a moment Raine flashed on how it would have been if

being surrounded by purple was the only bad thing that had happened to her. Bri came up and hugged her. "I'm glad you were found and I'm glad you're here. Fuck the Seamasters."

Raine suppressed a flinch. "Rather not."

"Don't blame you."

One last squeeze and Bri headed toward the door, her short, scarlet medica robe whirling around her, over the creamy thin silk pants. She'd started a fashion; more and more medicas were wearing their robes like Bri. Raine smiled.

"Um, one last thing," Bri said, glancing up and down the corridor outside. "Can't-make-it-to-Girls'-Night-In-tonight. See you tomorrow at some ungodly hour of the morning." She left fast.

"Ayes," Raine said. For the first time, she wasn't going to be the one on the hot seat. This was going to be fun. And interesting. She rubbed her hands and laughed.

47

Bri's courage failed her. She didn't want to be with the Exotiques. She sent a note that she was busy researching the frink and Chevalier sickness and couldn't make Girls Night In.

Instead she joined the evening walk in Castleton. Breathed better. Learning the city eased her scared inner child who still felt trapped. She wouldn't be good company anyway. If she was tired of herself, how much more would others be?

She'd taken a peek at Elizabeth's place that morning, had heard lovemaking noises and had immediately signed off. Elizabeth's Song had come through and it had sounded deeply happy. Of course Elizabeth had already dealt with her experience. Not surprising. Now it was time to grow up and Bri was having trouble.

Alexa, Calli, and Marian converged on her in a park near her tower. Her lame excuse hadn't been accepted. She should have said she'd would be doing an out-of-body trance.

Seeing their determined expressions, Bri knew that rationalization wouldn't have stopped them either.

"Oh, honey," Calli said, and hugged Bri as if she was one of Calli's children. Bri clutched her, wanted to cry, but stepped back. Calli kept a firm arm around Bri's waist.

So Bri set her feet and jutted her chin. "I've been having anxiety attacks."

"What, we couldn't see that for ourselves?" Alexa said, walked over and hugged her, too.

With a gesture, a smiling Marian herded them to a park bench. Bri sat with Calli and Alexa on each side. When they were settled, Marian stood before them. "Let's consider your stress factors." She lifted a forefinger. "Summoned to another world."

Alexa snorted. "Pretty much a zillion on a stress meter. Not sure why any of our hearts just didn't give out."

Marian spared her a cool look. "Because we're made of strong stuff." She raised a second finger. "You've been healing every day you arrived." Another finger lifted. "You faced the fact that only you could save a people."

Alexa's foot swung. "I've found that to be a rough stress factor, too."

Calli said, "Ahem. Ayes."

Raising a fourth finger, Marian continued, "You've watched people you loved die." That punched everyone into silence. They'd all watched people they loved die lately.

"You contracted a fatal disease and nearly died yourself," Marian said.

"Gonna run out of fingers soon," Alexa teased half-heartedly. Bri suspected Alexa's mind was still on the battlefield where Thealia had died. Great. This little Girls' Night In The Park session was depressing them all.

"Most of all…" Marian squeezed into the space between Bri and Alexa and wriggled her bottom to scoot Alexa aside, then put an arm around them, kissed Bri on the cheek. "You left your twin sister and your family in another world."

Bri sniffed hard, but tears dribbled down her cheeks anyway.

"That had to be the hardest blow. A new man and new friends aren't going to replace those bonds soon," Marian ended.

"That all makes sense to my head, but not inside." Bri swallowed tears.

Calli said, "You aren't a bad person for leaving them. Elizabeth made her choice, you made yours. They were both right."

"My parents and Elizabeth could all have come through." Bri set her chin. "I know it. My Mom and my Dad had heard those chimes and chants. Mom had a craving for potatoes."

Amazed silence. Marian recovered first. "We believe you. A couple who could raise *two* daughters to travel through the Dimensional Corridor could do the same."

Hugging Bri tighter, Calli said, "They aren't bad people for making that choice. They didn't abandon you. You didn't abandon them. You all had different choices and, well, destinies."

"Oh, man," Bri said and sniveled, gave up trying to control her tears and let them come. "I've done an awful lot of crying lately."

"You had reason," Alexa said, and shoved a grubby handkerchief in Bri's hand. "All those stress issues. Not to mention the idea of invading an evil Dark and trying to kill it. Probably weighed a little on your mind. Nibbled at you. Can tell you it does me."

"Me, too," Calli said.

"Me, too," Marian said. "Which reminds me, where is our newest Exotique? She was with us. We don't want to leave her alone as much as we did Bri." She looked at Bri straightly. "We left you in Castleton, worked more with Elizabeth—that was *our* mistake, not telling you how much we valued you. Just for being you."

"Elizabeth needed you more," Bri said, wiping her face and blowing her nose. "And you've tried making up for that lately, haven't you?"

"Ayes. I think it's imperative for us to—"

"Don't say 'assimilate'," Bri warned.

Alexa gave a crack of laughter.

Marian smiled. "Integrate Raine into our group. Or at least befriend her."

"I think she left people, too," Bri said, "Or was torn from them."

"I did," Raine said, stepping from the shadow of a tree. She stood awkwardly.

They all stood, Bri held out her hand, "Come sit with us."

"What are you doing here by yourself?" Calli demanded.

"Koz came with me." Raine looked over her shoulder. "He disappeared as soon as he saw you all hugging."

"Just like a guy," Alexa said.

Bri swallowed. "Speaking of guys." Even with these women, and logically thinking of the conversation, the anxiety in the back of her mind had only dimmed, not disappeared. Her breath came shallow. "Sevair is planning that damn *coeur de chain* Bonding Ceremony Ritual Whatever. I know he is. "

No one spoke, denied it.

"I guess I should say that we think once you've bonded with him, you'll settle down," Calli said.

"Settle down." Bri hopped up and paced a quick circle.

"When you have his blood in you, it will steady you," Calli said.

"Oh. My. God." Her own blood drained out of her head and her vision dimmed.

"Definitely a panic attack," Marian said putting an arm around Bri. Calli was up, too. They plunked Bri back down on the bench. She put her head between her knees.

Feeling like a fool, Bri struggled against it, strove to hear her own Song, and that of the Universe. Failed.

Maybe it was the upside-down business that blocked the Songs, so she drew in a breath and uncurled her spine vertebrae by vertebrae. Yoga. That helped, too.

"No one is going to force you to do anything you don't want to," Calli said. She reached out a hand for Raine, pulled her down on the bench, too. Good thing it was a long one, but Bri figured Alexa or Marian had noticed that when they'd found her here.

Staring at Raine, Calli repeated, "No one is going to make you do anything you don't want to, either."

Now it was Raine sniffing. Calli gave her a handkerchief. Raine blew her nose, nodded. "These last few days have been good. I've read all your Lorebooks." She glanced at Bri. "Except yours."

"Isn't done yet," Bri muttered.

"Of course not. You haven't learned your lesson," Marian said.

Bri gritted her teeth. She didn't want to hear any more, but of course Marian didn't stop.

"You have to know in your heart that this is where you belong. That you can trust Sevair and us and even Amee."

Alexa took out her baton and flipped it. What people had been left in the park faded away. When she looked at Bri, her eyes were deadly serious. "You have to accept that however long your life, being here was worth it."

"You aren't trapped here. You *chose* here," Calli said.

"We aren't going to fail," Alexa said.

She didn't say they'd survive, Bri noticed.

Raine slid to the end of the bench, "Maybe I should—"

Marian's long arm grabbed her. "You're with us."

Raine subsided. "Glad this is Bri's discussion."

"We'll get to you," the redhead said.

Bri was breathing deeply. "Okay. I understand with my head and not my heart. Yeah, I'm used to moving on when things get sticky. But everything has happened really fast."

There was a sudden shadow, the sound of wings, and Nuare glided in front of them. The roc didn't spare a glance for the other women. *I can take you anywhere on Amee.*

"But it's still here."

Here is where you chose to be. Why? FEEL the why. That's what you must do. Not think. Feel all the time the why. LISTEN to the why.

"Good advice," Marian murmured. "We can help by example."

They all linked hands and certainty infused Bri.

Alexa, Marian said mentally.

Alexa thought of Bastien. She was nervous since she hadn't bloodbonded with him, and was planning to. But the man held her heart. They'd fought together, saved each other's lives. Bri experienced Alexa's aching love for the Marshalls, her team, and her deep determination never to fail them. Her love for her new sisters. Her knowledge that she'd made a place for herself in this world.

Those feelings were layered by Marian: her questing mind, boundless curiosity. Her love for her man and her animal companion and her brother and her new true friends, fascinatingly different.

Calli's Song rang with complete devotion to her husband, children, volarans. New family, new world. Her emotional memory of the bloodbonding and how she'd found the loves of her life was filled with joy.

How their emotions helped! Bri *heard* Sevair's Song. The beat of his heart and his hammer as he worked in the tower on the final touches to the bathing room. After a long hard day of his own. His melody and his love for her came and buoyed her. He would never fail her, not like the rock star, not like Cassidy had failed Elizabeth. Never.

The Songs of the women near her. Like and unlike her. Once of Earth and now here. Always friends. Not going anywhere.

Bri felt other tugs, blinked her eyes open to clear dampness. Across the park, on the street, she saw people. People she'd healed. One or two raised their hands, and she understood some of them walked the same path that she did in the evenings, enjoying being close to her. They accepted her and valued her like no others in her life. Her gift was acknowledged and prized.

Suddenly she wanted to go home, to her tower. Sevair had finished the wonderful lower bathing room—a room she hadn't seen since her first day there—and was actually running the bath, scenting it, waiting for her. As he'd waited since the Snap.

"Thank you," she choked. She dropped their hands and the Song of the Exotiques faded, but still lilted in her ears and mind and heart. With a brief hug for each of them, and Nuare, she hurried home.

Sevair carried Bri all the way down the stairs to the spring in the bottom of the tower and proudly showed her the last carving on the fancy keystones. The place was no longer dank and gray. The air vents from the top of the tower funneled a sweet-scented breeze into the room. The barrel vaults had been scoured to a soft golden, the cheerful stone figures and faces restored by the man who dropped her into the pool and laughed, then followed her in.

They made love there, and then he carried her back *up* to the bed and they made love again.

"Tomorrow," he said as he pressed his body against hers. "The ritual is tomorrow."

Her insides jolted, then she *listened* to his heady Song and her own, winding around his, melding together, as their bodies moved together.

Sevair's side of the bed was cold when the pounding on the door woke Bri. The minute she opened her eyes she remembered everything. The ambush by the Exotiques, Sevair and the lovely bath. Lovemaking.

Bloodbonding ritual today. She wanted to crawl back under the covers.

She would not.

No doubt Raine was here to take her to the ceremony. Bri grabbed a robe, pulling it on as she ran downstairs. Raine was playing with the doorharp, sending her thumbnail up and down and up and down…

Bri flung open the door. "Hang on a minute." She spotted Nuare sitting in the middle of the cul de sac, ready to swoop down on her and take her to the ritual. Elizabeth's—Raine's volaran was there, too, ignoring the big bird.

"I'll be right down." Bri started up the stairs.

"I'm eager to see the house," Raine said.

Bri threw her a sour look. "I know you've come to take me to the *coeur de chain* bloodbonding ritual. I'm ready." Despite what felt like a flock of rocs flying around in her nervous stomach. Just as well they wouldn't have breakfast.

Raine smiled and looked beautiful. "Good. Everyone's looking forward to the wedding."

Hesitating, Bri said, "You, too? Feeling better?"

"Ayes."

"You're not alone," Bri said, reminding herself, too. She was not alone in this; Sevair would be with her. All her new friends would celebrate with her.

She concentrated on keeping her ears and mind open, listening to Songs. Sevair's was strong, steady, solid. As usual. Not even one tiny nervous note. Completely unflappable.

As soon as Bri and Nuare, Raine and Blossom, landed in Temple Ward of the Castle, Bri was whisked away for a quick bath infused with "special herbs." Herbs that contained Power. Herbs that were good for preventing infection as well as the circulation of blood, Bri saw, though no one mentioned that.

The Exotiques surrounded her and kept her spirits up and her nerves only slightly jittery as they helped her dress in a wonderful shimmering sleeveless gown of pale gray shot with silver. Sevair's colors. Bri wondered if he would be wearing medica red.

Then they were walking from the Castle keep to the temple and Bri was squeezing the juice out of the stems of the bouquet she carried. She was on her way to her wedding—more than wedding, because when she died, he did. Or vice versa. Pairbonding. Whatever. Her family wasn't here. No parents to give her away, Dad to walk down the aisle, twin as maid of honor. How had she thought she didn't want that? Too bad.

She listened to the whys she was here—Sevair's Song, those of everyone around her, all wishing her well.

Hearing them, and her heart thump, she understood something more about herself. In her heart of hearts she'd believed partnership wasn't achievable. That the man she married would try to force her into the mold of his own expectations of what she should be. Just like everyone else.

Though her parents had a loving relationship, she'd always thought her parents were the rare, lucky ones. Her own relationships, and Elizabeth's, had never been so loving. She yearned for commitment and permanence.

Sevair could give her that, would give her that. As she would give it to him.

The minute Bri walked into the great Temple, her anxiety was soothed by the saturation of Power. She saw the knives and they gleamed wickedly but no panic grabbed her by the throat. She let her inner child out, gave the simple creature full rein, felt delight and wonder. The little one liked the sensation of magic infusing her, enjoyed the colors of the stained-glass windows patterned on the gray stone floor.

All her friends spread around her, ready to celebrate with her. Be assimilated? Bri snorted to herself, looking at the colorful semicircle of Exotiques. The others weren't assimilated.

While she stared at them, flashes came. Marian had her camera. A mirror was propped on the long altar table.

Sevair stood in front of it. Sevair.

Sevair.

Her heart took a shock. Yes. Ayes. She wanted him. The inner child shrieked with glee. Someone of her own. Someone who'd put her first. Oh, yeah.

Then as she walked forward, almost seemed to glide, there was no inner child and Bri. There was just Bri. She wondered if she'd finally grown up.

More than magic suffused her. Love from her friends and Sevair. She scanned them. More than the Exotiques and their men were there, too. People from Castleton, even a Citymaster or two from the other places she'd visited, beamed at her. More photos.

When she returned her gaze to Sevair he was smiling at her, with that special look in his eyes, the one only for her.

All the residual tension of doubt drained from her.

This was what she wanted. A love. A home. Friends. Respect.

For an instant she thought of Zeres and missed his craggy face. She bit her lip.

She glanced at the mirror and her family waved. Elizabeth and her mom were crying. Her dad blew her a kiss, then clasped his hands and waved them in a gesture of triumph.

The knives came out and she only felt calm, kept her gaze locked with Sevair's as they said vows, slowly steadily, strongly.

Then they were joined and blood and magic and more cycled between them. Not only did she see and hear Sevair's love for her, but felt it, real and true.

She sent the same back to him.

It was a full three days before Bri showed Raine the medica's house in Castleton.

Bri kept a wary eye on her. Raine's melody was full of sweeping highs and lows. Her aura pulsed erratically.

"What a pretty house," Raine said, turning around and looking at the gleaming furnishings, the delicate murals, running her hand down the banister. Every detail spoke of the Lladranans, respect for their Exotiques. Respect that hadn't been given to Raine. Maybe this wasn't a good idea.

"A wonderful house," Raine whispered.

"It's yours," Bri said. "I have the tower. This place is yours for as long as you want—or until the Snap."

Raine's Song went ragged. She opened her mouth, but said nothing. Her eyes filled with tears. A couple of harsh sounds emerged from her. She gathered herself, then said. "How can you stand it? Stuck here, knowing your real life is going on back home, knowing people who love you miss you, every day. How can you stand it!" Raine crumpled.

Bri caught her, did the air glide thing to the sitting room and a fat, welcoming chair big enough for both of them. She cradled Raine and let her cry, stroked her hair. "You're all right now. You're here where people will cherish you. You're all right," she soothed. She kept it up until Raine's shoulders stopped heaving and her sobs became whimpers. Bri fished in her pocket and came out with a couple of hankies and gave them to Raine, who'd curled in on herself.

"You've had it *so* hard. Such a horrible time. I'm sorry for that." Bri kept patting Raine, cleared her own throat. "But Lladrana is my real life, my real home. I made that decision."

"That cruddy tower—shit, sorry."

But Bri only chuckled. "It needs a little more work to be a showplace. Like Lladrana needs work."

Raine's face set. "Guess I won't be going home until the last fight."

Bri didn't want her to go home at all. Wanted her to stay and find a place here in Lladrana. The depth of that feeling surprised her. Perhaps it was because she'd found Raine so quickly after losing Elizabeth.

"Let me show you rest of the house," Bri said, standing.

Raine blew her nose, smiled and rose with a grace Bri admired. She was the most graceful of them all. "I've heard the stories about you and Elizabeth, and have read the Lorebooks—"

"Our cue, ladies," Marian said from the doorway. Calli stood with her.

"Where's Alexa?" asked Bri.

"Getting chocolate from Elizabeth's alternate stash in the kitchen."

Bri looked around the formal sitting room. "The most comfortable place is the bedroom." She smiled at Raine. "Huge feather bed. Big enough to hold a girl confab."

"Confab?" Raine asked.

"It's a word my Mom uses. Confabulation. Twin and I use it."

"Confab." Alexa joined them repeating it. "It's a good Exotique word." She nodded. "I like it." Looking at Calli, she said, "You got the hats?"

Calli swept out the hand she'd been holding behind her back, with two white cowboy hats stacked. She separated them. One had a wide red band with medica symbols. The other had a deep blue band with stylized waves.

Alexa and Marian took hats that Bri hadn't noticed from the settle bench. Alexa's band was jade green with little flaming batons, Marian's purple-black with jagged lightning.

Bri took the medica hat, placed it on her head and wasn't surprised when it fit perfectly. Alexa took Bri's left wrist and turned it over. Marching up Bri's arm after the bonding symbol of Sevair's stone hammer were the symbols of the other Exotiques. "Still there."

"If they don't show up before, the planet Amee graces us with these after the Snap." Marian showed her own arm with even more tatts than Bri's.

Raine stared at her bare arm, let out a relieved sigh, lifted her chin. "I know Lladrana has troubles, and I know that you all barely escaped with your lives, so you've been hurt here, too. But—"

"But me no buts. We've all heard it before. You'll stay or you'll go. Your choice." Alexa shrugged. "The hat is yours regardless." She put it on Raine's head.

Raine adjusted it, then smiled and became beautiful. "I always wanted a cowboy hat."

"Connecticut." Alexa shook her head.

"Hey, it begins with a *c*, like Colorado," Bri said. "That counts for something. For a lot." She linked arms with Raine.

"Note the fancy carving on the side of the stairwell." Everyone oohed and aahed, though they'd seen it before. As they toured the house, each of the women pointed out items they'd proposed. Affection tugged at her heart. From the corner of her eye, she saw the same emotion curve Raine's lips.

"The best part is the private tub downstairs," Marian said.

"We all had a part in that," Calli said, touching Raine's hand.

A few minutes later they'd settled on the bed with two pieces of chocolate each. They'd made a circle on the bed and Calli was on Bri's left, then Marian, then Alexa and Raine on Bri's right.

"This place is yours," Bri repeated.

"Thank you," Rain said softly. "I accept." Her chest flattened with a big sigh.

"Ah, you are all still here," Sevair said. He walked in, wearing a stupid-looking hat with a wide brim and carrying a book under his arm. He took in the women, visibly braced himself, and continued. "I found this book on the marble-topped cabinet under the magic mirror in our tower."

Bri stilled and at her sudden quiet the others fell silent, looked at Sevair.

He held out the volume, large and bound in red leather tooled in gilt that looked brand new. "I can't read it," he said.

Bri hopped from the bed, took it, and brushed a kiss on his lips. When he turned to go, she said, "Stay."

Reluctantly he dragged up a chair to the bed as she plopped back down with the other women. She put the book in the middle of their circle and all gazes fixed on the title. *The Lorebook of Exotique Medica Elizabeth Brigid Drystan.*

Bri sniffed. She'd been able to hold it together when Raine had broken down, but this was a whole 'nother matter. She wiped her arm across her eyes, saw the white square Sevair offered, and took it, dabbed at her face, knew she'd need it again before she was done. Meeting his kind and steady eyes, she told him the title.

Then she drew in a deep breath and opened the book. A title page, with a caduceus at the bottom.

Marian reached over and fingered a corner of the page. "Acid-free paper." Her eyes narrowed and she touched the fancy lettering. "Bridgenorth font. I'd say Elizabeth typed this herself and had it bound."

"Eight-and-a-half-by-eleven paper," Alexa said.

"Yes." Bri cleared her throat. "Yes." She opened the book and there was a photo of her and Elizabeth in the Castle. "Oh, man, I'm gonna lose it."

Calli patted her shoulder as Bri wiped her eyes again. She scooted in and leafed through the book. There were photos, and drawings where Elizabeth spoke of something that they hadn't taken a picture of—like a dreeth. Pages of three-dimensional drawings from all angles.

"Cassidy did these drawings," Bri said, swallowing hard. "He's a good artist." She glanced at Sevair.

"I don't mind hearing about him—my woman stayed." His tone was so complacent, she frowned, then he picked up her hand and kissed her fingers and she melted a little inside, as always. Elizabeth's place was in Denver. She knew that in her head and her heart, but it would take a while to accept the loss and stop hurting. Same as her family at home.

Exclamations came as Calli continued to turn the pages. Sevair scooted closer, snorting at a picture of Zeres drunk—another grief that would eventually heal—then made a disgusted noise in his throat at the picture of the Lladranan men. "I'm much more attractive than Faucon or Bastien."

"Of course you are," all the women chorused.

He made the noise again.

Finally Calli turned to the last pages and Bri gasped. Cassidy and her father and her mother had handwritten letters to her. Her eyes blurred and when Calli withdrew her hand, Bri turned the pages. She didn't want to read the letters now, so she went to the last page, all cursive.

We know that you will fight the Dark and win.

I love you, Bri, Elizabeth.

You will win. I love you, Bri, Cassidy.

You will win. I love you, Bri, Dad.

You will win. I love you, Bri, Mom.

Tears rolled down Bri's face.

Three hawk feycoocus flew through the window, lit on the bed within the circle of women. Three magical mind-voices chirped, *We will win.*

Calli grabbed her left hand, stared into her eyes. "We will win." Hands clasped together around the circle. Raine hesitated, then completed the circle between Bri and Alexa. Bri's voice rose with the other women's along with a surge of incredible Power. "We will win."

Sevair sat on the bed, lifted her onto his lap, met her eyes and again she was connected with others so that they all spoke together.

"We will win."

Bri hoped so, but still saw the window darken as the

sun went behind clouds, felt the chill of an early autumn. She leaned back to look into Sevair's eyes. "Win or lose, I'm here forever."

* * * * *

One last Summoning before the final battle.
Don't miss
Singer for a World
Coming in 2009!